ARROWOOD

ARROWOOD

MICK FINLAY

mira

mira

Recycling programs
for this product may
not exist in your area.

ISBN-13: 978-0-7783-3094-3

Arrowood

For questions and comments about the quality of this book, please contact us at
CustomerService@Harlequin.com.

www.BookClubbish.com

Printed in U.S.A.

To Anita, John and Maya

Chapter One

South London, 1895

THE VERY MOMENT I WALKED IN THAT MORNING I could see the guvnor was in one of his tempers. His face was livid, his eyes puffy, his hair, least what remained on that scarred knuckle of a head, stuck out over one ear and lay flat with grease on the other side. He was an ugly sight, all right. I lingered by the door in case he threw his kettle at me again. Even from there I could smell the overnight stink of gin on his foul breath.

"Sherlock blooming Holmes!" he bellowed, slamming his fist down on the side table. "Everywhere I look they're talking about that charlatan!"

"I see, sir," I replied as meekly as I could. My eyes tracked his hands as they swung this way and that, knowing that a cup, a pen, a piece of coal might quick as a flash get seized and hurled across the room at my head.

"If we had his cases we'd be living in Belgravia, Barnett," he declared, his face so red I thought it might burst. "We'd have a permanent suite in the Savoy!"

He dropped to his chair as if suddenly tuckered out. On

the table next to his arm I spied what had caused his temper: *The Strand* magazine, open at the latest of Dr. Watson's adventures. Fearing he would notice me looking, I turned my attention to the fire.

"I'll put the tea on," I said. "Do we have any appointments today?"

He nodded, gesturing in the air in a defeated manner. He'd shut his eyes.

"A lady's coming at midday."

"Very good, sir."

He rubbed his temples.

"Get me some laudanum, Barnett. And hurry."

I took a jug of scent from his shelf and sprayed his head. He moaned and waved me away, wincing as if I were lancing a boil.

"I'm ill," he complained. "Tell her I'm indisposed. Tell her to come back tomorrow."

"William," I said, clearing away the plates and newspapers scattered across his table. "We haven't had a case for five weeks. I have rent to pay. I'll have to go work on Sidney's cabs if I don't bring money home soon, and you know how I don't like horses."

"You're weak, Barnett," he groaned, slumping further in his chair.

"I'll clean the room, sir. And we will see her at midday."

He did not respond.

At twelve o'clock sharp Albert knocked on the door.

"A lady to see you," he said in his usual sorrowful fashion.

I followed him down the dark corridor to the pudding shop that fronted the guvnor's rooms. Standing at the counter was a young woman in a bonnet and a billowing skirt. She had the complexion of a rich woman, but her cuffs were frayed and brown, and the beauty of her almond face was corrupted by a chipped front tooth. She smiled a quick, unhappy smile, then followed me through to the guvnor's rooms.

I could see him weaken the moment she walked in the door. He began to blink and jumped to his feet and bowed his head low as he took her wilted hand.

"Madam."

He gestured to the best seat—clean and next to the window so there was a little light thrown onto her handsome physique. Her eyes quickly took in the piles of old newspapers that lined the walls and were stacked in some places to the height of a man.

"What can I do for you?"

"It is my brother, Mr. Arrowood," she said. It was clear from her accent she was from the continent. "He's disappeared. I was told you can find him."

"Are you French, mademoiselle?" he asked, standing with his back to the coal fire.

"I am."

He glanced at me, his fleshy temples red and pulsing. This was not a good start. Two years before we'd been thrown into the clink in Dieppe when the local magistrate decided we were asking too many questions about his brother-in-law. Seven days of bread and cold broth had crushed all the admiration he had for the country right out of him, and to make it worse our client had refused to pay us. The guvnor had held a prejudice against the French ever since.

"Mr. Arrowood and me both have a great admiration for your race, miss," I said before he had a chance to put her off.

He scowled at me, then asked, "Where did you hear of me?"

"A friend gave me your name. You are an investigative agent, yes?"

"The best in London," I said, hoping a little praise would soothe him.

"Oh," she replied. "I thought Sherlock Holmes?"

I could see the guvnor tense again.

"They say he is a genius," she continued. "The best in all the world."

"Perhaps you should consult him then, mademoiselle," snapped the guvnor.

"I cannot afford him."

"So I am second best?"

"I mean no offence, sir," she replied, noticing the edge to his voice.

"Let me tell you something, Miss…"

"Cousture. Miss Caroline Cousture."

"Appearances can be deceptive, Miss Cousture. Holmes is famous because his assistant writes stories and sells them. He's a detective with a chronicler. But what about the cases we never hear about? The ones that do not get turned into stories for the public? What about the cases in which people are killed by his blundering mistakes?"

"Killed, sir?" asked the woman.

"Are you familiar with the Openshaw case, Miss Cousture?"

The woman shook her head.

"The case of the five orange pips?"

Again she shook her head.

"A young man sent to his death by the great detective. Over the Waterloo Bridge. And that isn't the only one. You must know the case of the dancing men? It was in the newspaper."

"No, sir."

"Mr. Hilton Cubitt?"

"I do not read newspapers."

"Shot. Shot dead and his wife almost killed as well. No, no, Holmes is far from perfect. Did you know he has private means, miss? Well, I hear he turns down as many cases as he accepts, and why do you think? Why, I wonder, would a detective turn down so many cases? And please, don't think I'm envious of him. I am not. I pity him. Why? Because he's a deductive agent. He takes small clues and makes large things of them. Often wrong, in my opinion. There." He threw his hands in the air. "I've said it. Of course he's famous, but I'm afraid he doesn't understand people. With Holmes there are always clues: marks on the ground, the fortuitous faggot of ash on the table, a singular type of clay on the boat. But what of the case with no clues? It's commoner than you think, Miss Cousture. Then it's about people. About reading people." Here he gestured at the shelf holding his small collection of books on the psychology of the mind. "I am an emotional agent, not a deductive agent. And why? I see people. I see into their souls. I smell out the truth with my nose."

As he spoke, his stare fixed on her, I noticed her flush. Her eyes fell to the floor.

"And sometimes that smell is so strong it burrows inside me like a worm," he continued. "I know people. I know them so badly it torments me. That is how I solve my cases. I might not have my picture in the *Daily News*. I might not have a housekeeper and rooms in Baker Street and a brother in the government, but if I choose to accept your case—and I don't guarantee that until I hear what you have to say—if I choose to accept it, then you'll find no fault in me nor in my assistant."

I watched him with great admiration: when he got into his stride, the guvnor was irrepressible. And what he said was true:

his emotions were both his strength and his weakness. That was why he needed me more than he sometimes understood.

"I'm sorry," said Miss Cousture. "I do not mean to insult you. I know nothing of this detective business. All I know is how they talk of Mr. Holmes. Forgive me, sir."

He nodded and harrumphed, and finally sat back in his chair by the fire.

"Tell us all. Leave nothing out. Who is your brother and why do you need to find him?"

She clasped her hands in her lap and composed herself.

"We are from Rouen, sir. I come here just two years before to work. I'm a photographer. In France they do not accept a woman as photographer, and so my uncle he helps me gain employment here, on Great Dover Street. He is a dealer of art. My brother Thierry worked for a patisserie at home, but there was a little trouble."

"Trouble?" demanded the guvnor. "What trouble?"

She hesitated.

"Unless you tell me everything, I cannot help."

"They accuse him of stealing from the shop," she said.

"And did he steal?"

"I think yes."

She glanced humbly at him, then her eyes brushed my own. I'm ashamed to confess that even though I was married more than fifteen years before to the most commonsensical woman in the whole of Walworth, that look stirred up an urge in me that hadn't been stirred in a while. This young woman with her almond face and her single chipped tooth was a natural beauty.

"Continue," he said.

"He had to go very quick from Rouen so he followed me to London. He found a job in a chophouse. Four nights ago he comes back from work very scared. He begs of me some money to go back to France. He will not tell me why he must go back. I've never seen him so much scared." She paused here to catch her breath and dab at her eyes with the corner of a yellowed handkerchief. "I say no to him. I could not let him go back to Rouen. If he returns he will be in trouble. I don't want this."

She hesitated again, a tear appearing in her eye.

"But perhaps more I wanted him here in London with me. This is a lonely city for a stranger, sir. And a dangerous one for a woman."

"Take a moment, mademoiselle," said my employer nobly. He sat forward in his chair, his belly hanging on his knees.

"He left in a great anger. I have not seen him since. He's not been at work." The tears began to flow properly now. "Where does he sleep?"

"Now, my dear," said the guvnor. "You don't need us. Your brother's no doubt hiding. He'll seek you when he feels safe."

She held her handkerchief over her eyes until she had control of herself. She blew her nose.

"I can pay, if that's what concerns you," she said at last, pulling a small purse from inside her coat and withdrawing a handful of guineas. "Look."

"Put them away, miss. If he's that frightened, he's probably back in France."

She shook her head.

"No, sir, he is not in France. The day after I refuse him I come from work and see that my clock is gone, and my second shoes and a shift I bought only this winter last. The landlady says me he was there that afternoon."

"There! He's sold them to pay his fare."

"No, sir. His papers, his clothes, they are still in my room.

How he enters France without the papers? Something has happened to him." As she spoke, she dropped the coins back into the purse and withdrew some notes. "Please, Mr. Arrowood. He's all I have. I have nobody to turn to."

The guvnor watched as she unfolded two five-pound notes: it was some time since we'd seen banknotes in that room.

"Why not go to the police?" he asked.

"They will say what you say. I beg you, Mr. Arrowood."

"Miss Cousture, I could take your money, and no doubt there are many private agents in London who would happily have it. But it's one of my principles that I never take money if I don't think there's a case, particularly from a person with limited means. I don't mean to insult you, but I'm sure that money you have there is either hard saved or borrowed. Your brother's probably holed up with a woman somewhere. Wait a few more days. If he doesn't return, then come back and see us."

Her pale face flushed. She rose and stepped to the grate, holding the banknotes to the glowing coals. "If you do not take my case I put this money in your fire," she said sharply.

"Please be sensible, miss," said the guvnor.

"The money's nothing to me. And I think you prefer it in your pocket than your fire?"

The guvnor groaned, his eyes fixed on the notes. He shifted forward in his chair.

"I will!" she said in desperation, moving them down to the flames.

"Stop!" he cried when he could bear it no more.

"You will take my case?"

He sighed. "Yes, yes. I suppose."

"And you will keep my name secret?"

"If that's what you wish."

"We charge twenty shillings a day, Miss Cousture," I said. "Five days' payment in advance for a case of missing persons."

The guvnor turned away and began to fill his pipe. Although he was usually short of money, he was always uncomfortable receiving it: it was too open an admission for one of his class that he needed it.

Once the business was conducted, he turned back to us.

"Now, we need the details," he said, sucking on his pipe. "His age, his appearance. Do you have a photograph?"

"He's twenty-three. Not so well-grown like you, sir," she said, looking at me. "In the middle between Mr. Arrowood and you. His hair's the colour of the wheat and he has a long burn on the ear, on this side. I have no picture. I am sorry. But there are not many in London with our accent."

"Where did he work?"

"The Barrel of Beef, sir."

My heart fell. The warm five-pound note I held now felt cold as cabbage. The guvnor's hand, holding the smoking pipe, had dropped. His eyes gazed into the fire. He shook his head and did not reply.

Miss Cousture frowned.

"What is it, sir?"

I held the money out to her.

"Take it, miss," I said. "We cannot take the case."

"But why? We have an agreement."

I looked at the guvnor, expecting him to answer. Instead, a low growl came from his lips. He took the poker and began to stab the glowing coals. As I held out the money to her, Miss Cousture looked from me to him.

"There is a problem?"

"We have a history with the Barrel of Beef," I said at last. "The owner, Stanley Cream, you've probably heard of him?"

She nodded.

"We came up against him a few years back," I said. "The case went badly wrong. There was a man who was helping us, John Spindle. A good man. Cream's gang beat him to death and we couldn't do nothing about it. Cream swore to have us killed if ever he saw us again."

She remained silent.

"He's the most dangerous man in South London, miss."

"So you are afraid," she said bitterly.

All of a sudden the guvnor turned. His face was glowing from staring so intensely into the fire.

"We will take the case, miss," he declared. "I do not go back on my word."

I bit my tongue. If Miss Cousture's brother was connected to the Beef, there was a good chance he really was in trouble. There was a good chance he was already dead. At that moment, working on the cabs seemed like the best job in London.

When Caroline Cousture had left, the guvnor fell heavily onto his chair. He lit his pipe and stared into the fire as he thought.

"That woman," he said at last, "is a liar."

Chapter Two

⬥————————————————————⬥

WE WERE JUST FINISHING THE PIE AND POTATOES I'd fetched for our dinner when the door from the shop burst open. There on the hearth, carrying a carpetbag in one hand and a tuba case in the other, was a woman of middle age. She wore grey and black; her bearing spoke of a well-travelled soul. The guvnor was immediately struck dumb. I jumped to my feet and bowed, quickly wiping the grease from my fingers onto the back of my trousers.

She nodded briefly at me, then turned back to him. For a long time they looked at each other, him with a look of surprised shame, she with a righteous superiority. Finally, he managed to swallow the potato he held in his mouth.

"Ettie," he said. "What… You're…"

"I can see I've arrived just in time," she replied, her noble eyes travelling slowly over the pill jars and ale flagons, the ash spilling from the fire, the newspapers and books piled on every surface. "Isabel hasn't come back then?"

His big lips pursed and he shook his head.

She turned to me.

"And you are?"

"Barnett, ma'am. Mr. Arrowood's employee."

"Pleased to meet you, Barnett."

She returned my smile with a frown.

The guvnor eased himself from his chair, brushing the flakes of pastry from his woollen vest.

"I thought you were in Afghanistan, Ettie."

"It appears there's much good work to be done amongst the poor of this town. I've joined a mission in Bermondsey."

"What, here?" exclaimed the guvnor.

"I'm going to stay with you. Now, pray tell me where I shall sleep."

"Sleep?" The guvnor glanced at me with fear on his face. "Sleep? You have a nurse's quarters of some kind, surely?"

"From now on I'm in the employ of the good Lord, Brother. It's no bad thing, by the look of this place. These mountains of papers are a hazard, for a start." Her eyes fell on the little staircase at the back of the room. "Ah. I'll just see the space now. No need to accompany me."

She put her tuba on the floor and marched up the stairs.

I made tea for the guvnor while he sat staring out the murky window as if he was about to lose his life. I broke a piece of toffee from my pocket and offered it to him; he put it greedily in his mouth.

"Why did you say Miss Cousture is a liar?" I asked.

"You must watch more closely, Barnett," he said as his teeth worked on the toffee. "There was a point in my speech when she flushed and refused my eye. Only one. It was the moment I told her I could see into a person's soul. That I smelt out the truth. You didn't notice?"

"Did you do it deliberately?"

He shook his head.

"It's a good trick, I think," he said. "I might use it again."

"I'm not sure it is. Lying's a way of life where I come from."

"It is everywhere, Barnett."

"I mean they won't flush if you accuse them."

"But I didn't accuse her. That's the trick. I was talking about myself."

He was making hard work of that toffee, and a little juice escaped the side of his mouth. He wiped it away.

"What was she lying about, then?"

He held up his finger, grimacing as he tried to work the toffee off his molar.

"That I do not know," he replied when he'd freed it. "Now, I must remain this afternoon and find out what the deuce my sister intends to do here. I'm sorry, Barnett. You'll have to visit the Barrel of Beef yourself."

I was none too pleased with this.

"Maybe we should wait until you're able to come," I suggested.

"Don't go inside. Wait across the street until a worker comes out. A washerman or a serving girl. Someone who could do with a penny. See what you can find out, but do nothing that'll put you at risk. Above all, don't let Cream's men see you."

I nodded.

"I'm quite serious, Barnett. I doubt you'd get a second chance this time."

"I don't intend to go anywhere near his men," I said unhappily. "I'd as soon not be going there at all."

"Just be careful," he said. "Come back here when you have something."

As I made to go he glanced up at the ceiling, where the scrape of furniture being moved could be heard.

The Barrel of Beef was a four-storey building on the corner of Waterloo Road. In the evenings it was patronized mostly by young men arriving in hansom cabs from across the river, looking for some life after the theatres and political meetings had shut down for the night. Downstairs at the front was a pub, one of the biggest in Southwark, with two floors of supper rooms above that. The rooms were often booked out by dining societies, and on a summer's night, when the windows were open and the music had begun, it could be like walking past a roaring sea. On the fourth floor were gaming tables, and these were the most exclusive. This was the respectable face of the Barrel of Beef. Around the back, down a stinking lane of beggars and streetwalkers, was the Skirt of Beef, a taproom so dark and so fugged with smoke you'd start to weep the minute you stepped in.

It was a cold July so far, more like early spring, and I cursed the chill wind as I set myself up on the other side of the street, slumped in a doorway like a tramp aside the warm cart of a potato man, my cap pulled low over my face, my body covered in an old sack. I knew too well what Cream's men would do if they discovered me watching the place again. There I waited until the young men got back into their cabs and the street went quiet. Soon a group of serving girls in drab grey clothes came out and marched down eastwards towards Marshalsea. Four waiters were next, a couple of chefs behind. And then, at last, just the kind of old fellow I was looking for. He wore a long ragged coat and boots too big for him, and he hurried and stumbled down the street as if in urgent need of a crapper. I followed him through the dark streets, barely bothering to keep hidden: he'd have no reason to suspect anyone would be interested in him. A light rain began to fall. Soon he arrived at the White Eagle, a gin palace on Friar Street, the only drinking place still open at that late hour.

I waited outside until he had a drink in his hand. Then I strode in and stood at the counter next to him.

"For you?" asked the fat bartender.

"Porter."

I had quite a righteous thirst and downed half the pint in a single swallow. The old fellow supped his gin and sighed. His fingers were puckered and pink.

"Troubles?" I asked.

"Can't drink that stuff no more," he growled, nodding at my pint. "Makes me piss something rotten. Wish I could, though. I used to love a drop of beer. Believe me I did."

Sitting on a high stool behind a glass screen was a man I recognized from the street outside the Beef. He wore a black suit, rubbed thin at the elbows and ragged at the boot, and there was not a hair on his head. His match-selling business suffered on account of his habit of exploding into a series of jerks and tics that made people passing him jump back in fright. Now he was muttering to himself, staring into a half-pint of gin, one hand grasping the other's wrist as if arresting its movements.

"St. Vitus's Dance," whispered the old man to me. "A spirit got hold of his limbs and won't let them go—least that's what they say."

I sympathized with him about drinking beer and we got to talking about what it was like to get old, a subject about which he had much to say. Presently I bought him another drink, which he accepted greedily. I asked him what was his occupation.

"Chief sculleryman," he replied. "You know the Barrel of Beef, I suppose?"

"'Course I do. That's a fine place indeed, sir. A very fine place."

He straightened his beaten back and tipped his head in pride. "It is, it is. I knows Mr. Cream as well, the owner. You know him? I knows all of them as run things down there. He give me, last Christmas this was, he give me a bottle of brandy. Just comes up to me as I was leaving and says, 'Ernest, that's for all what you've done for me this year,' and gives it to me. To me especially. A bottle of brandy. That's Mr. Cream, you know him?"

"He owns the place, I know as much as that."

"A very fine bottle of brandy that was. Finest you can get. Tasted like gold, or silk or something like that." He supped his gin and winced, shaking his head. His eyes were yellow and weepy, the few teeth left in his mouth crooked and brown. "I been there ten years, more or less. He ain't never had one reason to complain about my work all that time. Oh, no. Mr. Cream treats me right. I can eat anything as is left at the end of the night, long as I don't take nothing home with me. Anything they ain't keeping. Steak, kidneys, oysters, mutton soup. Don't hardly spend any money on my food at all. Keep my money for the pleasures of life, I do."

He finished his gin and began to cough. I bought him another. Behind us a tired-looking streetwalker was bickering with two men in brown aprons. One tried to take her arm; she shook him off. Ernest looked at her with an air of senile longing, then turned back to me.

"Not the others," he continued. "Only me, on account of being there longest. Rib of beef. Bit of cod. Tripe if I must. I eat like a lord, mister. It's a good setup. I got a room over the road here. You know the baker's? Penarven the baker's? I got a room above there."

"I know a fellow who works down there, as it happens," I

said. "French lad name of Thierry. Brother of a ladyfriend of mine. You probably know him."

"Terry, is that him? Pastryman? He don't work with us no more. Not since last week or so. Left or given the push. Don't ask me which."

He lit a pipe and began to cough again.

"Only, I'm trying to get hold of him," I continued when he'd finished. "You wouldn't have a notion where I can find him?"

"Ask his sister, shouldn't you?"

"It's her who's looking for him." I lowered my voice. "Truth is it might do me a bit of good if I help her out, like. Know what I mean?"

He chuckled. I slapped him on the back; he didn't like it, and a suspicious look came over him.

"Bit of a coincidence, ain't it? You happening to talk to me like that?"

"I followed you."

It took him a minute to work out what I was saying.

"That's the way it is, is it?" he croaked.

"That's the way it is. You know where I can find him?"

He scratched the stubble on his neck and finished his gin.

"The oysters is good here," he said.

I called the barmaid over and ordered him a bowl.

"All I can say is he was very friendly with a barmaid name of Martha, least it seemed that way to anybody with their eyes open," he said. "Sometimes they left together. You ask her. Curly red hair—you can't miss her. A little beauty, if you don't mind Catholics."

"Was he in any trouble?"

He drained his glass and swayed suddenly, gripping the counter to steady himself.

"I keep my nose out of everything what happens there. You can find yourself in trouble very quick with some of the things as goes on in that building."

The oysters arrived. He looked at them with a frown.

"What's the matter?" I asked.

"It's only as they go down better with a little drain of plane, sir," he replied with a sniff.

I ordered him another gin. When he'd just about finished off the oysters, I asked him again if Thierry was in trouble.

"All I know is he left the day after the American was there. Big American fellow. I only know 'cos I heard him shouting at Mr. Cream, and there ain't nobody who shouts at the boss. Nobody. After that, Terry never come back."

"Why was he shouting?"

"Couldn't hear," he said, dropping the last oyster shell on the floor. He held onto the counter and stared at it as if he wasn't sure he could get down there without falling over.

"D'you know who he was?"

"Never seen him before."

"You must have heard something?" I said.

"I don't talk to nobody and nobody talks to me. I just do my work and go home. That's the best way. That's the advice I'll give my children if ever I have any."

He laughed and called over to the barmaid.

"Oi, Jeannie. Did you hear? I said that's the advice I'll give my children if ever I have any!"

"Yeah, very funny, Ernest," she replied. "Shame your pecker's dropped off."

His face fell. The barman and a cab driver at the end of the counter laughed loudly.

"I could give you a few names to swear as my pecker's attached and working very well, thank you," he croaked back.

But the barmaid wasn't listening any more; she was talking to the cab driver. The old man stared hard at them for a few moments, then finished his drink and patted his coat pockets. His skin sagged from his bristling chin; his wrists seemed thin as broomsticks under the sleeves of his thick overcoat.

"That's it for me."

"Could you find out where he is, Ernest?" I asked as we stepped onto the street. "I'd pay you well."

"Find another fool, mister," he replied, his words slurring in the chill air. "I don't want to end up in the river with a lungful of mud. Not me."

He glanced bitterly through the window where the barmaid was laughing with the cabman, then turned and stomped off down the road.

Chapter Three

◆————————————————◆

THE GUVNOR'S ROOM WAS TRANSFORMED. THE floor had been swept free of crumbs, the bottles and plates had vanished, the blankets and cushions straightened. Only the towers of newspapers against the walls remained. He was in his chair with his hair brushed and a clean shirt on. In his hand was the book that had occupied him over the last few months: *The Expression of the Emotions in Man and Animals* by the infamous Mr. Darwin. Some years before, Mrs. Barnett had become quite enraged by this fellow on account of him seeming to suggest, or so she said at least, that she and her sisters were the daughters of a big ape rather than the generous creation of the good Lord above. She'd never read his books, of course, but there were people at her church very against the idea that the good Lord hadn't made a woman from a ribbone and a man from a speck of dust. The guvnor, who hadn't come to a decision on this matter as far as I knew, had been reading this book very carefully and slowly, and letting everyone know that he was reading it along the way. He seemed to think it held secrets which would help him see past the deceptions that were the everyday part of our work. I couldn't help but notice too that another of Watson's stories lay open on the side table next to him.

"I've been waiting all morning for news, Barnett," he declared, looking as uncomfortable as a hog in a bonnet. "I had breakfast many hours ago."

"I didn't reach home until gone two."

"She had me up early as she wished to clean the bed somehow," he continued with resignation. "Very early. But what did you discover?"

I explained what I'd found out, and immediately he had me send the lad from the coffeehouse to find Neddy. Neddy was a boy who the guvnor had taken a shine to a few years back when his family had moved into a room down the street. His father was long dead, his mother a quite disastrous washerwoman. Her earnings weren't enough for the family, barely enough to pay their rent, so Neddy sold muffins on the street to support her and the two youngers at home. He was nine or ten years or eleven perhaps.

The lad arrived shortly after, carrying his muffin basket under his arm. He was sorely in need of a haircut, and had a rip in the shoulder of his white jerkin.

"Have you any left, boy?" asked the guvnor.

"Just two, sir," replied Neddy, opening the blanket. "Last two I got."

I quite marvelled at the magnificent thick black dirt that framed his little fingerbits, and beneath his brown cap could see distinctly the slow crawl of livestock. Oh, for the carefree life of the child!

The guvnor grunted and took the muffins.

"You've eaten, Barnett?" he asked as he bit into the first. With his mouth full of dough, he gave Neddy his instructions. He was to wait outside the Beef that night until the waiting girl Martha came out, and then to follow her home and bring back the address. He made the boy promise to be extra careful and not to speak to anyone.

"I'll get it, sir," said the boy earnestly.

The guvnor popped the last bit of muffin in his mouth and smiled.

"Of course you will, lad. But look at your dirty face." He turned to me and winked. "Don't you prefer a boy with a dirty face, Barnett?"

"I ain't got a dirty face," protested the boy.

"Your face is caked in dirt. Here, take a peek in the looking glass."

Neddy scowled at the glass hanging on the wall.

"It ain't."

The guvnor and I broke out laughing; he took the boy to his chest and hugged him tight.

"You get off now, lad," he said, releasing him.

"Are you going to pay him for those muffins?" I asked.

"Of course I'm going to pay him!" snapped the guvnor, his forehead taking a flush. He pulled a coin from his waistcoat and threw it in Neddy's basket. "Don't I always pay him?"

The boy and I looked at each other and smiled.

When Neddy was gone, and the guvnor had brushed the crumbs from his waistcoat to the floor, I said, "She's made a good job of this room, sir."

"Mm," he murmured, looking morosely around him. "I must say, I'm not hopeful of a happy solution to this case. I fear what might have happened to the French lad if he's found trouble with Cream."

"I fear what might happen to us if they find we've been asking questions."

"We must be careful, Barnett. They mustn't find out."

"Can we give her the money back?" I asked.

"I've given my word. Now, I need a nap. Return tomorrow, early. We'll have work to do."

By the time I arrived the next morning Neddy had returned with the address. The boardinghouse that Martha lived in was just off Bermondsey Street, and we were there in twenty minutes. It wasn't pretty: the white paint on the door was flaked and grubby, the windows were misted all the way up the building, and a terrible black smoke poured out the chimney. At the sound of shouting inside, the guvnor winced. He was a gentleman who did not like aggression of any flavour.

The woman who opened the door seemed none too happy to be disturbed.

"Second floor," she rasped, turning away from us and marching back to her kitchen. "Room at the back."

Martha was every bit as beautiful as the old man had made out. She came to the door wrapped in two old coats, the sleep still in her eyes.

"Do I know you?" she asked. The guvnor drew in his breath: she had a resemblance to Isabel, his wife, except younger and taller. The long bronze curls were the same, the green eyes, the upturned nose. Only her slow Irish drawl was unlike Isabel's fenland lilt.

"Madam," replied the guvnor, a quiver in his voice. "Apologies for disturbing you. We need to talk to you for a moment."

I looked over her shoulder into the room. There was a bed in the corner and a small table with a looking glass on it. Two dresses hung from a rack. On a chest of drawers was a neat pile of newspapers.

"What is it you want?" she asked.

"We're looking for Thierry, miss," replied the guvnor.

"Who?"

"Your friend from the Barrel of Beef."

"I don't know no Thierry."

"Yes you do," he said in his friendliest voice. "We know he's a friend of yours, Martha."

She crossed her arms. "What do you want him for?"

"His sister employed us to find him," replied the guvnor. "She thinks he might be in trouble."

"I don't think so, sir," she said, and made to shut the door. I managed to get my boot in the way just in time. Her eyes dropped to my foot, then, seeing we weren't to be budged, she sighed.

"We only need to know where he is," I said. "We aim to help him, is all."

"I don't know where he is, sir. He don't work there no more."

"When did you see him last?"

A door slammed above and heavy footsteps began to come down the dusty stairs. Martha quickly pulled her head back into the room and shut the door. It was a tall man with a prominent, bony jaw, and by the time I recognized him it was too late to turn my head away. I'd seen him hanging around the Barrel of Beef when we were working on the Betsy case four years before. I never knew what his job was—he was just there, all the time, lurking and watching.

He glared at us as he passed, then stamped on down the stairs. When finally we heard the front door open and shut, Martha appeared again.

"I can't talk here," she whispered. "Everyone works in the Beef. Meet me later, on my way to work."

Her green eyes glanced up at the stairs and she paused, listening. A man began to sing in the room along the corridor.

"Outside St. George the Martyr," she continued. "At six."

With a final worried look upstairs, she shut the door.

I'd reached the first landing when I realized the guvnor wasn't behind me. He was still staring at the closed door, deep in thought. I called his name: he started and followed me down the stairs.

When we'd gained the street, I broke the silence.

"She's a little like—"

"Yes, Barnett," he interrupted. "Yes, she is."

He didn't speak again the whole walk home.

They had only been married a short time when I first knew Mr. Arrowood. Mrs. Barnett always wondered how such a fine-looking woman had married a potato like him, but from what I saw they seemed to get on just fine. He made a reasonable living as a newspaperman working for *Lloyd's Weekly*, and their household was a happy one. Isabel was kind and attentive, and there were always interesting visitors around their home. I met him at the courts, where I was earning a living as a junior clerk. I would sometimes help him gain certain information for stories he was writing, and he often invited me to his lodgings to have a bite of mutton or soup. But then the paper was sold to a new proprietor, who installed a cousin in the guvnor's position and ejected him onto his uppers.

Mr. Arrowood had by then some renown for digging up the sort of truths as others would like to have remained buried, and it wasn't long before an acquaintance of his offered him a sum of money to solve a small personal problem involving his wife and another man. This young man recommended him to a friend who also had a small personal problem, and that was how the investigational work began. A year or so later I found myself also out of work on account of losing my temper

at a particular magistrate who had a habit of jailing youngsters who needed a helping hand a good deal more than they
needed a spell in adult prison. I was out on my ear without so
much as a handshake or a pocket watch, and when the guvnor
heard what had happened he searched me out. After an inter-
view with Mrs. Barnett, he offered me work as his assistant on
the case he was working on. That was the Betsy bigamy case,
my baptism of fire, where a child lost his leg and an innocent
man lost his life. The guvnor blamed himself for both—and
rightly so. He shut himself in his rooms for the best part of two
months, only coming back out when his money was used up.
We took a job, but it was clear to anyone he'd taken to drink.
Since then, cases were irregular and money was always short.
The Betsy case hung over us like a curse, but what we'd seen
bound me to him as sure as if we were brothers.

Isabel put up with his drinking and the irregular work for
three years before he came home one day to find her clothes
gone and a note on the table. He hadn't heard from her since.
He'd written to her brothers, her cousins, her aunts, but they
wouldn't tell him where she was. I once suggested he use his
investigative skills to find her, but he just shook his head. He
told me then, his eyes shut so he shouldn't see me looking
at him, that losing Isabel was his punishment for letting the
young man die in the Betsy case, and that he must endure it
for as long as God or the Devil pleased. The guvnor wasn't
usually a religious man and I was surprised to hear him say
it, but he was about as raw as a man could be after she left
and who knows where a man's mind will go to when he's left
heartbroken and turning it all over night after night? He had
been waiting for her to return since the day she left.

Chapter Four

WE WERE LATE. IT WAS A DIRTY AFTERNOON, WITH rain and wind and mud in the streets. St. George's Circus was busy at that time, and the guvnor, whose shoes were too tight, was hobbling along with many grunts and sighs. He'd bought the shoes used and cheap from the washerwoman and complained almost the very next day on account of them being too small for his bloated feet. She wouldn't take them back so the guvnor, being careful with his coppers, had resigned himself to wearing them until such time as they split open or lost a heel. It was taking longer than he'd hoped.

When we finally got to the church we could see our Martha up ahead, wrapped in a black cloak and hood. She was holding onto the churchyard railing, just inside the gate, her eyes sweeping up and down the street. She was clearly anxious to find us, so the guvnor pinched my arm and hurried on. A crowd was gathered outside one of the cookhouses; as we fought our way through, a shortish man pushed past us from behind and darted away before us, the tails of his old winter coat flapping in the wind, his hat sitting back on his head.

The guvnor swore and grumbled as a coalman dumped a sack from his cart onto the pavement in front of us.

Just then there was a shriek up ahead.

A woman with a baby stood by the church gate looking around frantically as the short man who'd shoved us ran off towards the river.

"It's the Ripper!" she screamed.

"Get a doctor!" someone else called.

We both began to run. By now there were many others also rushing to the church gate to see what had occurred. We pushed our way through the crowd and saw Martha lying curled on the wet ground, her hair spread across the flagstones like a spill of molten bronze.

The guvnor let out a groan and fell to his knees next to her.

"Get after him, Barnett!" he called back at me as he lifted her head from the path.

I took off, winding and ducking through the crowds. The short man ran across the street ahead of me. His coat, much too big for him, billowed behind, his bandy legs moving at full pelt. He sped to the next intersection. As he turned down Union Street, I caught the side of his face, his oily grey hair stuck to his forehead, a nose with a prominent hook. A minute later I reached the same corner but was brought up short by a teeming wet mass of people and horses. I couldn't see him anywhere. I hurried on, my eyes searching frantically for his dark coat in the crowd, my way checked all the time by carts and buses and street vendors, further and further down the road.

I ran blindly, on my instinct, until I saw a flash of black coat turn down a side street up ahead. I pushed my way between the carts to the junction. Ahead of me was an undertaker knocking on a door. There were no other men in the narrow lane. My chest heaving, I turned back to busy Union Street, not knowing which way to go. It was no use. I had lost him.

When I got back to the churchyard the crowd was still

there. A gentleman paced up and down the path, shaking his head. The guvnor was kneeling on the ground, Martha's head cradled in his lap. Her face was ashen, the tip of her tongue resting at the side of her mouth. Beneath the thick black cloak, her white serving blouse was a slick claret.

I knelt and checked her pulse, but could see from the way the guvnor shook his head, by the desolate look in his eyes, that she was dead.

At that moment a constable arrived.

"What's happened here?" he asked, his voice booming over the noise of the crowd.

"This young woman's been killed," said the gentleman. "Just now. That fellow there chased the man."

"He ran off down Union Street," I said, getting up. "I lost him in the crowds."

"Is she a streetwalker?" asked the copper.

"What has that to do with it?" replied the gentleman. "She's dead, for pity's sake. Murdered."

"Just thinking about the Ripper, sir. He only did street-walkers."

"She was not a streetwalker!" barked the guvnor, his face burning with fury. "She was a waiting girl."

"Did anybody see what happened?" asked the constable.

"I saw it all, I did," said the woman with the baby, important and breathless. "I was standing here, right here next to the gate, when he comes up and chives the lady through her cloak like that. One, two, three. Like that, poor girl. Then he runs off. He was a foreigner, I'd say, by the look of him. A Jew. I thought he was going to do me for afters, but he just run off like they said."

The constable nodded and finally knelt to check Martha's pulse.

"He didn't have human eyes," she continued. "They was shining like a wolf, like he wanted to rip me as well. Only thing stopping him was all the people coming over when she screamed. That's what frightened him off. Too late for her, though, poor little thing."

The constable stood up again.

"Anybody else see the incident?"

"I turned when I heard the girl cry," said the gentleman. "Saw the chap hurtle off. He looked Irish from where I was, but I couldn't be sure."

The constable peered down at the guvnor.

"Were you with her, sir?"

"He come along after," said the woman.

"I recognize her from the Barrel of Beef." The guvnor's voice was grey and flat. "I don't know her."

The policeman took a description from the woman and the gentleman, who agreed it must have been a foreigner but couldn't agree whether it was a Jew or an Irishman, and then from me. Once he'd sent a boy to the station for the police surgeon, he dispersed us.

"What do we do now?" I asked as we trudged back.

The guvnor cursed, ignoring me.

"Damn Cream to hell!" he exclaimed. "He'll kill whoever he wants."

"We don't know he was behind it."

He cracked his walking stick hard against the kerb, a look of utmost misery on his face.

"We've led that dear girl to her death. That cur from the Beef saw us at the house. We might as well have killed her ourselves."

"We didn't know they all worked in the Beef."

"Damn it, Barnett. It's starting again. The whole cursed Cream business."

"Perhaps we should leave it to the police," I suggested.

"That idiot Petleigh will never find the killer."

The guvnor glanced back at the church. When we'd turned the corner he held out a small, twisted handkerchief.

"This was gripped in her hand," he said. "I'm sure she held it for us."

He opened the handkerchief. Inside was a single brass bullet.

Chapter Five

WE ARRIVED IN GREAT DOVER STREET LATER THAT evening, where a row of milliners, dress shops and shoe shops all had their lights on for the evening trade. At the end was a coffee grinder, and the breeze carried the rich smells of the roasting beans. There was only one photographer's studio, called "The Fontaine." A man in a green velvet jacket with hair reaching his collar stood at the desk constructing a picture frame. He held a small hammer in his hand and a pin in his mouth.

"Good day, sirs," he said with an insincere smile. "How may I help you? Is it a portrait you're after?"

"We're looking for Miss Cousture," said the guvnor, glancing around at the photographic portraits on the walls. "Is she here?"

"She's at work," the man replied, pulling back his long head disdainfully. "I'm the proprietor, Mr. Fontaine. Do you want to book a portrait?"

"Did you take these?" asked the guvnor, indicating the pictures. "They're very good."

"Yes indeed. All my own work. I could make a fine image

of you, sir, if you don't mind me saying. Your profile is quite wonderful."

"Do you think so?" asked the guvnor, his chest inflating. He smoothed the hair around his crown. "I've been thinking of commissioning a picture for some time. I think my sister would very much like a portrait above the fire."

I looked at him, unable to suppress a smile at the thought of such a gift.

"We can book it in now, sir. Shall we say Monday morning? Eleven o'clock?"

"Yes… Ah. Wait. On second thoughts, I'd better wait until I've taken possession of my new suit. But might we speak to Miss Cousture now? On a personal matter."

The artist looked down his long nose at us for some time.

"It's important, Mr. Fontaine," I said, growing impatient. "Is she here?"

With a theatrical sigh and a shake of his lank black hair, he disappeared behind a curtain at the back of the store. A moment later Miss Cousture appeared.

"Good day, Mr. Arrowood," she said quietly as she swept through the curtain. She was wearing a high-waisted black skirt, a white blouse rolled to her sleeves, her hair pinned up on her head. She nodded at me. "Mr. Barnett."

Mr. Fontaine appeared behind her and stood by the curtain, his arms crossed.

She flicked her eyes at her employer as if to warn us not to talk. There followed a silence. Her pale cheeks coloured. She looked at her boots.

"Would you mind if we have a private moment with the lady, sir?" asked the guvnor finally. Noticing that his tie had blown over his shoulder from the breezy street, I stepped forward and flipped it back. He took a quick backward swipe at me.

"This is my studio, sir," said the man with a sniff. He rubbed his long nose quickly. "The name above the door is mine, not the lady's. If you have something to say, get on and say it."

"Then will you come outside, madam?"

"Oh, *putain*, Eric!" she cursed, turning to her employer. "One moment, that is all!"

On the lips of this fine woman, the profanity turned the air cold. Fontaine threw his head back and ducked behind the curtain. We heard his angry footsteps on the stairs.

The guvnor pulled a chair from behind the counter and lowered himself down with a wince. He rubbed his feet through his tight boots. For some time he didn't speak.

"We need to ask you a few more questions, miss," he said at last.

"Of course. But I tell you all I know."

"We must know what trouble your brother was in," he said, a pained smile on his red face. "Any small thing he might have said. Please be quite open with us."

"Of course."

"Did you know his friend Martha?"

She shook her head.

"His sweetheart. You didn't know about her?"

"I never heard the name."

"Well, Miss Cousture, I'm afraid to say she was murdered this afternoon."

We watched as her face turned from surprise to sadness. She gripped the counter and lowered herself onto the stool.

"We had an appointment to meet but someone got to her first," explained the guvnor.

She nodded slowly.

"We also discovered there was some trouble in the Barrel of Beef just before Thierry disappeared. The only clue we have is that it might involve an American. Did Thierry mention any such thing to you?"

"An American?" she said, a disappointed tone in her voice. "No, never. What is the name?"

"We don't have a name. All we know is that the day your brother disappeared there was an argument involving an American. We don't even know for sure Thierry was involved. But please think again. Did anything happen before he disappeared? Was there any change in him?"

"Only when he comes to me for money. The last time I see him, I tell you he's scared." She paused, her eyes travelling quickly from the guvnor to me and back again. "Do you think he's dead? Is that what you mean by 'trouble'?"

The guvnor took her hand and held it.

"It's too early to think of that, miss."

She was about to speak again when Mr. Fontaine swept back through the curtain. This time he would not be budged.

We walked back towards Waterloo. The air was still and a fog had descended.

"Barnett," said the guvnor at length. "Was there anything that struck you as odd about what we've just seen?"

I thought for a bit, trying to guess what he'd noticed.

"Not as I could say," I said at last.

"Tell me, if Mrs. Barnett had disappeared without taking her clothes or her papers, and you'd appointed a detective, and let's imagine that two days later the detective came to see you. You're quite mad with worry, remember."

"Yes, sir."

"What would be the first thing you would say to him?"

"I suppose I'd ask if he'd found her."

"Exactly, Barnett." His brow tensed. "Exactly."

The guvnor continued home to ponder this development, while I returned to the White Eagle. I had myself a bowl of oysters and then a plate of mutton as I waited, and then a glass of porter, and then another. It was a noisy night, and I was happy enough to sit in the corner and watch my fellow citizens larking about under the great looking glass as stretched the length of the ceiling. Later on the match-seller trudged in. He looked at no one as he made his way across the syrupy floor, but held his face in a rictus in case he should launch into some anarchic pantomime. He paid, took his glass, and went to hide in his usual corner behind the glass panel.

When the crowd began to thin, Ernest stumbled in and stood at the same place at the bar as before. He took himself a gin and drank it quick, his back hunched over the counter. He wore the same thick clothes as before, and didn't appear to see anyone around him except the barmaid, who slammed his drink before him as if he'd insulted her mother.

"Good to see you again, my friend," I said, placing a second glass before him. "Come sit at my table. I could do with a bit of company."

He looked up with confusion in his eyes. He glanced at the gin, then back at me. A trickle of blood from his gums ran down his single remaining front tooth.

"Eh?" he said at last.

"We met the other night, Ernest. Here. Two nights ago."

Slowly his watery eyes cleared and he seemed to remember me. He pulled himself upright. Then he became suspicious.

"I ain't got no money," he declared, before quickly swallowing the whole glass in one.

"Come over. I'll get you some oysters."

"What is it you want?"

I lowered my voice. The cab driver I'd seen before was leaning against the bar in the corner, talking with the barmaid.

"I want some information is all."

He shook his head.

"I don't know nothing. I should never have spoke to you the first time."

He turned away from me. From behind the glass partition an arm flailed, followed by an irritated growl. A group of young men, their faces and hands black with coal dust, came over to look at the source, and the sight of the tortured matchseller trying to suppress his mania made them laugh. They returned to their table, but the ruckus went on for minutes. From behind the screen came another strangled yowl and a foul curse from the ticcing man, which made the young men burst into a second, louder round of laughter.

"Let me get you another drink," I said to the sculleryman. Before he could refuse, I gestured to the barmaid and placed a nice mug of gin in his raw fist.

"Let's sit. You look like you need to get the weight off your feet. You've been working hard, Ernest."

He followed me meekly to the table.

"Did you ever see Thierry's sister at the Beef?" I asked when we were sat down. "Good looker, dark hair? French, as you might suppose."

He breathed in sharply, then quickly swallowed his gin.

"Not as I ever saw. Never saw him with any woman but Martha."

"What about the American? What did you hear about him?"

"You said oysters?" he said, folding his arms over his matted coat.

I went to get him a bowl and another mug of gin. He'd got through half of it and survived a short burping fit before I asked him again.

"Mr. Cream has plenty of business acquaintances," he replied. "They was in day after day. Some of them you'd recognize, but this one I never seen before. Bald, with black hair around the crown. Black beard. Blue eyes that pierced you. I took them up some coffee and he almost stared right through me. There was an Irishman with him. I seen him in the place a few times before. Little fellow with a big voice. Stringy yellow hair. One of his ears was cut off. Horrible-looking he was."

"And you don't know his business, I suppose."

"They talk business in the office, not the scullery."

"I need to know anyone else Terry was tight with, Ernest. Who did he talk to? Give me some names."

"I give you a name last time. Martha. Ask her."

"I need another name."

"I've given you a name!" he protested, chafing now that he was flushed through with gin. "Ask Martha. If anybody knows anything, it'll be her."

I leaned in to him and whispered, "She's dead, Ern. Murdered on her way to work this evening."

His mouth fell open; he stared at me with his rheumy eyes. It seemed as if his pickled brain couldn't absorb what I'd told him.

"Did you hear me? Murdered. That's why I need to talk to somebody else."

Slowly, fear took him over. His arm trembled, his eyes blinked fast. He swallowed his gin; I gestured for another.

When it arrived he shook his head.

"I got to go, mister," he said. His voice was strained. "I don't know nothing."

He made a move to rise; I held his wrist fast.

"A name, Ern. One name. Someone he might have talked to. Who did he work next to? Who in the Beef did he spend the most time with?"

"I suppose Harry." He was talking quick now, looking around him at each noise. "You could try him. One of the junior cooks. He worked in the same part of the kitchen."

"And what does he look like?"

"Very thin. Unnatural thin, he is, and his eyebrows are dark but his hair's yellow. You can't miss him."

I let go of his wrist.

"Thank you, Ernest."

In a flash he was up and scurrying out of the gin-house. As I rose, I felt someone's eyes on me. I turned. The bald head of the match-seller had appeared around the side of the glass partition, and he was staring at me with curiosity. He sniffed, his shoulders twitched, and he disappeared back into his hole.

Chapter Six

THE NEXT MORNING I FOUND THE GUVNOR ALONE in his parlour. His face was red and had a peculiar shine to it as if he'd been buffed by a cleaning maid.

"She's out," he declared the minute I stepped in from the shop. "She's at an organizing meeting with the others."

"Organizing? What's she organizing?"

"They're to visit the poor. Now, what did you discover last night?"

I told him about the junior cook, Harry. Since neither of us had any particular inclination to show our face in the Barrel of Beef, he summoned Neddy and instructed him to take a note. The note was signed "Mr. Locksher," the guvnor's usual alias, and promised a reward of a shilling for "a very quick job indeed." Harry was to come that night, after his work was over, to Mrs. Willows' coffeehouse on Blackfriars Road, the only one open until such a late hour. "Your friend from across the Channel suggested your name" was all the explanation offered. Neddy was under instruction to hold tight to that note and not to give it to anyone other than the fellow called Harry. We told him to look out for the thin man with black eyebrows and yellow hair, and to walk direct into the kitchen and not to tell anybody who had sent him.

The boy scampered off while the guvnor refilled his pipe. When he had it lit again, he looked at me sadly.

"What do you think about the girl's death, Barnett? Do you think it was Jack on the prowl again?"

"It doesn't seem like it."

"Indeed. This murder wasn't Jack's work. His killings were all of a similar character. He did his work in solitary places. He preferred to butcher the bodies, and this takes time."

I waited, knowing from the way he stared into the air that there was more to come.

"I've been thinking about this man," he continued. "First, there's his precision. He hurries to the church, delivers three deadly blows and runs into the crowd. He leaves nothing, no clues, no knife. He's rapid and careful, so we can assume it isn't an act of passion. Neither was it robbery. A robber wouldn't choose a poor girl as his victim, not in daylight, and not on a busy street."

"He wouldn't have time to search her pockets."

"Quite so." He puffed on his pipe and thought. "And his clothes. He wears a winter coat when it's summer. It's too big for him. Therefore he's either a man of little means or in disguise. Tell me, as you chased, did he look back?"

"Not once. I had my eyes on him all the time until I lost him. I only saw the side of his face as he turned the corner."

"He didn't turn his head once to determine whether he was pursued?"

I shook my head.

"Tell me, if you'd murdered a person on a busy street and fled, how would you feel?"

"My blood would be up, I suppose. I'd be anxious not to be caught."

"Yes, yes, and would you turn your head to see if you were being pursued?"

"I reckon so."

"You wouldn't be able to stop your head turning, Barnett. Your strong emotions would make you do it. This man isn't like you. He's used to controlling his emotions. So what is he? A hired assassin? A police officer?"

"A soldier?"

He nodded, placing his pipe in the ash dish and pushing himself out of the chair.

"That's a start. And now we'll go and visit Lewis. I don't want to be here when Ettie resumes her reorganization of my life, and you'd better not be here either else she will begin on yours."

Lewis Schwartz was the proprietor of a dark weaponry shop not far from Southwark Bridge. It was where people came with pistols and shotguns they desired to sell; it was where people came when they needed to buy some self-protection. It wasn't a business I'd have wished to be in: I could only imagine the criminals who came and went from this boutique, but Lewis was as solid and unaffected by the danger of his trade as the river walls that seeped their yellow pus into the bricks of his dark shop. He was a fat man with one missing arm and stringy grey hair that fell onto his grimy collar. The guvnor and him were old friends. He used to go to Lewis when he needed information for the newspaper, and since we'd become private agents he continued to help us from time to time. The guvnor always brought a packet of mutton or roasted beef or a bit of liver from the cookshop, which he would slap on the little table foul with grease. I was in the habit of standing back on these occasions, just as I did now, my mind imagining all the diseases whose traces could no doubt be found on the mud-black hands of our friend.

Today Lewis ate carefully, chewing on one side of his mouth only.

"You got tooth problems?" I asked him.

"One of the devils is playing me up."

"Let me see," demanded the guvnor.

Lewis opened his mouth and tipped back his head. The guvnor winced.

"That tooth is black. You must have it pulled."

"I'm mustering my courage."

"Sooner the better," said the guvnor.

It was only when the beef was finished, and the fingers wiped on the trousers of these two old friends, that the guvnor fished in his waistcoat pocket and pulled out the bullet.

"Any idea who might use a bullet such as this, Lewis?"

Lewis put on his eyeglasses and held it under the lamp.

"Very nice," he murmured, turning the bullet this way and that, rubbing its shaft with his fingers. "It's a 303. Smokeless. But how did you come by something like this, William?"

"A dying girl gave it to me," said the guvnor. "A young innocent girl, murdered before our eyes. And we mean to find out who killed her. Do you know what type of gun it's from, Lewis?"

"The new Lee-Enfield repeating rifles." Lewis handed the bullet back. "Military rifles, only issued to a few regiments so far. This is no huntsman's rifle. She must have got it from a soldier. Did she have a sweetheart?"

"He was no soldier."

"Then another man. Was she a whore, William?"

"She was not a whore!" cried the guvnor.

Lewis looked at him in surprise.

"Why are you angry?" he asked. "Did you know her?"

"I don't understand why everyone assumes she was a whore. She worked in the Barrel of Beef."

"She might have been given it by a customer," I said, understanding that the guvnor had attached the same purity to Martha as he attached to his wife.

"Why would a customer give a girl a bullet?" asked Lewis, his nose twitching. "A tip, now that would be one thing. But why a bullet?"

The guvnor shook his head and stood.

"That's what we have to find out," he said.

As we reached the door, a match flared. The guvnor turned back. Lewis sat hunched in his chair at the back of the shop, surrounded by boxes of bullets and sheaves of gunpowder, a glowing pipe in his mouth.

"One day you'll blow yourself up," the guvnor said to his friend. "I've warned you about this for years. Why do you never listen?"

Lewis waved him away.

"If I started to worry now I'd have to sell up this shop and become a potato-man," he said. "You should see some of the individuals I have to deal with. One spark and they would explode themselves. Next to them, this is nothing."

Late that night we waited in Mrs. Willows' coffeehouse. I watched the street outside ebb and flow in the mud and the brown rain, the night-time people stagger and shriek, the horses clop by, their heads low and weary. Midnight passed and the dark new day took its place outside the grimy window. The guvnor read the newspapers like a glutton. He started with

Punch, stowing *Lloyd's Weekly* and the *Pall Mall Gazette* under his thighs. On the next table a thin fellow with the uniform of an undertaker ate a packet of whelks and watched him un-happily, waiting for the chance of a read before he wandered home. But the guvnor took his time, reading every column, every page, then just when it seemed he was finished he went back to the beginning and began scanning the columns again.

"Look at this, Barnett," he said, holding up a cartoon. It was of a tall Irish peasant holding a knife over a cringing English gentleman. The caption was *The Irish Frankenstein*. "They're printing these cartoons again. You see what they do? The Irish have monkeys' faces, covered in hair. The Englishman is defenceless. Good God, why does this never change? Why will they not see our own aggression?"

"I suppose they don't want to see it, sir."

The undertaker cleared his throat and nodded at the paper. The guvnor lit his pipe, then without a word thrust the paper at the man, before lifting his leg and continuing on to the *Gazette*.

Finally, the door swung open and in walked our man. He stood in the doorway, his long thin arms protruding from a brown woollen coat that was too long in the body and too short in the limbs. His yellow hair was tucked into a grey cloth cap pulled down over his ears. He looked at the undertaker, at Mrs. Willows standing in the door to the kitchen, then at us. His black eyebrows twitched.

"Mr. Harry," I said, standing. "This is Mr. Locksher. Have a sit down. You want a coffee?"

He nodded and sat on a stool.

"What's the job?" he asked.

"We have a parcel for your friend Thierry," said the guv-nor softly, leaning across the table. "Only we can't find him."

Harry stood.

"You said a job. That ain't no job far as I can see."

"We'll pay you for the information."

He looked back and forth between us for a moment, chewing his lip.

"No."

He was turning to leave when I grasped his arm.

"Let go," he demanded, his bristly face pinched. Under the thick wool of his coat I could feel the bones of his arm: he was thin as a workhouse pensioner. His skin was grey, the rims of his eyes red. The bones of his jaw were sharp like a skull.

It was no trouble to shove him back down on the stool. He was a good few inches taller than me but weak as a sparrow.

The undertaker quickly rose, shoved the remains of his whelks into his pocket, and made his exit. Mrs. Willows brought over the coffee, her face calm like nothing was happening.

"You be nice, Mr. Barnett," she murmured.

"We intend to be very nice to the gentleman, Rena," said the guvnor.

"I don't know nothing," said the man. "Honest. I can't help you. He's gone. Went off a few days ago now. Probably gone back to France. That's all I can think." He glanced up at me. "That's all I can say, sirs."

"You're a thin man for a cook," the guvnor observed.

"Cook's helper. I do the peelings mostly. Pull the bones out the fishes. I ain't no big cook."

The guvnor leaned over the table suddenly and shoved his hand in the man's coat pocket. Before Harry could respond, he pulled out a greasy packet and dropped it on the table.

"It's a pudding," said Harry, his tone defensive. "Half a pudding."

"What's in there?" asked the guvnor, indicating the other pocket.

"Couple of spuds. Bit of a ham bone. They was going to throw it."

"I doubt that," I said, having a bit of a look in his pocket. "Ain't nothing wrong with that food. Even if it was on the turn, they'd sell it in the Skirt or outside to those as sleep in the alley."

"Don't tell him, mister. Please. I'll take it all back. Last thing I need right now is to be out of a job."

"No need for that, sir," said the guvnor. "We're not on friendly terms with your employer."

"Why are you so thin?" I asked. "Are you sick?"

"If six children be called a sickness. And one of them only two this month."

"But you've a regular job," said the guvnor. "Is your wife alive?"

The man nodded, his eyes twitching towards the window where a hansom trotted past.

"Doesn't she feed you?"

The knuckle in Harry's gullet rose as he swallowed.

"I can't help you," he said.

"We do mean to give you a shilling, Harry," said the guvnor, his voice gentle. "We're investigative agents, working for Mr. Thierry's family. They say he's gone missing. They're worried."

Harry continued to stare out the window, unsure whether to trust us.

"We couldn't come to the Beef because Mr. Cream has a particular dislike for us," continued the guvnor. "That's why we sent the boy."

For another minute Harry considered it. Then he rose.

"I can't help you. Thierry just left. I ain't heard from him since, and even if I did know something I don't know as I'd tell you. I don't want to be mixed up in what ain't got nothing to do with me."

Yet he didn't leave. The guvnor looked at him in silence, his face puckered in thought.

"We were there when Martha was stabbed, Harry," he said at last. "She was waiting to meet us. I held her until the constable arrived."

The cook froze. His eyes filled with brine. I put my hand on his shoulder, and he let me support him as he sat back down.

"We think that had something to do with Thierry going missing," the guvnor went on. "We're going to find out who killed her. But we need information."

"You were there?"

"She asked us to meet her. She wanted to tell us something."

All of a sudden Harry began to talk quick. He leaned across the table, his voice low as if not wishing Mrs. Willows to hear. "Something was happening at the Beef," he said. "Not the usual. Something bigger. I don't know what for sure, but there was a gang of them in and out of there. Mr. Cream asked Terry to go and get a delivery for him last week. I told him not to go but you never can say no to Mr. Cream. Not if you want to work there, you can't. One day they come in, two of them, up to Mr. Cream's office and start wrecking it. We could hear it from the kitchen. Not a one of Mr. Cream's men went up to stop them. Not Mr. Piser, not Long Lenny, not Boots. They all stands down next to the front bar, quiet as mice."

"Who were they?"

Harry shook his head.

"Were they American?"

"And Irish, but that's all I know. It was secret. They come

in and go straight upstairs, never a word to anybody, like they was in charge."

"Come, Harry," said the guvnor. "Think. You must have heard something about them."

"There was some talk of them being burglars. You know Mr. Cream's a fence, I suppose? Somebody reckoned they was doing the big houses up in Bloomsbury and so on. The big houses around Hyde Park as well, the ministers' houses, the embassies too. Jewellery and silver. You know, things easy to move on. That's where Mr. Cream comes in. That's the whisper I heard. Didn't hear any names."

"Why did they turn over his office?"

He shrugged. "Could of been any reason. He swindled them. Let slip something to the coppers. Made a promise he couldn't keep. Could of been anything."

"What did Martha have to do with it?"

"Nothing, far as I know. Except Mr. Piser was always sweet on her. That's the only connection far as I can see. But she was sweet on Terry. Mr. Piser, well, he didn't like it."

"Did they have an argument?" asked the guvnor.

"Mr. Piser never had an argument with no one. Doesn't talk enough to argue."

"Why do you think she was murdered, Harry?"

He drained his coffee and straightened his back.

"Probably on account of going to meet you," he said, holding the guvnor's eye. "That'd be my guess, sir."

The guvnor looked like he'd had the wind knocked out of him. I don't know why. He knew it as well as I, knew it the minute we saw the girl lying on the church path. Sure as day we'd gotten her killed.

"Tell us about Terry's friends," I said. "Know any of them?"

"I only know him from the kitchen. Don't know what he does outside."

"You never talked about his life?"

"I know he went out drinking, but I couldn't say who with. Never had the money myself to go out for a spree."

"Where did he go? Which pubs?"

"Sorry, sir. I don't recall him ever saying."

I gave Harry his shilling along with a little ticket with the guvnor's address on it.

"If you hear anything else."

"Yes, sir," he said, standing. He pointed at the pudding. "Can I take it?"

"'Course you can. Take it all."

"And you won't tell no one you talked to me, will you?"

"You have our word," said the guvnor. "But tell me, Harry. How long has your wife's drinking been a burden?"

Harry's mouth fell open.

"Her…" he began, but seemed unable to continue.

"You tolerate her so far?" continued the guvnor, then left his special silence that I knew well enough by now not to fill. He looked kindly at the thin man, who shifted from foot to foot. Finally, Harry cracked.

"But how did you know? Somebody tell you, did they?"

"Nobody told me, my friend. I saw it in you."

"It ain't easy, sir. I don't get no sleep, what with the youngsters. But I work such long days, she got no one to discipline her. And the old crow next door leads her astray."

The guvnor stood and grasped his hand. "Such things are sent to test us. I know you have the strength to pass the test, Harry, but you must nourish yourself. You're too weak to be a proper father. You must eat more."

"Yes, sir," said Harry, his eyes on the floor, ashamed.

"Thank you for your help."

When he was gone, we stood and wrapped ourselves up in our coats. The sky was clear, but though it was summer the air was cold. Mrs. Willows cleaned and swept and turned out the lamps.

"How did you know about his wife?" I asked as we stepped out onto the pavement. On the other side of the road a copper walked his beat.

"I sensed it, Barnett."

"Give over. How did you really know?"

"How much do you think a junior cook makes? Thirty shillings a month? Forty? It's enough to feed his family and pay for their room without him starving himself. Yet he steals food and risks a job that he badly needs. It must mean his money is going elsewhere. He doesn't have the money to go drinking himself, he told us that much. So where?"

"Plenty of other places," I said. "Gambling debts, maybe."

"Too sensible for that. He was very careful in what he told us until we gained his trust. That doesn't speak of a gambler. But did you see how he looked away when confessing his wife was alive? Did you notice how he changed the subject when I asked if she fed him?"

"She might have been bed-bound. She might have been put away."

"He would have told us if she was ill. There's no shame in illness—half of London is ill. Drinking was a guess, Barnett. I admit it. But this city is drowning in drink. It was a good guess."

"A lucky guess."

He laughed.

"I'm a lucky man, Barnett. In some respects."

As we wandered back through the early morning streets,

past the piles of bodies wrapped in rags outside the workhouse and the cab station where an old fellow swept up a great pile of horse manure, he laughed again. His hollow laugh echoed in the quiet street like a thunderclap.

Chapter Seven

I ARRIVED THE NEXT MORNING TO FIND ETTIE IN a considerable fury.

"Were you out drinking with him?" she demanded. "He hasn't been home since yesterday!"

"No, Ettie. I wasn't."

It seemed as if the room had grown in size since the last time until I realized that all his stacks of newspapers were gone.

"Did he go to a woman? Is that what he did?"

"We met a man about the case around midnight. I parted with him at the corner of Union Street, not five minutes from here. He said he was going home."

"The truth?" she asked sternly.

"The truth."

She looked me steady in the eye, her nostrils flaring with each intake of the fresh London air.

"I see," she said at last. "Perhaps he's been garrotted, then. It would serve him right."

I shook my head. "There's a place he goes when he's upset. An all-night oasis, he calls it. I think he'll be there."

Ettie raised her eyes and sighed.

"What's upset him this time?"

"He blames himself for the death of the serving girl. The man we questioned last night said as much. I reckon he wouldn't have taken it half as bad if the girl didn't remind him of Isabel, though. You know, he held her off the ground until the police surgeon arrived—wouldn't leave her on the wet path. He near enough wept in front of the crowd."

She thought for some time.

"Has he been drinking since Isabel left?"

"Not constant. Occasional. Not constant at all."

She shook her head with impatience. "This city is awash with drink. Bottles and jugs are the soldiers of Lucifer, Norman. The poor are in its thrall, according to Reverend Hebden. The working men drink up the children's food and batter each other and end up standing in the dock. The women scream and fight. They lose their husbands and walk the street. The Ripper was God's punishment for the drink, there can be no doubt about that. Chinese gin is the latest thing, did you know? And good men like my brother fall into its arms at times of vulnerability. You do not drink yourself, I hope?"

"In moderation."

She nodded, stooping to pick up a feather from the floor.

"We have a fight on our hands, Norman. I'm with Reverend Hebden. The city's been a monster to the poor. Have you read the accounts of Charles Booth?"

"No, ma'am."

"He says it all. We're currently ministering to a filthy place called Cutler's Court. Have you heard of it?"

I shook my head. We stood in the middle of the room, facing each other. She held her back straight, her arms crossed. Her face was solemn as she explained, "Over four hundred people living in twenty small houses, and on each side a slaughterhouse. Ten souls asleep in each room. One standing pipe for water and two latrines. Can you imagine? And everywhere you look are piles of oyster shells and bones."

I could imagine. I had lived in such a place myself not twenty years before. I knew this city. I knew all its evils and all its games.

"All the dirty trades surround these quarters," she went on. "The waste from the slaughterhouses sinks into a ditch which runs through the centre of the court. And this is where they empty their toilet pans. The stink's an insult to Jesus, Norman. The whole court is owned by one man who refuses to install more sanitation. One landlord. But we are there."

Ettie spoke with passion, and for the first time I caught sight of the spirit which drove her. I felt I understood her a little better for it. She looked at me in silence, expecting an equally strong reply, but I knew that on this subject I'd have to fail her. Though I'd left the court-dwellers behind long ago, I couldn't talk of them as strangers.

"What do you do there?" I asked instead.

"We campaign for improvements. We help. We pray for guidance. There's a programme that our organization follows across London: we teach basic hygiene; we hold prayer meetings and provide medicines. The Ladies' Association for the Care and Protection of Young Girls work closely with us. Do you know them?"

"I've seen the women about town."

"I had little sense of the scale of the problem before I came here. You know that William and I were raised in…" She hesitated, and a flush came to her cheeks. "That is to say, our father had means."

"Yes, I knew that, Ettie."

"Of course. Anyway, half the women in the court work as prostitutes. In some families both mothers and daughters earn money this way. We try to help the younger ones. There are sanctuaries they can go where they're taught to do useful work. We try and save them before it's too late."

"Noble work, Ettie."

"It isn't easy. The men don't like them to be saved, so there's trouble sometimes, but the poor are our burden and our responsibility. Such it says in the good book, Norman. The war is here. The war is in our backstreets and alleys."

Her chest heaved with passion beneath the black bodice of her dress. Her forehead was red, and I was pleased when she hesitated and drew a slow breath. I didn't want to hear any more about the people of the court, my people, for all the bad things they did I had done myself, or watched, or encouraged. I knew everything she described, but I knew it from the other side.

"But now I worry for my brother. You know where he is, you say?"

"Don't worry. I'll bring him back."

"Very good." She turned to the stairs. "And tell him to bring some muffins. Hot ones, mind. Tell him to pay the full price."

There was only one other punter in the Hog that morning, a great lascar with a knife in his belt and his hair tied back like a pirate. He lay asleep on a bench by the fire, snoring, his mouth hanging open. A fat woman stood by the counter rinsing out glasses in a tin bucket. The place stank of tobacco smoke and the spilt beer that lay like a slick over the stone floor. The guvnor was sat upright at a table in the corner, his back to the door. In his clasped hands was a bottle of porter. It was only when I got up close I could see that his eyes were closed. I lay my hand on his shoulder and shook him. He groaned and protested.

"I've instructions from your sister to return you," I said.

He opened his bleary eyes for a second to look in my direction, then immediately let his head fall onto the table.

I put my arm under his and hauled him up. He was heavy. He was heavier each time.

The woman tutted and sighed as I struggled with his leaden carcass.

Slowly, his feet began to shuffle in irregular steps. He groaned again and wiped his mouth; his eyes opened to slits; his red face puckered up. He belched in my ear. But at least he was walking, after a fashion.

"Lovely making your acquaintance, Hamba," he mumbled at the sailor, who continued to snore on the wooden bench.

"Take him with you, why don't you?" said the woman with a laugh.

The guvnor turned and bowed loosely at her.

"A pleasure, my petal," he burbled.

"I hope you ain't thinking of leaving before you give Betts the crown you owe her, Mr. Arrowood. She made me promise to collect it from you."

"Ah," he spluttered, fumbling in his waistcoat for his coins. "Of course. Yes."

The coins spilled onto the floor. I scooped them up, gave the woman a crown, then stuffed the rest into his pocket.

Without letting go of my arm, he bowed once more. When we gained the street he grunted at the sudden light and covered his eyes.

"Carry me, Barnett."

"Walk on."

"I'm suffering."

"As am I, but I don't deserve it."

We plodded and swayed through the busy streets. When we reached his rooms behind the pudding shop, Ettie was sitting upright darning a sock in his favourite chair. A look of great disappointment crossed her face.

"Do you need help getting him upstairs?"

"I'm fine, Sister," he grunted, only now letting loose my arm and standing by himself. "Help me up the stairs, Barnett."

It was a struggle to get up the narrow staircase, but finally we gained the top and he fell onto his mattress, panting and clutching his forehead. I was breathing heavy myself now.

"Barnett," he slurred as I turned back to the stairs. "Is Nolan out of prison?"

"Out last week."

"Go see him."

I'd decided the very same myself the night before when I guessed the guvnor would be sloping off to the Hog after leaving me, but I didn't tell him that. It wasn't our way.

"Get me the chamberpot," he mumbled.

"Get it yourself," I said as I set off down the stairs.

He was snoring before I reached the bottom.

Ettie watched me in despair.

"One moment, Norman," she said as I reached the door. "Did you get muffins as I asked?"

"I'm sorry. I had my hands full."

"Quite so."

Her mouth turned down in sadness: Ettie enjoyed her food just as much as the guvnor.

"You must ask Mrs. Barnett to come to a meeting," she said. "Reverend Hebden is always looking for new recruits. She'd find it enriching, I'm sure. I shall tell you the time of the next one."

"Thank you, Ettie."

Her eyes narrowed as a queer noise came from her stomach. Next moment, a light flush came to her cheeks.

"That's arranged, then," she said, picking up her darning again. We both pretended we hadn't heard the gurgle in her innards.

Nolan lived in two rooms of a lodging house on Cable Street. He was an old friend of mine from Bermondsey days. His business had always been just the other side of the law, and we often went to him if we wanted to know about things as were happening in the Irish parts of town. A few days ago he'd come out from fourteen moons' stir for the theft of an overcoat from a Chinaman on the Mile End Road and now he was back in his old life, fencing carriage clocks and cooking pots to the good women of Whitechapel.

"You ain't looking so good," he said as we sat at the table. His wife Mary, his mother, and two cousins had been dispatched to the front room to allow our conference. Despite the sunshine outside, the back room was cold, the light from the window cut out by a taller building not five yards behind. He wore broken spectacles on his nose, one of the arms being a chewed pencil tied on with a thread of hairy string.

"Apologies for not visiting you in the nick, mate," I said. "I've an aversion to criminals."

"Forgiven, Norman. How's the old boy?"

"Suffering after a night in the Hog."

He laughed and slapped his thigh.

"He never could absorb it. Weak body, that's his problem. Weak stomach. Now, me old mate, what is it you're after this time?"

"You heard anything about a gang of Irish or Americans? Thieving from the big houses in the West End?"

He got up and closed the door. When he came back his smile was gone.

"I'd leave that one alone, my friend. The two of you don't want to be asking after them lot."

"It's connected to a case."

"Well it might be, but you don't want anything to do with them. Stay well away."

"The guvnor won't do that. A girl's been killed. He's taken it personal. It seems as this gang is connected to—"

"Don't tell me any more!" he barked, his spectacles falling from his face. "Did I say I wanted to know?"

I shook my head.

"Right, here it is." He leaned over and collected his eyeglasses from the wooden floor. "Those lot are Fenians. You remember them?"

I nodded. Who in the country didn't remember the Fenians? Ten years ago the city was in a panic for bombs exploding all over the shop. There were stories every day of new targets and plots foiled by the police. Explosives had been planted in the underground railway, London Bridge, even the Houses of Parliament. People were so scared they stopped using the trains. The guvnor himself had written many a story for the paper on the hunt for the skirmishers and the Irish Americans behind it all. They'd brought the fight for Ireland to the heart of England, and all of us who lived here knew it.

"But I thought they'd given up?"

"Most of them did, but a few of them went their own way, like. Them as still believe the only thing the British will listen to is war. I heard they were connected to the burglaries in some way. And that's all I heard."

"Names?"

"I only ever heard one name. Fellow called Paddler Bill. One of the Invincibles, they say. You remember them?"

"The assassins?"

"That's them. He was one that got away, never even named at the trial. Big, red-haired fellow—not as I ever seen him myself. They say he carries the executions of those men with him still. That's why he keeps up the fight. Killed his brother for informing, so they say. Killed him in a sweet factory. Boiled him up in toffee."

I shivered.

"Christ, Nolan. I don't like this case."

"These are people you don't want to anger," he said. "Stay well away."

He watched me as I thought about it, as I wondered if I could persuade the guvnor to walk away. But I knew that was a fantasy: once he gave his word he'd never give up.

"Why housebreaking?" I asked at last. "What's that to do with the campaign?"

"For the money, I shouldn't wonder. Costs money to fight a war."

"And you don't know any other names?"

"Don't know nothing about the others. And before you say anything, I ain't going to ask around neither. Those lot ain't afraid of tying a person up and dropping him in the river on a cold night and that's a fact."

"I wouldn't ask if it wasn't important, Nolan."

He shook his head, jamming his hands in his pockets. A cat appeared from behind the oven and padded up to him, rubbing its side on his trouser leg. He kicked it away.

"Mary's Irish too, ain't she?" I asked.

"She was born here. Her mother and father, they come over

after the famine, but they don't know nothing about these Fenians. Most of them lot's American."

"What does she think of them?"

"Her cousin Kate's the one who goes to all the land reform meetings. But the whole lot of them's for a free Ireland. Father was too, before he croaked."

"How couldn't they be, living with you?"

More than once Nolan had bent my ear on self-government. He'd come over himself during the depression twenty years ago; his brother who stayed behind was thrown into Tralee gaol for helping tenant farmers resist eviction. The more he'd told me about what was happening over in Ireland the more ashamed I was at what my people were doing. The guvnor was with Nolan on this, and that was one of the reasons they'd grown to have such respect for each other.

"A lot of yours see us as no more than filth," said Nolan, nodding. "There are plenty of law-abiding Irish round here, mate. Not me, of course, but plenty of others, yet any crime that's done, they says it's us. If there's work we're the last to get taken on. Our people got good cause to take against you. But listen, Norman. I'll be for the liberation of my country till I die, but I don't go along with the bombs. Never have done."

He crossed his arms and shook his head, and from the look on his face I could see he was about to start up on some more serious talk. But just then the door squeaked open and his Mary's head appeared. "Potboy's here, lads," she said.

Nolan made a noise like he'd been holding his breath. He smiled.

"You want a drop o' porter with me?" he asked.

I had a bit of porter with him and Mary, and then she went

out for whelks. Still I couldn't persuade him to make any enquiries. He was frightened of these Fenians. And Nolan wasn't usually frightened of anything.

Chapter Eight

❖━━━━━━━━━━━━━━━━━━❖

THERE HAD BEEN AN ACCIDENT OUTSIDE THE FON-
taine when we arrived that afternoon. A horse had fallen over
and died, pulling its carriage onto its side. A lady was sitting
on a step howling, blood all over her face and a posy of flowers in her hand, while the cabman tried to uncouple the carriage from the horse's corpse. A crowd had gathered to poke
at the horse and stare at the howling woman. The guvnor bent
down to her as we passed.

"Are you hurt, miss?" he asked, holding out his handkerchief. "Here, take this."

Her crying calmed as she peered through her teary eyes at
the guvnor, then at the tattered red cloth. Seeing the tobacco
stains and the dangling threads crusted with who knows what,
she shuddered and turned away.

He quickly pocketed his rag.

"Can I send for someone?" he asked.

"Don't touch me," she hissed, covering her face with her
hands. "I don't need your help."

He tapped his stick against his boots and nodded, a look
of sadness on his face. He didn't seem to know what to do.

"Come along, sir," I said, taking his arm. "Cabman'll sort her out."

Eric stood in the window of the studio, watching the crowd. As we pushed open the door he stepped quickly behind his counter. He wore a spotted cravat and a high-collared shirt of some yellow fabric. He recognized the guvnor immediately.

"Ah, sir. You've come to make an appointment for your portrait. I'm so pleased. I'd absolutely relish the opportunity to record your noble features for posterity. You've precisely the profile that I'm in this business for."

"Well, yes indeed," burbled the guvnor, blown off course by this rare flattery. I'd never heard anyone describe his great potato head in such a way before. Never before.

"When did you have in mind?" asked Fontaine. "Mm?"

He had opened his appointments book and taken up his quill.

"But first we'd appreciate a short meeting with Miss Cousture, sir," said the guvnor. "If that's not too much trouble. Only a brief meeting."

Fontaine's firm lips drooped, revealing two front teeth that overhung his bottom lip like a hare.

"She isn't here. She went out for soup at midday and didn't return. And if you see her you can tell her I'm very close to finding another assistant. You know, sir, I hired a woman because I believe in the emancipation of the female species."

"My sister also," said the guvnor firmly.

"Well, this is how I am treated."

He had got irked, just for a moment, and it was then his accent slipped. I could distinctly hear a flavour of Irish in his vowels. The guvnor shot me a glance.

"It certainly does you credit, sir," replied the guvnor. "How long did you say she's been working here?"

Fontaine sighed and raised his quill.

"You said an appointment?"

The guvnor nodded and looked around the portraits on the wall. "You have a very fine eye," he said, scratching his chin. "I see such spirit in these people."

"That is my goal as an artist," replied Fontaine seriously. He pointed to a portrait of a soldier that hung behind the counter. "This one is my finest."

"Ah! It is indeed a work of art," declared the guvnor.

Fontaine gazed at it for some time.

"You have a good eye yourself, sir," he said, turning to the guvnor.

"I wonder if perhaps you might have time now for my portrait?"

"Why yes! I believe I do. Just enough time before my next sitting, I believe. Come, come." He gestured for the guvnor to go through the black curtain. "Enter! A man like yourself should absolutely have a representation of his fine visage for his hallway or his drawing room or perhaps his library—absolutely."

He was still talking as he disappeared behind the heavy curtain. I waited a moment or two before taking the opportunity to explore the drawers of his counter. They were full of screws and plates and bulbs. In the bottom drawer I found his accounts book, and from that learned that he'd begun to pay Miss Cousture on January of this year—not four months previous. I hunted for an address and eventually found it written in the back leaf of a small notebook.

The guvnor appeared twenty minutes later, his side-hair combed and greased down, his whiskers trimmed, his cravat tied neatly at his neck.

"Yes, sir," Fontaine was saying. "One week. And your address?"

"Fifty-nine Coin Street. Behind the shop."

"I'll put a small frame around it, the same one as around the soldier's portrait. Your sister will be most taken with the picture, I assure you." He held open the door. "No doubt at all, sir."

"Well, that was interesting, Barnett," said the guvnor as we turned the corner at the end of the street. "It would appear that our client was not introduced by her uncle the art dealer as she says. According to Mr. Fontaine, it was a minister of the church who approached him, last Christmas if you will. The minister offered the lady at half the wage Fontaine would have to pay anyone else. She knew nothing about the art of photography, it seems. Nothing at all. But, you know, a pretty face and the soft persuasion of the Church can make up for much."

"And the cheap labour."

"Indeed."

"He only began to pay her in January," said I. "Least that's what his account book says."

"I see you've been busy too. And something else: Miss Cousture has turned down Mr. Fontaine's intimate advances, and yet he will not give up the possibility of bedding her."

I laughed.

"I'm amazed what people'll tell you, sir."

"Oh, he didn't tell me. I read it in him."

"You read it in him?"

"Yes, Barnett. It seems that her disappearances are quite regular and unexpected. He told me as much. More regular than one would tolerate from an employee. Yet still he doesn't dismiss her, despite his obvious anger. Why? As Mr. Darwin tells us, we need look no further than man's essential animal nature. It is because she's beautiful and he yearns to find himself between her thighs, as I'm sure many men do. No doubt, given his position, he believes it's his right. It isn't his fault. It is the lion's right to take the females of his pride, and Mr. Fontaine is his own little lion. I've no doubt many shopkeepers on this street bed their assistants. The city is awash with little lions. It must stick in his craw that she doesn't offer herself. It's as if he has purchased a beautiful cake, which sits all day on his counter. Yet he cannot eat it."

"Perhaps he's married."

"Oh, Barnett. You are quite sweet sometimes."

"How can you be so sure he desires her?"

"Because she's beautiful. I desired her. You desired her."

"I didn't."

"You did, my friend. I saw you lose your usual brute composure in my room. Despite your commitment to the formidable Mrs. Barnett, even you were taken by her."

We had to stop as a costermonger pushed a wide cart piled with coats across the pavement and into an alley.

"Your deductions are more like Sherlock Holmes than you think," I said when we were walking again.

"No, Barnett. I decipher people. He deciphers secret codes and flower beds. That man and I are not alike, and frankly I'm getting tired of your jibes about him."

I laughed to myself as we walked.

"Why did she lie to us?" I asked as we passed under the railway bridge.

"I don't know. And since Mr. Fontaine wouldn't agree to tell me where she lives, we're going to have to wait until she reappears to find out. Another job for you, Barnett, tomorrow. Pray the rain doesn't return."

I held out the scrap of paper on which I'd scribbled the address.

"Lucky I found this, then, sir."

A smile broke over his ruddy face. He clapped me on the back.

"Excellent, Barnett. Let's hope she is in."

I noticed the fellow as we turned into Broad Wall. He wouldn't have been a noticeable man ordinarily except he had a piece of torn, brown paper stuck to his trouser leg. I'd seen it earlier in the coffeehouse, and wondered as I drank my brew if it was stuck on there by a smear of treacle or some-such. And there it was again, attached to the same man who was walking along the other side of the road looking up at the high windows.

"Shall we turn down this alley, sir?" I asked as we approached a narrow lane on our right.

"But why?"

"There's a man might be trailing us. Don't look back. He's on the other side of the road. Medium size in a grey coat."

The guvnor clenched his hands and bit his lip, itching to have a little peep as we made our way forward.

"No, don't," I said. "Don't look."

"Yes, yes, Barnett," he replied, chafing against this restriction and trying hard to keep his eyes on the way ahead. He was limping with his tight shoes and puffing with his weight. "I heard you the first time."

"You were about to look."

"No, I wasn't."

Presently we reached the alley. It was a narrow, dark track, the workshops and factories on each side built high and leaning in towards each other as they rose to the grey sky. Most were closed for the night but a few had faint lights behind their grimy windows. Tired people trudged past us, their clothes thick and frayed, their eyes cast down. The ground beneath us alternated between gravel and mud. Up ahead a cart was being loaded with crates. We continued past it, then turned again into an even smaller passage. We didn't look back, and at the end turned into another alley, this one darker still. I pointed at a bend in the road ahead where a small wall jutted out.

"Yes, ideal," said the guvnor.

We hurried towards it and concealed ourselves there, myself peeking out the way we'd come, the guvnor behind me, leaning against a door, catching his breath.

Very soon the man appeared, walking quick towards us.

"He's coming," I whispered.

"Hold tight," murmured the guvnor.

There was a sudden noise behind us. The door the guvnor was leaning on was wrenched open and there stood a woman in rags holding a chamberpot full to the brim with a filthy stew. She looked taken aback to see two gentlemen standing on her doorstep awaiting the delivery of her family's ordure. Perhaps unable to stop her muscles from doing what they were surely accustomed to doing at such a moment, she swung the pot back as if to chuck it into the street.

The guvnor, startled, backed away quick from the woman and straight into full view of our pursuer. Seeing him, the man turned and ran back the way he came.

"Curses!" exclaimed the guvnor, and as he spoke he received half the woman's delivery on his trousers.

I set off after the man. As I turned the first corner I saw him running up ahead, dim against the black brick. All the way down I was gaining on him, so that by the time he reached the next alley I was sure I would catch him. He turned right, leading us further away from the lamps of Broad Wall, further into the maze of damp buildings. I was slowed by a cart trying to turn, the horse blocking my path.

"Hold up, hold up," whined the deliveryman. "You'll spook him."

I scrambled over the empty cart.

"Bloody prick!" shouted the man, taking a swipe in the air with his whip.

The alley ahead was empty. I ran on, soon coming to a junction. On an instinct I turned left again, seeing the lamps of a proper street some way up ahead.

It was as I was noticing this that I felt my legs swiped from under me and came crashing down hard onto the gravel. And right when my hipbone hit the ground another blow fell on my spine. I cried out in pain, just managing to twist my head to see the man, his narrow eyes burning in his bearded face, raising his truncheon to strike me again. My eyes fixed on his hand clasping the truncheon, on the bruised and crushed fingernail of his first finger, and in that moment the ruined nail seemed angry and vengeful, as if the man himself was only its tool. I held out my hand to stop the blow, receiving it instead on my forearm. Immediately a great wave of nausea came over me and the strength flew from my body. My ears were ringing like the bells of Christ Church; my eyes were full of tears. I was helpless. I wrapped myself up tight in a ball, clenching, clenching even my eyes, readied for the next blow.

It didn't come. Afraid to turn my head in case I was smashed in the mush, I listened. Slowly the bells faded and I could hear a woman's voice talking from inside one of the buildings. I got my courage up and turned my head. The man was gone.

I sat up, not sure I could stand. Every little movement made me jerk with pain. I looked up and down the alley until I was sure he was gone, then, leaning against the wall, pushed myself to my feet.

A mighty ache in my back caused me to sit down on the ground again, where I rested, rubbing my arm, waiting for the sick feeling to leave my belly.

A woman came round the corner ahead, a heavy cooking pot in her hands.

"You fall over, mate?" she asked.

"Just a bit, mum," I said, trying to make my voice sound normal. "Tripped myself up."

"Want a lift?"

She put her pot down and helped me to my feet. She was as well built as Mrs. Barnett, and her presence alone made me feel stronger.

"You pass a short man with a beard up there?" I asked her. "Would have been running, most likely."

"He was in a right hurry," she replied, picking up her pot. "He rob you, did he?"

"You might say that."

"Well, you don't want to bother with the police, less you want to waste half a day or more."

"Did you see what he looked like?"

"Not much in this light. Thin little eyes, though, suspicious-looking, I'd say. But like I say, you don't want to bother with the police this time."

We walked along side by side. With each step I had a jarring pain in my back.

"Ask me why," she said.

"Why?"

"'Cos he had a police truncheon in his belt. And it was a police belt, mate. Wasn't wearing a uniform, though. Just the standard copper's boots."

"You know a lot about copper's clothes, do you?"

"My old man was a constable," she said. "Before he croaked. I was the one used to polish up those boots each day. You married?"

I nodded. We walked together until we reached the main road, where she waddled off towards the bridge. When she was out of sight, I lowered myself down onto the steps of the Home and Colonial to give myself rest from the pain. It was an hour before I had the strength to go on.

Chapter Nine

WHEN I REACHED THE GUVNOR'S ROOMS HE WAS sitting with a tankard in his hand. Ettie was in the chair by the window, her hand flat on her forehead. She acknowledged me briefly then shut her eyes. The guvnor shook his head as if to warn me off, then, still shaking his great turnip, took a long swallow of his ale. He looked guilty for what had happened but, as was his way, gave me no apology.

I lowered myself down onto the small sofa with care, sure there must have been a great bruise across my spine. The guvnor noticed my swollen hand.

"Good heavens, Barnett! What the blazes happened to you? Shall I call the doctor?"

"I suppose that'll come out of my money again, will it?" I replied, more sharply than I intended.

He looked hurt.

"I'm only bruised," I said more gently.

I did wonder if Ettie, being a nurse as she was, might have taken a look, but she didn't stir from behind her hand.

"You need some attention," he insisted. "I can get the doctor to see to Ettie at the same time. It'll be cheaper that way."

"I don't need one," she said quickly, her eyes still closed.

"Nor me," said I. "Though a drink would help my nerves."

He passed me a small blue bottle.

"Chlorodine," he said. "A quite magical medicine. It will help."

I took a draught while the guvnor poured me a mug of ale. Feeling the good medicine warm my throat, I told him how I'd been beaten in the alley.

"Oh dear, Barnett," he said when I'd finished. "This case becomes more complicated by the day. I've been sitting here puzzling over why Miss Cousture would lie to us. She was here while we were out, you know. My sister spoke to her. It appears she's suddenly impatient to know if we've made any progress. But she hasn't left an address. Doesn't that seem queer, Barnett?"

"There's nothing about this case as doesn't seem queer."

"And now a constable follows us, gives you a beating, but doesn't attempt to question you."

Ettie let out a sigh and shifted in her chair, a grimace on her pale face.

"What ails your sister?" I whispered.

"She's come over weak and unwell." The guvnor's voice rose in volume as he spoke. "She will not go to bed. She just sits there."

I detected a slight flicker in her eyelids. It was clear she was listening but was resolved not to respond.

The guvnor raised his eyes to the ceiling. He tapped out his pipe.

"We'll visit Miss Cousture first thing tomorrow, before she leaves for work. We'll search her room for clues."

"You think she'll let us?"

He laughed.

"I'm sure she won't, but it might at least provoke her to tell us the truth."

The shop bell began to tinkle. With some pain, I rose and went through to find Inspector Petleigh at the door. Behind him was the young constable with the booming voice who had taken charge of the murder scene at St. George the Martyr. I led them through to the parlour where the guvnor now sat alone. The creaking boards above told me that Ettie had retired.

"Are these the men?" Petleigh asked the constable.

"They is the men, sir," bellowed the young man. "Him and him."

"I knew it," said the inspector. "The moment you described them, I knew it was these two."

He laughed unkindly. We'd had plenty of dealings with Inspector Petleigh over the years, some of them good, some of them not so good. He didn't approve of the work we did, but he knew that there weren't enough police to look into all the crimes as were happening around our parts. He wasn't a bad sort, though you'd never get the guvnor to admit that.

"The tall one is him who gave chase," said the constable. "The other was holding her head. They knew her. They said they did."

Petleigh sat without being invited and addressed the guvnor. "I'm disappointed with you, William. Most disappointed. I thought you'd learned your lesson. You agreed to stick with pilfering servants and infidelities. Now I find you on the scene of a murder again."

He twizzled his moustache and stretched out his legs. He wore new leather boots, the soles wet with fresh mud. I noticed that the young constable, who stood by the door gripping his helmet by his side, hadn't wiped his feet either. I went to the cupboard for the broom.

"I am glad they've put such a keen mind as yours on this case," said the guvnor, relighting his pipe. "Tell me, have you caught the devil?"

"We're investigating. It looks like a street robbery gone sour, although the girl hadn't much to steal. There's also the possibility that the Ripper is back. The Commissioner is keeping an eye on that one."

"Oh please, Petleigh!" cried the guvnor. "That's ridiculous. Jack never worked in daylight in a crowded street."

"Quite so. We're working on some various leads. But we'd be nearer our solution if information were not being withheld from us."

"May I ask what these leads are?"

Petleigh sighed and shook his head. A pained smile drew wide his thin lips.

"Do you take me for an idiot?" he asked.

"Not at all, sir. I take you for an imbecile."

Petleigh's nose flared; he spoke sharply, "You know, sir, I can take you before the magistrate for obstructing us."

"I've done nothing, Inspect—"

"You're working on a case connected to the murder," interrupted Petleigh loudly. "Am I wrong?"

"No."

"Therefore you have information which you didn't tell us about at the relevant time. Several days have now elapsed, enough time for the culprit to get away. A magistrate might say you were protecting the murderer."

"We don't know who the murderer is," replied the guvnor. "He brushed past us. Barnett gave chase but lost him."

"What case are you working on?"

"We're trying to find the girl's sweetheart. We were due to meet her at the church."

"She hired you," declared Petleigh.

"No."

"Then who?"

"I cannot tell you," replied the guvnor, shaking his head. "Our client requested privacy."

"Tell the inspector!" barked the constable. "Otherwise we'll haul you off to the clink for the night."

Petleigh held up his hand to the young man.

"We can help you catch the murderer, Inspector," said the guvnor.

"You've a very high idea of yourself, Mr. Arrowood," said Petleigh, crossing his legs. "Who do you think you are? Sherlock Holmes?"

The guvnor snorted.

"Let me make this plain. We are the police. We deal with murders, violations, robberies. Dangerous men. You look for lawyers who have doctored their contracts. You search out husbands who have run off with the maid. We don't give you information—you give it to us. So, once again: who are you working for, and what do you know about this murder?"

"I'll tell you what I can if you find out the name of the officer who gave Barnett a hiding this afternoon," said the guvnor.

They looked at me.

"He was following us, Inspector," I said. "I wondered if maybe it was you who put him up to it?"

Petleigh looked at the constable.

"Did you know about this?" he asked.

The constable shook his head.

I showed him my swollen arm, then lifted my shirt to reveal the bruise on my back.

"Ow!" exclaimed the guvnor, shifting in his chair. "What a corker! That must smart. It's the colour of kidneys, Barnett. I think we will call that doctor after all."

"No, sir. I cannot afford him." I tucked my shirt back in and addressed Petleigh. "He was a copper, though. And you didn't answer the question. Did you put him up to it?"

"No, Norman," said Petleigh. "I swear it. Tell me what happened."

When I'd explained and described the man as best as I could, he said, "Are you sure he was an officer?"

"He wore a police belt, and it was a police truncheon that damaged me."

"I don't recognize the description. Constable?"

"There's one works over Elephant and Castle way who fits the picture," replied the young man. "I don't know his name. But I can't think one of our men would do such a thing as this."

"If this is an officer—and we don't know that for certain, mind—but if it is, do you wish to raise a complaint?" asked Petleigh.

"We want the name," said the guvnor, looking at me. "That's all at the moment."

Petleigh considered this for a while.

"We'll make enquiries. Now tell me what you know."

The guvnor filled him in with all the facts we knew. Petleigh scribbled in a notebook as he talked, trying again and again to get the names of our client and our informants. The guvnor resisted.

"The girl had this in her hand," he said, fishing the bullet from his waistcoat. "I believe she meant it for us."

Petleigh held it under the lamp and inspected it. Then he placed it on the table.

"Could be a sweetheart gave it to her. Or she might have picked it up from somewhere. I don't think it's important."

"Oh really?" said the guvnor. "Well, I suppose we must trust your judgement on that. What's your theory then, Inspector?"

"Oh no, no," said Petleigh in a tired voice. "You tell us yours, Arrowood."

The guvnor cleared his throat and sat forward.

"The simplest story is that the French boy was involved in some business between Cream and the Fenian gang. Something went wrong and the boy either fled or was killed. Martha was murdered because she was about to give me information, which means it's a serious business. More serious than we realized when we took the case. That's my best guess. Now, what have you found out?"

Petleigh stood, brushing some imaginary dust from his jacket.

"Much the same," he replied as he examined his sleeves. "Or similar."

I couldn't help but laugh. Petleigh's face soured.

"I need the names of your informants," he insisted.

I stepped to the grate and began to rouse the last embers of the fire. The guvnor tutted and fiddled in his pockets for matches. He said nothing.

"You cause me much annoyance, Arrowood," said Petleigh at last. He placed his hat carefully on his head. "Leave this to the police, sir. If Cream or the Fenians chose to dispose of you they'd smash you like a…like a…" He stood before us, his mouth open, the weight of his warning lost in his inability to find a suitable idea. "Like a cow on a dumpling," he said at last. He turned to me. "That goes for you also, Norman."

"Also like a dumpling, Inspector?"

"They would break you like a biscuit."

"Of course, sir."

"I'm serious!" cried Petleigh in a fury. "You're no match for them. We know Cream's men are behind a wave of deaths in the last few years, and it sounds like we can add this girl's murder to the list. You don't know the half of it, Arrowood. Drownings, beatings, arson—anything you can think of. The most appalling things. They'll kill anyone who gets in their way and they've people so afraid that we can't get anyone to testify against them. I don't have to remind you of the Spindle case, do I? You saw what they did to that man!"

The guvnor nodded.

"Do you want that to happen to you?" demanded Petleigh.

The guvnor sat thinking, his hands clasped on his belly, his eyes on the fire.

"You'll send me the name then, Petleigh?" he asked at last.

"Yes, I'll send you the name," replied the inspector with a sigh. "But leave the murder of the serving girl to us. If you learn anything, you must tell me at once. Send the muffin boy with a message. Do not follow that trail yourselves, I'm warning you."

When they'd gone and we were sitting in the warm parlour drinking another mug of ale, the guvnor let out a humourless laugh.

"Much the same!" he declared. "Much the same, Barnett! Idiot. He knows without us he's no chance of solving this murder."

"What of tomorrow, sir?"

"Tomorrow we see what the French lady is all about."

Chapter Ten

I DIDN'T SLEEP MUCH THAT NIGHT, THOUGH I WAS tired enough and badly in need of rest. I couldn't get comfortable with the bruise on my back, and my arm was burning like a little beggar. All night my thoughts went round and round, and every way they turned there were men ready to kill us. If it was up to me, we would have handed the money back as soon as Miss Cousture mentioned the Barrel of Beef, but now we had the Fenians to worry about as well. A girl had already died and I'd had a beating. There was only one way it could go: the deeper we got into this case the worse it was going to get.

As we walked down the Old Kent Road, past the people hurrying off to work, the omnibuses full to bursting, I laid it down plain. "We'll most probably get ourselves killed before this case is over."

"Not if we're careful," the guvnor replied.

From the way he spoke, I wasn't sure he believed it himself.

"You must be worried about the Fenians, William," I said.

His face darkened. Even though he argued fierce for Irish self-government, the Fenian bombing campaign we'd gone through ten years before had terrorized him. He'd covered the

dynamitards for his newspaper, and sat through the trials of
the Invincibles, the Mansion House bombers, the Dynamite
Sunday plotters. He'd investigated the Skirmishing Fund and
the Triangle and the tangled connections between Clan na
Gael and Parnell. He became a changed man in those years,
and it was maybe this that lost him his job in the end. Before
then he was fearless, chasing up a story wherever it led. But
the years of panic in the city affected him. He stopped taking
milk in his tea, believing the stories of the Fenians poisoning
the urns with strychnine. After the underground railway plot
was discovered he wouldn't go in the tunnels no more, and to
this day he'll only travel across town by bus. For a whole year,
like so many other fearful people, he bought his water off a
cart from the countryside in case they'd tainted the pumps.
I'd never seen a man so badly feared from something. It was
this partly as drove Isabel to run off, and it took him some
years before he started to regain his old self. But some of that
fear still remained, and you could see it round the edges of
him sometimes, mixed in with the tantrums and the kindness
and the jumble of other qualities that made up his character.

"What do you say we get out now?" I said. "Give the lady
back her money. Something else'll come up in time. As soon
as Cream or the Fenians find out we're interested, we'll end
up in the river. And now we've got a bent copper. How do
we know anything we tell Petleigh isn't going to get back to
them?"

He was silent. No doubt he was remembering the Betsy
case, when John Spindle was beaten to death by Cream's men.
It seemed a simple job when we took it on. Mrs. Betsy wanted
a watch on her husband, a stevedore on the docks, on account
of how short his wages had got. She reckoned he was gambling, though it turned out the money was going on a sec-

ond wife he was keeping down near Pickle Herring Stairs. It was a few bob's easy work for us, we thought. A couple of days following him when he finished at the docks of an evening, then on to the next case. And it would've been, except for the guvnor taking a shine to Bill Betsy's other wife, and her tricking him into helping her cousin out of some trouble he'd gotten into. It was through that we'd caused John Spindle's death. Without knowing what we were doing we'd exposed him, then hadn't arrived in a cab to pick him up as we said we would. We'd left him in the hands of Mr. Piser and Boots, to be clubbed to death in the coal cellar of the lodging house we'd hidden him in. The guilt had lain heavy on us ever since, and so far we'd kept our promise to steer clear of jobs that could turn bad. For four years we'd kept to that resolution, yet still the memory of the case could make us feel the most wretched men in London.

The guvnor stopped walking.

"Barnett, listen to me," he said, his voice strong and fierce as the people flowed past us on the pavement. "We made a terrible mistake before, but we've learned from it. I knew the day would come when we'd have to atone for what happened, and we'd have to use all we've learned." He stood there looking up at me, his eyeglasses perched on his red nose. He jammed his hands in his pockets. "This case has chosen us. They killed Martha, that poor girl, killed for the sake of their secret. We have to keep on this case for her sake. They cannot get away with it again. Petleigh won't solve it, you know that. Unless there's clear evidence, the police can do nothing. They don't have the men."

"You got a penny for the baby, mister?" croaked a filthy woman in a coarse wrapping of rags who'd come up behind us. "He ain't too well, poor thing."

The guvnor fished out a coin and handed it over. He peered at the baby's dirty face, at the snot which ran over its lips and the yellow gum that glued its little eyes, and pulled out the brand new yellow handkerchief which had appeared in his waistcoat pocket the day before.

"Wipe his face," he said to her.

She looked at the cloth as if it was a trick. With an impatient sigh he rubbed the child's face himself, then stuffed his new handkerchief into the child's blanket.

"Don't sell it," he said to her as he walked away. "It's not for you. It's for the baby."

Further down the street he turned to me.

"This case has chosen us, Barnett. This is our chance to make things right."

The address turned out to be a grey-brick villa on a wide avenue of comfortable houses. On the wall was a brass plaque with a cross and the letters CSJ. The door was opened by a matron in a black dress, a white scarf tied over her head. She was none too pleased to have visitors so early in the morning and asked us to come back at a more decent hour. We held our ground, and eventually she allowed us in while she went upstairs to find Miss Cousture.

The parlour was a gloomy room. A piano stood in one corner, a long sofa along the wall. There were no ornaments save for one silver crucifix with the twisted figure of Christ hung from its wings. We sat on two heavy chairs by the small fireplace. As we waited we could hear movement at the back of the house, and women's laughter on the floor above. There seemed to be quite a number of women in the place.

"This is a respectable enough house for a shopgirl," commented the guvnor.

"Perhaps her uncle arranged it for her."

"If indeed she has an uncle."

We heard the clatter of plates further into the house, and the smell of food drifted in to us. I hadn't yet eaten and found my mouth filling with spit. A groan arose from the guvnor's belly like the bellow of a birthing cow.

Just then Miss Cousture swept into the room.

The guvnor and I rose as one, smelling her freshly bathed skin, admiring her perfect outfit and hair which shone even in that dark room.

She bade us sit, and took her position in a small wing chair.

"Your sister told you I called yesterday?" she asked.

"Indeed," replied the guvnor. "We wish to give you our news."

"But how do you find me? I did not leave an address."

"We're detective agents, Miss Cousture," he said. "It's our job to discover such things."

"You have some news for me?"

"Before we begin, it is imperative we examine your room," said the guvnor, rising to his feet and stepping to the door. I did the same. It was a trick of his: he believed it was harder to refuse an act already begun than an act merely suggested.

The lady didn't move.

"But why?" she demanded.

"There might be a clue in his possessions. Something only an agent would notice."

"There is not."

"You mean there is nothing you've noticed, or there is nothing?"

"They are the same."

"Pardon me, Miss Cousture. We must satisfy ourselves that is so." He held his arm out to the hallway. "Shall we?"

She did not budge from her seat.

"You wish to find your brother, don't you, Miss Cousture?" I asked.

"You cannot go to my room. Men are not permitted upstairs."

"But your brother was permitted."

A flush of anger crossed her pale cheeks. She breathed out heavily.

"He was not permitted. This is a holy house."

The guvnor sat down again. He gazed at her kindly, using another of his psychological techniques: generous eyes atop a pinched mouth.

The lady bore it well for a minute, then became uncomfortable. She glanced at me, then at the fireplace, where her eyes remained until she finally broke.

"Putain!" she exclaimed, slapping her hand onto the arm of the chair. "Yes, I admit! I did not say the truth before. He did not stay here. There. That is what you want me to say?"

"But why, mademoiselle?" asked the guvnor. "We're trying to help you."

She looked at him defiantly, the anger still in her eyes.

"Do not treat me as the criminal," she replied. "I was afraid you did not take the case seriously. I know you will say he goes home to France, so I say he left the papers."

"He didn't even leave his papers?" exclaimed the guvnor, throwing his hands into the air.

Her gaze fell.

"I do not know," she admitted.

"And I don't know whether to believe anything you've told us, Miss Cousture," said the guvnor.

"The rest is true," she said urgently. "Everything. Please,

Mr. Arrowood. You must find my brother. I've paid you. You've given your word."

He gripped his walking stick and stared at her.

"Please, Mr. Arrowood. I'm sorry for deceiving you."

The guvnor looked at me and raised his eyebrows. I could see he was thinking.

"Where did he stay, then, miss?" I asked. "If he wasn't with you?"

"Doss-houses. He goes from one to the next. I don't know the last one."

"Do you know any of them?"

"No, sir."

"Why didn't you live together?" asked the guvnor sharply.

"I feel safe here. It's a Church house, for women on their own. Thierry isn't good with money. He drinks. I cannot pay his rent and mine too." She bent forward very suddenly and gripped the guvnor's wrist. "Please, sir. Do not leave the case. I know there is trouble. He was frightened. More than I have seen in him before."

"And so he might have gone home," I suggested. "Surely that's right."

"He would not leave me without saying where he goes. He would send a message. He drinks, yes, but he is loyal."

She relaxed her grip and the guvnor sat back in his chair. He began packing his pipe. Slowly, he explained what we'd found out.

When he'd finished, she sat in the gloom of the parlour, her face a knot of worry.

"Terrible," she whispered. "It's very bad, isn't it?"

"Shall we give your name to Inspector Petleigh?" asked the guvnor.

She shook her head.

"Then we shall not. Might we know why you wish to remain in the shadows?"

She blinked and swallowed. For the first time she seemed unsure. After a good deal of scratching and frowning and twitching her button nose, she replied, "It is Mr. Fontaine. He would not be happy with me to bring the police to his shop."

The guvnor's eyebrows were raised.

"Mr. Fontaine would be unhappy?"

She nodded, edging forward towards us. She spoke quietly now.

"He takes pictures of some things, of women, you know? It could be scandal. I don't know."

"What pictures?"

"For gentlemen."

"You mean intimate pictures?" he asked in a whisper.

"Sex pictures, Mr. Arrowood."

The guvnor blinked violently, as if a fly had gone into his eye.

"And you help him with this?" he asked, his eyes watery. He rubbed them.

She did not reply. The door opened and the matron entered.

"We must ask the gentlemen to leave, Caroline. You're needed in the kitchen."

The lady stood.

"Yes, ma'am. I'll be right through. The gentlemen are going."

The matron looked at the guvnor and me with irritation, then retreated into the hallway. Miss Cousture shut the door and addressed us.

"You must find my brother, Mr. Arrowood." Her hand lingered on the doorknob, her brow creased with a frown.

"You must get into the Barrel of Beef and find what they have been doing."

"They'd kill us if we showed our faces there," I said.

"Then you must make a burglary. When it is shut."

The guvnor glanced at me, as surprised as I to hear the lady say it.

"Yes?" she demanded.

The guvnor nodded. I cleared my throat.

"We need another payment, miss," I said.

She pulled her purse from a fold in her skirt.

The guvnor rose.

"I'll wait for you outside, Barnett. Good day, Miss Cousture."

Chapter Eleven

LATER THAT NIGHT I FOUND MYSELF BACK AT THE White Eagle. Ernest was in his same place, hunched over the bar, a mug of gin grasped in his gnarly hand.

"Holy Christ," he grumbled. "Not you again."

"Buy you a drink, old man?"

"I ain't answering no more questions," he announced loudly, his eyes darting around to make sure he was heard. "You can bugger off and leave me alone."

The barmaid turned and frowned. Three streetwalkers sat at a table in the window, ignoring us. Behind the partition was the match-seller. He caught my eye and held it as the left side of his face twitched and winked. Struggling to control the movements, he grinned, then covered his cheek with his hand.

I ordered drinks.

"I don't want that," said Ernest.

"Just a few questions. Then I'll leave you alone."

I put a shilling in his hand.

He scowled, then slipped it in his pocket.

"I need some information about Martha. What do you know about her?"

"Nothing. She was friendly with Terry. That's all. They had a laugh together."

"They were lovers?"

"Don't know for sure. Seemed to me she thought she was too good for the likes of all them as works in the Beef. Waiting for a gentleman to come and set her up somewhere, that's what I thought. Waiting for a gentleman. She was a right toffer, she was. Thought she'd meet one upstairs."

"So she wasn't a Judy, then?"

"Too particular to be a Judy."

He tipped the gin into his mouth.

"You ever see a soldier with her?"

"I'm in the kitchen. Don't see nothing what goes on upstairs."

"You hear any talk about a soldier or an officer or somesuch as came into the place?"

He sniffed, then wiped his wet nose on the sleeve of his ragged grey coat.

"I ain't heard nothing."

"There a back door to the kitchen?"

"There's a door into the yard."

"You got a key for that?"

"If I had I wouldn't let you have it. Anyways, they bolt that door at the top and bottom, so even if you did have a key you wouldn't get in."

A woman was shouting in the street outside, a copper holding her arm behind her back. He pushed her past the big window as she kicked and twisted.

"What good's it going to do you getting in anyways?" His eyes narrowed. "You planning a click or something?"

"I need you to do a favour for me, Ern," I said. "Leave a

window open in the back tomorrow night, is all. Take you a minute. Half a minute."

"Not a chance," he said, his pink eyes watering. "Mr. Cream's done right by me and I'll do right by him."

"There's half a crown in it for you."

"Go to hell. You could give me five quid and I wouldn't do it."

He drained his glass. As he turned, I took hold of his arm and pulled him back.

"Leave off me," he said, angry now.

"I haven't finished, chuckaboo."

He tried to pull away but I tightened my grip. I felt his wiry arm through his coat.

"Leave off!" he cried again, trying to wrench himself free. "Let go, you bastard!"

"What's this?" asked the barmaid, coming over to us. "I hope you two's just having a lark."

I let him go.

"Family business," I said, smiling as nice as I could at the woman. I brushed the front of the old man's coat and straightened his lapels. "Right as rain."

Ernest scowled at me and scurried out of the shop.

When I got to Coin Street the next morning, the guvnor wasn't too pleased to hear I'd failed.

"Tell me what he said," he demanded.

He sat in his chair in the now perfectly tidy parlour. I began to retell what had happened, but I'd barely got started when one of Ettie's prayer books came flying through the damp air towards my head.

"Not last night!" he cried. "The first time! From the first

time you met him! And I want every word you can remember."

I breathed in and out slow, calming myself. Never in my life did I like being shouted at, and he knew it. I glared at him, sat in his chair, his face red and spongy. His shoulders fell.

"I apologize, Barnett. I promised I wouldn't throw my possessions at you again, I know I did. My sister's been driving me insane. That's all I can say. I won't do it again."

"Just see you don't," I said. "Not one more time. Otherwise I'll jam that book so far down your throat you'll be saying your prayers out your arse."

He blinked in surprise, then regained his voice.

"You have my word, Norman. Now tell me. Everything he said. As close to his words as you can."

When I'd gone through each of the three times I'd spoken with the sculleryman, he questioned me further about each detail, about how much he pissed when he drank beer, about the gift Cream had given him, about how the barmaid and cabman had laughed about his pecker. Then he sat in silence, puffing his pipe as the clock ticked away on the mantel. Finally, he spoke.

"I have a plan. Now, listen carefully."

When I arrived at the White Eagle later that night, the guvnor was sat on his own at a table near the bar, a plate of oyster shells in front of him. He wore his best suit, his hair combed and perfumed, his fingernails cleaned. He supped from a mug of wine. Ernest was hunched at the bar, his nose running, the ragged coat down to his knees. The same cabman was there, talking to the barmaid. A few others stood quietly staring into their mugs. I walked up and banged a coin down on the counter.

"Pint for me," I told the barmaid. "And whatever my mate here is having."

The old man started as if I'd woke him from a dream.

"Oh, Christ. Not you again. I ain't doing it, I told you before. I don't want that drink neither."

I bought him a gin anyway and stood there drinking my pint. The fat barman came through with a crate of bottles.

"Ernest!" called the cabman from the other end of the bar.

"What?" snapped the old man.

"Something in the paper about you."

"Eh?"

The cabman held up the paper and showed him the headline.

MAN FALLS INTO PRIVY! it declared.

Everyone at the bar laughed.

"Go fuck yourself," growled Ernest.

When the barmaid went out back, he drained his glass and turned to the door. I took his arm.

"Leave off me!" he spat, a thread of drool falling out of his mouth onto the front of his coat. His woollen sleeve was damp and greasy. "I've had enough of you!"

"Just a window, mate," I whispered in his overgrown ear. "That's all I want. I'll make it worthwhile for you."

He jerked his arm away, but I gripped him tighter.

"Ow!" he cried. "Let go, you bastard!"

"Let him go!" commanded the guvnor, rising from his table. "He doesn't wish to speak to you, sir."

"This is none of your mind," I replied. "You sit back down, mister. We're only having a chat."

The guvnor lifted his walking stick and cracked it hard on my forearm. I let go of the old man, cursing. It hurt like the blazes: it was a lot harder than he'd said he'd hit me, and, even though he swore he wouldn't, he'd gone for the same arm as the copper almost broke two days previous.

"There, sir!" exclaimed the guvnor. "And don't let me see you worry this man again."

I backed away from him as if I was afraid, hiding the fury I felt.

"Now you come over here and sit with me," said the guvnor to Ernest. "You come and sit with me until you've recovered. That must have been a nasty shock, there."

"Thanks for your help and all, sir," replied Ernest. "I do appreciate it, but I'd just as well be on my way now. Get away from him, like."

"Of course. Of course," said the guvnor, stepping between Ernest and the door. "But might I trouble you, sir, to stay a few more moments? I won't let him near you. I'm not from these parts, you see, only here for a couple of nights, and am sorely in need of a bit of advice about this part of town. I'm thinking of investing in a business down the road." He leaned close to the old man and whispered, gesturing around the bar, "These others in here strike me as half-wits, some of them, but you look like you're a man who knows what's what. Would I be right about that, sir?"

"Well, you're right about that, I reckon, sir. Been living and working around here near on sixty year, so if I don't know then I don't know who do. Just don't want to be around him, is all," he said, jerking his head in my direction.

"I'll make sure he doesn't bother you," said the guvnor, leading the old man to his table. "Please. Sit with me a while. You'd be doing me a great favour."

"Well, all right, then," said Ernest, taking a seat. "I suppose I could do that."

I turned my back to them and supped my pint. For some

time the guvnor asked his opinion on local matters. How far it was into the West End, which hotels had the best reputation, the location of theatres and so on. When the barmaid came through, the guvnor signalled her.

"Another for me, and a glass of gin for my friend please, madam."

"Well, I suppose another wouldn't hurt," said Ernest.

"I do not like to see a man put upon," said the guvnor. "I do not like to see that. Coves like that have no right to disturb a working man like yourself. I assume you've just come from your work. Is that right?"

"Just come direct."

"Where is that you work, sir?"

"A place called the Barrel of Beef. Waterloo Road, if you know it."

"Ah! I've been there. A very fine place indeed, that is. I think it's the best place to eat in this part of town, or so I've heard."

"Works in the kitchen there," said Ernest, gulping his gin. "Been there ten year, more or less."

"Ten years! Your employer must value you."

"He does that. Mr. Cream's his name. Rich man, he is. One of the richest around here and no word of a lie."

"I own a hotel in Gloucester," said the guvnor loudly. "Twenty rooms. I've a man just like you there, been with me since the start. I swear I'd get rid of all the others before I'd lose him. Never been late, never missed a day except through sickness. I'd wager you're the same?"

"Yes, sir. Never missed a day."

"I knew it. You know, you can tell a good man by the look in his eye. I saw it in you the minute I spoke to you. Look, my friend, I'm having some more of these oysters. Could I persuade you to join me?"

When the oysters and more drinks were ordered, the guv-nor started up again.

"No, I do not like to see a man put upon. A man thinks that because he's younger and has a bit more muscle on him that he's better. But he doesn't see what's inside. The wisdom of age. When I see a younger man putting upon an older man, I'd like to break his arm. It makes me wild with fury."

"That's how I see things too, sir."

"Say, I'm just thinking here. You wouldn't come and work with me, would you? I'd give you a good position and a wage you'd be very happy with. I need another man I can trust."

"Well—"

"Of course," interrupted the guvnor. "You'd never de-sert your employer. You aren't that kind of man. No, no. I shouldn't have asked, I apologize for putting you on the spot. Ah!" Here the guvnor gasped and clutched his leg. "Damn! Oh, this knee is hell itself. All my joints seem to cause me nothing but pain these days. It's no pleasure getting old, is it, my friend?"

"None, sir," said Ernest. "I'm up at the chamberpot five or six times a night these days. I'm tireder when I wake than when I go to bed. Age is no friend to a body, that's for sure."

"Ah, that sounds appalling," said the guvnor, shaking his great head in pity. "It must make life a misery for you."

"It does that, sir. But I don't complain."

"You're not the sort to complain. I noticed you holding your back when you came in. Does that trouble you also?"

"Pain is constant. I tries not to take too much Black Drop as it sends me sleepy, that's the thing. I do use a lot of that, though, and no word of a lie."

"I will not let a man work if he's in pain. My man, the one I mentioned, he also suffers with his back. When I see him in pain I tell him to go to bed. I still pay him. It's a matter of principle. Age takes us all in the end. I suppose your employer does the same?"

"Well, no, as it happens. He expects me to work through, pain or no."

"What? A loyal man like yourself?"

"Yes, sir."

The guvnor shook his head. "I must say, I'm surprised."

The oysters and drinks arrived and for a few minutes they didn't speak. When the guvnor had finished, he said, "How much does he pay you, this Mr. Cream, if you don't mind my asking, sir?"

As Ernest answered, the guvnor brought his pint to his lips. "I gets six shillings a week."

The guvnor choked on his drink, spitting a gob of beer onto the table. He clutched his chest, coughing and wheezing, shaking his head.

"This cannot be true!" he exclaimed at last, a right fury on his face. "Six shillings for a loyal, hard-working man such as you? It's an outrage!"

Ernest nodded.

"You, who's never had a day off sick in his life? Works through his incessant pain? Up five times a night due to a bladder condition? Six shillings each week?"

Ernest nodded again.

"I'm losing respect for this Mr. Cream, Ernest. I really am. I'm sorry to say it, with your being so loyal to him, but it seems to me that you're shockingly maltreated by this gentleman. I suppose he at least gives you a rise each year?"

"I never had a rise, sir."

The guvnor stared at him open-mouthed. Ernest looked around uncomfortably, scratched his balls, then gulped down the rest of his gin.

"What, in ten years?" asked the guvnor finally.

"Never, sir. Now you come to say it, I suppose I should have had one by now."

"Not only one, my friend. I cannot believe this. But what about days off?"

Ernest shook his head again.

"To visit your family?"

"Don't have no family."

"No wonder your back is causing you pain. Not a day off?"

"He should really give me a day off from time to time, shouldn't he?"

"He's making you ill."

The guvnor ordered more drinks for them both. When they arrived, he took a long swig, then wiped his mouth.

"My man gets half a sovereign a week. For the same job as you. I increase this by a penny each year. He's allowed two days off every month. I hope you don't mind me saying this, Ernest, but I believe, and many employers share this belief, that every man deserves respect. If a businessman makes a healthy profit, he must treat his best workers with dignity. I believe you are being abused."

"I just thought it was the way things are, sir."

The guvnor nodded, his eyes looking kindly at the old man.

"Drink that one up. I'll order more. I do enjoy talking to you, my friend."

When the next round arrived, the guvnor said, "I'm sorry for speaking plain, sir. I couldn't help myself. I hope I haven't caused offence?"

"If you says it's true then true it must be, sir," said Ernest, the quick drinking of three mugs of gin making his words come loosely now. "You're a gent and a businessman and you'd know what's what, far as I can see. Truth is, sometimes I don't believe he treats me right, sir. I felt that way for some time now. He lets his men make fools of me too on account of me being old and all. One of them's worse, Long Lenny's his name. I'd happily see that one in the river, I would."

"I knew it," replied the guvnor, slapping the table hard. "Your loyalty prevented you from telling me that. But I could tell there was something."

I heard the old man sigh and wheeze at the same time. The guvnor's voice dropped.

"What did that chap at the bar want with you, my friend? Trying to rob you, was he?"

"No. He's got some lark going." Ernest was quite drunk now, and the words ran into each other. "Wants to break up, up into the pub. Wants me to leave a window open night, open a window. That's right, offered me half a crown, he did."

"A burglar, is he?" whispered the guvnor. It was all I could do to hear him.

"Must be. I told him no, but he's come again, back here again. Won't leave me alone, will he?"

"See what I say? You're just the type of man an employer should value."

"Hasn't done me much good, by the sounds of it," mumbled Ernest with a burp.

"Honestly, my friend, it sounds to me like Mr. Cream deserves to be burgled the way he treats you, and may the Lord forgive me for speaking plain. The money he must earn from the place and he hasn't given you a rise in ten years! Well, maybe you deserve a bonus after all that, not least as your body suffers so with overwork."

"Maybe I do. I am in a deal of pain, sir, won't deny it."

I glanced back at them. Ernest was swaying on the little stool.

"How much did he offer you, did you say?"

"Half a crown."

"Ask him for a crown."

Ernest took a big breath and steadied himself on the table. His lips were smacking each other, his wet tongue ran over his broken teeth. It didn't seem like he could talk at all at that moment.

"It's only your due after all these years," the guvnor went on. "After the way you've been swindled by that man. After your back has almost been broken by overwork. It sounds safe enough, leaving a window open. Nobody will know. Look, I'll call the man over."

The old man let out another burp. "Ouch. Sorry, sir, just comes out like that sometimes, from out of nowhere, like. But you…you reckon it's…it's right, what you're saying about the window?"

"It's the rightest thing in the world. Believe me. I'm giving you advice from a businessman. What's right is right, and you cannot argue with it."

"Well, I suppose."

The guvnor stood and buttoned his coat. He shook the old man's hand firmly.

"I'm afraid my knees are so very painful I must retire now, my friend. I'm honoured to meet such an honest, hard-working man. Really I am. It's been my pleasure to talk with you. If you're ever in Gloucester, you must come and see me. We'll have a spot of lunch."

"I—"

"Yes, indeed. It will be good to see you again. Now, look

here." He stepped across the room and tapped me on the back with his walking stick. I turned. "The price is a crown, you wretch. No less, do you hear? My friend at the table will do what you ask, but he wants the money now."

"Yes, sir," I said. As I fished the coin out of my pocket a bolt of pain went through my arm. Cursing, I stepped over to Ernest and put it in his pink hand.

"He'll do it tomorrow night," continued the guvnor. "Which window, my friend?"

Ernest blinked.

"Which window?" I growled.

"In the courtyard down the side," burbled Ernest. "Little one next to the kitchen door."

"How little?"

"Suppose you'll need a boy to get in."

"I'll return tomorrow," the guvnor said to me. "If I hear you've stolen this money back from my friend you'll answer to me. Do you hear?"

I looked down as if I was scared of him, and tipped my cap.

"Good night, sir," said the guvnor, and stumbled out of the shop.

Chapter Twelve

THE NEXT NIGHT, WHEN ALL THE PUBS AND ALE-houses were shut, when those without lodgings were snoring in the alleys under bundles of old rags and only the occasional hansom troubled the streets, we made our way to the Beef. It was three hours before sunrise. Behind us, stumbling tired along the paving stones, was little Neddy. We didn't talk much on the way: it was the first time in four years we'd be going back inside the place. I went to the lane at the back, near the entrance to the Skirt of Beef, and hid in a doorway where I had a good view of the windows. The guvnor took Neddy to check the front.

The building was dark and quiet. When I was sure there was no sign of life inside I went round the front to find them. We crept down the narrow alley that ran aside the building until we found the gate. Rats scuttled away as we stepped inside the small yard. The ground was strewn with peelings and rinds, which spilled from the overflowing bins. A sewer grate was cut into the middle: from the smell of it this was where the kitchen workers did their piss.

Next to a heavy oak door was our window. I had it open in a second.

Neddy stood by the gate, quivering.

"You cold, mate?" I asked as hushed as I could.

"A bit."

"You scared, then?"

"I never did a robbery before."

"It ain't a robbery, Neddy. We ain't stealing. We're looking for clues."

"I know. But the coppers don't know that, do they?"

"Listen, Neddy darling," whispered the guvnor, sitting on a crate and clasping the boy's shoulders. He spoke very low and reassuring. "You're a brave boy, I know you are. The first time I met you I could see you were something special. I said it to Mr. Barnett. I said, "That boy's going to go far." That's why we're teaching you how to be a detective agent."

"I know, sir."

"That's the spirit. Now, it'll take you one minute, perhaps two, and then you'll be out again. We'll lift you. When you're in, unlock the door. There'll be bolts at the top and bottom. Stand on a stool if you need. As soon as you have them open, you'll be out again."

"What if there's men inside?" asked Neddy. He moved from one foot to the other. One boot was black, the other brown. They were men's boots, twice as big as his little feet.

"Nobody's inside. Look. There are no lights anywhere."

"They might be sleeping."

"They don't sleep in the kitchen," I said. "Now come on. Here, give me your hat."

The boy was brave. We lifted him up to the window and he slipped through easy. We heard him fall head first onto the floor on the other side with a little grunt. It didn't take more than a few seconds before the door was open and Neddy was out again.

"Good boy," I said. "You done us proud."

He sniffed, and I could see in the dim light that his eyes had watered at the fall. He rubbed his elbow.

"Brave lad," said the guvnor. "Now you wait for us out on the street, at the front. You keep watch for us. If you see any of the lights go on, or if anybody comes along and unlocks the door, I want you to throw this through the window."

He held a pebble out to the boy.

"But what if I break the glass?"

"I want you to break the glass. Make sure we hear it. Then run. Get home as quick as you can."

"Yes, sir."

The guvnor ruffled his hair.

"Go on, now."

The kitchen was warm from the embers still aglow in the fires. We stopped for a moment to listen, but the only sound in there was the skitter of a mouse behind the wall. The guvnor lit the candle stub he'd brought, and we crept across the stone floor to a corridor where we found the stairs. The first step creaked something awful. I froze, the guvnor yanking at my coat from behind: if there was anyone in the building they'd surely have heard. When there was no sound from upstairs, I carried on, and we climbed as quiet as we could to the stair-head. There we found a wide front supper room laid out with long tables and chairs, and two more private rooms at the back. All were dark, all were silent. The next floor was the same. The stairs leading up from here were blocked by a heavy green door with a window in the middle. I got out my betty and had it open in a minute or two. Before climbing the last flight we paused again, listening. The guvnor was wheezing from the stairs, my own breath coming quick now too. There was no sound above.

On the top floor was the gaming room, with a long hazard table in the middle, a roulette wheel, a few smaller card tables scattered around. A bar ran the length of one wall. As the guvnor nosed around, I went to the window and looked down on the street four floors below. It had started to rain; Neddy was crouched in a shop doorway opposite, his cap down tight on his head, his arms wrapped around his knees. Otherwise, the street was empty.

Cream's office was at the back of the building. Out came the betty again and soon the door swung open.

"You've very delicate fingers, Norman," whispered the guvnor.

We listened one more time for movement downstairs, then went in.

The guvnor swung his candle slowly around the room. There was a heavy desk by the back window, a safe in the corner next to a cabinet, a smaller desk by the wall. The bookcase held shelves of ledgers.

"Where do we start?" I asked, lighting my own candle. We had to work quick. If Cream's men came back while we were upstairs, we'd be trapped.

"I'll take the desk," he replied. "You start on that cabinet. Find anything unusual written down around the time Thierry disappeared. Or any names you recognize, Irish connections, anything to do with rifles."

Both the cabinet and desk were easily opened. I'd been taught the art of lock picking by my Uncle Norbert when I was a lad. He was a locksmith, and was preparing me to work with him when he fell between two barges one night and died. They said he was drunk and I've no reason to doubt it. I never had much use for the skill working in the courts, but it made me a valuable assistant for Mr. Arrowood as long as the locks were simple. Expensive ones like those on the outer doors of the Beef were too much for me, but I was good enough at the little ones and the old ones.

Inside the cabinet were ledgers going back years. I looked through them. They were nothing more than account books for the Beef and Cream's other businesses. Payments made, invoices. Nothing that helped us.

The guvnor sat at the desk with a thick red notebook open in front of him, scribbling something into his own pad. Every creak and scratch, every gust of wind made us freeze, afraid it was Cream's men come back downstairs. I tried the safe but knew it'd be shut. Norbert hadn't taught me that art, and so I started on the shelves.

It was right then as we heard the glass shatter below.

"Time to go," hissed the guvnor.

We got out of the office quick as we could. At the top of the stairs we stopped and listened. There was no sound below. We crept down, taking care to put our weight at the corner of each step so as not to creak. We listened again on the next landing.

Now we could hear them: the muffled sounds of men talking down below, something heavy scraping across the floor. We waited, the guvnor trying to control his wheezing, my heart beating like a hammer.

"Hide?" I whispered.

"We've got to get out," he replied, his lips in my ear.

I knew he was right. Cream's men carried knives and pistols. If they found us in here we had no chance.

The voices seemed to go outside, then come back in. More scraping. The guvnor nudged me: we crept down the next flight to the first floor. The sounds of the men moving about were louder now.

Again we waited. The guvnor took my hand and gestured to one of the private dining rooms at the back.

"In there," he whispered.

Before we had time to hide there was a shout from downstairs. Then came the sound of heavy boots running out of the building and onto the street.

We took our chance and stumbled fast as we could down the stairs, through the kitchen and out into the alley where we turned down towards the Skirt, away from the front of the Beef. The guvnor couldn't run too well with his shoes and the weight he carried, so when we got to the end of the alley and were sure we hadn't been followed we slowed, quick-marching through the streets behind the Beef and crossing the Waterloo Road further up. It was raining heavy now, the moon hidden behind clouds, the streets black as hell. We wound our way through the alleys on the north side until we came out a few shops down from the pub. There we hid behind a stack of rubble from a half-demolished building.

Outside the Beef stood Cream's landau, the driver having a smoke while sheltering in a doorway. Next to it was a cooper's wagon loaded with barrels and a couple of long crates. A slack-shouldered nag stood before it, drenched in the rain, his head hanging pathetically like he thought he was too old to be out so late. The door to the Beef was open, and we could hear the sound of the men's low voices inside. A dim light spilled onto the street.

"That was quite a jolly," whispered the guvnor when his breathing had returned to normal.

"We were lucky," I said.

I shifted around to get myself more comfortable on the pile

of wet bricks. My back was paining me from where the copper had beaten me, and I was hoping the guvnor would call it a night so I could go home to bed. For maybe ten minutes nothing changed on the street.

"Tell me, Barnett," he whispered, lowering himself to sit on a pile of stones. The rain fell in a thin stream from the brow of his hat. "What did you think when Miss Cousture proposed we burgle the Beef?"

"I was surprised a lady like her'd suggest something like that."

"Miss Cousture has a hard side to her character, doesn't she? I wonder where she learnt such a tactic?"

"In a penny dreadful, might be," I whispered.

He was about to reply when three men came out the door. One was Cream, holding an umbrella, his back upright. He removed his derby, smoothed down his hair, and replaced his hat. Behind him was Long Lenny who I knew by sight from the time I spent watching things in the Beef during the Betsy case. The other was a stranger to me. He was wrapped up against the rain, a scarf around his face, a black cap pulled low. The man jumped on the back of the cart and began putting the lids back on the barrels, latching each one with a click that echoed in the dark street.

Cream climbed into the landau and the horses moved off. As the carriage trundled away, the two men pulled one of the long boxes from the cart and carried it inside the Beef. Then the second was pulled off and hauled inside. They came back out carrying a heavy chest which they loaded onto the wagon next to the barrels. The man with the scarf exchanged a few words with Lenny, got on the cart, and drove away. Lenny went back inside the Beef.

We waited for some time in case Lenny left and we could

get back in. It rained steadily: the street had turned to puddles and mud, water poured over the blocked guttering and down the walls of the buildings all around us. Our clothes were soaking wet. After half an hour the guvnor jogged my elbow and pointed at the first-floor window, which had a hole the size of an apple in it, lines spreading out like a spider's web.

"He's a good boy," he said. "I'll give him another shilling for that. Did you find anything in those ledgers?"

"Nothing."

"I think I might have found something in the notebook."

As he spoke a dark figure stepped out from a doorway further down the road and began to walk quickly towards us through the rain. I pulled the guvnor's head down behind the pile of rubble. As the man passed, I peeked out.

At first I thought maybe I was mistaken on account of the dark and his cap pulled down so low over his face, but the cocksure way he walked told me it was him all right, and I felt a rage take hold of me as I remembered how he'd stood over me with his burning eyes and his truncheon and beat me before I'd had a chance to fight back. I wanted so bad to repay that copper for the great aching bruise that spread over my spine like a burn and kept waking me at night.

I drew my cosh and stood up. But as I stepped forward to make my move I was struck by a heavy blow on my thigh which had me cry out in surprise. I stumbled back onto the sharp stones, my leg deadened, feeling I was going to puke.

The sound of the copper's boots echoed in the street as he fled. The guvnor stood above me, a bit of old pipe in his hand.

"I'm sorry, Barnett. But that really wouldn't have been a good idea."

I gritted my teeth and rubbed my leg until it felt half normal again.

"Are you all right?" he asked, chucking the pipe onto the rubble. "Shall I get a hansom?"

"If you ever do that again, Mr. Arrowood, I shall knock your teeth out, so I will."

"I understand, Norman."

I allowed him to help me up, and we hobbled away down the street until we found an early morning cab. The church bells were just sounding four o'clock.

"Would you mind if he drops me off first?" he asked meekly when we were sat down in the back. "My gout, you see."

"Sod your gout, sir," I replied, and leaned across to give the cabbie my address.

Chapter Thirteen

I ARRIVED THE NEXT AFTERNOON TO FIND ETTIE entertaining six ladies in the parlour. They sat on stools brought in from the shop, each holding a cup of tea in their capable hands. The chill had finally left the air and it was a stuffy day. The window stood open.

"May I introduce you to the ladies of the London Mission, Mr. Barnett?" asked Ettie. "Mrs. Boothroyd, Miss Crosby, Mrs. Campbell, Mrs. Dewitt, Miss James, and our organizer, Mrs. Truelove."

I nodded to each in turn.

"I've heard of your good works," I said.

"We're instruments of the Lord, Mr. Barnett," replied Mrs. Truelove, her head tilting, a most engaging glimmer in her eye. "We deserve no credit. There's too much to be done."

"Did you pass on my invitation to Mrs. Barnett?" asked Ettie.

"She's a little sick at the moment."

"Oh dear. I hope it's nothing serious."

"Thank you, Miss Arrowood."

"Please pass on my best wishes."

I nodded. The ladies examined me as I stood by the door, my hat gripped in my hands.

"He's upstairs," Ettie said at last.

The guvnor lay on his bed, his waistcoat open, one fat red toe bursting from a hole in his yellow sock. His bald head was also red with the heat and running with sweat. In his hand he held a book.

"They've ejected me," he complained. "Their clucking comes right through the floorboards."

"They're trying to do some good."

"They are, Barnett. Do not mistake me. I'm only peeved that I haven't had my cup of tea yet this afternoon."

I sat on the other bed. A curtain, which separated the two beds, had been drawn back and tied to the wall. The small open window looked across the alley to a brick wall, black with soot. No breeze blew through to ease the heat of the day.

He pointed at a tray on the chest.

"I brought something in for you. Have you eaten?"

I shook my head.

"Good. I'll have something with you. Go on, help yourself."

There was a wrap of sliced ham, a packet of still-warm spuds, a nice loaf of bread, half a pound of cheese. I served myself a plateful and sat back on the bed. He got up with a grunt and did the same.

We ate, listening to the outlines of the discussion through the floorboards. I took some more ham and ate. It was good ham, and I hadn't had the like for a long while. I knew this was his apology. Ham was always the guvnor's apology.

"You know we had a housekeeper when we were children?" he said, his cheeks bulging, a crumb of wet bread stuck to his chin. "It wasn't thought fit for our mother to carry out household duties. I'd like to have one again, but I suspect I never will. I don't suppose you had one, Barnett?"

"My mother was a housekeeper for someone else."

"Oh, yes. You did tell me."

Yes, I did tell him. But I didn't tell him that she was only a housekeeper until her employer, old man Dodds, died. After that she couldn't find another position, for who would take such an ugly servant into the house, her face being burned down one side like a pound of raw liver? And who had held her face onto the side of the cooking pot one night but Mr. Dodds himself? I was only about ten years old when we moved to Weavers Court in Bermondsey, and what a shock that was for both of us. Being big for my age, I had to learn quick how things were in that stinking court. I had to learn to fit in, and I had to learn to use my fists. From those early years I carried two things which weren't always helpful to me as a grown man. First, a prejudice against all those who treat their servants as less than themselves, and, second, a heavy guilt over some of the things I did to get along in the three years my mum and me lived in that court.

"I've been reading something interesting," said Arrowood, putting aside his plate and taking up a book. "Henry Maudsley, the psychiatrist. He has much to say on crime and insanity." He flicked through the pages until he found his spot. "He writes there are two types of creative men, those of serenity and high intellect, and those of limited intellect but great energy. These are the two types that influence the world. But listen to this and tell me if it does not describe my sister. The second type are *"Persons who are clever but flighty, talented but unstable, intense but narrow, earnest but fanatical; all sorts of persons who are plunging into new movements, good or bad, and pursu-*

ing them with intemperate zeal lack the just balance of the faculties."
Now. Does that not describe her perfectly?"

"I don't know her well enough, sir."

"It's incredible. It's as if Maudsley is married to her himself."

"You find it hard to see the good in your sister, sir."

He looked at me in surprise, then turned back to his food.

"Have you heard from Petleigh?" I asked at last.

"Nothing. I'll send him a message when Neddy comes
along for his money."

"Neddy hasn't been yet?"

He saw the alarm on my face.

"He'll be on the street with his muffins," he said. "Or re-
pairing some damage his mother has done."

"The boy's usually eager for his money."

"There were at least five minutes between the window
breaking and their running out into the street. Neddy isn't a
fool. He would have been off the minute he let fly the pebble." He put his book back on the dresser. "The boy has a
good mind."

"I know. I just want to be sure he's safe." I returned my
plate to the chest. "So tell me, what did you read in Cream's
notebook?"

"It was a list of dates going back a few years. Prices and
names, but rarely the two together. There was only one that
struck me. Do you recognize the name Longmire, Barnett?
Colonel Longmire?"

I shook my head.

"If it's the one I'm thinking of, he's a high official in the
War Office," he continued. "The name appears irregularly
over the last four or five years. No information, only dates
and the name."

"A connection to the bullet?"

He nodded. "Perhaps a connection to our Martha. If it's the same Longmire."

We heard footsteps coming up the wooden stairs and the door swung open. It was Ettie.

"There's a woman below requesting to see you about Neddy," she said. "She's in the shop."

The guvnor nodded.

"I'll get my shoes on. Bring her in."

"I'd rather leave her in the shop, William."

"You'd—"

"She's distraught," she said sharply.

He heaved a long sigh and glanced at me.

"Tell her we'll be down presently."

The pudding shop was usually busy at that time of day, but today it was more choked than usual. Albert's thin and gloomy face was wet with sweat as customers tried to attract his attention. He was a slow man, and not suited to this type of frantic commerce. His wife, Mrs. Pudding, was stirring a huge vat of dough, while their sons John and Small Albert were tending the ovens and cooking pots.

"What's happening here, lads?" I asked as we pushed our way through the door at the back of the shop.

"Fire at Gleason's," replied John, stopping for a moment. "Last night. Everyone's come down here today. We can't keep up. Hottest day of the year too."

"Ready to come out!" barked Albert. "You wouldn't mind getting out of the road, Mr. Arrowood? Emergency situation, as you might see. All Gleason's customers are down here."

"Of course," murmured the guvnor, somewhat dazed to be amid the hungry throng.

At the sound of the guvnor's name, Neddy's mother appeared through the crowd.

"Mr. Arrowood?" she asked. Her voice was strange and high-pitched, as if her tongue were glued to the roof of her mouth. Her hair was matted and tied up on top of her head like a bundle of rotted sacks. Her neck was grimy; many of her teeth were missing, the others brown and yellow. A long dress fell to the floor beneath a very old coat which looked like it had once been worn by a rich lady. She was the only one in the shop with a coat.

"Now look here," she began straightaway. "I don't so much mind him going off into service or learning a trade and so on, nothing wrong with that, happy for him and for us his family as you see and very happy he has one such as you, sir, and you, sir." Here she acknowledged me with a nod and a twitch of the nose. "Just so long as he doesn't forget his family, his sister with the twist in her foot and the other which can't seem to learn to speak proper. Just so long as he keeps earning a share, a few shillings here and there, keeping us in a few potatoes and so on, sir, as to taking care of us his blood when I fall sick as I do regular with the weak lungs I got in here." She thrust up her chest and produced a delicate cough.

"What is it you're asking me, madam?" asked the guvnor, trying to free himself from her claw. She held tight, pulling him in closer to her. "You know I cannot pay you, much as I'd like to."

"Now, sir, wherever he is you make sure he remembers to send the money back to us down here every day, or every week, like. And today we got nothing and the nippers could do with a bit of this pudding since they haven't had nothing today at all."

"Tell him to come along to collect his money. He's earned it."

She stopped her monologue. Her baby's chin jumped to the side; her eyes narrowed.

"I ain't seen him. That's why I come here."

"He didn't return home last night?" asked the guvnor.

"I ain't seen him since he come to you yesterday for a job."

The guvnor looked at me.

"Are you sure he didn't come home?" he asked her again. "Is there somewhere else he might have gone? Aunties? Friends?"

"You don't know where he is?" she asked.

"No. He left us about three."

"Oh, Lord," she groaned. "Oh, Blessed Lord."

The other customers were watching her now as she took the guvnor's other wrist.

"He's been picked up by the coppers, that's what," she said, her voice sharp now. "What did you have him doing so late? I trusted you, sir. I trusted you. Or he's had a beating. What was you up to? Eh? So late at night with a little boy? What was you up to?"

"We had a delivery, that was all, missus," I said. "Now listen. Is there anyone else he could've gone to?"

"Nobody. He never went to nobody. Oh, Lord. The coppers have got him from being out and about so late. They'll say he was up to no good. What we going to eat while he's in the pokey?"

I fished in my pocket and handed her a few shillings.

She snatched the coins from my hand and dropped them in the pocket of her coat.

"Now I suppose I have to find him," she said, turning to leave. "Lord Josh, what troubles I got."

We watched her in silence as the customers, desperate for their pies, pushed and chattered around us. Without looking at him I knew the guvnor was feeling the same panic as me.

Chapter Fourteen

WE WAITED IN THE STATION UNTIL INSPECTOR Petleigh appeared. He brought us through the back and up some narrow stairs to a dark office. The window was jammed open by a block of wood, but the room was still baking hot. Without sitting, the guvnor began to tell him about Neddy. Petleigh dropped himself onto a chair behind the crooked desk and listened. When the guvnor finished, the inspector pressed his fingers together and pushed his chair back.

"You fools," he said.

"You need to search the Beef, Inspector," continued the guvnor, his fists clenching and unclenching. "Make Cream aware that you know he has Neddy. There's no time to lose. Oh, Lord, I hope to God it isn't already too late."

"Mm."

"Let's go now." The guvnor put his hat back on his head and moved to the door. "Right away."

"I take orders from the Chief Inspector, Arrowood. Not from you."

"Inspector, please. I wouldn't be so forthright if it weren't so urgent. You know Cream's ruthless. He'll hurt the boy. He will enjoy hurting him."

"I told you not to interfere."

The guvnor's eyes were bulging.

"Petleigh, listen to me! We've made a terrible mistake, I admit it. But Cream will be wild when he discovers someone has burgled him. He'll do anything to find out who it was. He'll tear up that boy until he talks, then he'll throw his skin into the river. You must come now!"

Petleigh looked at us for some time. Finally, he spoke.

"I think we'll give it a little while before blundering in to the Barrel of Beef. Most likely Neddy will have met a friend and got diverted. A boy such as him maybe likes a bit of house-breaking, eh? Or he's gone off on a bus and got himself lost in the West End. If he's not returned by, let's say, tomorrow evening, then we'll think of visiting Mr. Cream."

"What?" spluttered the guvnor.

"You might remember we have a murder case on our hands? Our officers are busy with enquiries. I'm sure he'll be back in a jiffy."

The guvnor slammed his fist on the desk. "No!" he roared. "That will not do! It was three in the morning. There were no buses, no friends he would run into. The streets were empty. And Neddy is as honest as you are. The boy's in danger, I swear it!"

"Do not shout at me, Arrowood." Petleigh stroked his moustache rapidly in irritation. "I won't be argued with."

"I'll shout as long as a boy's life's at risk! Go to the Beef, you lazy cur!"

"Out of my office!" cried Petleigh, getting to his feet.

"Not until you agree to do your job!"

"I will decide how to do my job!"

"I'll expose you in the *Gazette* if that boy is harmed! I'll name you!"

"Out! Out!" Petleigh strode to the door and bellowed down the stairs. "PC Reid! Come immediately!"

"You do your job, sir!" cried the guvnor again. He was overheating; his face was crimson. I took his arm and pushed him out of the office.

"Wait for me outside," I whispered firmly. "Don't say another word."

Maddened as he was, he knew better than to resist. Reid appeared at the bottom of the stairs.

"Make sure the gentleman leaves, Reid," called Petleigh, then retreated into his office. I stepped back inside and shut the door.

"Inspector, I'm sorry," I said. "Mr. Arrowood's an emotional man. His heart sometimes overpowers his head. He don't mean no harm."

"I'll have him arrested for assault."

"And there's no one could blame you for that."

He sat wearily behind his desk. He seemed to be suffering a great strain. I took a chair next to the door.

"Your job's difficult," I said.

"You've no notion how hard it is."

He wiped his brow with a handkerchief, then pulled a cigar from his pocket and lit it.

"The boy's like a son to him," I said. "Neddy's father's dead, his mother's simple. Mr. Arrowood's watched over him these last few years. He's desperate with worry, and it's only because he knows you could find him that he's so upset. He knows your skills well enough."

Petleigh nodded and drew on his cigar.

"Barnett," he said. "You must consider me stupid."

I watched him puff.

"Were you playing with him?" I asked.

"I admit I was. I do enjoy his tantrums. I will visit the Beef, of course I will. Cream's a disease in this part of London and I'd dearly love to send him to prison. But I don't like receiving orders from the likes of Arrowood. I don't even like them from the Assistant Commissioner."

I stood.

"Did you find the name of the constable who gave me a beating?"

"It wasn't the officer from the Elephant and Castle we had in mind. Poor chap's down with consumption and hasn't worked for months. But there's a man that fits the description at Scotland Yard, or so I hear from the detective who sits in this office with me. They attended a ceremony together but unfortunately weren't introduced, so I don't have his name. He's not a constable, though. I'm not sure of his position."

"Can you find out?"

"I'll ask about."

"Thanks, Inspector. When will you be back?"

"I'll go immediately. Come back around six."

He pulled another cigar from his pocket and held it out to me.

"Smoke it outside, will you, Barnett? Go and put your employer out of his misery."

At six I was waiting at the station house. Petleigh hadn't returned. For an hour or so I sat on the bench watching the good citizens of Southwark come and go, making complaints, telling of their misfortunes, waiting, protesting, fighting. Finally, Petleigh stepped in with PC Reid behind him. He beckoned me to follow him up the stairs.

"Cream is vexed," he said once the office door was closed.

"Something's happening there, I swear it. Something that has him worried."

"Did you find the boy?"

He shook his head with a frown. "We searched everywhere. If they have him, they're holding him elsewhere."

"We saw them take a trunk out and load it on the wagon. Mr. Arrowood reckons they might have locked him in there. Did you question his men?"

"Piser and Long Lenny, yes. Got nowhere."

"Can you bring them in?"

"And beat them?" he asked, staring hard at me.

"Yes."

"No, Barnett. We don't use those methods in this station."

"But the boy!"

"We cannot beat them, Barnett. You know that. Anyway, they know we suspect them now. It might be enough to save the boy."

"It's not enough, Inspector."

"Have you a better idea?"

I turned and left the office.

The Beef had closed for the night. I waited across the street, hid behind the same pile of rubble as before. Cream, elegant as always, had left earlier in a landau with Piser and Boots. The windows upstairs went dark, then the serving girls came out, the kitchen workers, the barmen. Ernest appeared on his own again, but I let him get on with it. I was not after him tonight. Finally the door opened and Long Lenny came out. Though it was still warm, he wore his raincoat as he always did, his cap pulled down over his eyes.

I followed a few hundred yards behind as he strode down the empty street. Shouting from a window above a pawnbroker's made him pause and look up, then he walked on. Behind me I could hear the clack of horse-steps as the growler wandered along.

We passed the shuttered shops of Lambeth Road and the long wall of Bethlem. Lenny didn't look back. He was taking his tired body home, away from all he'd been put through that day by Cream and the others. When I was on the watch in the Betsy case I spent some hours drinking in the Beef, gathering information on who worked there, what they did. I followed Lenny a few times when he was out on a delivery. He never clocked me, and by the time we did show our hand he was in the clink for assault. Lenny was a rough, and that was all. He did what they told him. He made mistakes and got shouted at. He made no decisions himself, but he did enough, and he did it so well the thieves and whores would get out of the way if they saw him coming.

He turned into an alley, out of sight. I ran to catch him up. When I reached the corner he was only twenty yards away.

He stopped and jerked his head back, squinting at me through the darkness.

"What do you want?" he growled. I could see he thought I was about to rob him.

"I come to say sorry, Jack," I said, staggering and slurring my words just right as I approached him.

"Get to fuck," he mumbled, turning to walk away. "I ain't Jack."

I had the chloroform over his mouth quick, my other hand taking his wrist and wrenching it hard up his back. Lenny might have been taller, but I was stronger. He struggled, then, as the liquid took its effect, became weak. I knew chloroform wouldn't put a man as big as him right out, but he was confused enough to lose the fight in him.

A window opened in the doss-house behind us and a bucket of filth was thrown out. As it closed again the growler stopped at the entrance to the alley and my brother-in-law Sidney jumped down.

He took Lenny's legs and I his arms, and we dragged him back to the carriage. It wasn't easy on account of Lenny being so tall and still half-awake, but we got him in. The street was empty: we had luck with us.

I clambered inside, where the guvnor was waiting. He took care of Lenny's wrists while I wrapped his ankles in strong twine. When he was secure, the guvnor forced open his mouth and poured a vial of ether down his throat.

Sidney climbed onto the box and roused the horses. Though he now ran cabs, Sidney had spent his early life at sea where he caught a taste for using his fists. With two kids and his wife dead in childbirth, my brother-in-law had his ups and downs, but he was always ready to help when we needed a third man.

The growler was moving quick now, bumping us up and down over the cobbles. Soon we pulled up by the wharf steps just past London Bridge. It was high tide; the boats were roped up and bobbing in the dark river. I gave Lenny another long sniff of chloroform, then we dragged him onto the furthest wharf, right down to the end where we were hidden from the bank by a barge. He was mumbling but he wasn't too much trouble, confused as he was with the medication. There we lined him up, his waistband right on the edge of the floating wharf, me and Sidney sitting on his legs.

When his head touched the water he came around quick: he started twisting and throwing his legs about and shouting. But the more he thrashed the more his head went under. He came up coughing and choking, hacking up the stinking water, his shoulders jerking around, trying to free his hands from behind his back. We were patient: he wasn't going to last too long that way as his only hope of keeping his head out the water was with his belly muscles.

"Now listen, Lenny," I said, taking a grip of his wet hair and pulling his head up. "If you tell us what we want to know we'll get you up and that'll be you and us, the best of friends."

"Let me up," he croaked. "I work for Mr. Cream. He'll kill you."

"We're just going to ask you some questions."

He began to shout. I stamped down hard on his ankle and heard him groan. His head disappeared in the water again.

He surfaced, gasping. Then came a wild jerking of his legs; he took a big breath and fell back again into the river. After a moment he came up retching and choking. Sidney grabbed his coat-front and held his head out of the water.

"If you don't tell us, we'll have to tip you in the water," I said most politely. "You see, Lenny? The current's on its way out right now. Fast here as well, isn't it?"

"Treacherous," said the guvnor, lighting a cigar. He stood crow at the edge of the barge, keeping watch over the street.

"And seeing as your hands and feet are tied up," I said. "Well, I don't have to say, do I?"

"Cream'll get you," he groaned, his voice hoarse.

"The police'll think it was Cream done it," I replied. "And Cream won't know it was us, will he? A man like that's got enough enemies." I patted his wet cheek. "See, you're in a difficult situation, mate."

I shoved his head under the water again.

He thrashed about while I held him there a bit too long for comfort. When I pulled him out he was gasping and wheezing.

"Where's the little boy? The boy who broke your window last night. Where is he?"

"I don't—"

I shoved him under again. The same routine. He thrashed about. I pulled him out.

"Please," he begged when he'd got control of his lungs. The big man started to cry.

"Where's the boy?"

He began to cough again; there was water spurting out his mouth. I brought my elbow down hard into his belly, making him scream. Even Sidney groaned at that one.

"I don't know," he gasped, sobbing. "Honest. I didn't see a boy."

"Last night when you were at the Beef, you picked up a boy. Where is he?"

"I didn't see a boy!" he cried. "You got to believe me. Please."

"I understand," I said, all friendly. "You want to be able to tell Cream you didn't tell us about him. So I'll ask you an easier question."

"I don't know about the boy!"

"Shut it! Now listen. Where did the cart go last night? After it left the Beef? Where was it taking the chest?"

He looked at me like he was dazed. I grabbed his coat and pushed him back over the river.

"I'll tell you!" he cried. "Pull me up and I'll tell you!"

Sidney helped draw him back onto the pier and he sat there, his trussed legs out before him, his hands tied behind his back, breathing hard. The water ran off him onto the planks of the wharf.

"Milky Sal's place on Southwark Bridge Road," he said, his voice hoarse. "Number hundred and twelve."

"Is that where the boy is?"

He retched up another load of water.

I crouched down and looked in his miserable face.

"Is the boy at Milky Sal's, Lenny?" I asked.

"I told you, I don't know about a boy," he answered. "Honest. We didn't see a boy."

"If he's not there we'll come back for you, Lenny."

The fight had gone out of him. He just looked at me.

"What happened to Terry the pastry cook?" I asked.

"Eh?"

"The French lad."

"Who are you?"

"Answer the question."

"I've answered your bloody questions. Let me go now."

Sidney took hold of his sopping coat and I his legs and we pulled him over to the edge again.

"No!" he cried, twisting about, trying to edge back on the jetty.

We shoved his head back under.

"Oi!" came a shout from the street. We looked up. A policeman stood by the river wall, peering out. It was a dark night, and his lamplight could barely reach halfway across the water to us. Lenny's thrashing body was hid by the barge.

"Help us, Constable," called the guvnor. "This man's fallen in the water."

We pulled Lenny up. He was limp, and for a moment I thought he might be drowned.

"Have you got him out?" called the constable across the water.

"We have. He's a drunk."

We heard the policeman swear and walk back to the wharf steps. Sidney quickly cut loose the twine with his knife and threw it in the water. Lenny fell to his side, gasping and heaving.

The three of us strode up to meet the policeman as he stepped onto the wharf.

"We saw him from the road," said the guvnor. "Lucky we came along just as he fell in. Drunk out of his mind."

"I'd better take him in," said the policeman.

"Thank heavens for people like you," said the guvnor, patting him on the shoulder. "You're a good young fellow."

"Thank you, sir."

"Now we need to be off. That drunkard has made us late for our appointment."

Chapter Fifteen

MILKY SAL'S PLACE HAD THREE FLOORS ABOVE AND one below. There were no lamps on as far as we could see, but daylight was beginning to break and people would be starting to wake soon. We waited until Petleigh and his men arrived in two Black Marias. They wasted no time hammering on the front door with their truncheons. It soon opened, revealing first a man with Portuguese trousers and a long moustache, then Milky Sal's morning face, pale and tired, below a yellow sleeping cap. When Petleigh explained their purpose, she began cursing him in the most filthy terms. The inspector nodded to the constables behind him and they filed inside, pushing past her flapping arms.

Sidney had gone off home by then, and it was just the guvnor and me who waited by the police wagons. From indoors we could hear shouting, women's voices protesting the sudden awakening, heavy boots up and down the stairs.

The basement door opened and three young women, coats thrown over their nightdresses, crept up the stairs to the street. They stopped when they saw us. When it was clear we weren't going to challenge them, they hurried away.

Next, two girls no more than fourteen years old were brought out and put in the wagons.

"Is the boy there?" the guvnor asked one of the coppers.

"We haven't seen a boy, sir. Plenty of women, though."

The constables locked the wagon and returned to the house.

Presently the Portuguese man was brought out. He was bare-chested, a long scar down his arm. The officer who had him in handcuffs was bleeding down the side of his face. He threw the man down the stairs so he landed painfully on the paving stones, then picked him up roughly and tossed him in the back of the other wagon.

"Any sign of the boy?" asked the guvnor.

"No, sir."

It was too much for him. He hurried up the stairs and into the house.

"Find anything else there?" I asked the officer.

"It's a brothel." He chuckled. "I never seen so many ladies in their nightshirts."

"What about those young girls?"

"Probably illegal."

The door opened again and Milky Sal came out with an officer holding each arm. She now wore a tight black dress, a small hat pinned to her head from which a most elegant veil fell over her face. She was talking bitterly.

"Interfering with a woman who's only running a business," she said. "You should be ashamed of yourselves, disturbing all my girls when they need their beauty sleep. There's a few important men who won't like you taking me in, I'll tell you."

The officers said nothing.

"Don't bloody pinch me," she cried, jerking her arm from the taller of the two coppers.

"Yes, ma'am," he replied.

"What are you looking at, bruiser?" she spat at me as they escorted her to one of the wagons.

"Did you find the boy?" I asked the coppers when they'd got her shut up.

"Ain't no boy in there," the shorter one replied. He wiped his face with a cloth and looked up at the dark clouds that were gathering to the north of the city. "Bring on the storm. I can't hardly breathe in this heat."

I found the guvnor on the stairs, climbing up from the basement. His face was the colour of beet.

"No luck?"

He shook his head.

"What's down there?" I asked.

"A kitchen and a coal hole."

"The backyard?"

"There's nothing there but washing."

Petleigh came out of the front room.

"What did Milky Sal say?" asked the guvnor.

"She isn't saying anything," said Petleigh. He wasn't happy. "She claims to know nothing about a boy, nothing about those young girls either. Never heard of Cream, she says."

"Let me question her," said the guvnor.

"Do not try me, Arrowood. Not one of the girls has seen a boy, so they say. If it weren't for finding those young girls this would have been an utter waste of time. You may consider yourself lucky."

While the guvnor protested, I decided to have a look below. At the bottom of the stairs was a wide kitchen that took up most of the basement floor. At the front, the windows and door opened onto the stairs up to the street; at the back was a door to the yard and another to the pantry. The windows, rippled with black dust, let through a gloomy light. A long table stood at the back wall. The stone floor was sticky, with crumbs and vegetable rinds collected in the corners.

At the range, stirring a great pot, was an old woman. She looked around at me without interest then turned back to her gruel.

"Did you see a boy here yesterday?" I asked.

"Ain't no use asking me about a boy," she replied with her back to me. "I don't get upstairs. Only know what comes down here for food."

"You been here long?"

"Long enough."

"You got any children yourself, Cook?"

"That your business is it?" she asked, banging her ladle on the side of the pot and placing it on the side.

"I suppose not."

I sat at the table.

"Someone snatched a little boy, around ten years old," I said. "A right little imp, he was. We got told he was brought here."

She put a lid on the pot and wiped her hands on her apron.

"They're going to hurt him," I said.

"I had seven," she said. "Six of them dead before five years old. My last boy's at sea."

She walked slowly to the table and sat opposite me. Her grey hair was very thin on her head. She had a growth like she was carrying a baby in her stomach yet her limbs were thin as sticks.

"He have any children?" I asked.

At last she smiled, revealing two drunken teeth in her top gum.

"Four. Saw them Christmas last. Gave them each a wooden horse, I did." She cackled. "They're taking me to the races next month."

"That'll be a fine day out. You like the horses?"

"Always did. From when I was a nipper."

I leant forward at the table and nodded at the pile of blankets by the yard door.

"You sleep down here?"

"On the floor."

"Bit hard, is it?"

She shrugged.

"I'm used to it, I reckon. Got the fire, which is more than what some got."

She winced and clutched her belly.

"You're sick, ain't you, Cook?"

"Who ain't?"

"I'm no copper, you know."

"Could be one of those plainclothes agents. How would I know?"

"I just want to save the boy before they hurt him."

She nodded and looked at me with her foggy eyes.

"Did you hear anything two nights ago?" I asked. "Anybody arriving? Would've been almost morning."

She thought for a moment, her fingers tapping on the table.

"The wagon came. Portuguese let him in. Almost morning, as you say."

"D'you know what they were doing?"

"They brought out a few things for the wagon—heavy, from the way they was grunting. I don't sleep proper at the best of times. Didn't get up to look, if that's what you're going to ask."

"Did you hear a boy?"

She shook her head. "Didn't see nor hear a child. Wagon was off soon after, anyway."

"Is there anywhere in the house they could hide a boy?"

"Ain't never been upstairs. I can say he ain't down here."

"You sure you didn't see what they were loading?"

"Just saw the horse's legs through that bit of glass there." She pointed at the grimy window that looked onto the basement stairs: at the top, through the bottom of the railings, could be seen the wheels of the police wagon and the legs of its horse. "Big white fella he was, with black stockings."

"Who drives the cart?"

"That's Sparks. Has a cooperage down by Cutler's Court. Nice-looking old mare he has but they don't treat her right. Me and that mare both." She cackled again. "Oh, but we understand each other. Sometimes I take her up something when she's stood out there. An old carrot or something. Bit of water when it's hot."

I got up.

"Eh, mister, you won't tell Sal I been talking to you, eh?"

"'Course not. Will you see a doctor?"

She hunched her shoulders and screwed her face into an ugly brown knot.

"Hope you find the boy, dear," she said, pushing herself to her feet with a groan.

Chapter Sixteen

THE LANES WERE BUSY. WOMEN CARRIED GREAT bundles of umbrella frames and hat sacks to and from the factories that were packed together in that part of town; dockworkers and labourers were on the move. The sky started to spit out a few drops of rain, but the heat drove it back up almost right away and so it remained close and sticky. I was worried about the guvnor: he was wheezing from his bad chest, limping with his gout, and sweating so bad it was even coming through his thin blue jacket. It was quite a collection of discomfort to observe and it made me feel tired just to watch him drag himself along the busy morning streets. I told him to go home and I'd get Sidney to help, but he scowled and waved his stick at me.

"It's been a day and a night," he said. "The boy must be desperate with fear."

He pushed on, the guilt heavy on his suffering face. We'd neither of us spoke about what we were really afraid of—that Neddy was already abroad, sold by Cream to a foreign gentleman. Or he was already dead.

"We'll find him," I said.

We walked on.

"I've been thinking about how Neddy was taken," he growled, his breath short and strained. "What if he didn't run home when he threw the stone?"

"We told him to run as soon as he warned us."

"But Neddy likes to impress me, doesn't he? He always wants to do more than we ask. It isn't enough for him to provide for his sisters and his mother, he wants to do something for me, so that I am happy. What if he stayed there in case we needed him? What if he decided to find out what Cream's men were doing?"

We'd turned the last corner before the cooperage when, with no warning, the guvnor grabbed my shirt and pulled me into a narrow alley.

"Good Christ," he murmured, peering out into the lane. "It's her."

"Who?"

"My sister," he whispered. "And all the women. Hide yourself."

We hunched in a door as the women marched past on the main lane. They were all there: Ettie, Mrs. Truelove, Miss James; Mrs. Campbell; Miss Crosby; Mrs. Boothroyd and Mrs. Dewitt. They strode along, each with a determined look on her face, each holding a basket. They carried on past the cooperage and entered another alley on the right.

"What's the name of that place in there?" he whispered.

"That's Cutler's Court."

He groaned. "I should have remembered. It's the place she's been saving."

When the last of their bonnets and skirts had disappeared, we stepped back into the lane. The cooperage opened onto it with two wide-open barn doors. Inside, men were pounding hot metal ties into shape. Others were operating saws. Outside stood a wagon. Attached to it was the big white horse with black stockings that the old cook had made friends with. Its eyes were dull and suffering, its great head bowed; foam lined its black lips.

We crossed the lane and entered the workshop. Inside, the heat was raging from the small forge. The men worked with no shirts. Barrels large and small lay on the stone floor and were stacked against the walls. Everywhere, hanging from the walls, on the barrels, in the men's hands, were saws, hammers, axes, wood with raw, jagged cuts, its wounds damp and pink in the glow of the fires. At the back, two more barn doors opened onto a yard where rows of barrels stood in the open air. We found Sparks at the back, talking to one of the drivers.

"What can I do for you, gentlemen?" he asked as we approached. His face was freckled. He wore a jacket with no shirt beneath it. The toes of his boots were worn away.

"We've come for the boy," declared the guvnor.

Sparks frowned.

"No boys here, sir."

"We know he's here," I said. "Hand him over."

His eyes hardened. He raised his voice.

"I told you, there ain't no bloody boy here. Now go on, get out."

Behind us the hammering stopped and the men looked on. They were rough men, scarred, battered, dirty with soot. There were a lot more of them than us.

"Sir," said the guvnor. "We won't cause you any trouble as long as you hand him over. But we must have him. I'm asking politely. We're not leaving until we have him."

"Lads!" ordered Sparks. "Over here."

A big bald fellow put down his saw and came over to us. Another who looked like his brother came from the other side, an old police truncheon in his fist. Two younger men, one with a poker, another with a pair of pincers, ran over from the forge. Four others blocked our way to the door.

"Now, now," said the guvnor shifting on his feet, his voice losing the confidence of before. "There's no need for trouble, sir. Tell us where the boy is. Otherwise we'll have to get the police here to search the place."

I realized straightaway the guvnor had made a mistake. The slightest twitch of a smile came across the cooper's lips then fell away. We were on our own, and he knew it.

"Who are you two mumpers?" asked Sparks, looking us up and down with a sneer.

"His guardians, sir," replied the guvnor, hooking his thumbs in his waistcoat in a show of confidence that his nervy twitching betrayed. "Now make it easy on yourself. Where is he?"

Sparks nodded at the roughs: the two brothers seized my arms and held me tight. The younger lads took the guvnor. A fellow with a mop of curly hair and the build of a street-fighter strode towards us, his great sledgehammer swinging in the heat of the forge.

"Get the doors, Dennis," said Sparks.

As a short man began to pull the doors to the alley shut, the street-fighter stepped before us. He held the iron hammer up across his chest, his head tilted to the side, waiting. There was no trace of kindness in his pale eyes.

"Gentlemen," said the guvnor, his mouth dry. "There's no need for violence. You'll only make it worse on yourselves."

I tried to pull away but the men twisted my arm hard up my back, making me groan with pain. The guvnor looked on with alarm, his own arms clamped by the two lads.

Sparks scratched his armpit under his jacket. The doors slammed shut.

"Now, sirs," he said slowly. "Tell me who you are and what the bloody hell's going on here."

"Your cart was seen last night," said the guvnor, his words quick and nervy. "Outside Milky Sal's building."

"And what's that got to do with a boy?"

"The police got a tip he was there, but he wasn't. You took him before they got there."

"Oh, I did, did I?" asked Sparks.

"We believe so," said the guvnor.

A hammer began to tap against a barrel behind us, then a second against an anvil, tapping like two clocks out of time. Sparks stared at the guvnor as the noise echoed in the great workshop. Again I tried to wrench free my arms, but they held me fast. The street-fighter rested his sledgehammer on his shoulder, his cold eyes burrowing into me. The slow hammering continued, the guvnor flinching each time as if the noise was striking him. It was starting to rattle me too.

"Who gave the coppers a tip?" asked Sparks.

"We don't know," said the guvnor quickly. "They didn't tell us. They just called us to meet them at this woman Milky Sal's house."

Sparks nodded at the two men holding him. One of them kicked the guvnor's legs from under him and he fell to the floor with a cry. The lad wrenched his arm behind his back while the other dropped on his ankles. The hammers got louder.

"Let me up!" demanded the guvnor.

Sparks placed his boot on the guvnor's neck and pressed his face to the floor. "Why'd you think I took this boy?"

"Coppers took Sal and the rest of them to the station," I said. "We were just leaving when the neighbours come out. It was them as told us about your cart."

Sparks crossed his arms and looked down on the guvnor pinned on the floor. He thought for a moment.

"That means the rozzers don't know you're here," he said. He looked at the curly-haired man with the hammer. "It all sounds bloody queer, don't it? What do you say, Robbie?"

"It's queer, all right," agreed the street-fighter.

Sparks stepped over and looked me hard in the face. His was wet with perspiration, his eyes yellow.

"Start on this big one, I reckon," he said.

I pushed back as hard as I could, trying to fell the men who held me. But they were too strong.

"They do know we're here," cried the guvnor, raising his head from the floor, his eyeglasses hanging from one ear. The two lads held him fast. "We sent a message before we arrived."

Sparks looked at him hard, then, with no warning, the back of his hand flew through the air. I saw it coming but the brothers held me so tight I couldn't get out of the way. It landed full square in my face.

I cursed, spitting blood from my mouth onto the stone floor.

"Surely you don't think we'd just come in like this?" said the guvnor. "On our own? We aren't fools, Sparks."

Sparks thought for a while, looking down at the guvnor's red face with disgust. I kept my eye on his thick hand as he rubbed his knuckles. He made to strike me again, causing me to flinch. But he didn't land the blow. He sneered as if I was a coward, then said, "Get them out of here, lads."

"No!" cried the guvnor as they hauled him up. "Give us the boy, Sparks!"

Sparks grabbed the guvnor's coat and pulled him so their faces were almost touching.

"I don't know about no boy," he hissed. "Fuck off and count yourself lucky I ain't putting you in that furnace."

As the guvnor struggled, they marched us across to the doors and shoved us out. Dennis took the white mare and led her and her wagon into the workshop. Then the door was slammed shut again.

I spat more blood from my mouth. I was angry as a man could be. The guvnor dusted the dirt from his shirtfront.

"He's in there all right," I said. "Did you see Sparks twinge when you mentioned the boy?"

"I did," replied the guvnor, looking back at the cooperage. "But I wasn't sure… How's your mouth?"

"Forget my mouth. How are we going to get the boy?"

"I'm still puzzling over Lenny, Barnett. I tell you that man seemed as if he really didn't know about Neddy. I'm not sure his will would have been strong enough to hold out with all that dunking you gave him."

I didn't care to think about what the guvnor was saying. This was our only chance to find Neddy. If we didn't find him in there, I didn't know what we'd do.

"Sparks is up to something," I said. "Why would he shut those doors on a hot day like this? There's a forge in there and ten dripping men. And why bring a horse sorely in need of some cooling down inside with him? I reckon he's going to get Neddy out of the shop."

The guvnor walked across the alley, thinking.

"Or some stolen property he doesn't want the police to see," he said.

The sun beat down on us in that dusty lane, and I was getting irritated with him.

"We have to do something now!" I exclaimed. "If he's in there, Sparks'll have him out in minutes."

"I know that!" he barked back at me. "Damn! We'll have to get back in, Barnett. There's no time to send for the police."

He paced up and down in despair, his collar now soaked in sweat. Then all of a sudden a gleam came into his eye.

"I've a plan. Hurry, follow me."

He stumbled as quick as he could past the cooperage and down to the entrance of the court. I followed him in. It was dark there, the buildings packed tight and rising up high on all four sides, blocking out the sun. Between them was a long yard of mud with an open drain in the middle. The stink was something awful. Oyster shells were piled all over the place. Dogs wandered amongst naked children.

None of the buildings had doors, just gaping holes where doors should have been. All the ground-floor windows were boarded up. A drunken old hag sat on a step burbling a song, adding oaths to every other line, her eyes shut. A crowd of loafers in filthy shirts eyed us up. In the doorways here and there stood the missionary women talking to the denizens of the court. A young woman listened to Mrs. Truelove sullenly, a brown parcel in her hand; an especially thin man talked loudly and hurriedly to Mrs. Dewitt, who stood back from him as if in danger of catching the eruptions which covered his face; two mothers holding babes nodded politely as Mrs. Campbell explained something.

The guvnor made his way to Ettie, who was handing a packet of carbolic soap to an old man sitting on a crate.

"William!" she exclaimed. "How did you find me?"

"We've an urgent situation, Sister. Neddy's been taken. Cream's men have him in the cooperage back in the lane." He pulled out his handkerchief and mopped his face. "They've beaten Barnett here and were about to take a hammer to me."

She gasped and clutched her breast.

"We need your help to search him out. I hazard they won't lay a hand on you women."

"You want us to go in and rescue him?"

The old man let out a cackle which turned into a great, bone-rattling cough.

"I think he might be in a trunk," the guvnor replied. "But they could have him tied up somewhere. The whole place must be searched."

"But this is dangerous, William. How many men are there?"

"About ten."

"There are only seven of us."

"I'm sure they wouldn't lay a hand on women. Hold your crosses out."

"Oh, William. Don't you read the papers? Women are killed every day by men. You have to get the police."

"We don't have time to get them. The gang thinks the police are on their way. We have to do it now before they spirit the boy away."

Ettie gripped her hands together and looked around the court, her brow drawn down.

"These are the people you're investigating?"

"Yes, Ettie."

"I told you not to use the boy for your work, William. Did I not tell you that?"

"Please, Ettie. They're about to move him. This might be our only chance to save him."

She continued to frown at him, her nose-holes twitching as she breathed. Then suddenly she turned to the women and clapped her hands; immediately they stepped out of the doorways and looked around.

"Ladies!" she announced. "My brother needs our help. In

the cooperage a boy is imprisoned. We must try and rescue him."

There were expressions of outrage from the ladies.

"The devil is here before us," proclaimed Mrs. Dewitt.

"He's ten and is called Neddy," continued Ettie. "We must go in and search for him. Look for a trunk. If not, look anywhere a boy might be concealed. There are men working in there—you must pay them no mind."

"Are the men likely to stop us?" asked Mrs. Truelove.

"It's possible," replied Ettie. "We must move quickly and with faith. The Lord will strengthen our hand."

Mrs. Truelove now clapped her hands.

"At once, ladies!" she commanded.

We followed them as they marched out of the court and hammered on the door of the cooperage. When it opened, the ladies pushed their way in and without a word spread out and began peering in the barrels around the workshop. We held back in the alley.

"Oi!" cried Sparks, coming through from the yard. "What are you lot doing?"

"Leave us, sir," replied Mrs. Truelove. "We're searching for the boy."

"There's no boy here!" Sparks was in a fury now, his face red, throwing his hands about wildly. "I told the guardians he wasn't here. Now go on! Out of the shop."

Mrs. Truelove didn't reply. The ladies continued to search, lifting barrel lids, peering in corners, calling out Neddy's name. The workers stood in their bare chests, not knowing what to do. Mrs. Truelove strode to the pile of barrels stacked against the wall and began to look inside each one. She paused.

Again she clapped her hands.

"Ladies, look for a trunk! And only search the barrels with lids. Mrs. Dewitt, Miss James, you see if there's a storeroom."

Sparks ran over, seized her arm and jerked her back viciously. Ettie, who was searching in the stable, was over in a moment.

"Unhand her!" she demanded, pulling his coat.

Ignoring her, Sparks slapped Mrs. Truelove hard across the face and continued to drag her over to the door. She fought hard against him but he was too strong. He shoved her into the lane.

"Get out of here the lot of you!" he shouted, turning back to the workshop. "Lads, take a hold of them and get them out!"

The workers spread out across the cooperage. Mrs. Dewitt screamed as she was thrown to the floor by one of the brothers. Landing on a pile of bolts, she raised her hand in horror, a wide gash on her palm already coursing with blood. The big man took hold of her foot and began pulling her along the floor. At the same time, Sparks had Miss James trapped at the end of a row of tuns. He grabbed at her hair and began to drag her out. She wailed, her hands swinging and scratching at his face. He cursed.

"Fucking help me, Robbie!" he shouted to the street-fighter.

We assisted Mrs. Truelove to her feet. Her mouth was already swollen up, but she straightened her skirts and marched straight back inside. Me and the guvnor followed and were just through the door when the guvnor tapped my arm and pointed at the cart, tethered to the tired white nag by the forge. It had been loaded with the same long wooden boxes we'd seen outside the Beef the night before. There were more now, thirty at least. A tarp lay in a pile on the floor.

As the men began to catch the women we searched for the trunk. Mrs. Truelove, a look of rage on her matronly face,

grasped the handle of a coal shovel and was hurrying up behind Sparks when there was a shout from the yard.

"He's here!" cried a Scottish voice. It was Mrs. Campbell.
"I've found him!"

All at once the boy was running through the workshop,
dodging here and there as the men stood on, none of them
knowing whether they should be trying to hold the women
or stop the boy. His face was smudgy with soot; his eyes red
from tears. His shoes were gone. His cap was gone.

"Get him!" shouted Sparks, dropping Miss James. "What
the hell are you all doing standing there?"

But it was too late. Neddy reached the door.

"Keep running!" called the guvnor. "Get away from here."

"Run, boy!" I cried.

The boy raced on down the lane, and by the time Sparks
had got his men going on the chase, Neddy had turned the
corner and disappeared into the crowd.

Chapter Seventeen

WHEN WE ARRIVED AT COIN STREET, NEDDY WAS sitting on a high stool in the shop eating a large pudding. He gave us as cheery a smile as he could with his swollen mouth; without a word the guvnor went over and wrapped his arms around the little imp.

"Aw," said Mrs. Pudding, pausing her sweeping. "Ain't that sweet. I give him a pudding, Ettie, as he looked half-starved when he got here."

"Thank you," she replied. "He's been sealed in a barrel all night."

Ettie and I watched the guvnor hug the boy. We watched his great lumpy head, red from the exercise and the heat, his face clenched, his eyes tight shut behind his eyeglasses. A single tear squirted out from his eye and rolled down his fat cheek.

Immediately he let go of the boy and wiped the tear away.

"Neddy, Neddy, my boy. What a brave lad you are."

"It wasn't nothing, sir."

It was only then we noticed the boy's front tooth was gone.

"They knocked your tooth out?" I asked.

"The barrel fell off the wagon," said the boy. "It didn't hurt, sir."

"See how brave he is," declared the guvnor, turning to us with pride.

"I'm glad you found me, sir. I didn't much like being in a barrel."

"I wouldn't like to be in a barrel either," said the guvnor sympathetically. "Not on a hot day in particular."

"It was real hot. I thought I'd get cooked in there. I didn't know where I was."

"Tell us what happened, Neddy."

"I'm sorry, sir. I should have run like you said."

The guvnor turned to me again and nodded, a triumphant smile on his face.

"But when they went inside I thought I could get a listen of them," continued Neddy. "They was talking about something and it seemed real important. I wanted to find out for you, Mr. Arrowood. I only went under the wagon. I made sure they didn't see me, just like you learned me."

"Go on, Neddy."

"Then the landau came along and parked up in front and I reckoned they'd see me so I climbed into one of the barrels. But when the men came out they latched it over and I couldn't get out no more."

"Did they hurt you, boy?"

"They didn't know as I was in there, sir. I kept quiet all night, even when they was moving the barrel. I knew you'd come and rescue me, Mr. Arrowood. That's why I never called out. I knew you'd come."

"You were lucky, Neddy," said the guvnor in a stern voice. "How long could you have lasted in there?"

"Not much longer," said the boy, very quiet. "I was almost ready to shout for them to get me out. It was so hot I was getting a crust, sir."

"You must never do that again, do you hear? I'm disappointed with you. Don't you understand those men might have killed you?"

Neddy's little head dropped.

"We might never have found you."

The guvnor looked at Neddy's downturned head for some time. The boy's shoulders twitched. Ettie came over and whispered to me, "Is he weeping?"

I nodded.

She nudged the guvnor.

"Well, Neddy," he said softly, putting his hands on the lad's shoulders. "Let's forget it. You were trying to help us. I understand that. You were being brave."

The little head nodded.

"Is your lip sore?" asked Ettie.

"I'm all right, missus. I can take it."

"Would a slice of cake help?"

Finally, he looked up. His eyes were blurry.

"Might help a bit, missus."

"Then you finish up that pudding and we'll go through."

"I wouldn't have told them nothing, sir," said Neddy, regaining his composure. "I would've said I was doing a click, after their cooking pots for the marker. I had it all planned out."

"Good thinking," said the guvnor, fiddling with his purse. "But next time remember the first detective rule: do not put yourself in danger. Now, here's the shilling I promised you."

Neddy nodded seriously, then took the money and pocketed it.

"Sir?" I said.

When the guvnor looked over I gave him a glare.

He patted the boy on the head and gave him another quick hug.

"That's my boy," he said.

"Sir?" I said once more.

"Right, boy," said the guvnor, ignoring me. "Your mother's worried. Get your cake and go home. Buy your family some pease pudding. Better yet, Albert will give you one of the puddings he has left. I'll pay, Albert. With the usual discount, of course."

"There was that bonus you mentioned," I said.

"Bonus? I mentioned no bonus."

"You said you'd give him an extra shilling for his trouble. He's lost his shoes."

The guvnor's nose rode up and his eyes narrowed.

"I do not rem—"

"Yes, William," said Ettie, now catching up and giving me the wink. We shared a smile. "Give him that extra shilling you said you'd give him."

The guvnor snorted, then reluctantly fished in his purse for another coin.

"Thank you, sir," said Neddy, his eyes shining at how rich he had become.

"You're most welcome," said the guvnor. "Now go through to the parlour and Ettie will clean your face up."

Petleigh was still there when we reached the station. He was pleased to hear we'd found Neddy.

"Well, you'll be glad to know you didn't completely waste my time earlier," he said. "One of the young girls we found says she's been maltreated by many different men. She wasn't allowed to leave the house. At least we can take Sal to the magistrate on that evidence, so something has come of your false lead, Arrowood. A French girl, only fourteen. There's nothing she wants more than to go back home."

The guvnor shook his great turnip head and said, "She's already ruined, I fear."

"You don't believe in reform, William?" asked Petleigh.

The guvnor shrugged. "She's lived as a whore. Her mind has changed. Can it change back?"

I didn't like to hear the guvnor talk like this: I was no expert on the topic of opinions, but it did seem to me that some of his didn't fit together too well. At times he was willing to see the good in the most miserable wretch in London, then at other times some of the more unforgiving beliefs of his class would tumble from his mouth as natural as breathing.

"Well," said Petleigh at last. "These questions are not for the police. For today we've rescued her. That's as much as we can do."

"What's her story?" I asked.

"Her father died of fever. Her mother was in service. Four younger brothers. The grandmother raised them until the mother lost her job. Without the wages the grandmother couldn't afford to keep them." Petleigh sighed and leant back in his chair. "They'd heard of an English woman looking for girls to go into service over here. It seems that some of our gentlefolk prefer French girls in the house. More polite. More honest, is the belief. Anyway, it was a blind. The woman was Milky Sal. She brought the girl over from Rouen, away from her family, and that was that. The other girl's also French but she isn't speaking."

Me and the guvnor looked at each other.

"Are they both from Rouen?" asked the guvnor.

"Both."

"The maiden tribute?" I asked.

Petleigh nodded.

"Still very much alive, I'm afraid, despite what they write in the papers. The trade goes both ways. Our young flowers are transported over there and theirs over here. The fact is we don't have enough men for all the crimes in this wretched city." The skin around his black moustache was dotted with sweat. He rose and opened the door, trying to get a bit of air through the office. His window was now wedged up with a pickle jar. "Curse this foul heat," he growled, kicking the wicker bin next to his desk in a sudden show of irritation.

"Let me talk to Sal," said the guvnor, hoisting himself to his feet.

"I've already talked to her."

"Give me five minutes with her."

"She claims to know nothing about the murder."

"There's something else I need to ask her."

"About the murder?"

"About our case. It might help you."

Petleigh emitted an exasperated sigh. He flipped off his black coat and carefully placed it on the back of his chair.

"We can do without your help, Arrowood."

"We found the boy," the guvnor reminded him.

"You lost the boy!"

"And another thing: when Sparks thought the police were on their way he started loading the same wooden crates onto his wagon as he brought out of the Beef the other night. He's hiding something."

"Oh, Arrowood. We're pursuing a murder case. D'you think I've time to go after stolen goods?"

"Just let me talk to Sal."

"Again. No."

"Damn you, Petleigh!" cried the guvnor, much agitated by

this obstinate policeman. He wiped his face. "The lad we're looking for is from Rouen. Sal might know something that would help."

Petleigh crossed his arms. A belligerent look had come over his eyes.

"I've had enough of this," he said. "Get out of my office, both of you. We've nothing more to discuss."

"Listen, Petleigh," began the guvnor.

"Sir," I said, taking his arm. "This isn't the way."

"Get out," demanded Petleigh, now stroking his moustache frantically. "Go on. I've no time for your tantrums."

When we reached the street, I spoke.

"Next time I'll see Petleigh alone, sir. You cannot control your temper. For someone who sees into people's souls, you seem awful blind to that man."

The guvnor growled and waved his hand in the air.

"He irks me."

Over the road was a coffeehouse, and the smell of baking cake reached us. The guvnor took my arm and led me across.

Lewis was also in a bad mood. His cave, rammed to the roof with items he would never sell, was hotter than a cookshop, and there was no back door or window to let the air through. Outside, tied to the doorposts, hung bushels of boxing gloves and holsters. From the lintel of the door was suspended an array of hunting knives. On the pavement were boxes of swords, bows, walking sticks and umbrellas, while a display of handguns was laid out in the window. He sat in the full sun amongst this forest of goods, his face blotchy and shiny, his hair stuck to his scalp in oily strands. He was perspiring so much his thick black coat was wet through, the sweat dripping onto the hot dirt. When he saw the package

of fried fish I held he perked up. We pulled a bench over to
the shady side of the street and ate. When we'd finished, the
guvnor asked him if he knew of Longmire.

"War Office? I've heard of him."

He hurled his greasy paper across the alley, rose with a
groan, and waddled inside the shop. When he emerged he
held a book.

"Ah yes, of course," he muttered as he leafed through it.
"Colonel Montague Longmire. Serves in the Department of
the Master-General of the Ordnance under Sir Evelyn Wood."
He looked up. "This is connected to the bullet, eh?"

"It might be. What else can you tell us?"

"Second son of Lord Longmire. A Gloucester family. I've
a memory he's an ally of the Commander-in-Chief."

"Did he serve in Ireland?" asked the guvnor.

"That I do not know."

"Catholic?"

"I doubt it."

"Is he married?"

"What respectable man isn't?"

"You, Lewis, for one," said the guvnor.

The fat man laughed.

"Have you heard from Isabel?" he asked.

The guvnor shook his head sadly and passed the notebook
to his friend.

"Recognize any of these other names?"

Lewis glanced through them.

"No," he said. "Only Longmire."

We lit cigars and sat awhile in silence, watching the carts
trundle in and out of the warehouses along the street. Lewis
asked about the case: we told him all we knew. He concentrated hard on each detail, asking question after question. More

than once in the past he'd helped us with a suggestion or a bit of extra information. When we told him about the women saving Neddy at Sparks' cooperage, he laughed.

"I do know a little about that cove Sparks," he said, turning serious again. "The cooperage is one of Cream's safe places. Easy to keep things hid in a few barrels when the police would have to search a hundred to find one. And no danger of being robbed either."

The guvnor stared across the alley at the shop, nodding his head as he pondered this.

"And easy to move around the city on a cooper's cart, I suppose," he added.

"Cream's no fool," said Lewis. "He has his systems."

The guvnor stood as a truck piled high with tea chests passed for the wharves.

"If you think of anything else, we'd like to hear it, my friend."

"Be careful, William," replied the gun merchant. "The Fenians are fanatical. To them the cause is everything. If you're in their way, they'll dispatch you."

"I know the Fenians, Lewis," said the guvnor softly.

"Are you sure this case isn't too much for you?"

The guvnor looked at me, a glimmer of weakness appearing in his eyes.

"We're going to find Martha's killer," he replied, holding my gaze. "After that, I'm sure of nothing."

Chapter Eighteen

FONTAINE WAS TALKING TO A GENTLEMAN WHEN we arrived. The man had great white whiskers around a pink face, a grey top hat with a black band, a fine frock coat. Despite the heat he wore white gloves. Outside stood a brilliant black carriage with a coachman in livery. Two white horses snorted and moved from one foot to another, impatient to be gone. The gentleman glanced at us as we stepped in, dipping his head as if he didn't want to be recognized.

"In any case, you will send a message," he said, hastening to bring his conversation to a close.

"Of course, sir. It will be two days, no more."

Fontaine bowed and hurried around the counter to let the gentleman out. As he did, Miss Cousture swept into the shop from behind the curtain.

"Gentlemen," said Fontaine before she had a chance to speak. "How good to see you. You'll be pleased to know the portrait is ready."

He smiled and rubbed his hands together.

"Splendid!" replied the guvnor, immediately recovering from his heat exhaustion. "Bring it, please. I cannot wait a moment longer."

"I think you'll be delighted, sir. I have it just here."

The moment he slipped behind the curtain I thrust a note into Miss Cousture's hand. She quickly pushed it up her sleeve.

"Have you anything to tell me?" she asked under her breath.

"Read the note," I whispered.

Carrying the large picture, Fontaine backed through the curtain.

"I must say how well it has come out," he said with a grunt. "It has ennobled you, sir. This portrait would grace the finest country houses."

"Let us see!" demanded the guvnor.

"Help me, Caroline."

They hoisted the picture onto the counter and carefully removed the brown paper in which it was wrapped.

There stood the guvnor, against a sallow background, his elbow resting on a lectern. A parrot stood on a perch behind his shoulder. One hand was tucked inside the breast of his coat in the style of Napoleon.

"Bravo, Mr. Fontaine!" exclaimed the guvnor. "I couldn't have hoped for so good a likeness."

I noticed that the sepia tones had erased many of the crevices and irregularities of his ox-like face. It was quite a marvel.

"I do believe I have brought you out. I could see your spirit, Mr. Arrowood. Adventurer. Hero. Noble. There you are, as you really are."

The guvnor continued to examine it, nodding, muttering in appreciation.

"I hope you don't mind, sir, but I took the liberty of showing it to my good friend Mr. Flint, who has a position in the College of Fine Arts. He has a very highly developed appreciation of the human form. I was so exceptionally pleased with this portrait I felt I must show it."

"Indeed. Of course. And what did he say?"

"He saw something in you which reminded him of Moses, sir."

"Moses!" exclaimed the guvnor. "Did he really?"

"He thought it uncanny."

"Moses," repeated the governor, nodding, his chin in his hand, his eyes devouring the portrait. "Well, well. I am humbled. What do you think, Barnett? Will my sister enjoy it?"

"She'll worship it, sir."

Appearing not to hear me, he gave a contented sigh and turned to Fontaine: "It feels as if I've been reunited with a long-lost friend."

Fontaine ran his fingers through his shiny hair and smiled again. "It was my honour, sir. Having a subject like yourself makes all the humdrum sittings worthwhile. You've done me a favour, sir."

"Barnett, you must get one done. Mrs. Barnett would surely appreciate it. Or..." he glanced at Fontaine, "perhaps you do not see something in him as you did with me, Mr. Fontaine?"

"*Au contraire*, sir," replied Fontaine, his eyes now fixing on me, travelling from my nose slowly down to my boots. "I could ennoble you equally, Mr. Barnett. Such a well-grown man."

"Not equally, surely?" said the guvnor, looking at me with disapproval. "Not equally. But still, I'm sure Mrs. Barnett would like one."

"I cannot afford such things."

"Oh," said Fontaine quickly, turning from me. "Well then. Can I assist you, Mr. Arrowood, to a cab? Perhaps you would appreciate a portrait of your sister?"

We waited for Miss Cousture in Willows' coffeehouse. The portrait, wrapped in brown paper, lay up against the wall be-

hind the table, the guvnor sitting beside it. Once again he
had snatched up the newspapers, storing the two he was not
reading under his leg.

"Here's an interesting case," he said, smoothing out the
Daily Chronicle on the table. "Miss Susan Cushing, a fifty-year-
old widow from Croydon, has been sent two ears in a card-
board box. On a bed of salt. Lestrade is on the case."

"Human ears?"

"Of course human ears," he said quietly. He continued to
read the account intently, rubbing his hands in delight. "But
what a case, Barnett! Why do we never get cases like that?
They suspect three medical students who she'd evicted from
their lodgings. Revenge, they say. Well, well. But that doesn't
explain the salt. They appear to have missed that. I'd wager
the salt is meant to indicate something to the lady. But what
could it be?" He turned the page and snorted. "Ah. No other
information."

Rena brought over a beef sandwich and a cake slice for each
of us. The only other customer, a footman, finished his coffee and left us alone.

"They're still reporting Martha's death," said the guvnor as
he ate. "Three pages in this paper."

"Anything useful?"

"Tittle-tattle. A neighbour says she was Welsh. Idiots. And
here, a constable is saying it could be the Ripper. Interrupted
before he could carve her up. And a whole two pages describ-
ing the Whitechapel murders again in the most appalling detail. Oh, dear. I thought we'd left those in the past."

"Any other theories?" I asked.

"*Lloyd's Weekly* suggests she was recently insured. It points
to her father."

"Where does that information come from?"

"It doesn't say," replied the guvnor. "But at least that would accord with the killer being a hired assassin."

"No mention of Cream or the Fenians?"

"Nothing."

The door opened and Miss Cousture entered. Her face was red with the heat and she was breathing heavy.

"Mr. Arrowood," she said before she'd even sat down. "Give me your news. I do not have so much time."

"We've made some progress, miss," he replied. "It seems Cream has some dealings with a Colonel Longmire who works for the War Office. It might be our connection to the bullet."

"If the bullet is so important," she said sharpish. "Are you sure there's a connection?"

"Cream met Longmire often over the last year. We also know that the bullet was from a rifle that's only just been issued to the army."

"And?"

"Cream uses a cooperage to store stolen goods. He moves them around town in the cooper's wagon. We also know he has a brothel, run by a woman called Milky Sal."

Here he stopped and ripped off a piece of the sandwich with his teeth. Miss Cousture, still standing, was looking at him intently, both hands clasping a small handkerchief.

"Do have a seat, miss."

"You have been to the brothel?"

"Yes, we have."

"And what you find?"

A butcher, still wearing his bloodstained apron, tried to push open the door. I blocked it with my boot, shaking my head. He snarled but moved on. Rena was a good sort: she said nothing, instead retiring to the back room.

"Would you like a nice coffee, miss?" I asked, swallowing down the last of my sandwich.

She didn't seem to hear me.

"What you find in the brothel?" she asked, her eyes fixed on the guvnor. "Something that leads to Thierry?"

He continued to chew, looking up at her pale face. When he'd swallowed his mouthful, he asked, "Do you have something to tell us, miss?"

"What do you mean?"

"You don't seem interested in the bullet, although it's the best clue we have. You're not interested in Cream's stolen goods operation or the cooperage either. But when I mention the brothel you come alive."

"I am interested in the bullet. Of course, yes, but I do not understand if it will lead to my brother. That's all."

"You appear most interested in the brothel."

She was silent for a moment, her eyes scanning the street outside.

"Because my brother visits brothels," she said at last. "So of course it is possible you find clues of him there. That is why."

"I see, I see," said the guvnor, his tone now soft and full of sympathy. "But I must ask you again. Is there something you're not telling us?"

She scowled, her nostrils flaring. She heaved her breast.

"*Mon Dieu!* You take my money each time and you give me nothing."

"Miss Cousture," said the guvnor, his voice still gentle. "I know this is difficult for you. You're desperate, and in this great city it's hard to know who to trust. But we can't help you find your brother if you don't tell us the truth."

"I have told the truth."

He breathed heavy and delivered his trick: pursed lips below the most generous eyes he had. He waited, the silence so full of possibility even the flies stopped to watch. But instead of confessing she crossed her arms, refusing to look at him.

"Please sit for a moment," he said at last.

She huffed and puffed and glared, but at last she perched on the stool opposite him. I stood against the door.

"We know your uncle didn't find you the job. We know it was a minister." Here the guvnor paused to stir his coffee. He blew on it, then took a noisy slurp. Only when the cup was back on the table did he continue. "You didn't come to London to pursue your career at all, did you, Miss Cousture?"

She looked up at me, and right then I felt sorry for her.

"How do you know this?" she whispered.

"Your employer, Mr. Fontaine."

She scowled. "Of course."

"Now, miss. Believe me when I say we don't blame you for deceiving us. You have your reasons, I'm sure."

She nodded but said nothing.

The guvnor touched her hand and whispered, "Why did you lie?"

"Oh, Mr. Arrowood," she replied softly, her eyes cast down on the table. "It is shameful for me to say the truth of my life. I am so much ill-treated by Eric. He pays me almost nothing. I am like a slave."

"And the minister?"

"The house I live, it is a mission house. It provides shelter for unmarried women in the city, I tell you this before. I am grateful for it, but the truth is I live on charity." She looked at him now. "For this also I am shamed. When I came to London I thought I would be more. My family are proud people and I also. I would not put up with Eric but the Reverend found the position and I must accept it, else I will be on the street. He accepts no disagreement. But I decide I will not return to France until I learn the skill. One day I will walk from his shop and return home, perhaps as the first female photographer in France."

As she spoke, the guvnor stuck his knife in the mustard pot and absent-mindedly slathered a thick sheet of the yellow paste inside his sandwich. Then he got another load and pasted that in too. And then another, so that the mustard was thicker than the beef.

"Guvnor," I said.

He waved his hand at me.

"If you're paid so little," he asked her, "how came you to have so much money in your purse?"

"Please do not ask me this question," replied Miss Cousture. "I did not steal it."

"I'm not suggesting you stole it."

"Please do not ask this question."

"But how do I know this isn't also a lie?"

"I tell you the truth now." She dusted her hands against each other. "No more lies."

"Then where did the money come from?" I asked.

She turned and looked at me, her almond eyes pure. Strands of hair fell from her hat onto her pale neck, moist with the heat of the day. She shook her head.

"I won't tell you."

The guvnor and I shared a look, both thinking the same thing. It was not uncommon for a single woman to earn a little extra this way. I didn't judge her for it, and I knew the guvnor wouldn't either.

"You told us you lived with your brother," he said.

"To make you take the case. But please, Mr. Arrowood. I tell you he's in trouble. I know it."

"Don't worry, miss," I said. "We've learnt enough to know that's true."

"I'm going to ask you something now," said the guvnor, his voice the very essence of kindness and care, "and you must tell us the truth."

Miss Cousture nodded.

"What do you know of Milky Sal?"

"I do not know this Milky Sal!" she exclaimed. "Who is she? Why do you ask me again?"

"We didn't ask you before."

She hesitated for a moment.

"Oh. I thought so."

"Tell me what decided you to come to England. The truth this time."

"I came with my brother. He was in trouble, as I said to you before. In trouble for stealing. There are cruel men in Rouen who seek him."

As she spoke, the guvnor did a most singular thing. He brought the sandwich to his lips, holding it at a tilt, and squeezed hard. A thick stream of mustard shot from it and alighted on his shirtfront, from where it continued down in a yellow trail to his belly. At this he spread his arms and sat back on his bench, placing his unbitten sandwich back on the plate.

Miss Cousture carried on speaking throughout his strange performance. Although her eyes were fixed on him, she didn't appear to take in what he'd done.

"He is not so sensible, my brother, and I was afraid he will only return to France if I'm not here in London to stop him. We came together, and I am responsible for him. This is why I am here. It was not to work as a photographer. I confess it now, but I said it because—"

"Were you hired in Rouen to work in England as a servant?" interrupted the guvnor. Still his arms were spread wide, the mustard like a yellow wound on his white shirt.

She swallowed.

"No, sir."

"Did you know of any girls in Rouen hired by an English woman to come and work in London?"

"No, sir."

"You see, Mademoiselle Cousture, we have a strange connection. Cream owns a brothel run by Milky Sal. She was in Rouen pretending to recruit girls for service in England. When they arrived, of course, they were put into service in her brothel. Ill-treated. Imprisoned."

Here he left his silence, but again it didn't work. Miss Cousture looked out of the window at the street, the horses drooping in the heat, the children quiet and wilted as they plodded past the shop. One thin fingernail scratched the table. The mustard, watery in the heat, slowly made its way down the guvnor's shirtfront.

"You see," he continued. "We need to understand the connection."

She shook her head and went on gazing out the window at the wagons and carts trundling past on the dusty street. "I do not know anything of this, sir. It is not connected. Unless…"

She thought for a moment.

"Unless Milky Sal knows the men who chase my brother." Her eyes widened in excitement. She looked up at me, then at the guvnor. "Yes, yes. That must be it! She has told them he is working at the Beef. She must know them from France. You must keep working, Mr. Arrowood. She knows where he is! Please. Find out all about her business. Find who she deals with, who is her customers. Investigate her, Mr. Arrowood."

She brought her purse out and took two guineas from it.

The guvnor cleared his throat and looked away as I took the money from her.

When she'd gone, my employer asked Rena for a wet towel to mop his shirt.

"Ettie will have something to say about this," he said morosely. "It was all I could think of in the moment."

"You did it deliberate?" I asked.

The door burst open and three urchins came bustling in.

"You got any money, you little scamps?" demanded Rena.

"We have, missus," said the girl, holding up a coin. "And we wants some fruit cake. Big slices too, if you please. We been doing sacks all day."

"Yeah and we're right hungry, missus," piped a boy half her size.

The guvnor spoke loud, as if he was trying to drown them out.

"Did you notice how she didn't react to my mishap, Barnett?"

"It was right peculiar."

"Not so peculiar if you understand a little of the mind. We can assume it's harder to lie than tell the truth. So when one's attention is concentrating on invention and concealment it has little to give to other things."

"It was a test of deceit?"

"It was. And she failed."

"I haven't seen you do it before."

"I've only just been thinking about this."

"You might be wrong. The brain might be more vigilant when lying."

"It's possible, but then how do we account for her behaviour?"

"Politeness?"

He scowled.

"Embarrassment?"

"Oh, Barnett. You must admit she didn't appear embarrassed."

I hadn't seen the guvnor so pleased with himself for a long time.

We walked back to Coin Street together. To the guvnor's disappointment, Ettie showed no great liking for the portrait. Indeed, she seemed quite angry and hectored him for the price he'd paid. He refused to tell her, and I was about to take my leave when all of a sudden she calmed and persuaded me to stay for a cup of tea and a bit of almond cake. As we sat in the parlour she quizzed the guvnor on the latest developments in the case. Ettie was very interested in all as had happened, but the guvnor would only give her the most sketchy details. This didn't satisfy her, and she pushed him for more. As I sat, enjoying the cool evening breeze through the shutters and the sounds of their bickering, a boy arrived with a note.

"The copper says you got to come straightaway, sir," said the boy, panting for breath. "I run all the way, sir. Fast as I can, like he told me."

The guvnor gave him a ha'penny and sent him away. He tore open the envelope. His mouth fell open.

"Lace your boots, Barnett," he said, getting to his feet.

"What is it?" asked Ettie.

"It's from Petleigh," he said, holding the note out to me.

Come immediately to mortuary in Dufours Place, it said. *Your Frenchman might be found.*

Chapter Nineteen

WE TOOK A HANSOM AND WERE AT THE MORTUARY within twenty minutes. PC Reid stood in the corridor outside the room, his helmet on the seat beside him, a small packet of Peak Freans in his hand.

"The inspector said you was to go straight through," he said, wiping the biscuit crumbs from his black coat.

Petleigh was seated inside the door, waiting for us. At the other end of the cold, vaulted room was a man in a brown apron. He was tall and grey-haired, and his back was bent. In front of him, on a wooden table, we could make out a misshapen and naked white body.

"I think it might be your man, William," said Petleigh.

"The body's been in the water some days," said the surgeon, wiping his hands on a rag. "Quite swollen and most of the hair is gone. Nothing around the pubis, under the arms, just a few strands on the head. Flesh is either swollen or gone. The face is so bloated that I've had to remove the eyeballs to identify the colour. Come over and see if you can identify it."

The guvnor stood where he was, gazing over at the surgeon, his mouth open, his eyes quite glazed.

"Come along, William," said Petleigh, walking over to the table himself. "Have a look."

Still the guvnor didn't move.

"Never seen a corpse, Mr. Arrowood?" barked the surgeon. "I was under the impression you were a detective of some kind."

"I am a detective," he murmured. "I've never seen a corpse like this, that's all."

"Where did you find him?" I asked.

"Past Dartford," replied Petleigh. "A lighterman found him in the reeds. Pulled him up."

"Any reason for thinking it might be Thierry?" I asked.

"Well, his clothes were gone, most of them, except a sleeve. But there was a length of rope attached to his neck, and tied to the other end was a barrel stave and iron collar. I thought of your cooper, you see. They probably weighted a barrel with mud and tied him to it. But come and see if he fits your description."

I began to move towards the table, hearing the guvnor follow silently behind me. The police surgeon stood back and crossed his arms. Even from across the room I could see the body was in a horrible state, but as I neared it got horribler and horribler. The stench almost made me bring up my tea. The skin, where it remained, was bright red with something grey behind it, and parts of the arms and legs were bloated like they were soon to explode. In other places long strips of skin were peeled off, so we could see the muscle and bone beneath. A great cut ran from the neck down to the belly, and the flesh was opened out so the surgeon could stick his tools into the organs inside. The guvnor stepped away and fell heavily onto a chair by the wall.

My eyes seemed glued on the insides of the man, and it took

some moments before I could look at the head, and then moments more before I could speak.

"But where's the face?" I asked.

The surgeon pointed with his scalpel. "Look, this thing is the nose. The cheeks have enclosed it." He inserted the handle of his tool into a crevice and pulled it apart. "See the nostrils buried in here? And this purple bloom, these are the lips." Here he pushed his scalpel in and with his other hand pulled down hard on the chinbone, which was clean of both skin and flesh. Inside the purple bloom were small yellow teeth. "The eye is here. It was the only way of identifying the colour."

He picked up a china bowl from the shelf behind him and held it out. The eye stared up at me from inside, a mess of deep blood across the squashed orb, a tangle of blue nerves like a tail. Its iris was brown.

"Is it him?" asked Petleigh.

"How can we identify it?" I asked. "There's no face."

"But what about the eye?"

"You wish me to identify him from a single eye?"

"We've never seen him anyway," said the guvnor from the chair.

"You've never seen him?" exclaimed the surgeon. "Then what in blazes are you doing here? Petleigh, what have you brought them here for?"

The inspector winced.

"Did your employer tell you his eye colour?" he asked.

"No," I replied. "But there's a burn on his left ear."

The surgeon examined each side of the head carefully.

"There isn't enough flesh on the ears to tell. You must get the relative here to take a look, Petleigh. I don't know why you didn't do that in the first place."

"We had to consider that the relative might be the murderer, Mr. Bentham," said Petleigh. "That's one theory we're working on."

"No, it isn't!" cried the guvnor. "She's not the murderer. Why would she hire us? Honestly, Petleigh. I despair."

"So it's a woman!" replied Petleigh, as if he had been very tricky in getting this information from us. "Tell me her name. You're now obliged to."

I glanced at the guvnor. He sighed and finally gave me the nod.

"Miss Caroline Cousture," I said. "You'll find her at 56 Lorrimore Road, Kennington. A mission house. She's the sister of the missing man."

"Reid!" barked Petleigh.

When the young constable came in, Petleigh dispatched him straight off.

"Barnett, go with him," said the guvnor to me. "She may need comfort."

"No," said Petleigh. "Reid will go alone."

The guvnor heaved himself to his feet. "But, Inspector! She'll be distraught."

"I'll allow you to wait outside in the corridor for her. And you should thank me for that."

"Can't we do this in the morning, Petleigh?" asked Bentham with a loud sigh.

"I'm sorry, sir. It cannot wait."

The surgeon scowled. "I'll go for some refreshment in the Hand and Flower. Call me when she arrives."

The police surgeon returned without being summoned an hour later, smelling of mutton and wine. He was more friendly but would not meet our eyes, not knowing how to display himself now that he was half-drunk. He slipped into the mortuary with Petleigh at his heels. Soon after, PC Reid arrived with Miss Cousture and led her quickly down the corridor towards us. Her face was shaded by a badly repaired black veil which hung unevenly from her hat. Mr. Arrowood had been worried at how she'd be affected by the corpse and wanted to prepare her, but she didn't stop nor reply when he tried to speak to her, and when we tried to follow them into the mortuary, Petleigh blocked our way.

"Wait outside," he said, and shut the door.

We sat back on the hard wooden chairs and waited. Within minutes the door opened again and Miss Cousture stepped out. She had lifted her veil.

"It is not him," she said.

A weak smile flickered across her face, then her eyes seemed to roll. The guvnor jumped up just as her knees buckled, catching her under the arms and lowering her to a seat.

"I'm sorry," she said, her eyes remaining shut. "That poor soul."

She pulled a grey handkerchief from her sleeve and held it over her mouth.

"The smell."

"Are you sure it's not him, miss?" asked Petleigh.

"Of course. My brother had hair like wheat. In there, on that, is black. Not so much, but black. It's not him."

"I'm sorry you had to see it," said Petleigh.

She looked at the guvnor.

"But I say to you, like wheat?"

She looked at me questioningly.

I glanced at the guvnor and knew from his guilty face he felt as shamed as me. Idiots. Shocked as we were by the sight of the body, neither him nor me even thought about the few strands of hair. Fine bloody detective agents we were.

"You told them his hair colour?" demanded Petleigh. He turned to us. "And you didn't think it might help?"

"I must admit I was quite ill at the sight," said the guvnor.

Just then, something struck me about what I'd seen earlier. Without waiting to hear the guvnor justify himself in more detail, I pushed my way back into the mortuary and strode across the cold floor to the monstrous form on the table. The surgeon was pulling a blanket over it.

"Wait," I said.

"What's he doing?" asked Petleigh, hurrying over behind me.

I swallowed and took hold of the cold wrist. Even before I touched it, my stomach heaved. It felt like tripe, and almost the moment I touched it the stench filled my mouth. Gritting my teeth I turned the hand over. There, on the first finger, was a crushed nail, only now it didn't seem angry like before. It looked soft, innocent, like it belonged on a baby with a smashed up hand.

"I know who he is," I said. "It's the plainclothes copper that beat me. The one from Scotland Yard."

"A policeman?" asked the surgeon. His speech was a little wavering. "Good God."

"What is it, Mr. Bentham?" asked Petleigh.

"Here, let me show you something else."

The surgeon peeled back the blanket from the legs of the corpse.

"You call yourselves detectives. How about you try to explain this?"

He pushed the end of a broomstick under its calves and lifted both legs. As they rose, the feet flopped down, bent back at an unholy angle, as if they were only attached by threads to the ankles. It made me feel unsteady for a moment. With his free hand the surgeon took one foot and bent it very sudden so the heel touched the back of the calf.

Miss Cousture gasped.

The guvnor groaned.

"No idea?" asked Bentham.

"Have the bones dissolved in the water?" I asked.

The surgeon waved his hand dismissively.

"Petleigh?" he asked with a grim smile.

"Just tell us before we're sick."

"Both Achilles have been severed and the ankle bones crushed. Next question for our detectives. Why would the killers do that?"

Not one of us replied this time.

"To stop him running away. If you cut the feet off, which has the same effect, there's too much blood loss. The captive dies. This way, the captive remains alive, either to prolong his torment or to continue to interrogate him."

"Mon Dieu," gasped Miss Cousture.

"I've seen this before, several years ago," continued the surgeon. "I was working in Manchester. A pathological thief. Four previous convictions. Then found dead with exactly the same injuries."

"Did they find the killers?"

"They did not. But clearly it was a grievance over some criminal activity or other. I suppose the police there didn't think it worth the time. There were only two inspectors for the whole city."

"Wait," said the guvnor. "It cannot be the policeman. We saw him alive two and a half days ago. How could his body be so decomposed?"

"Are you sure?" asked the surgeon.

"Could his body go like that from two days in the water?"
I asked.

The surgeon shook his head. "Unlikely. But it would explain something else I was wondering about. His skin is so
red, and there are what look like burn marks on the bones
of his palms and the bottom of his feet. I assumed they were
old injuries."

"Burn marks? But the body isn't burned," said Petleigh.

The surgeon wrinkled his nose and shut his eyes.

"No," he said. "Not burned. But you would get these ef-
fects if it was boiled."

A moan came from Miss Cousture. She dropped her head
into her hands, her body trembling.

Silence filled the cold room. I gripped the back of a chair,
feeling unsteady. We all looked at each other, not wanting to
believe what the surgeon was telling us.

"The evil bastards," I said at last.

"You must find out what case this man was working on,
Petleigh," demanded the guvnor. "And why he was following us. It must be something to do with Cream: we saw him
watching the Beef."

Petleigh threw his hands in the air.

"You never learn, do you, William? My job is not to assist
your cases. I'll hand this over to the Criminal Investigation
Department. He's their man. They'll deal with this case now."

"So you do know who he is, Petleigh."

The inspector looked uncomfortable for a moment.

"I don't have his name. I haven't spoken to the commander
yet."

"Well, you should have," said the guvnor. "Our case must
be connected to theirs."

"Be quiet, William. I cannot interfere with the work of the CID. And they'll want to see you tomorrow no doubt."

"Good!" cried the guvnor. "Because I want to see them!"

Petleigh looked as if he were about to lose his temper when he paused, breathed slowly, then turned to Miss Cousture.

"I'm sorry you had to see that, Miss Cousture."

She nodded.

"Let's run you home, miss," said the guvnor, taking her arm.

Her veil had fallen, and in the gloom of the mortuary I couldn't see her face. But I reckoned she might be crying. If it was me, I reckoned I'd be afraid that the same thing had happened to my brother.

"Yes, Mr. Arrowood," she said, only barely loud enough to hear.

"Come to the station at nine tomorrow morning, miss," said Petleigh as we were leaving. "I have some questions for you. And William, expect a visit from CID."

Chapter Twenty

THE GUVNOR ASKED ME TO TIP UP EARLY THE NEXT day in my best suit. He had a plan of sorts. By the time I arrived he'd already sent Neddy off to Scotland Yard with a note for the CID. It said only that it concerned their drowned officer, and asked them to send someone to meet us at Willows' at midday. The guvnor believed that a man was only such a man as others treated him, and that officials became more like ordinary men the more they were stripped of the costumes and offices that went along with their jobs. So we'd approach them first and on our turf, we'd look better than them, and we'd manage the meeting on our terms. This, he thought, would confuse our roles just enough to get them to tell us something about the case the dead copper was working on. I wasn't so sure it would work, but I can't say I had an idea of my own, and sometimes, as I've learnt with the guvnor, you must to do something even if you aren't sure it's right.

When I arrived he was wearing his best black suit, with a green waistcoat and a milky white cravat. His boots had a high polish, his hair combed down flat over his great bald head. I was stunned for a moment: the guvnor was grinning like a cat. Above the fire hung the photographic portrait.

"Oh dear, Barnett," he fussed. An eccentric smile lay across his lips. "Look at your hair. Didn't Mrs. Barnett see you before you left the house? Your head is like gorse. That'll do us no good at all. Ettie, come down!"

Ettie was down sharply, and the moment she saw me her face softened.

"Norman. I hear there are developments in the case."

"Things are moving along, that's for sure."

"What did you discover at the mortuary?"

I was about to answer when the guvnor interrupted.

"Can you fix his hair?"

Her brow turned quizzical. She brushed the waistband of her high skirt.

"His hair, William?"

I glanced in the looking glass by the door.

"Yes, cut it," continued the guvnor. He was moving from one foot to another, a crazed look on his face. I wondered if he'd had a drop of coca-nut already this morning. "Put some lotion in it. Comb it. As you've done with me. We're meeting CID today."

"No, Ettie," I said, trying to relieve her embarrassment. "It wouldn't be proper. I'll visit the barber if it's really so bad."

"You misunderstand," she replied. Her steady gaze unnerved me, and a queer flicker had lit up her eyes. "My hesitation isn't for propriety's sake, Norman. In Afghanistan I've done a great deal more intimate things with men I didn't know than cut their hair. The body's no more than a vessel lent to us by the good Lord. It's the soul which is sacred, is it not?"

"Yes, I suppose."

"Indeed, I'm happy to help, but I hesitate for Mrs. Barnett's sake. What will she think?"

"I suppose she'd understand if it was necessary for the case," I said. "But I don't want to put you in a difficult situation."

It didn't seem right. A woman of her upbringing shouldn't be called on to attend to the hair of a man so much less refined than herself. I hadn't had a good wash for a few weeks and couldn't account for what she might find in that jungle upstairs. The singular thing was that I had the impression she positively wanted to cut my hair.

"Is Mrs. Barnett feeling better now?" she asked.

The question came at me unexpected, and I couldn't find my words right. I don't know if it was just the way I'd come to live that last month, but the kindness in Ettie's eyes bore into me so true it was as if for a short moment she touched that part of Mrs. B that was lodged there in my heart. I wanted to talk, but I knew I couldn't clamber over the sadness her enquiry had caused in me. Instead I shook my head.

"I'd like to pay her a visit, Norman. To discuss what we're doing in the mission."

"I see."

"Could you ask her when she's feeling better? Perhaps later in the week?"

"I'll ask."

"Good," she said, pulling a chair from the table. "Now, sit here by the sink."

No sooner was I seated than she placed a towel over my shoulders. In a flash she had a comb and a pair of scissors in her red hands and was dragging out the tangles in my barnet.

"We'll go in an hour," said the guvnor, sitting in his usual chair and picking up his book about the emotional life of man and animals.

"Have you finished those mysteries you had the other day?"

I asked as innocent as I could, trying to shake off my melancholy. "In *The Strand Magazine*?"

"I had a look," he grunted.

"Learn anything?"

Ettie let out a quiet laugh.

"I did not."

"Oh!" exclaimed Ettie. "Did you hear about the woman in Croydon who received two ears in a box of salt?"

"We read about it yesterday," he said. "A most interesting case."

"Sherlock Holmes has been asked to help. I saw it on the front page this morning."

"I might have known," said the guvnor, and for the first time that morning I detected a tittle of anger in his voice. "The most interesting case of the summer so far. No doubt Dr. Watson will be pleased."

"They said it might be medical students," said Ettie.

"I doubt it," replied the guvnor. "Stealing ears from corpses would be a serious matter. Why would they risk their careers to frighten an old woman? And I doubt Holmes would have been invited along if it was as simple as that." The anger passed from his voice and he became playful. "What do you think? Will he taste the salt in which these ears lie and identify it is from a particular mine he happens to know in the Baltics? Or perhaps he has quite by chance been writing a treatise on regional variations in the shape of ears."

He was silent for some minutes as Ettie continued to comb my hair.

"I wonder if he'll solve it," he said. "If we don't hear of this case again, we can assume he's failed."

"You want him to fail, Brother."

"Not in the slightest."

"Admit it for once, William," said Ettie. "Sherlock Holmes has a great mind. He's second to none."

"The man makes too many mistakes to be great."

She tutted. "You're just jealous."

To my great surprise, he laughed. "Not at all, dear Ettie. Not at all. But Providence looks more kindly on some than others. Even you'd admit that, Sister. From what I read in Watson's stories, many of Holmes's deductions rely more on good luck than genius. And what about all the cases that don't make it into *The Strand*? No doubt he's less successful there."

She turned to him. "Ever since you lost your position with the newspaper you resent those with more success than you, Brother. And don't you dare deny it."

"Tripe, most excellent Sister," he said with a fraternal laugh. "But it's true that Holmes has never suffered for his art. D'you know how much the King of Bohemia paid him for three days' work?"

"Is that why you won't give him his due?" she asked. "You see yourself as neglected?"

"You must admit I haven't been fortunate in my career. Nor in love."

Such a conversation would ordinarily have turned his face red, yet here he was, giggling and squirming as if being tickled.

"I believe you're jealous, William. What do you think, Norman?"

It was something I'd noticed from time to time, but I didn't think it wise to say anything. The guvnor was in a happy mood, and I wanted to keep him there. Without waiting for a reply, he jumped spryly from his chair and retired to the outhouse.

"A letter arrived this morning," said Ettie when he'd gone.

"From Isabel. That's why he's behaving like a fool. She proposes to come and meet him in a few days."

"Is she coming back?"

"He believes so, but I doubt it. I think she'll demand money from him."

"What'll you do if she does return?"

"I don't think that will happen. Now, will you tell me what you discovered at the mortuary? William's trying to protect me, but he doesn't realize I've seen more of the world's evil than he has himself."

As I told her about the mortuary, she stood behind me and resumed her work on my head. I shut my eyes to guard against the falling hair, and soon began to relax. She'd clearly done this before. She moved swiftly, and I felt her bodice brush my back as she positioned herself. By the time I'd finished telling her what had happened the day before, my hair was untangled and she'd begun to use the scissors, snipping with her customary confidence. She worked in silence: there was only her breathing and the ticking of the grandmother clock to listen to. After several minutes of this she brushed the hair from my shoulders and then scraped away at my neck with a razor. Then she picked up her comb again, but instead of using it she began to run her fingers through my hair, rubbing my scalp, palpating my head muscles and behind my ears. When I first felt her fingers up there I gave a start, so unexpected was it. My own barber never once touched my scalp in all the many years I've been going. But it wasn't unpleasant, and I settled back in the chair and relaxed, wondering if I should be guilty over the pleasure I was feeling.

It was over too soon. She whipped off the towel and began tidying up my side-whiskers and moustache. I sat up again in the chair and opened my eyes, thinking it was over, when all of a sudden she placed her hands on my cheeks and slowly pulled them back to my ears. Her breathing deepened as she did this, and I sensed her head near my shoulder. I tensed, wanting to turn to see what was happening, but I feared that this might bring attention to what she was doing and cause her embarrassment. She raked her fingers gently from my neck up through my hair to the crown and then back again. I felt her hot breath on my neck.

"Have you finished, Sister?" said the guvnor, bursting back into the room. "I could do with some tea."

She pulled her hands away from my head and stood back.

"Yes, yes," she muttered. Her voice had lost its hard edge. "I think so."

"Turn and let me see, Barnett," he said.

I stood, catching Ettie's eye as I turned. She flushed and looked away.

"Excellent," said the guvnor. "Most wonderful. Some lotion, Ettie, to finish it off?"

"The bottle's on the sideboard," she replied quickly.

"Perhaps we shall have some cake as well?" he suggested.

I stood gazing at her, unsure what had occurred.

"There's a looking glass by the door," said the guvnor. "Take a look at yourself. And spray some of that perfume on you, cover up the stink. I told you to visit the bathhouse."

"It was shut so early," I replied.

Ettie caught my eye and again I saw that flicker. She turned away quick.

"Hurry and fill the kettle, Sister," said the guvnor. "We have to be off soon."

She threw her hands into the air and turned on her brother.

"Fill it yourself, you lazy toad! You've been sitting doing nothing all morning."

"Ettie!" cried the guvnor, both surprised and hurt. "What's wrong?"

"Oh, be quiet," she said, and stormed up the stairs.

We watched as she disappeared.

"What was that all about?" he asked when we heard the door slam.

"She thinks you're trying to shield her," I said, still feeling the shadow of her fingers on my scalp and the quick beat of my heart.

"I do wonder if she might be happier in Afghanistan. I've tried to suggest it."

"That's maybe why she's cross with you."

The guvnor sighed and stared at the ceiling. "You'd better make the tea then, Barnett," he said at last.

We'd not had two sips when small Albert rapped on the door.

"Two gentlemen, Mr. Arrowood," he said. "I left them in the shop like you said."

As I stood to retrieve them, the two men swept past small Albert and into the room. I sized them up fast. The older one wore a brown suit. His beard was run through with grey and his eyes were red and watery: he wouldn't be too much trouble. The younger one was a different story. He wore a dusty black jacket that had seen better days and as soon as he came in the room he was looking me up and down, searching out my weaknesses. Although he couldn't make my height he had the face of a pugilist: two teeth missing from his bottom jaw, a nose that seemed to be sniffing his right cheek, and eyes so wide apart it made you queasy just to look at him. It was the face of a gargoyle. He stood with his hands at his sides in a stance I knew meant he was ready to use his fists. I'd seen that stance many times before in pubs right before a ruckus broke out. His boots were scuffed and old, the lace of one of them broken.

"You was supposed to wait in the shop," complained small Albert.

"We don't need you any more, son," said the older of the two men. He spoke in an Irish accent. "Thank you kindly but we'll be left alone now."

Small Albert looked at the guvnor, who stood clutching the heavy walking stick he kept by his chair. I edged over to the fireplace, my eye on the poker. We were both thinking the same thing: Fenians.

"Go on, son, it's fine," said the guvnor to small Albert. He looked at the older man. "And you are?"

"Detective Lafferty," said the older one. As he spoke, I reached down for the poker. "This is Detective Coyle."

The younger man looked at me like he'd taken a dislike to my hair.

"CID," continued the older man. "I take it you're Mr. Arrowood?"

"I am," replied the guvnor.

He turned to me.

"And you're Mr. Barnett?"

I nodded.

He pointed at my hand and said: "You'll not be needing that poker, sir. You try and use it and we'll shove it up your arse."

I didn't move.

"We need the both of you to come to Scotland Yard with us," continued Lafferty.

"Oh, really," I said. "Scotland Yard?"

"Yes, really. Concerning the murder of one of our officers. I assume it's not inconvenient?"

"We did say midday," objected the guvnor.

"Well, we treat the murder of one of our own as urgent, you see," said Coyle. His voice was wide and flat. And Irish.

"How do we know you're from CID?" I asked.

"And why would you doubt it?" asked Coyle, stepping up to me.

"You're surprised that the Irish can work as police," said Lafferty, taking Coyle's arm and pulling him back a few steps. "I know it's hard to fathom, but what can you do? Our countries are shackled together. We might not have welcomed your lovemaking but now we're married, so we are. And the truth is that you English don't wash any more than we do, do you now?"

"I'm sure you're correct," said the guvnor.

"Now, we've a carriage outside. Let's walk out there nice and civilized."

Seeing the guvnor start to shift himself, I spoke up, "If it's all the same with you, gentlemen, I don't think we will. But have a seat and maybe we can have a little talk here."

"Yes, we can talk here," said the guvnor, pulling out two chairs from the table. "My sister will make us tea."

"This isn't a discussion, Mr. Arrowood," said Lafferty. "Now, let's go."

I wasn't going anywhere. I was pretty sure these two were Fenians, and after seeing what had happened to that copper I was ready to kill them before I'd let them take me.

"You're not fooling anyone," I said, gripping the cold iron of the poker. "You're no more policemen than we are. We've no quarrel with you, gents. We're only trying to find a young French lad for his family. Thierry's his name. We've got no interest in what you're doing. We just want to find the lad."

The guvnor was studying their faces as I spoke, trying to

detect signs of emotion when I mentioned Thierry's name. What he saw instead was Coyle pull something from his jacket pocket.

It was a revolver.

"We're not asking again," he said. His voice was hollow. His eyes were like tacks. "Drop your weapons."

"Oh, Lord," moaned the guvnor, his eyes wide with fear. He threw down his walking stick. "There's really no need. Gentlemen, there's no need for that. I believe in a free Ireland. Barnett also. We aren't your enemies."

"That's interesting, sir," said Lafferty.

Briefly, Coyle met Lafferty's eyes. Seeing my chance, I raised my poker to strike him, but Coyle was too fast. He spun around, his gun at my chest.

"Drop it," he hissed.

I had no choice. I let it fall from my hands. Coyle kicked it away.

"Gentlemen, please!" cried the guvnor. "Let's talk about this! We're no danger to you, I give you my word."

"Calm yourself, Mr. Arrowood," said Lafferty. "He'll only shoot you if you make trouble. Now, do we need to use the handcuffs or will you come like the gents I know you are?"

"Handcuffs?" asked the guvnor.

Lafferty sighed and pulled a pair of irons from his pocket.

"Yes, handcuffs," he said. "I told you, we're from CID. Petleigh gave us your address."

"Petleigh? You mean you're really from CID?"

"The murder of an agent's an urgent matter, Mr. Arrowood, just as Mr. Coyle said. Inspector Petleigh came to see us shortly before your boy arrived."

The guvnor turned to me, a question in his eyes.

I nodded, although in truth I still found it hard to believe.

I'd never heard of an Irish policeman and now we had two standing here in front of us.

"Now, if you don't mind," said Lafferty. "The horse'll be getting impatient. He don't like the sun."

Chapter Twenty-One

THEY DIDN'T TALK TO US ALL THE WAY TO SCOTLAND Yard. The guvnor sat opposite me, a serene smile on his face, his eyes turned vacantly to the window. I could see he was still preoccupied with Isabel's letter. When we reached the Yard they led us down into the basement and into a grey room with one small, clouded window up high by the ceiling. In the middle was a table with six chairs around it. When we were seated Lafferty and Coyle left the room, locking the steel door behind them.

For nearly two hours he remained calm and serene. It was most unlike him. But then his stomach began to growl and his mood changed.

"They've done this deliberately," he said, standing up then straightaway sitting down again. "Trying to influence our minds."

When they did finally return, after nearly four hours, they offered no apology.

"Where have you been?" demanded the guvnor. "You've kept us here half the day."

"We had business to attend to," replied Lafferty, dropping a tin ashtray onto the table along with a memo book and a pencil.

"So had we," protested the guvnor. "You'd better make this quick."

They acted as if he hadn't spoken. Coyle stood by the door, while Lafferty strode up and down asking us questions. We told him all we knew, holding nothing back except what might get us charged if looked at a certain way. We told him about Milky Sal and the cooperage and Martha's death. We told him about the Fenian housebreaking gang. We told him that Longmire was an acquaintance of Cream, but not how we came by that information. When we'd told all we knew, Lafferty sat down at the table opposite us and nodded to Coyle, who put his notebook away, stuck his hands in his pockets, and began to ask all the questions again just using different words this time. As it went on, I could see the guvnor getting more and more riled.

"Does that ever work, lad?" he asked at last. If there was one thing the guvnor didn't like, it was being dominated by a younger man.

"Sometimes," said Lafferty. "If they're tired or making up a story that's too complicated for their minds."

"Perhaps we shall use it, Barnett?" said the guvnor, turning to me. "You can be Detective Coyle and I'll be Inspector Lafferty. Let's study their methods. See now how Coyle uses a threatening posture? What authority! Why have we never used this strategy, Barnett?"

"Maybe because you ain't a detective," said the gargoyle.

"I'm a private investigative agent," replied the guvnor. "And I've worked on more cases than you could imagine."

"Not like Sherlock Holmes though, are you now, sir? We ain't read about you in the papers, have we?"

The guvnor shook his head, a great sad frown on his face. "Oh dear, oh dear. So the CID idolizes Sherlock Holmes just

like the rest of the country. How disappointing. I'd hoped
Scotland Yard would have better men."

Coyle flushed. "You think a lot of yourself, don't you, Arrowood? Don't tell me you could solve the cases he did. Holmes
has the mind of four men."

At this, Lafferty rolled his eyes. He clearly didn't share
Coyle's opinion.

"Take the Mormon case," Coyle continued, gripping the
back of his chair. "D'you know that one?"

"The corpse found in a house off the Brixton Road," replied the guvnor wearily. "Thomas Drebber."

"There ain't a man in England could of pieced that case together the way he did. CID couldn't have done it. Not even
Whicher could of solved that one."

"But Holmes didn't solve that case," said the guvnor firmly.

"'Course he solved it. It's all there, written down. He got
the name of the murderer—"

"Hope!" interrupted the guvnor. I could see he was brew-
ing up again. "The murderer's name was Hope!"

"—and even led him to Baker Street so they could take
him in," continued Coyle.

The guvnor hopped to his feet, his voice raised. "For pity's
sake! All Sherlock Holmes did was phone the Cleveland police, who told him Drebber was being pursued by Hope. He
was told the name of the killer, you imbecile! How is that
solving the case?"

Coyle shook his head stubbornly, saying, "What about the
nose bleed and the horse tracks? What about the man's ruddy
face and the ring? Holmes read all those clues. None of the
others pieced it together."

"All lucky guesses," replied the guvnor, clasping his head
in exasperation. "For each clue he finds, Holmes identifies a

couple of possibilities, dismisses one, and declares the other the solution. Take the motive for the murder. It wasn't burglary, that was clear. Holmes decides it was therefore either over a woman or for a political purpose. He appears ignorant of any other motives for murder. What about vengeance? Perhaps the man's brother had been killed by Drebber. Perhaps he'd been swindled out of a family fortune. Perhaps Drebber scuttled his ship. What about a crime of insanity? What about blackmail? No, Holmes doesn't consider any of these nor any of the other possible motives for murder on God's earth." The guvnor's speech quickened. He was glaring intently at Coyle, not allowing any interruption. He hurtled on. "And then he rules out a political purpose because the footprints reveal the murderer had paced around the room after Drebber's death. Holmes declares this would never happen in a political assassination. Poppycock! Nothing is so straightforward. Perhaps there was someone on the street and the killer had to wait. Perhaps he wanted to be sure Drebber was dead. Perhaps he was tortured by horror over what he'd done. So by pure chance Holmes arrives at the conclusion that the motive was a woman. He was correct, yes, but only because he blindly stumbled on the motive through a quite astounding failure to understand all other possibilities."

"But the ring!" said Coyle. "That was proof it was—"

"It was not proof!" roared the guvnor, swiping the ashtray and with it Coyle's hat to the floor as if a demon had possessed him. "The presence of the ring could be explained in many other ways! Perhaps in the scuffle it fell from the man's pocket. Perhaps he was on his way to pawn it. Perhaps it was left as a blind. Holmes dismisses the writing on the wall as a blind, so why not the ring? Why not the ring, I ask you! Perhaps Drebber is trying to buy the killer off! And the most serious problem is again something Holmes doesn't see. If the ring is really so important, how is it that the killer leaves it at the scene?"

The guvnor was now shrieking, his hands waving wildly in the air. His red face shone, his head appeared to have swelled to almost double the size. He slammed his fist on the table. Lafferty and Coyle both watched him in surprise, their mouths open.

"Any fool can see that this should mean the ring is *not* important! But again, Holmes is lucky. Against all odds, the killer does leave it! It's a one in a million chance, I tell you! Holmes is proved correct, but only because he's missed all the possibilities. And Watson writes it out for *The Strand* declaring the man a genius!"

The guvnor stood at the edge of the table panting, his eyes travelling from Lafferty to Coyle to me. Lafferty tapped his pencil on the table. Coyle leaned against the wall, his arms crossed. Nobody spoke. The guvnor continued glaring at us, chewing his lip. Finally, Lafferty said, "You seem to know a lot about that case, Arrowood."

The guvnor's face twitched: he didn't seem so sure of himself all of a sudden.

"He reads a lot," I said, standing and taking his shoulder. He was unnaturally hot and even through the thick fat of his arm I could feel his pulse beat wildly. I helped him to sit. I retrieved Coyle's hat and put it back on the table. "Mr. Arrowood's always in a book."

"We'll have to put the handcuffs on if you erupt like that again, Arrowood," said Lafferty.

"No need to restrain him," I said. "He'll be good. But it doesn't help if you try and rile us up like that."

Under the table I felt the guvnor pat my knee.

"You ain't no match for Sherlock Holmes, Arrowood," said Coyle, not wanting to let it go. "Look at you. You're a worn-out old hound who makes his pennies chasing debtors with your strongman here. They say you're quite a hand at following women for their cuckolds. They say you enjoy it."

I could feel the guvnor tense up again beside me.

"Now, now," said Lafferty, turning to his companion. "Let's not start again."

"How old are you?" the guvnor asked Coyle, his voice quiet now.

"And what's that to you?"

A quack emitted from the guvnor's stomach. He clasped it quick.

"I'm only enquiring about your experience in this line of work. You look rather young."

Coyle's lip curled. His fists clenched. He looked at Lafferty, who was sitting at the end of the table with his hands clasped behind his head.

There was a knock at the door and a young copper's head poked through.

"Inspector Lafferty?"

"What is it? We're busy here."

"Inspector Lestrade requests you come to his office when it's convenient, sir."

"About what?"

"About the Whitehall case. That's all he said."

"Tell him I'll be there presently."

The copper withdrew and the door closed again on us.

"You know Lestrade?" asked the guvnor.

"Who we know and don't know isn't your affair," said Lafferty. "Now, gentlemen, how about we try this again, eh? There's no need for a fight. Will you take a cigar?"

The guvnor thought about this hard before finally agreeing. I retrieved the ashtray from the floor. When we'd all lit up, Lafferty said, "Someone's killed our man. You can understand that we aren't in the best of humour. I'd appreciate it if you'd answer our questions, even if you find them repetitive."

"Of course, Inspector," said the guvnor. "But how about you tell us the victim's name?"

"That ain't your business," replied Coyle.

"It would help us in this conversation we're having," I said.

Lafferty looked at me, curious.

"Petleigh has a high regard for you, Barnett. Says you'd make a good police officer."

"I'm flattered, sir," I replied.

Lafferty puffed on his cigar. He didn't look so sure.

"Do you have any idea who killed him, Detective?" asked the guvnor impatiently.

Lafferty raised his eyes to the ceiling and sighed.

"Well, at least tell us what case he was working on," continued the guvnor when no response came. "I assume it's the murder?"

"The murder?" asked Lafferty.

"The girl!" exclaimed the guvnor. "Great Scott, don't tell me you're not working on the murder?"

Lafferty pulled on his cigar but said nothing.

"Are you after Cream, then?"

Lafferty smiled.

"The young girls?" asked the guvnor. "The Fenians?"

"Shut up," said Coyle.

"Gentlemen," said the guvnor in the most reasonable fashion. "We've told you what we know. Just give us an idea."

"That we cannot do, sir," said Lafferty with a laugh. "Now,

let's get back to this bullet you mentioned. Are you quite sure it's from an Enfield repeating rifle?"

"It's only what we've been told," replied the guvnor.

"Who told you this?" asked Lafferty.

"Someone unconnected to the case."

"I see. Where is it?"

"I have it at home."

"Hmm," murmured Lafferty. "I don't think it's important, but you'll have to fetch it for us anyway."

"You can come back with us and collect it, if you must," said the guvnor, folding his arms.

"I think we'll stay here." Lafferty pulled his watch from his waistcoat. "Let's say you'll be back in two hours or less, eh?"

The guvnor pushed himself to his feet with a sigh.

"Let's get off then, Barnett," he said. "You'll have to bring it back for them."

"I don't think so," said Lafferty slowly. From the smile on his face, he was enjoying himself. "Mr. Barnett will stay here until you get back, Mr. Arrowood. It isn't as I don't trust you, sir, but we're taught to be cautious."

The guvnor's face reddened. "You mean I have to bring it back here? You want me to travel all the way across the city and then all the way back? I've better things to do, sir. I have gout. Send a policeman with me. He'll bring it to you."

Lafferty stood and opened the door.

"The sooner you do it, Mr. Arrowood, the sooner you and Mr. Barnett will be back on the streets."

"So, your case is connected to the bullet," declared the guvnor.

"Don't get ahead of yourself, Mr. Arrowood. We always tie up loose ends in case they return to lash us in the next heavy wind. We're trained that way, that's all. We've no reason to think the woman wanted to give it to you. There aren't any reports of anyone being shot recently. Have you heard any, Coyle?"

"None."

"I didn't think so. And Cream isn't known for using rifles. Knives, yes. Fists and boots. The river, yes, a pistol if you must, but not rifles as far as we know. I'm thinking maybe the girl just picked it up from the street on her way to meeting you, or maybe she stole it from one of the men she knocks about with."

"If you think so," said the guvnor.

"I do. But we'll have it in case our superior asks to see it. That's all."

I stayed in my chair as the guvnor followed them out.

It was an hour before the two coppers returned. The room was cool on account of being in the basement and I'd been pacing, trying to keep myself warm. They told me to sit. Lafferty took a chair opposite, with Coyle standing behind me.

"You aren't telling us everything," began Lafferty. He'd removed his jacket and now sat in his waistcoat and shirtsleeves. I could smell beer on his breath. "I understand. In this work it can be dangerous to reveal your full hand. But we need to know everything. One of our men's been killed, and we can't let it lie now, can we? So where d'you want to start?"

"We told you everything," I said.

Almost the very moment I finished speaking there was a flash of cold pain that went through my body from my upper arm. The sick came into my mouth, and I clutched at the spot where I'd been hit, turning to see Coyle holding a truncheon. There was hatred on his face, the kind of hatred you feel when you hurt a man.

"Now, Mr. Barnett, I'll ask you again," said Lafferty.

I jumped up, grabbing at Coyle's neck with my good arm,

but the pain as I moved sapped the strength out of me and he pushed me back down hard on the chair. Lafferty now had a pistol in his hand, pointed at my chest.

"Go to hell," I spat at him.

Coyle struck me again in the same place on my arm; I felt a low, animal groan come out my mouth. It bent me double, my head cracking onto the table.

"We want to know about Longmire," said Lafferty. "What does he have to do with Cream?"

"We don't know," I said, my face twisted. I was turned so Coyle couldn't reach my arm again, but I knew my back was exposed to him. I never hated a man so much as I hated that young copper; I swore I'd get him back when I had the chance. "All we got was the name. That was our next job."

"Where did you get the name?"

Feeling Coyle tensing behind me, I thought for a moment. Just for a moment. Then I told him.

"We broke into the Beef. Found a notebook full of names. Longmire kept coming up. More regular than any other in the last couple of months. That was all. Really. We knew he worked at the War Office. Didn't recognize none of the others."

I stood up. If I was going to take another blow, I wanted to be facing him. The young copper stared me in the eye, his crooked nose twitching, slapping his thigh slowly with the truncheon.

Lafferty was silent for several minutes. Finally, he said, "Take this."

He put a sovereign on the table.

"What for?"

"We want you to keep us informed. That's all. When you discover something, you send us a note."

I moved away from Coyle to the end of the table. Each small movement caused me more pain, so much so I thought my arm must be broke.

"Why don't you just clout me again?"

"Take the money," replied Lafferty. "It's less painful."

To avoid another blow, I picked up the coin.

"What case are you working on?" I asked. "If you want my help I got to know."

"We're after the housebreaking gang."

"It's a lot of effort for burglars, isn't it? Why's CID involved?"

"They've upset some powerful people," said Lafferty.

"Who? Longmire?"

"They've stolen property from some high people in government. Those people would like the property back."

"What property?"

A copper knocked at the door. Lafferty went into the corridor for a moment, then returned.

"You can go. Mr. Arrowood's back."

"So if I get information about the housebreakers, I send you a note?"

Lafferty smiled and hitched up his trousers. "That's it. And anything else about Cream's network as might be relevant. Longmire, for example. And perhaps it'd be best not to let your employer know about this, eh? Tell nobody. One more thing. It's likely we'll ask you to do things from time to time. To keep a watch on a person, to follow someone. Perhaps to open a lock. For this you'll get ten shillings a week."

"I have a job already."

"It'll only be occasional."

"Why not get a copper?"

"Some things are handled separate from the constabulary,"

replied Lafferty. "Sensitive matters as this is. Now, Coyle'll
see you out."

I followed Coyle along the dark corridor, holding my arm
so it wouldn't move. Lafferty walked behind. Every slight
jump or swing shot a bolt of pain through me, and each bolt
made me want to slice through the gargoyle's dirty throat. Before we reached the stairs there was another steel door with a
small window looking into a room just like the one we'd left.
I glanced in. Sat with his back to me at a table was the guvnor.
I was about to open the door when Lafferty took my battered
arm roughly from behind, bringing me up short with pain.

"Leave, Mr. Barnett, there's a good bloke."

I waited outside the Yard for near an hour. Being parched
by then, hot with the afternoon sun and my arm giving me
merry hell, I got a pot of porter from the pub down the road
and stood out on the pavement watching the entrance to the
police station. It was late afternoon and the street was busy
with omnibuses and traps. Newsboys were calling out, trying
to shift their piles of papers. I had myself a couple of sausages
and another pot and waited some more. The pub began to
fill up with coppers coming off duty. Two hours had passed
and the guvnor still hadn't showed, so I decided to give up.
I took the pot back into the pub, and as I was leaving I spied
Coyle coming out of Scotland Yard. I ducked into a doorway
and watched as he crossed the road and entered a coffeehouse.
A milk wagon came trundling along the road just then and
blocked my view for a moment. When it had passed I saw that
Coyle had come out and was now walking along the road towards Waterloo Bridge. He was talking and laughing with a
short man who hurried along beside him.

I looked after them, stunned. On this hot day, the man

didn't wear the same long coat whose tatters had danced be-fore me as I chased him on that wet and windy day in the Borough, but I couldn't mistake that square body and those bandy legs. They stopped at the Bridge and the man turned side on, revealing the awful hook of his nose. Coyle was shak-ing hands with the man who had killed Martha.

Chapter Twenty-Two

❖

I WENT TO THE APOTHECARY ON THE WAY HOME.
It was the same arm as the other copper had gone for in the alley,
and it hurt so bad I thought it might be broke. The assistant
didn't think it was fractured and sold me a box of Black Drop
for the pain instead. I slept deep that night and woke with my
head in a fug and my arm purple and swelled out. I took another Black Drop and stared at the envelope that had laid on my
table for days. Finally, I picked it up and set out for Coin Street.

I found Ettie standing on the street outside the pudding shop
with Mrs. Truelove, Miss Crosby, and the Reverend Hebden.
I wasn't sure how to act with her since she'd grappled in such
an intimate way with my scalp, but it didn't matter: she was
more concerned about her brother than what passed between
us the day before.

"Where is he?" she asked after introducing me to the holy
man.

"I haven't seen him since yesterday, Ettie."

She sighed and took me aside.

"Is he drinking again?" she whispered.

I explained what happened at Scotland Yard.

"Do you think he's been arrested?"

"Chances are they're trying to sweat more information from him."

"Then why was Inspector Petleigh here this morning looking for him?" she asked.

"Petleigh works local. The other detectives are from CID. Likely they wouldn't tell him what they're up to."

This seemed to satisfy her. She looked over my shoulder at the street ahead.

"Are you off somewhere?" I asked.

"Cutler's Court. We're just waiting for one of the ladies. Did you ask Mrs. Barnett about my visiting?"

"She's a bit busy at the moment," I said.

There was something curious in the look she gave me, and I was relieved when Reverend Hebden came over.

"Will you come with us, Norman?" he asked. He was younger than the three women, a fine, high-shouldered man, a wave of glossy black hair reaching his collar, a strong chin.

"I can't, sir. Got too much on with this case."

"Shame. We're smuggling out a young girl. We've arranged to take her to a safe place. It's taken weeks to persuade her."

"I wish you luck then, Reverend."

"Are you sure you won't come, Norman?" asked Ettie softly. "We're short of menfolk."

"Perhaps another time."

"Well. Let's hope so."

"Shall we go, ladies?" said Hebden. "I think we've waited long enough."

He shook my hand firmly. As they turned to go, Ettie quickly squeezed my elbow.

I'd been putting it off for days, but that squeeze gave me a deal of comfort I'd been missing, and I knew the time had

come. I walked to the register office at St. Olave and joined
the queue, listening as each person in the line before me set
out their details to the registrar. The old fellow wrote slowly,
asking for their papers, dipping his quill again and again in
the ink, blotting the ledger. Some of the poorer folk couldn't
spell out their names, so he suggested a letter here and there,
and the job got done.

"What do you wish to register?" he asked when it was my
turn.

I made to speak but the word caught in my throat. I blinked
against the tears. He nodded slowly, his eyes kind through the
thick spectacles. He scratched his whiskers.

"Death?"

I nodded.

"Could you give me the name, sir?"

"Elizab—"

I took a deep breath, covering my eyes from him.

"Take your time, sir," he said.

I swallowed hard, steadying myself, and spoke again.

"Elizabeth Barnett."

His quill scratched at the paper.

"And you're her husband?"

I nodded.

He took our address, her date of birth, her work at the milliners. My eyes were blurred, my voice unsteady. He wrote it
down and blotted the paper.

"'Cause of death?"

I opened my mouth to speak but again couldn't bring out
the words. Instead, I handed him the envelope with the death
certificate. He read it slowly.

"She died in Derby, sir?"

"I didn't even know she was ill."

He frowned.

"By rights, you should register it up there. And you should have done it within five days. Did you bury her?"

I nodded again, his words swimming in my head. She was off visiting her sister when it happened, only a week before Miss Cousture appeared at Coin Street. She got the fever and that was it. She never came home again.

"They don't normally permit burial," he said.

I heard him, but was numb. I held the edge of his desk to steady myself.

"Sir?" he asked.

"The doctor got sick. I only just got the letter."

The registrar was silent for some moments. Then he began scratching the paper with his quill again. He tore off a slip and passed it to me.

"I know it's hard, sir. You be strong."

I went into the pub across the road and got myself a brandy and hot water. My hand trembled as I held the mug. I drank it off in one, then had another. That one I couldn't finish. I went out into the crowded street, walked up to the river and crossed Tower Bridge, into the noise of Katherine Dock and the great ships stinking of tar and salt. I couldn't bring myself to tell the guvnor when it happened, couldn't tell anyone. I suppose I was afraid of what would happen if I just came out and said it. Then a day passed, and another, and another, and still I couldn't say the words. I just wanted to keep moving. I knew that he and Ettie would be kind, and that would hurt even more. Each question they asked, each hand they placed on my shoulder, would pain me, and I was tired of pain. But I knew I couldn't put it off forever.

I walked and walked, on to Western Dock, back around the

Tower and on up Lower Thames Street, until I started to see the people around me again, until I heard their voices. When I felt I was myself once more, I crossed London Bridge, back to the south, and on down to the familiar streets of Southwark.

With a free Saturday ahead and needing some company, I decided to pay a visit to my old friend Nobber Sugg. Nobber still lived in Bermondsey, just round the corner from where we grew up. He'd done well in his life, better than anyone I knew from our neighbourhood: he'd worked as a market porter since his father died and now lived with his family above a chandler's with four rooms all to themselves. Nobber and I had a few pints in the Bag o' Nails and I began to forget my troubles. In fact, I developed quite a tolerable feeling about me on account of the porter and the Black Drop I was dosing myself with, so when he suggested chuntering over to East Ferry Road, where Millwall was playing the Royal Ordnance, I didn't take much persuading. It wasn't until seven or so as I got back to Coin Street.

The guvnor looked tired and beaten, and his gout was playing up. I could see he'd taken laudanum before I arrived as he sat in a flop on his chair, his shirt open to the belly. He told me how Lafferty had kept him all night in that room with nothing to eat or drink. Wouldn't even let him out to relieve himself. He was none too happy with it.

"At least we've learnt something from this," he said with a sigh. "The bullet's definitely important."

"Didn't Lafferty say it wasn't?"

"He made a special point of saying it wasn't. Out of all the things we told him, it was the only thing he wanted to make sure we believed wasn't important. Not Martha, not the young girls, not the brothel, not even the Fenians. Make no mistake, Barnett, that bullet is the most important part of their case."

It was only when I told him about seeing the murderer with Coyle that he sat up. His eyes became hard.

"At last we have something."

"But what?"

"A conspiracy, Barnett." He plucked a cigar from the box on his side table and lit it up. "I think it's time to introduce ourselves to Colonel Longmire."

Chapter Twenty-Three

WE MET AT WHITEHALL THE NEXT DAY, WHERE A little blessed rain was falling. The streets were full of day-trippers and tourists come to see Big Ben and the Parliament, all wandering up and down, cheery in the warm rain. The soldier at the door of the War Office told us that Longmire wasn't in, that there wasn't none of them in on a Sunday.

"Come back Monday, gents," he said, putting down the slice of bread and cheese he'd been eating. He couldn't have been far off retirement, and he didn't seem such a bad bloke, though his yellow eyes would have troubled a doctor some. "We can help you better then, I should think."

"I thought the War Office would always be working," said the guvnor, irritated. "We're always fighting a war somewhere, aren't we?"

"Soldiers do the fighting," said the man. "Not this lot."

He moved his plate to the side of the desk, revealing the *Daily Chronicle* underneath. In big, bold letters, the headline read,

SHERLOCK HOLMES SOLVES IMPOSSIBLE CASE OF SEVERED EARS IN ONLY 2 DAYS! DOUBLE MURDERER ARRESTED AT ALBERT DOCK!

I saw the guvnor's eyes drop to the paper and sweep across the words. For a moment his lips pressed together and his brow hardened. He swallowed. Then he looked back at the old soldier and said, "This is extremely urgent. Could you give us his address?"

"I don't have it. Come back tomorrow and we can get a message to him."

"Isn't there anyone who would know?"

"It's only me here," he replied. "Come back tomorrow."

We stood on the steps, sheltered from the rain by the grand doorway of the War Office. Just as we made up our minds to leave, Arrowood pointed across the road. There stood a line of hansom cabs by the kerb.

We approached each driver in turn, asking whether they knew Colonel Longmire. The first few didn't recognize the name. The fourth, who was hooking a nosebag to his horse for his dinner, said he did.

"They asked me to pick him up the other day," he said. "Smart fellow, is he? Some sort of mole by his eye?"

"D'you know where he lives?" I asked.

He shook his head. "Can't help you there. I was bringing him back here."

"Any of these other cabmen who might know him?"

"There's a lot of officers and suchlike work in there," he said, patting the horse's neck as it ate. "We don't usually get their names."

"Come on, Barnett," said the guvnor. "We'll have to come back tomorrow."

"Picked him up from the Junior Carlton Club," continued the cabbie. "You've heard of it, I suppose? The one as got bombed by the Irish a few years back?"

"I know the one," said the guvnor. "I reported on it for my newspaper."

"St. James's Square," said the cabman. "That's where they all go, politicians and the like."

Fifteen minutes later we were at the club. It had been repaired since the explosion eleven years before, and through the windows we could see the heavy curtains, the glittering chandeliers and ornate ceilings of its stately rooms.

The doorman wouldn't let us in.

"I can give him your name," he said, looking at my repaired trousers, at the guvnor's white shirt grey with sweat and grime around the collar. He knew we weren't the right sort to walk into a gentlemen's club, no matter what the guvnor's accent was like.

The guvnor gave his alias, Mr. Locksher, saying it was urgent that we speak to the colonel. The doorman gave it to the porter, who disappeared along the corridor. He came back a moment later.

"The colonel asks you to make an appointment at his office tomorrow."

"This is important," said the guvnor. "We must speak to him today."

"I'm sorry, sir," said the porter. "He doesn't wish to be disturbed. He's in conference."

The guvnor fished inside his waistcoat pocket and pulled out the bullet.

"Give him this. Then he'll see us."

The porter scowled. "You must be joking."

"He'll understand. I need to talk to him."

The porter shook his head and shut the door on us.

"You didn't give it to the coppers?" I asked.

"I stopped with Lewis on the way and picked up another

bullet for them. I assumed we'd need this one when we spoke to Longmire."

"Lewis had one of the same?"

"It was the same colour. The world isn't perfect, you know Barnett. You can't have everything."

I couldn't help but laugh.

"Listen, when Colonel Longmire comes out, will you give him this note?" he asked the doorman, scribbling a few words on his notepad. The doorman looked at it with a dull silence. The guvnor pulled a shilling from his pocket and stuffed it in the doorman's waistcoat pocket.

"We're detectives working on an important case," he said.

"Coppers?" asked the doorman.

"Private agents."

The doorman looked uncertain.

"Like Holmes and Watson," I said.

"Once the colonel sees this note, he'll want to talk to us," the guvnor continued, pretending I hadn't spoken. "He'd be unhappy if you didn't give it to him. So be a good chap. You'd be helping the country."

Longmire's carriage pulled up outside Willows' at seven. The colonel was a medium-sized man with a mole the colour of potato skin touching his eye, in which he held a monocle. He wore a drooping moustache, plaid trousers, a brown derby on his bald head, and a sour expression on his face. He stood on the threshold of the coffeehouse, his eyes travelling with annoyance over the customers. For a moment they rested on Rena as she wiped down the counter. I rose from the bench and beckoned him to our table. His coachman stood outside the window, watching us closely.

"Will you have a coffee, Colonel?" asked the guvnor.

Before replying, Longmire dusted the stool with his hand-kerchief and sat down. He looked around again at the other customers: four ladies just out of church, a cabman eating his tea, a family finishing off their slices of seed-cake.

"The note said Mr. Cream wanted to see me," he said at last. It was clear from his face he thought the coffeehouse might give him a disease, and he wanted us to know it. A gold watch chain hung from his waistcoat pocket. "Who are you?"

"Associates of Mr. Cream," said the guvnor.

"Why are we meeting here and not in the Beef?" His voice was nasal and contemptuous.

"This is more convenient for us," said the guvnor.

"And who are you?"

The guvnor took a bite of his sandwich and chewed it slowly, all the time keeping his eyes fixed on Longmire's monocle. The shop was hot, and perspiration was beginning to break out on the military forehead.

"Mr. Locksher," said the guvnor. "This is Mr. Stone. I'm afraid I lied in the note. Mr. Cream doesn't know we're meeting. We'd prefer to keep it that way."

"I only speak to Cream," hissed Longmire, leaning over the table towards us, his voice low. "Do you understand?"

At this he stood and made to leave. The guvnor hooked his finger into his waistcoat pocket and pulled out the bul-let. He stood it in the middle of the table, then winked and tapped his pitted nose.

Longmire stared at it, swallowing. He glanced around at the other customers. His lips twitched, but he couldn't seem to decide what to say.

"Aren't you interested in how we came by it?" asked the guvnor at last.

"A bullet? I have no interest. Perhaps you bought it in a shop."

The guvnor sat back and raised his eyebrows.

"You know these bullets cannot be bought in shops."

"I know no such thing. Now, if you try and contact me again I will have you arrested."

The guvnor laughed. I also laughed. It was one of his tricks, to laugh when a character lies to your face. Laugh long, as if you cannot help it. The other customers looked around as we laughed; Longmire stood, his thin nose flaring, the humiliation and ire plain in his eyes.

"Please, Colonel," said the guvnor. "You only make yourself look small. We know what this bullet is and where it came from. As do you. Would you like us to spell it out in this busy coffeehouse?"

Longmire's lips narrowed. He glanced outside at his coachman, then sat down again. As he reached for the bullet, the guvnor snatched it away and buried it back in his waistcoat pocket.

"Where did you get it?" asked Longmire.

"We found it in the hand of a dead girl."

"What girl?"

"A girl called Martha," replied the guvnor. "She served in the Barrel of Beef. Do you know her?"

"You mean the murdered girl? I read about the case in the paper."

"But do you know the girl?"

"I only deal with Cream."

"You use the gaming tables."

"There are many girls who serve. I don't know their names."

"Do you know who killed her?"

He threw his hands in the air. "No! I know nothing about

this, and you're severely trying my patience with these questions."

"Yet you stay at the table," said the guvnor, a warm smile on his face.

This was Mr. Arrowood's skill, how he worked on people. And as long as he wasn't in one of his emotional states, he was good at it.

"You stay because of the bullet," continued the guvnor. "It's only supplied to the army, for the new Enfield repeating rifles. An interesting story for the *Gazette*, do you think? I'm quite sure your superiors would want to know how it came to be in the hand of a serving girl."

Longmire looked up.

"All right," he said. "I do know the girl. I gave it to her."

"Explain."

"I had an occasional association with Martha," he whispered. "There. I confess. When I put an end to our liaison she requested something to remember me by. A memento. I believe she was implying I should buy her jewellery. It tickled me to give her this."

The guvnor looked hard at me. For moments he didn't speak, but this time it wasn't a trick. We were both thinking the same thing: if what Longmire was saying was true, what we thought was our most important clue was worth nothing.

"You want money, I suppose?" asked Longmire.

"We don't want your money," I said.

"I'll pay you not to go to the papers."

"We don't want your money," repeated the guvnor. "Why did she want to give us the bullet?"

"Did she give it to you?" asked Longmire.

"It was in her hand when she died. She was waiting for us."

"I suppose she was clutching it because she was in love with me. Perhaps it comforted her as she died."

"Did you love her?" asked the guvnor.

"Of course not."

"Why was she killed?"

"How would I know?" hissed Longmire. "The papers say it was the Ripper. A robbery gone wrong? I don't know. Now tell me, Mr. Locksher. What do you want of me?"

I looked at the guvnor, who was thinking hard. He seemed lost.

"Sir?" I asked.

He blinked and took a long breath. "First we need to find a young man," he said. "A French lad called Thierry. He worked in the kitchens at the Beef. He's disappeared and his family are worried. Do you know him?"

Longmire's eyes narrowed.

"You think I know who works in the kitchens? I've never been in the kitchens! I know no French boy. I only speak to Cream and a couple of his men."

"You don't understand, Colonel," said the guvnor with a kind smile. "We'll take what we know to your superiors and then to the papers. I've many friends in the press. Your wife will find the story interesting, I'm sure."

"Listen to me. I do not know this boy. In truth I do not know him."

"You'll forgive us if we doubt you. But if you really don't know then you must find out."

"How in the blazes do I do that?" Longmire demanded.

"Ask your friends in the Beef. We'll give you two days."

The colonel covered his face with his hands, his elbows on the table. He breathed heavily. Finally, he spoke.

"How will I contact you?"

"We'll contact you. Tell your office and your club to accept our notes next time. And write your address here."

The guvnor pushed his notepad over the table.

Longmire wrote quickly, then pushed the notebook back.

"You said first," he said with a scowl. "What else are you asking?"

"We'll tell you that another day," replied the guvnor.

Longmire stood, knocking his stool to the floor. He slammed the door of the coffeehouse as he left.

Chapter Twenty-Four

AS SOON AS LONGMIRE'S TRAP MOVED OFF WE LEFT the shop and crossed the road to where Sidney's growler was parked. We followed the carriage down to St. George's Circus, then up the Waterloo Road to the Beef. There, Longmire jumped out. He was back after no more than ten minutes and the trap moved off.

"I wonder if they were talking about Thierry or the bullet?" said the guvnor.

"Most likely he's asking Cream to give us a swim in the river tied inside a coal sack."

The guvnor sighed.

"Perhaps," he said at last.

We crossed Waterloo Bridge as the evening sun began to peek out from the breaking cloud, and followed the trap down the Mall, through Green Park, and along the south side of Hyde Park. The growler gave none too smooth a ride, and all the jumping about aggravated my arm, now swollen and black. I swallowed another Black Drop and grit my teeth. In Kensington the trap turned up towards Notting Hill, then finally came to a rest outside a villa on Holland Park Avenue.

We kept our distance as Longmire climbed out, strode up

the wide steps, and rang the bell. A butler opened the door and ushered him in.

I climbed out of the growler and walked towards the gate to see if there was a nameplate. Night had now fallen, and the street was dim. I could see no plate, and neither was there anyone on the street to ask.

I returned to the growler and we waited, watching the house. After several minutes the guvnor spoke, "There's something I need to ask you, Norman."

He leaned forward, placing his hand on my knee.

"I've noticed you're not yourself these days. Ettie's noticed something also. Are you ill?"

"It's the Black Drop, William," I answered. "That copper hurt me bad."

His hand remained on my knee.

"And is there something else?"

"I'm fine," I said, though the words almost choked in my throat.

"I see."

He seemed disappointed in my answer. It felt wrong to deceive him, but I just couldn't say it. I wondered to myself if it was always going to be this way.

"We'll trail Longmire," he said after some time. "You stay here and see what you can find out about the owner of that house. Come to my rooms in the morning. But please, Norman, watch yourself. You know what they're capable of."

I nodded, my nose wrinkling as the image of that copper came back to me, his skin boiled off, his crushed ankles. The guvnor squeezed my hand and looked seriously at me. I knew he was remembering it too.

After fifteen minutes Longmire came out, climbed into his

trap, and they moved off. I jumped out of the growler and took up my position on the other side of the road.

The villa was set back from the street, a neat row of miniature box hedges out front. Including the basement, it was five floors, with balconies above the front doors. Inside, the lights were blazing. It was a quite magnificent house, but the outside was in need of a new coat of paint and it looked tired next to its well-tended neighbours.

There wasn't much traffic on the road. A few omnibuses chugged past towards the West End. Now and then a hansom came along or a cart of produce on its way to the market. My arm was starting to pain me again, so I swallowed another Black Drop. After an hour a man came out from the side of the villa and turned up towards Shepherd's Bush.

I called out to him and hurried across the road.

"Excuse me, friend," I said. He was a younger man, his hair cut very short and greased down on his head. He wore a plain brown suit. "Do you work in there?"

"I'm the footman."

"Evening off?"

"That's right. You looking for work?"

"I'm a house painter. Saw the house was in need of a new coat."

"You'll have to speak to Mr. Carstairs about that. The butler."

"What say I buy you a drink and ask you a few questions? Always helps to have a bit of information first."

"Well…" He thought about it for about a second. "Just a quick one, maybe."

He took me to a little pub called the Rising Sun on Walmer Road, where we had a pint of Old Six and a pot of periwinkles. The footman told me the house was owned by Sir Herbert Venning, the Quartermaster-General to the Forces. He worked in the War Office, heading the department as supplied equipment to the British Army. Hearing this, I ordered two more pints and set about asking who did their painting and whether there were any outbuildings also needing a lick of paint.

"There's nothing out back," he said.

"Stables?"

"Round the corner in Stewart Street."

"The house looks like it hasn't been painted in a while."

"It was going to be done," he told me, supping his pint down quick now that I was being so loose with the coppers. "Two or three month ago we had a painter as started on the back. They got rid of him when we was burgled. Must have thought he was involved, I suppose."

"What do you think? Was it him?"

"Don't know. Master was in a terrible rage about it all. Sacked the butler as well and he'd been there more than twenty years. We was all surprised. But the master was in such a temper about it. He would have turfed us all out if he could, I reckon."

"How'd the burglars get in?"

"Come in through the window in the middle of the night," said the footman. "Nobody heard them. Some of us sleep downstairs, some others up in the garret. Butler's room's below the stairs and he didn't hear nothing, so he said. Master and mistress slept through it too. Someone must have left a window unlatched, that was the only way they could of done it. That's why the housepainter was turfed out."

"But why the butler? Did the coppers think it was him?"

"That's the thing we don't understand, see? Master never called the coppers."

He finished off his pint and I ordered two more. My head was swimming a bit with the ale and the pain tablet, but I felt very relaxed and comfortable in that little pub. A singsong started up in the other room.

"He didn't call the coppers?" I asked. "Didn't they take anything?"

"Only papers from the master's study. We think they heard someone downstairs. Cook always gets up early to start things. Maybe they heard her. They come in through the music room window and went straight across to the study. Didn't take any of the valuables, and there's plenty of them in the drawing room. Paintings and ornaments and so on. Didn't take none of them."

"Those papers must have been valuable."

The footman lit a Capstan without offering me one. He drew in hard and blew a couple of smoke rings.

"Master was beside himself," he said. "I never seen him like that. I never seen him drink like that, and shouting at us for every little thing."

"What was in those papers, do you think?"

"We don't know. We've been going over that question ourselves, but none of us know. Could be government papers, that's what we think. Something important."

"And he never called the police?"

"Coppers were never involved."

The guvnor was excited to hear my information when I arrived the next morning.

"So the two people he thought would be most concerned about our meeting are Stanley Cream and Sir Herbert Venning," he said, pacing up and down the room. He puffed on his pipe and thought for a bit. "This is good. Now we have a line that connects the three men with the bullet."

"But he might have gone to Cream about Thierry, not the bullet."

The guvnor stopped pacing and frowned.

"You're right, of course," he said. "Thank you, Norman."

He tamped out his pipe, put the windcap on it, and found his hat.

"Now we must return to the War Office. I only hope we don't have to wait so long for an omnibus this time."

"The underground would be quicker, sir," I said, as I always do.

He ignored me, as he always does.

The same old soldier sat at the desk in the entrance to the War Office. He sent a message to Venning's secretary, which came back promptly. Sir Venning was unable to see us. However, if it was important, we were welcome to write a letter. It was no more than we expected.

We tried his home later that evening.

"Sir Herbert has asked not to be disturbed," said the butler. He was more short and more round than was usual for a butler.

"This is an urgent matter," said the guvnor.

"Do write a letter, sir. His secretary will be able to deal with it."

"We have some information about a burglary committed here. I'm sure he'll want to know it."

The butler thought for a moment.

"I'll ask."

He shut the door.

When he returned, he said,

"Sir Herbert says there's been no burglary in this house. Perhaps you've mistaken the address?"

"But there was a burglary," replied the guvnor. "You know it well."

"I've only recently begun service here, sir."

"But you know there has!" exclaimed the guvnor. "That's why your predecessor left!"

"Good evening, gentlemen."

The door swung shut in our faces.

Chapter Twenty-Five

WE REACHED THE STABLES WHILE IT WAS STILL dark the next morning. Sidney had agreed to come out with us again and play the coachman. It being early, only one of the stables in the alley was open. I went in without knocking.

"Hello, matey," I said to the coachman. He was brushing down a fine black horse, working by five thick candles stuck on the posts around him. "Which one of these is the Venning stables?"

"This one," he said. His voice was thick, like he had a cold.

"Got a delivery for you outside," I said.

The coachman followed me into the alley. Sidney, who was hiding behind the door, coshed him as he stepped outside. We caught him before he cracked his bald head on the ground and carried him back inside.

"Nice shot, Sidney," I said.

"Thank you, Norman."

We tied the poor bloke's hands and feet and put a gag over his mouth. Then we lashed him to a post at the back wall of the stables with a set of reins that were hung on the wall. He struggled a bit, but nothing that troubled us. The guvnor, who didn't like to see violence, stepped inside and poked a couple of shillings in the coachman's waistcoat.

"I do apologize for that, my friend," he said to the chap, who was staring up at us in a daze. "That's for your troubles. Now, what time is your master expecting you?"

The coachman moaned something through his gag. I pulled it off his mouth.

"Don't hurt me," he groaned. His eyes were full of water.

"Answer the question," I growled at him.

"Half six. He's to be in early today."

"What's your name?" asked the guvnor.

"Bert."

"Who's got the stable next door?"

"Mr. Warner."

I slipped the gag back on his mouth. The guvnor patted his head and said, "Don't give the police our description. Do you understand that, Bert?"

The man nodded.

"Say you were knocked from behind."

He nodded again.

"You don't want us coming back, do you, Bert?" I asked.

He shook his head.

Sidney hooked the horse up to Venning's landau while I pulled over the roof and fixed it on. We blew out the candles and shut up the stables. I knew Bert would be making a noise as soon as he heard the other stables open up in the alley, but there wasn't nothing we could do about that. Me and the guvnor got inside the carriage and pulled the curtains, while Sidney drove us round to the villa.

Venning must have been waiting outside his house because Sidney jumped down as soon as we stopped. We kept still and listened from inside the carriage.

"Bert's sick, sir," said Sidney in his chirpiest voice. "Got a fever on his liver. Asked me to stand in for him. I'm from Mr. Warner's household, sir. Master said I wasn't needed today."

"I see," said Venning. His voice was quick and confident, if a little girlish. "And will you be able to bring me back this afternoon?"

"Yes, sir."

The carriage door opened and Venning began to climb up. Before he even saw us, I got hold of him and pulled him inside.

"What the blazes!" he cried, struggling against me. I shoved my hand hard over his mouth and sat on top of him on the floor as Sidney slammed the door shut, mounted the box, and set off.

Venning was short and made of soft, loose flesh that felt bad to touch. His face was quite round, with a small, baby mouth and a sharp nose. His wide eyes bulged as he tried to decipher what was happening in the little carriage, and his feeble body tried uselessly to get me off. My rear end felt very warm, and I realized that I'd never before in my life sat on a toff. I quite enjoyed it, what with the bouncing and the rolling.

Until he bit my hand.

I howled, jerking my hand away and giving him a back-hander with the other.

He shouted for help. The guvnor very quick pulled out his old red handkerchief and stuffed it into Venning's mouth.

"Now listen, Sir Herbert," he said, calm as you like. "We're not here to hurt you or rob you. We were unable to make an appointment and this was our only way to see you. We just want to ask you some questions. My colleague will remove himself from you and we'll take off the gag, but only if you do not shout out. When we reach Whitehall, we'll let you go. Do you understand, Sir Herbert?"

The quartermaster nodded frantically.

As soon as I was off him, the gentleman got up on the seat and dusted himself down. His little owl's face was white. His gloved hands were trembling.

"What is it you want from me?" he asked, his eyes darting from the guvnor to me.

"We're private detectives, sir, investigating a missing person," said the guvnor. "Do you know a young French pastry chef called Thierry Cousture, or Terry? He used to work in the Barrel of Beef."

"You're the men who are trying to blackmail Colonel Longmire," said Sir Herbert.

"We've had a consultation with your colleague."

"I think you're playing with words." He shifted in his seat, trying to move his knees so they didn't touch mine. Noticing his hat on the floor, he bent to collect it, fumbling it as he did so. "I do not like this situation, sirs. I do not like it at all."

"Nor us," agreed the guvnor. "It's quite wrong."

"Then what say we have this discussion in my office, gentlemen?" His voice quavered as he spoke. He'd become quite short of breath. "It would really be more comfortable. We can have tea. I'll send for some breakfast."

"Do you know Thierry Cousture?" asked the guvnor again.

"No, sir." He shook his head as if his life depended on it. "I do not know him. My life doesn't bring me into contact with pastry chefs."

He raised his trembling hands and began to push back the curtains. I stopped him.

"Do you know Stanley Cream?" continued the guvnor.

There was a short hesitation as he touched his whiskers.

"Stanley Cream?"

"Yes, sir. Do you know him?"

"I know of him. He owns the Barrel of Beef and a good amount of land south of the river."

"Have you ever met him?"

"I do not believe so."

"What about Colonel Longmire?"

"What about him?" asked Sir Herbert.

"Is he acquainted with Stanley Cream?"

"You know he is."

"Why did the colonel come to your house last night?"

The quartermaster touched his whiskers again. He picked his hat from the seat, his hands in thin white gloves, and dusted it once more. He reached for the curtains but stopped himself, glancing at me as if I might strike him.

"Did he come to my house?" he asked.

"We followed him," replied the guvnor.

"He's worried about a scandal. He came to ask my advice."

"And what did you advise him, Sir Herbert?"

"To try and help you with the missing man."

The guvnor sat back and crossed his arms. I peeked out the curtains. We were crossing Hyde Park.

"Tell us about the burglary," said the guvnor.

Sir Herbert shook his head and frowned.

"So you also know about that," he said. "Well, I cannot tell you who burgled me. I did not wish to involve the police."

"What did they take?"

"Some ornaments from the drawing room. Not a great deal."

"What, exactly?"

"Oh." He hesitated, his eyes raised to the ceiling. "A carriage clock. A pipe rack. That manner of thing."

The guvnor breathed slowly out of his nose-holes, his lips clenched, his head atilt, looking at the nervous toff in a friendly way. We said nothing. Sir Herbert glanced from the guvnor to me, his fingers scratching the armrest. The seconds ticked by.

"A small watercolour," he continued at last. "A silver ink-well. A globe, I think."

"You think?" said the guvnor.

"No, I'm sure they took the globe. My wife took charge."

"Why didn't you report it?"

"It was so little, really. But why do you ask? How does this concern your missing Frenchman?"

"We're just making enquiries," said the guvnor, wincing and rubbing his feet. "Your burglary happened at the same time he disappeared, and we know Mr. Cream's involved with stolen goods. There might be a link, you see, sir."

"Whatever's happened to the cook doesn't involve me."

"Why did you dismiss your butler?"

"How did you know that?" Sir Herbert asked, his temper rising.

"We're detectives. So, why?"

"That's my business," declared Sir Herbert, regaining his confidence. "Now, I demand you stop the carriage and get out. I've answered enough of your questions. Stop the carriage."

"No," said the guvnor. "You will answer our questions, sir. Remember, we hold information about your friend Colonel Longmire. Why did you dismiss the butler?"

Sir Herbert sighed. "I believe he helped the burglars."

"Why didn't you go to the police?"

"He was with me over twenty years. He started as a valet. I can only think he came to resent me, although I was always very good to him. I don't know why. Perhaps they forced him to help them. I didn't want to see him in prison. It was enough to send him off without recommendations."

"That's very noble of you," I said.

He shrugged. We sat in silence for several minutes as the coach jiggled across the park. Finally, the guvnor said, "Tell me, Sir Herbert, how many regiments have received the new Enfield repeating rifle at present?"

Venning blinked his shilling eyes.

"How many regiments?" repeated the guvnor when no answer came.

"What are you getting at?" asked Sir Herbert. His eyes were fixed on the guvnor; his small mouth hung open like he might be sick.

The guvnor played his silence again, tilting his head, raising his eyebrows. Venning looked at me, but I said nothing.

"What's that to do with your case?" he asked at last.

The guvnor puckered his fleshy lips as if he was about to kiss someone, but still he said nothing.

"Did somebody tell you to ask me that?" demanded Sir Herbert. "Is that it? Did Cream send you?"

"I thought you didn't know Mr. Cream?" said the guvnor.

"Don't play with me! Did Cream send you?"

The guvnor smiled and shrugged. "He might have done."

"Is there a message?"

"Tell us about the rifles, Sir Herbert."

"That's classified government business." Venning's face had become pink. He clasped his hands together on his lap.

"Tell us the part that isn't government business, my friend."

"There's nothing," stuttered Sir Herbert. "I don't know what you mean."

"But we already know."

"Know? What do you know?"

"More than we should," whispered the guvnor with a wink.

Sir Herbert looked at me for a moment. He shook his head.

"You don't know anything," he declared. "You're taunting me. Tell me what you know…or what you think you know."

"That would be rather stupid of us," said the guvnor.

"You don't know anything. There's nothing to know."

"Really?"

The landau came to a halt.

"Piccadilly!" cried Sidney from outside.

"Ah. This is where we leave you, sir," said the guvnor, opening the door.

"I don't understand!" spluttered Sir Herbert. "Are you private agents or are you with Cream?"

"Good day, sir," replied the guvnor, backing down the steps.

"Is that it?" asked Sir Herbert in alarm.

I waited until the guvnor had puffed and grunted his way to the pavement before getting down myself.

"Good day, sir," I said. "Sorry for sitting on you."

Sir Herbert leaned out of the carriage. "But who are you? Did you have a message for me?"

"Our business is concluded for today," replied the guvnor.

"You'll have to walk from here, sir," Sidney called from the footplate. "I've to take the carriage back."

"Oh, dear," said Sir Herbert.

The well-fed man climbed down onto the pavement and looked around him as if he didn't know where he was.

I hopped up on the step and whispered to Sidney, "Try and get the last butler's address from the coachman."

"Will do, Norman."

"How are the kids?"

"Good as they can be, I reckon. Fancy coming over Sunday? They'd like to see you."

"Most probably be working, mate," I answered. "But I'll come soon."

Sidney glanced over at the guvnor and lowered his voice. "You said anything yet?"

I shook my head.

"Want me to?"

"I'll be all right."

I jumped down to the street while Venning stepped over. He looked up at Sidney and asked, "But you will be able to pick me up this afternoon like you said, Coachman?" He put his hat on. "Two thirty?"

"I'm with them, sir," replied Sidney. "With the detectives."

"Oh blazes!" exclaimed Sir Herbert.

As we walked away towards Leicester Square in the cool morning air, the guvnor began to laugh.

"The man's a blinking idiot," he said. "God knows what trouble he's in."

Chapter Twenty-Six

SIR HERBERT'S COACHMAN DIDN'T HAVE THE ADDRESS of the butler who'd been dismissed, but he told Sidney that the man's niece still worked in the house as a laundry maid. We sent Neddy to hide in the bushes by the washing lines that afternoon, and when she appeared to hang out the clothes he told her he had an urgent message for her uncle about some money as was owed him. He was back with the address within three hours.

George Gullen lived near Earls Court. The street started respectable enough, but the longer you walked along it the darker and more broken down it got until you reached the end, a horrible court that was even more bad-smelling and evil than the one Ettie was saving. A press of filthy children in rags approached us as we tried to locate the address, swelling around us, asking for pennies. We shoved our hands into our pockets to protect against pickpockets and pushed through. Dossers slept in the dirt in the corners; old women with no teeth, rags wrapped around their heads, sat on stools staring at us.

The butler's room was on the second floor of a block with no front door. The banisters had been ripped from the staircase for burning. It was a warm day, and flies swarmed at a pile of shells and peelings on the first landing. A woman opened the door. Her hair fell in tangles onto her shoulders; snot ran from her nose to her lip. A baby cried in the room behind her.

"We're looking for George Gullen," I said. "His niece told us he was here."

"He ain't here," she croaked.

A child screamed from the room.

"Quiet, Mary!" the woman barked back.

"He does live here, does he?"

"When he ain't in the pub he does."

"Which pub would that be?"

A small boy with no shoes pushed past her.

"Got a penny, mister?" he asked me, holding out his sooty hand.

"Don't beg, Alfred," said his mother. "I told you before."

The boy ran off down the stairs.

"You make sure you bring something back for tea," she cried after him. She crossed her arms and leaned against the doorjamb. "What is it you want with him?"

"We're trying to find someone's gone missing," I told her. "Thought George might be able to help us."

"He wasn't in on the click."

"We know. We're trying to find out who did it."

She looked at us unhappily.

"Can you help him find work?" she asked.

"We just want to ask a few questions."

"He'll be in the Crosskeys. Across the court and down the alley. And you can tell him not to come back least he has some food for the children."

The pub was one room with a hole in the wall for serving. The floor was specked with shells and ash, sticky with ale. A grey-haired woman leaned through the hatch, listening to the four men who sat on a bench by the door. Two aged grey-hounds stood up when we entered and approached us, their heads bowed low.

"Any of you George Gullen?" I asked.

"That'd be me," said the man on the end of the bench. He was broad-chested and flat-faced, and he clutched a pint pot in his hand. He wore a red neckerchief, a heavy workman's shirt, and a brown felt cap. He looked like a labourer, but his voice and his neat black hair marked him as different. "Who are you?"

"Private detective agents," said the guvnor. "Trying to find a missing man. We need some information from you."

"Private what?" asked an old man sat next to Gullen. He had no teeth and his neck was bent so that to look up at us he had to twist his head. "What did he say? Are they coppers, George?"

"Private agents," said the old woman in the hatch. "Like Sherlock Holmes."

"Is that what you are?" asked Gullen, a bitter scowl on his face.

"What'll you have, gents?" asked the woman.

I ordered two pints of porter for me and the guvnor.

"What are you having, George?" I asked.

"Same," he said, finishing off the pot in his hand. "And same for these." He gestured the three other men on the bench.

"Now, steady on," protested the guvnor, his hand in his pocket. "It's you we wish to talk to."

"Maybe I don't wish to talk to you."

When the guvnor handed over the money and the drinks were passed out, Gullen took us to a table in the corner.

"Your wife said you aren't to come home without food for the children," I told him.

"They aren't my children." He gulped at his drink, spilling it on his thick shirt. Up close, I could see he was already drunk.

"We've been speaking to Sir Herbert," said I. "He told us you had something to do with his burglary."

"I had nothing to do with it!" he roared, bringing his fist down hard on the table. "You hear me? I had nothing to do with it! Is that why you're here? Did he set you on me?"

"No, mate," I said. "Truth is, he didn't want to talk to us. We're not after you. We just want to know what happened. We think it could be connected to our case."

The door swung open and the biggest, most ragged bloke I'd ever seen came stumbling in. The three men by the door picked up their pints and held them under the table. The man looked around the pub slowly, then staggered towards us. Gullen picked up his drink and held it to his chest.

The bloke reached for the guvnor's pint and spat in it.

"What the hell are you doing, man?" spluttered the guvnor.

As he spoke, the man bent down and spat in my pint.

Gullen chuckled.

"We can't drink these now!" exclaimed the guvnor. "You buy us another, sir!"

The man straightened up. His head reached the low ceiling; he had an infection that started below his eyes and travelled right down his neck to the grey rags he wore on his chest.

"No money," he mumbled. He pointed at the tankards. "You going to drink those, or what?"

"Of course not!" cried the guvnor.

The man picked up the two pints and carried them to a table at the far side of the room.

"Should have warned you about Cocko," said Gullen. "I'll have another, since you're going."

The guvnor gave me a shilling. When I put the next three pints on the table, Gullen began. "It was three or so in the morning: everyone was asleep." He spoke slowly, pausing every few words, his eyes half-shut, his pint clasped to his chest. "I heard something upstairs so I got up to check. They were in the study. Three of them. They'd broken open all the drawers in the bureau." He looked at the floor, seeming to think hard. "It was four or so, or three," he finally declared.

"You said that already," said the guvnor. He held his pint next to his belly, one eye on Cocko on the other side of the room.

"Right. One of them pulled a knife when he saw me, told me to keep my mouth shut or they'd chive me. They made me unlock the front door, then they were off. Three of them. And that was it." He brushed his hands together. "They ran off into the night."

"What did they take?"

"They had a carpet bag. Nothing else."

"Not a globe?" asked the guvnor.

"They didn't take any valuables. Didn't even go in the parlour. The mistress went through everything."

"Did Sir Herbert report anything missing?"

Gullen swilled his porter and burped. His eyes were glassy. He wiped his nose on his sleeve.

"Those aren't my kids," he said. "She expects me to feed them."

"Yes, yes," said the guvnor. "Did Sir Herbert say anything was missing?"

"He didn't, no, but he started drinking that night and was still drinking next afternoon when he threw me out." He paused, his face twisting in a grimace as he remembered. When he began to speak again he was more sober, like he'd been putting on a bit of an act before. "I've never seen him so upset. He was shaking, pacing up and down all night. Wouldn't even let me get the police. I knew they'd taken something important from that desk, but when I asked him outright he shouted out at me."

"Why did he think you were involved?" asked the guvnor.

"He knew I wasn't involved."

"He told us you were."

"He told everyone in the household I was. But I wasn't."

"Then why did he dismiss you?"

"Because I saw them. I wanted to get the police in. Now, get us a pennyworth of gin," demanded Gullen. "You're bringing back bad memories. He ruined me, that bastard. Refused to write me a letter of recommendation. I haven't worked since. He ruined me. Look where I'm living! Look at this stinking place. Half of them here make a living through robbing. The other half send their missus out on the streets." He clenched his tankard so hard his knuckles went white. "If I saw him on a dark street I'd kill him. Straight up. I served him loyally for twenty years."

The guvnor gave me a penny.

"I don't understand why he dismissed you," I said when I'd brought him his gin.

"It gave him an excuse not to go to the police."

"An excuse?"

"For the mistress, his children, the rest of the household. He told them he wouldn't go to the police to spare me from prison. He made out he was doing it out of kindness."

"Perhaps he really did think it was you?" said the guvnor.

"I'd been with him twenty years!" said Gullen, his eyes blazing. "He knew me. He knew I wasn't like that. No, he did it as an excuse not to call the police, all right, and you know why? Because I knew who one of them was."

A loud screeching laugh came from outside and the door burst open. A woman in a stained green dress and a blue bonnet rushed in, chased by a man in a pair of bang-up kicksies. The old fellow on the bench shouted at them and an argument started up.

"Who was he?" I asked when it had quieted down a bit.

"I recognized him from the races. He's always there at the Frying Pan. Bill is all the name I know, Paddler Bill. An American. Big belly, tall, with great curls of ginger. He's always there."

"Did he recognize you?"

Gullen swallowed half his gin and shook his head. He winced and pounded his chest with his fist.

"I'm just one of the crowd. Nothing special about me. He's loud, though. Spends money. Champagne, women. You can't help but see him."

"What about the others?" I asked.

"I didn't know them. One was bald with a black beard. Middling height."

"American?"

"He didn't speak. The other was a little fellow. Blond hair. One of his ears was missing."

"But why didn't Sir Herbert want them arrested?" asked the guvnor once he'd drained his pot.

"I've been thinking that over for the last few months," said Gullen. "They must have taken something that he shouldn't have had. He didn't want it discovered, that's what I think."

The guvnor stood.

"You've been very helpful, Mr. Gullen. Just one more question. What do you think they took from the study?"

Gullen shook his head.

"I haven't the first idea. I never knew what was in his desk. But look. You couldn't lend me a shilling for the children, could you, sir?"

"You'll spend it on gin," said the guvnor.

"Honest I won't, sir. Those children need to eat."

The guvnor was poking his hand in his pocket when I stopped him.

"We'll go to the cookshop and bring them something," said I. "No need to interrupt your day."

Gullen was still scowling as we left.

Chapter Twenty-Seven

AS WE WALKED BACK TOWARDS EARLS COURT, THE guvnor was silent. He was thinking, his gnarly head tilted upwards, his teeth chewing his bottom lip. When we reached the main road it was choked with buses and wagons. His nose caught a whiff of fried fish in the air, and he looked for its source like a dog who has a scent of fox. His stomach groaned.

"What do you think of Gullen, Barnett?" he demanded, his eyes searching left and right.

"Reckon I believe him. His story matches the footman."

"Did you know, my friend, that the signs of rage are universal? The same signs found in the English are also seen in the copper-coloured Indians of South America."

"I don't doubt it, sir."

"So says Mr. Darwin. Gullen displayed all these signs when I said that Sir Herbert accused him of the burglary. Dilated nostrils, glaring eyes, blood to the face. No momentary signs of uncertainty. I cannot believe he was acting, which means that Sir Herbert was playing us false."

I decided it was time to say something as had been on my mind these last few days.

"What if it's got nothing to do with the case, sir? We find

a piece of information and follow it until the next piece of information, and then the next, but each one might just be leading us further away from the trail. Could be the Fenians have nothing to do with Thierry's disappearance. Maybe the bullet was never meant for us. Maybe Venning's problem is a family one."

"But we must pursue them," he said softly. "What else can we do?"

"Sometimes I lose sight of the case, is all."

"Our case is the murder of the girl, Barnett. We must solve it for her sake. And we must discover what happened to Thierry."

A horse reared up on the street next to us, a wild look in its eyes. As it rose, it took with it a costermonger's cart, tipping a load of cough lozenges and unguents onto the ground. Some children began stealing the medicines while the costermonger tried to beat them off, all the while shouting at the cab driver whose horse had caused the trouble.

"D'you think Longmire was lying about the bullet?" I asked when we'd got round the hubbub.

"I don't know." The guvnor stroked his stomach, his eyes still searching for the fish-seller. "But it's clear he lies easily. And if we don't follow these trails what can we do? We'd have to start from the beginning again."

"We could try to find Thierry's drinking pals. Or we can find out how Coyle knows the murderer."

"We should have searched out the drinking pals straightaway, Barnett," he said sharply. "Why didn't you suggest it before?"

"Why didn't you suggest it?"

"There's no need to get irritable. That's your task for tomorrow; I need to think about Coyle. But now we must talk to Sir Herbert again."

"He won't see us, not after being kidnapped and all."

"Once he knows we've seen Gullen he may change his mind. Ah! Over there," he said, pointing down towards the underground station where the fish-seller was standing.

We took a package of fried fish back to the children and ate our own as we waited for the omnibus back to Notting Hill. It was early evening and the bus was jammed: we were forced to stand all the way. When we reached Venning's house, dark was falling.

As we turned off the pavement onto the wide steps, the front door opened and the page ran out, pushing past us rudely.

"Hold on, boy!" protested the guvnor.

The boy ignored him, gaining the street at full pelt and turning up towards Notting Hill Gate.

The door stood open.

The guvnor hushed me and we climbed the steps silently. There was no sound from inside.

"Let's see if we can find him," he whispered.

We waited for a moment in the grand hallway. The house was fitted up with electricity, the lights as bright as Piccadilly Circus. A stairway rose before us to a balcony; high above our heads was a chandelier of glittering crystal. Dark portraits of toffs hung frozen on the walls, and colourful china things stood in alcoves and on plinths. There was some commotion going on upstairs: hurried footsteps, conversations behind doors. No sound came from the parlour.

To the right, the door to the study stood ajar. The guvnor gently pushed it open and stepped inside. I followed, shutting the door behind us.

Sir Herbert was slumped over the table, his head twisted to

the side, staring at the fireplace. In his left temple was a grisly red hole. Scarlet blood ran across his forehead, into his big owl eyes, and down onto the desk, where it was absorbed into a jagged pool by the blotter. His mouth was open, his tongue hanging out. A pistol lay next to his hand.

The noise of footsteps came from the stairs. We heard a woman's voice, low and steady. Then a man, the butler. "I'll sit with him until the police arrive, madam. It would upset you to see him. It is…untidy."

"Thank you, Carstairs." The lady who spoke was calm. There was no trace of grief in her voice. "Did you send the boy?"

"Yes, madam."

The door opened and the butler stepped in.

When he saw us he threw up his hands.

"Who are you?"

"We're here to see Sir Herbert," replied the guvnor quick. "What's happened here?"

The butler's expression changed. He backed to the door.

"Help!" he cried.

"No, no," said the guvnor calmly, a smile on his face. "You misunderstand. We've just arrived."

"Help! Help!"

His cries brought others.

"What is it?" shouted a man.

"In here!" cried the butler. The door burst open and there stood the footman, the very one I'd shared a drink with. And then another man, and a housemaid, and finally the lady of the house herself. I was worried the footman would say I'd been asking questions, but he kept his mouth shut. I appreciated that.

"We've got you," declared the lady. "Take them!"

"No, no," protested the guvnor. "We only arrived this minute. This is nothing to do with us."

"Oh, my Lord," said the lady, her eyes only now falling on the body of her husband. "Poor Herbert."

"I'm so sorry for your loss, madam," said the guvnor. "But we're quite innocent. When he returns, your boy will confirm that we were arriving when he ran off for the police."

I took the chance to sit down on the sofa while he explained.

"Well, we will see what the police have to say," said the lady when he'd finished. "You will stay here until they arrive. My men will prevent you leaving."

With that she swept out of the room.

The pageboy returned shortly with a constable. The boy agreed we'd been coming in from the street as he left: only then did the suspicion leave the eyes of the servants who were gathered in the room.

The constable, a cheerful Welshman whose belly had outgrown his uniform jacket, told us to stay calm while he examined the corpse. Then, writing his observations in a notebook, he looked carefully around the room, at the carpet and the shelves, at the over-large statue of the naked athlete with his privates on display, at the globe that stood by the window. He asked each servant in turn where they'd been and what they'd seen. None of them had seen a thing.

The guvnor joined me on the sofa while this was going on. Soon enough there were more footsteps in the hall, and in walked Petleigh with Bentham, the police surgeon.

When he saw us, Petleigh simply shook his head. The guvnor stood and opened his mouth to speak, but the inspector didn't give him the chance. "Sit down! I will talk to you later."

He took the details from the constable, then watched as the surgeon examined the body.

"Death is clearly from the bullet wound," said the surgeon. "Very recently."

"Did you find a note?" Petleigh asked the constable.

"No, sir. I had a good look."

Petleigh turned to the butler.

"When did you hear the shot?"

"About half past eight, sir."

"When was the last time you saw him?"

"About five, sir. He told me he wasn't to be disturbed. The servants were down below until we heard the shot. The mistress was in her bedroom."

"Any children?"

"Two boys, sir," replied the butler. "Grown-up. One's in India. The other's with the forces."

"Did he seem disturbed?"

"A telegram arrived this afternoon for him. After that he didn't come out of the study."

"Did he have any visitors?" asked Petleigh.

"Not that I know of, sir."

"Where were you all afternoon?"

"In the butler's pantry. I would have heard the bells if anyone had come, sir. All the bells of the house ring there."

Petleigh sighed and paced slowly around the room, his hands in his trouser pockets.

"Was there any change in him recently?"

"I'm new here," replied the butler. "But they say he's been acting queer for the last couple of months."

"Queer in what way?"

"Tempers. The mistress and him rowing. Shouts at the servants."

"Melancholy?"

"Drinking," said the housekeeper. "Let's be plain. He's been drinking steadily since the burglary."

"The burglary?" asked Petleigh.

"About two months ago," replied the housekeeper. "There was a burglary."

The inspector thought for a moment.

"I see," he said. "Now, I need you all to clear the room. Can you tell the mistress I'll speak to her shortly in the parlour? And perhaps some tea would be a good idea."

The servants left us alone in the room.

"What in damnation are you doing here?" asked Petleigh when the door was shut. "Everywhere there's a dead body I find you've been there!"

"We needed to ask him some questions, Petleigh," replied the guvnor. "We arrived just as the boy was sent out for the police."

"What questions? What do you know about Sir Herbert?"

"He was worried about something that was stolen in the burglary," said the guvnor. "We don't know what it was, but he didn't want the police involved. His last butler, a fellow called George Gullen, saw the burglars. Yet instead of going to the police, Venning dismissed the butler. He must have been worried about something."

"Worried enough to take his own life?"

"Perhaps," replied the guvnor. "But he didn't take his own life, Petleigh."

The surgeon stopped sketching the position of the body in his ledger and looked up.

"He was murdered," continued the guvnor.

"Murdered?" exclaimed Petleigh. "Why do you say that?"

The guvnor rose and went over to the corpse. The pistol

was by his left hand. The wound was on the left side of his head. He lifted Sir Herbert's left arm and showed us his hand. The thumb was quite normal, but where the fingers should have been were just knobs made of shiny skin. It looked as if he had been born with the deformity.

"My Lord," I said.

"You didn't spot it, Barnett?" asked the guvnor.

I shook my head. "He was wearing gloves earlier."

"Nor me," said Petleigh, though it was plain it pained him to say it. He frowned. "I don't know why I missed that."

"I didn't want to mention it when the others were in the room," said the guvnor.

Petleigh stared at the corpse for several minutes, then sat in the wing chair, lit a cigar, and crossed his legs.

"Tell me everything," he said. "And do not leave anything out."

Chapter Twenty-Eight

WHEN WE'D FINISHED, PETLEIGH ROSE AND BEGAN pacing before the fireplace.

"Could the butler Gullen have reached here before you?" he asked.

"It's possible," replied the guvnor. "We stopped for food on the way. But remember the telegram, Petleigh. Sir Herbert received a telegram just before shutting himself in the study. That wouldn't have been Gullen."

The inspector nodded.

"It must still be here," he said.

We searched Sir Herbert's pockets and the drawers in the desk; we checked the bookcases, the grate, the floor. The telegram was not to be found.

"Yet it must be here," said Petleigh.

"Unless the killer removed it?" suggested the guvnor. "Here's one possibility. The letter announced a visitor. Sir Herbert was anxious to see this visitor."

The guvnor stepped over to the other side of the desk and looked out the long window in the corner of the room.

"You will confirm, Barnett, that nobody's touched the windows since we arrived?"

I nodded.

"Notice that the shutters are drawn in every window but this one. This window gives a view of the front door and the street. Now, why would Sir Herbert have the shutters of this window open? Perhaps because he was watching for the visitor. That way he could get to the front door before the bell was rung."

"So the servants wouldn't know that someone had arrived," said Petleigh.

"Exactly. It's possible that Sir Herbert let the murderer in himself."

"He lets the murderer in," said Petleigh as if he had thought of it himself, "who shoots him and then removes the telegram. Yes, yes. That might be how it played out. Any idea who it was, Arrowood?"

"My guess, Inspector, is that he was killed to stop him telling us what was taken in the burglary that night."

"Yes," agreed Petleigh, picking up his hat from the table. "Quite possible, although Gullen remains my first suspect. I think we'll bring him in tonight, and tomorrow I'll pay a visit to this Colonel Longmire. See what he knows. But listen. I want you to leave this to us. I'm most serious. Sir Herbert's an important man. You cannot meddle in this investigation."

"We're going to try and find Miss Cousture's brother," said Arrowood. "We've no choice. We've been paid to do so."

"Then stick to that. But this murder is a police case. Do you understand?"

The guvnor grunted.

"Now, William," said Petleigh, his tone softened. He scratched his wrist; he seemed suddenly uncertain. "How is your sister?"

"My sister?" replied the guvnor, the surprise clear in his voice.

"I called when you were out the other day." Petleigh hesitated, glancing at me. Even in the gloomy room I could see his pale cheeks flush. "Does she live there with you?"

"For the moment. Until her next position."

"She isn't married, then?" The inspector shifted from one foot to the other, gripping his hat tightly before his belly. His elegance was gone: all of a sudden his neat black suit didn't seem to fit him so well.

"No," said the guvnor hesitantly. As he examined Petleigh, a smile came slowly over his face. "I wonder…perhaps you might come for lunch one day, Inspector?"

"That would be most agreeable, William. If that would be acceptable to Ettie, of course."

"Splendid. I'll consult her over dates. I'm sure she'll be pleased to see you. Now, Barnett, let's go. We have things to do." The guvnor stood and made his way to the door. "Oh!" he exclaimed, as if remembering something important. He turned back to Petleigh. "I wanted to ask you a question. Do you know of two CID detectives, Lafferty and Coyle? Both Irish."

"I've heard of them."

"They pulled us in to Scotland Yard on Friday and interrogated us. It seems the dead officer was their agent. I'm afraid to say they brutalized us, Petleigh. I was locked up all night with nothing to eat. Barnett was beaten with a truncheon. Quite viciously. Coyle almost broke his arm."

"Their methods are different to ours," said Petleigh.

"Who the blazes are they? They wouldn't even tell us what case they were working on."

"No, they wouldn't do that."

"Why's that?"

"They aren't CID agents, William. They're SIB."

The guvnor looked puzzled.

"Special Irish Branch," said the Inspector.

"I know what the SIB are, Petleigh, thank you. I covered the Fenian attacks for ten years, if you remember. But I thought they were disbanded when the bombing ceased?"

"That's what the Home Office want people to think. They operate in the shadows. Nothing's recorded. Apart from the deputy commissioner and a few detectives such as Lafferty and Coyle, it's all unofficial. They have a network of undercover agents, all unknown to CID and the constabulary. Most of them are criminals, ex-members of Clan na Gael, those with a grudge: basically anyone that can get the job done."

"Get what job done?" I asked, glancing at Sir Herbert's lifeless body.

"Surveillance, intelligence-gathering, infiltration," replied Petleigh. "Some are agent provocateurs. None of them go through the books. They have a secret services fund. But you must know that they've always worked outside the law, William."

"That would explain why they were happy to give Barnett a thrashing," said the guvnor.

"I'm afraid so."

"They tried to recruit me," I said.

"You didn't tell me this," said the guvnor with a frown. "What did you say?"

"I didn't. I thought it might come in handy somehow."

"Good man," said the guvnor. He turned to Petleigh. "You'll be talking to Lafferty about Sir Herbert's murder, I presume."

"Yes, but I doubt they'll tell me anything in return. The SIB never share their information with the police. They think we'll ruin their cases. It causes many problems at Scotland Yard."

"There's something else you should know, Inspector," said the guvnor.

"Oh no," said Petleigh, his self-assurance now quite recovered. "What in Christ have you done now?"

"Barnett saw Coyle in a coffeehouse with the man who murdered our Martha."

It was several moments before the inspector replied.

"Are you sure?"

"I saw them," I said. "And they were very friendly with each other."

Petleigh nodded for a long time, his eyes vacant. A carriage clock ticked in the heavy stillness of the room.

"That is not good news, gentlemen," he said at last.

It was nine o'clock when our bus crossed the river again that night. We were packed tight next to each other in a double seat on the lower deck, my legs out in the aisle on account of the width of the guvnor's rear. Every other seat was taken.

"Why'd you invite Petleigh to lunch?" I asked him. "I thought you didn't like him."

"Perhaps I've judged him too harshly."

"Doesn't seem likely you'd change your opinion so easy."

He sighed and shifted in his seat, pushing me a bit further into the aisle.

The bus stopped and more passengers crammed themselves aboard.

"We're in trouble, Norman," he said as we moved off again. "We're going to need an ally in the police."

"Petleigh isn't so bad. You just never could see it."

He snorted.

The guvnor decided we should start enquiring after Thierry in the pubs and gin-houses around the Beef that very night. It was something we should have done right from the start, and would have done if we hadn't been led away by Martha's murder. We parted at St. George's Circus, each reminding the other to be careful and watch out for anyone following. Probably we should have stayed together: we knew there were people out there who could do to us what they'd done to the copper. But we had so much turf to cover and it felt like time was running out: it couldn't be long before Cream or the Fenians found out it was us as had been asking questions.

I took the triangle of streets between Blackfriars Road and Waterloo Road. The guvnor, whose feet were playing him up again in his tight shoes, took the smaller area between Waterloo Road and Westminster Bridge Road. I had a quick pint and a bit of mutton pie in the first pub I came to: they didn't remember any young Frenchman. It was the same answer in the next five places. I had another pint and, as my arm was playing up, I took another dose of Black Drop. Soon I was feeling more acceptable. Nobody remembered a French lad who liked a drink on New Cut, nor on Cornwall Road, nor in the stinking, violent pubs on Broad Wall. Finally, I reached Commercial Road, the last street before the river, and the pubs that served the wharves and warehouses. I was tired. Six more alehouses and I was finished. Nobody remembered Thierry Cousture.

Chapter Twenty-Nine

I ARRIVED AT COIN STREET THE NEXT MORNING TO find a big crowd gathered. The police had put up barriers to stop wagons coming through, while two fire engines stood halfway down the road. As I pushed through the press of people come to have a look, the smell of burning wood got stronger, until at last I saw the smoke rising from the roof of the pudding shop. Firemen were running in and out of the building, while others were pumping water. One hose disappeared up the side alley, another was led through the front door. The windows were blown out; inside all was black.

I fought my way through the crowd to the other side of the street, and there outside Church's coffeehouse sat the guvnor and Ettie. He was eating a big slab of bread and cheese, his face sooty, his side hair sticking out. Ettie sat silent and pale, shaking. Each had a blanket over their shoulders.

"Norman!" exclaimed Ettie. She took my hand and pressed it, clinging on to me. "It was horrible. They had to carry us out of the window!"

Still gripping my hand, she began to cough.

"Smoke," said the guvnor, his mouth full. He too let out a sharp cough.

"What happened?"

"The first we knew was when the firemen broke the bed-room window and woke us up," he said, wheezing. "They got us down on a ladder. Saved our lives."

"They carried you out?"

"We were almost passed out with the fumes, Norman."

Here he began coughing again. He held out his breakfast to me as he tried to control himself.

"But how did it start?"

"The firemen found paraffin cans," replied Ettie, finally letting loose my hand. "Whoever it was broke through a win-dow in the shop."

She held my eyes, and it was at that moment I had a change in my perception of her. She appeared uncommonly graceful sitting there on the stool with soot on her face, and maybe a little vulnerable. The woman who had stamped through the door with her tuba case seemed a different person.

The guvnor had stopped coughing; he took his bread and cheese back from me.

"Who do you think it was?" I asked.

The guvnor put a finger to his lips to silence me.

"Let's go inside for a moment, Barnett," he murmured.

"Oh, for goodness' sake!" exclaimed Ettie. She clasped her chest and stifled a cough. "Will you stop trying to protect me? In Afghanistan I saw more awful things than you could imagine, William, and now I've almost been killed. I think I have a right to be involved."

The guvnor looked at her with sorrow in his eyes. He nod-ded.

"It seems the people we're tracking have found out where I live, Ettie. It isn't safe for us here anymore."

"But who are they?" asked Ettie.

"Cream's men, the Fenians, Longmire," replied the guvnor with a sigh. "Take your pick."

"Oh my Lord," she said. "They want to kill us."

"They won't kill us, Ettie," said Arrowood. "We won't let them. We'll have to find lodgings anyway until this is repaired. They won't know where we've gone."

A horde of street children appeared through the crowd and pushed between us to the other side of the pavement.

"Are we insured?" asked Ettie when they'd got through.

Arrowood bit his lip and looked down. "Now, Ettie, don't be angry, but I'm afraid I didn't have the wherewithal to pay the premium last year. We didn't have a great deal of work at that time."

"Oh, William!" exclaimed Ettie, pulling the blanket tighter over her shoulders. "That was foolish."

"I didn't have the money, Ettie."

"Well, I can pay the builders. I have a little savings."

"You have savings?" asked the guvnor, surprised. "You didn't tell me this before."

"I said I'll pay," she said sharply.

The guvnor turned and rapped on the window of the coffeehouse.

"Albert! Come out here."

Albert emerged. He looked gloomy and tired.

"Where do you live, Albert?"

"Mint Street. By the workhouse."

"Can you take in my sister and I for a few weeks? How many rooms do you have?"

"Only two rooms for the four of us, Mr. Arrowood. We're packed tight as it is."

"Well, your sons can sleep with you and Mrs. Pudding. We'll have the other."

Albert looked uncertain. He didn't like to make such decisions himself.

"We'll pay half the rent while we're there," continued the guvnor.

Albert shifted from foot to foot and scratched his head. "Well," he said slowly. "I suppose. But only temporary. Only so long as the builders are in."

"Thank you, Albert," said Ettie.

"Actually, half the rent wouldn't be fair," said the guvnor. "There are four of you and two of us, so that would make it one third of the rent. You agree?"

Albert hesitated, his face screwed up as he tried to calculate.

"Good," said the guvnor before he had a chance to reply. "It's agreed. Tell Mrs. Pudding."

But Mrs. Pudding had overheard and was standing in the door of the coffeehouse.

"You can't stay, Mr. Arrowood," she said firmly. "My sister and her three are coming tomorrow. Ain't no space for another two."

"You can't come, Mr. Arrowood," said Albert. "Ain't no space."

"Well, then," replied the guvnor, taking a great long breath, "Lewis will have us."

"Does he have space?" asked Ettie.

"He has a house in Elephant and Castle."

"A house?" I exclaimed. "How does he have a house? He buys more than he sells in that shop."

"His father was a goldsmith," explained the guvnor. "He was left the house."

"Why isn't Lewis a goldsmith, then?" I asked. "Why's he trying to make a living in that old shop?"

The guvnor pulled the blanket from his shoulders and

dropped it in Ettie's lap. "He was trained by his father but says he didn't have the precision, even when he had use of both arms. And Lewis always loved weapons. From a young boy he was only interested in weapons."

Just then, a figure we knew only too well came through the crowd. He wore a brown derby, plaid trousers, a blue frock coat. In his hand he held a cherrywood walking stick. The guvnor gripped my arm.

"So we meet again, gentlemen," said the man.

It was Stanley Cream. He smiled, revealing the whitest, most regular teeth in London. His face was clean-shaved; he smelled of perfume. Boots appeared behind him. His eyes held mine, a cocky smirk on his ugly face, doing his best to remind me how badly he'd beaten me when we last met four years previous. He'd only got the better of me that time because I'd slipped on the beer spilled on the floor, but most likely he didn't remember that. I held his eye, bristling, my fear overcome by wanting to smash his ugly face in.

"You'll pay for this, Cream," said the guvnor, his nerves making his wheezing worse. He coughed, clutching a handkerchief to his mouth.

"Actually, I think you'll have to pay, Mr. Arrowood," replied Cream with a chuckle. He wasn't one of those as fake a refined accent: his was real. How he'd ended up in his line of work I never understood. "There looks to be rather a lot of repair work to your hovel, I'm afraid. I must say, you're a pitiful sight with such grime on your face. Is this your wife?"

"I'm his sister," replied Ettie.

"Oh dear, madam," said Cream, his voice dripping with false sympathy. "You might have been killed."

"Did you do this?" she asked, standing to confront him.

"Are you also a detective, madam?"

"A nurse."

"Admirable. Most admirable." He looked at me, his lazy smile disappearing. His voice became hard as steel. "I told you never to come near me again. I was very clear about that, Mr. Barnett. The two of you have been bothering my acquaintances. So listen carefully. Desist. Walk away or we shall be forced to do something very unpleasant. Very, very unpleasant. Do you understand? Or shall I get Boots here to translate for you?"

"We're looking for Thierry Cousture," I said. "Used to work in your kitchens. D'you know where he is?"

Cream shook his head. "Young Terry disappeared a few weeks ago without any warning. He left us short-handed. I was angry about that." He tapped his walking stick against his boot. "Very angry indeed. I'd like to find him myself."

"What was he doing for you?" I asked.

He tutted and turned to the guvnor. "If you do find him, I want to know about it. It's important I talk to him, you see. But don't go near my acquaintances again. You're lucky to be alive, Mr. Arrowood. You won't be lucky next time. That I guarantee."

Cream raised his stick and poked the guvnor in the belly with it. Then they turned into the crowd and were gone.

"Check if there are any more of them," said the guvnor, breathing heavily. Ettie began to cough again, her eyes searching anxiously in the mix of onlookers. I tracked around the back of the crowd, checking faces, making sure there weren't more of Cream's men waiting to get us. On the other side of the road I ran into Neddy.

"Is Mr. Arrowood safe?" he asked. He looked scared. He wore a man's cap on his dirty little head; the peak was half-torn off and fell over one of his eyes.

"They're both fine, Neddy. How's your mouth?"

He smiled at me, revealing the black gap in his front teeth.

"Makes me look pretty, don't it, sir?"

I laughed, though in truth I was faking it. Seeing Cream had rattled my nerves.

"What's your mother up to, son?"

"Having one of her bad days, I'd say. I got to get some money for her."

"I think Mr. Arrowood'll need your help today."

I led the boy back to the coffeehouse, where the guvnor was sitting on the stool again.

"I'm sorry for your troubles, sir," said Neddy.

The guvnor smiled and patted the boy's head. "Are you on the muffins today, my dear?"

"Only at four. I can help you before, sir."

"We'll need you to pull a cart. Can you do it with those big shoes? Why don't you tie the laces?"

Neddy bent to lace up the unmatched man-sized shoes he wore.

"When the firemen allow us back, we'll pack some bags and move to our new lodgings," said the guvnor. "But first, tell me how you're feeling after your adventure, lad. You know these things can affect our minds more than our bodies. How are you sleeping? Any nightmares?"

"Not as I remember, sir. I don't think so."

"Good. What about melancholy?"

"I'm just the same as afore. You don't need to worry about me."

"Feelings of terror?"

The boy shook his head.

"Good, good. You're a soldier, my boy. A good little soldier. And an army must take care of its soldiers." Using my arm, he pulled himself to his feet. He turned to us. "Now, I'll go and arrange it with Lewis. Ettie, you stay here with Neddy. Pack some bags when they let you in, but make sure there's a constable with you. We must be careful now. Be alert to anyone watching you."

"Don't worry about me, Brother. I can take care of myself."

"Make sure you collect my portrait. I'll return for you presently."

"I'll keep a watch, sir," said Neddy.

"Good lad. Remember, tell no one of our new lodgings. Barnett, you might as well continue with the pubs. But be careful. Watch out for anyone trailing you. They might pick you off when you're alone."

"How's your arm, Norman?" asked Ettie.

"Much better, long as it doesn't get nudged."

She smiled, the creases in her face darkened with soot. I dropped my eyes: her concern made me sad somehow.

"Well, be careful with it," she said.

"Meet me at The Fontaine at six, Barnett," ordered the guvnor. "We need to report to Miss Cousture. She's left several messages for us."

"Do you need me at The Fontaine too?" asked little Neddy.

"No, my little soldier. Just until four. Then you'd best sell some muffins."

This time I covered the pubs between Blackfriars and Borough High Street. By the end of the day I'd gotten nowhere and my feet were hurting. Nobody remembered a young Frenchman with hair the colour of wheat. Nobody remembered any Frenchman at all.

It was early evening when we opened the door of Fon-

taine's shop. Miss Cousture was behind the counter. Her face
was severe.

"Gentlemen," she said. "I come looking for you. But why
you do not come to see me? I sent two messages."

"A lot's happened, mademoiselle," said the guvnor. "We
had to follow the trail while it was still warm."

"You speak to Milky Sal?"

"They wouldn't allow us."

The anger left her face, replaced now with disappointment.

"Is your employer here?" asked the guvnor.

"He takes some pictures to a customer."

"Private pictures?"

"I think."

"These private pictures," said the guvnor. "Have you ever
seen them?"

"He keeps that side of the business separate from this. But
yes, I see them once. I looked in his bag."

"Where does he usually keep them?"

"In his house. The sittings he does at night, when I am
not here."

"Has he ever asked you to sit for them?"

"No!" she exclaimed. "Why you say that?"

"I'm only trying to understand. Please don't be offended."

She shut her eyes and shook her head as if trying to get the
idea of it out of her mind.

"Now, Mr. Arrowood. Tell me what you find."

The guvnor explained what had happened with Longmire
and our kidnap of Sir Herbert. He told her about the burglary and what Gullen had told us. Here she interrupted him.

"Tell me about this man Sir Herbert," she asked.

"He works in the War Office as Quartermaster General,"
explained the guvnor. "Large house, carriage."

"What age?"

"Perhaps fifty."

"And what does he look like?"

The guvnor glanced at me, puzzled.

"He's short, balding. A round face."

"Fat," I added.

"Have you heard of Sir Herbert Venning, miss?" asked the guvnor.

"No."

He tried his kind-eyed silence again. It had no effect.

"There's something you aren't telling us," he said at last.

"No." She crossed her arms.

"You've deceived us before."

"I say there is not, Mr. Arrowood." Anger flared on her face. "So I want to know about Longmire now. He is also short?"

"Why are you asking?" demanded the guvnor. "Do you recognize his name?"

"Perhaps I see him with my brother."

"He's average height." A burst of coughing took over him. He gripped the counter, his eyes shut tight until it subsided.

"Quite slim," I added. "Wears a monocle. There's a mole by his eye, size of a sixpence."

Her eyes blazed for the shortest time, as if a spirit had passed through them.

"Do you recognize him?" asked the guvnor, moving a picture so that he could sit on a stool by the door.

She shook her head.

He told her about Venning's death. As he spoke she gazed out the window at the street, her back erect, her shoulders high. She cleared her throat twice, then reached for a mug of water on the counter. I wasn't sure she was listening. When he described the fire at the pudding shop she simply nodded.

"Did you ever see Thierry's drinking friends, miss?" I asked.

"No," she said, her voice sticking in her throat. "I never saw him with anyone."

"Do you know where he used to go drinking?"

She shrugged. Her eyes fell to the counter. She seemed weak, as if the blood had drained out of her.

"He pretends to me he does not go drinking," she said softly.

The shop was silent.

Finally, she spoke again.

"Eric will be back soon. You must go."

"We'll find him, you know," said the guvnor, hauling himself to his feet. "We'll return when we know more."

I stayed behind while he stepped out onto the street.

Her almond eyes met mine, but they seemed empty. Her hair was tied up on her head and the high neck of her blouse was grubby around its frills, yet she was more fine looking for it. I felt the sweat prickle under my collar.

"We need another payment, miss," I said at last.

Chapter Thirty

WE STARTED ON THE PUBS AGAIN THE NEXT MORN-
ing. The guvnor took the streets south of Westminster Bridge
Road, I the section between New Kent Road and Great Dover
Street. His shoes had been burnt in the fire, and now he wore
a pair borrowed from Lewis which gave him another reason to
moan about his feet. Since he wasn't hobbling as bad as when
he had a gout attack proper, I let him get on with it.

We met in Willows' at dinner time. The sky had turned
grey and the air was close. The guvnor needed to go back to
his rooms to arrange builders and so I plodded on, this time
taking the streets from Bethlem down to the Oval. Still nobody seemed to know the young Frenchman. I had a few
pints along the way just to make the day pass easier. In a place
called the Bear, sitting in a dark corner, was a pale, bent little
bloke I was sure I'd seen in the street earlier. I felt his eyes on
my back as I stood at the counter, and each time I looked at
him he turned his head away, pretending to talk to himself.
I drank my pint down quick and left the pub, hiding behind
a wagon parked a couple of doors up the road. He came out
right away, into the middle of the road, looking up and down.
He cursed and hurried off towards the next junction, where

he had another look up and down, then slowly plodded back to the pub. I thought about going back in and making him tell me what his game was, but that would likely make things more difficult. Better to carry on.

When it began to rain my arm started to play up again; I had another dose of Black Drop, which made things easier still. By six I'd been to every pub and gin palace within half an hour of the Beef. I decided to move further east, into the poorer areas off Tabard Street. At ten o'clock, in a wedge-shaped hovel in the basement of a crooked tenement, I finally got lucky.

"There used to be one as come in here," said the barman. "Right trouble, he was. Hasn't been in for a while."

Over his shoulder lay the filthiest rag I had ever seen.

"You know where I can find him?"

"Ask his mate." The barman pointed with his cloth at a lone figure hunched on a bench by the piano. "They was always together."

The man wore a waistcoat made for a fat man though he was thin as straw himself. His topper was bent. His beard was scabby and bald in patches. In front of him was an empty tankard. I bought two pints and took them over.

He peered at me with watery eyes. Now I was close, I saw he was much younger than he looked—maybe twenty years old. Drunk. Badly fed.

"I'm looking for Terry," I said, putting a pint in front of him and sitting down. "Landlord says you're his mate."

It took him a long time to answer.

"Ain't seen him," he mumbled at last.

"Where can I find him?"

"Nowhere."

"His sister's looking for him. She's worried about him."

He laughed quickly, then swallowed half the pint. Beneath his giant waistcoat he wore a dirty vest. Blood was crusted at the corner of his mouth.

"What's funny?" I asked.

He shook his head as if I was a fool.

"When's the last time you saw him?" I asked.

"Saw him, uh…" His hand rose and swiped the air in front of his face, as if he thought flies surrounded him. His head swayed. "Maybe…maybe a month, two month. He's gone, anyways."

"Where did he go?"

"Don't know. Just left."

"Why did he leave?"

"Don't know, mate. Don't know." He finished the pint. "He disappeared."

I pulled a shilling from my pocket and put it on the table. He stared at it like he couldn't focus.

"That's yours if you tell me where he is," I said.

He took a moment to speak.

"Hassocks, near Brighton," he said eventually. "Works in a baker's."

"How d'you know that?"

"Told me, didn't he?"

"Why'd he leave town?"

"Boss trouble, weren't it."

"What trouble?"

He shrugged. "Don't know. He was right scared, though. Tell you that for nothing."

When he reached for the coin I slapped my hand down on it.

"Did he tell you anything about the Barrel of Beef? Anything as was going on there?"

He scowled at me, then shut his eyes. As he spoke, his head swayed just enough to make me queasy.

"We never talked about working," he mumbled. "Just drinking, looking for women, horses. He only told me he's in trouble. That's it."

"You didn't ask?"

"He wouldn't say."

He burped and clutched his belly, wincing. The burp popped his eyes open again.

I pushed the coin across the table towards him.

"A shilling," I said. "Price of your friendship, boy. Lucky I'm not out to get him."

He stared at me with his watery, pink-rimmed eyes, his head swaying, insulted but too drunk to care. He picked up the money and staggered to the bar.

We took the midday train to Brighton. It had rained all morning, and there weren't many people travelling south that day. The guvnor sat on the edge of his seat, fidgeting, preoccupied. The day before, as he was packing up his gear, another letter had come from Isabel. She proposed they meet at midday tomorrow at the Imperial Restaurant, a luncheon bar in the West End. A pricey place for lunch, all right. But Isabel always did think she was made for something better.

"If she's coming back then my sister will have to find lodgings," he said, staring intently out the window at the rows of grey roofs. "Can you and Mrs. Barnett put her up until she finds somewhere?"

"We've only one room."

"Only one room!" exclaimed the guvnor. "You're codding me! You live in a single room?"

I looked at him coldly.

"Can't afford more space," I said.

He sighed.

"I'm sorry, Norman. I didn't realize things were so difficult."

We didn't speak again until we were out of the suburbs and in the countryside. The train stopped at an empty station. Nobody got on.

"You know she might not be coming back, William," I said as we pulled away again. Though I said it out of concern, I caught a note of cruelty in my voice that surprised me.

"I know," he said, gazing out the window as the green fields of Sussex ran past. "I'll just be glad to see her again."

Hassocks was a tidy village with a station at the end of the high street. There was only one bakery. A woman with a baby in her arms stood behind the counter; she told us Thierry was in the bakehouse in the yard. We went back onto the street and down a side alley to an opening in the wall. The bakehouse stood on a patch of grass, its doors wide open to the breeze. As we approached, a young man in a white apron came out, a tray of bread on his shoulder. He had hair of wheat; the ear next to the tray carried an ugly scar.

"Thierry," said the guvnor.

The man stopped, looking at us suspiciously.

"Who are you?" he asked in a thick French accent.

"Mr. Arrowood. This is my assistant, Mr. Barnett. Your sister employed us to find you."

"I take in the bread," he said politely. "You wait. I come back."

He disappeared through the gate.

"Follow him, Barnett," ordered the guvnor.

I reached the street just in time to see Thierry dump the

tray outside the shop, turn, and start running. He ran straight into me.

I pulled his arm quick behind his back until he squealed, then marched him into the yard. He was younger than me but not so good with his muscles.

"He tried to run away, sir," I said.

"How impolite. We've come all the way from London, Thierry."

The young man's face was white. Sweat soaked through his shirt.

"Please, sir," he pleaded. "I don't make trouble for Mr. Cream. I come here to get away. I swear it, sir. I only keep away. I don't make trouble for him."

"We aren't from Mr. Cream," said the guvnor softly. "I told you. Your sister sent us. There's no need to be afraid of us, Thierry."

Thierry threw his other arm back, landing a sharp blow to my face, and for a moment I let go of him. He made to run off but I tripped him up and he fell onto the grass. My nose was smarting like it might be bleeding, and I landed on him harder than I needed to. It didn't do my arm any good at all.

"You little fool," I hissed in his ear as he struggled under the weight of my body. "We're your bloody friends. Your sister sent us."

I hauled him up to his feet again.

"I know you are from Cream," he protested, almost crying now.

"Listen!" exclaimed the guvnor. "Listen carefully! Your sister sent us to find you. We're here to help."

"My sister does not send you! She knows I am here."

"Thierry, lad, she hired us to find you."

He shook his head. "Why would she? She helps find the lodgings here."

It wasn't often the guvnor and I were both speechless, but we were now. We stared at him, trying to make sense of what he'd just said.

"She knows I am here," he whimpered.

"Don't lie to us, Thierry," said the guvnor at last. "We've been deceived enough already by your sister."

"I swear it, sir. She comes with me from London. She pays my first week's rent."

It was too much for me: I let go his arm and spun him round. Then I whopped him a good one right across his face with the back of my hand. He cried out and fell to the ground.

"Barnett, was that necessary?" asked the guvnor.

"I'm sick and tired of everyone lying to us."

Thierry shuffled out of reach of my boots, wedging himself between a barrel and the yard wall.

"I do not lie," he said miserably. "It's true. She knows I am here. I don't know what she tells you."

The guvnor raised his voice.

"Then why did she hire us to find you?"

Blood was coming out from the lad's mouth. He cupped his face in his hands, looking at me like a frightened pup.

"Ask her. I don't know."

"Well, have a guess, then. Help us, Thierry."

"I don't know, sir."

The guvnor nodded to me, then turned his back on us.

I pulled Thierry up and marched him back to the bakehouse. He struggled hard, but it was no use. There was a window in the iron door of the oven: inside the wood glowed orange.

"That looks hot, Thierry," I said.

"No, please," he sobbed.

I took his hair and pulled his head back hard, pushing him forward. With one hand I jerked the oven door open, feeling the roaring heat straightaway. He struggled best he could, throwing his fists about, but I was the stronger. Slowly I brought his head towards the door. It wasn't until his face was six inches away that he cracked.

"OK! OK, I tell you!"

I hauled him around and marched him back out into the yard, relieved to get away from the terrible heat. The guvnor was sat on a crate smoking a cigar.

"The truth, my boy," he said.

I let go and dusted the lad down a bit. He was trembling, his face red and damp, his mouth bloody.

"Why did she hire us?" I asked.

"She wants to find information on Mr. Cream," he said, trying to catch his breath. "I was helping her, but I must escape. Too much danger for me to stay."

"Why was there danger for you?" I asked.

"They ask me to deliver boxes. Always they are in the basement room. One time I find crates of rifles and bullets. I am looking inside when one of them, Mr. Piser, come down the stairs and see me. He is very angry, beats me onto the floor, kicks me, my back, my face. He locks me there for Mr. Cream, but I have a friend in the kitchen. When I don't return, he comes to search me."

"Harry?" asked the guvnor.

He nodded. "He lets me out. That's it. I don't go back to the Beef no more. I know I see something they don't want me see. I come down here so they don't find me."

"You took a bullet?"

He nodded.

"In case I can use it against them."

"We talked to Harry. He didn't tell us about this."

"I ask him to tell no one."

"He's a good friend," said the guvnor. "Now, who were the guns for?"

"I don't know, sir."

"Where did Cream get them?"

"I don't hear of them before I open the boxes."

"You gave a bullet to Martha?"

"You talk to Martha?" His eyes became concentrated. "How she is? She never comes to see me since I left. All this time she never comes."

"You haven't heard?" asked the guvnor cautiously. A look of great pity came over his face.

"Heard?" whispered Thierry, looking at the guvnor with terror.

"I'm very sorry, son," said the guvnor, laying his hand on the lad's shoulder. "Martha was murdered. We'd arranged a meeting with her. She was stabbed as she waited for us."

Thierry's face broke. He wiped the blood from his lips, he clasped his forehead. He opened his mouth to speak, then shut it again. Finally, the tears began to fall.

We sat with him for some time. The woman from the bakery came into the yard. When she saw him, she pursed her lips, turned, and left.

The sky became blue for a while, then white clouds returned, then grey. With a sigh, the guvnor spoke again.

"I'm so sorry, Thierry. We're trying to find who killed her. But we need to ask you more questions. Are you able to answer?"

The lad nodded, his eyes shut.

"Why did you give her a bullet?"

He answered softly, choking. "If something happens to me."

"Why not your sister?"

"I must make Martha believe I am in danger." He was whispering, his hand over his eyes. "She thinks I leave her. She don't believe I love her. The French, you know, they think we chase women."

He began to weep again.

"Thierry, she did know you loved her," said the guvnor gently. "She came to meet us, but the murderer arrived a minute before we got there. She was holding the bullet when she died."

The guvnor went to him, took him in his arms and held him, stroking the young man's hair as if he was a child.

"It's OK, lad," he murmured.

When Thierry was calm again, the guvnor continued. "Why is your sister trying to find information on Cream?"

"She's not my sister. She's my friend. I help her escape to come back here."

"Back here?"

Finally, Thierry looked up. His eyes were red and blurry.

"She's English. When she was a girl her mother saw a notice for girls to go for service in France. But when she arrives in Rouen it is not service. It is a brothel. A woman called Milky Sal, she is behind it. She works for Cream. Caroline was thirteen when she arrives in France, and eleven more years before she run away. I help her escape the house."

"How do you know her?"

"I am deliver from patisserie. My job. Before I begin to bake."

"But why didn't she tell us this?"

"She is ashamed for it, for being a whore. She tells police, but they do nothing. She wouldn't take it. We wanted information on Cream for the police will arrest him. So I take the job in the Beef. I couldn't find about selling girls, but he is the fence, you know? We thought we can find evidence for the police to arrest him. We want to see him in prison."

"So when you left she hired us, hoping we'd find out more about Cream's activities," said the guvnor wearily. "She could have told us that. You're amateurs, you and Caroline. Do you know how dangerous Cream is?"

"I know." Thierry bent over on the crate and buried his face in his hands again. "You think I don't know?"

We left him in the yard as the light August rain began to fall again.

Chapter Thirty-One

WE TALKED OVER THE CASE AS WE WAITED FOR THE train. I was tired of being duped again and again by Miss Cousture, but the guvnor hardly seemed to mind, and that vexed me more. It was always that way: I could never fathom where his pride would fall. Some minor slight would make him erupt, while now he accepted the discovery that Miss Cousture knew all along where Thierry was as just another piece of the puzzle. Maybe it was meeting Isabel tomorrow as made him so noble today.

The train was busier on the way back to London. We chose seats opposite a nervous young woman in a light, summer dress. A picnic hamper lay by her feet, a slim amber bonnet hid her eyes. She was tucked into a corner, a tattered magazine open on her lap. When she turned the yellowed page, I could see she was reading one of Holmes's old cases. The guvnor also noticed and groaned so as she would hear. The young woman glanced up to find him staring at her, shaking his head in disapproval. Her pale cheeks flushed; she dropped her eyes to the magazine once more.

"May I ask what you're reading, miss?" he asked.

"An old Sherlock Holmes case, sir. 'A Scandal in Bohemia.'"

"Ah yes. And how do you find it?"

"It's diverting. I've read it before, though."

"It's the case of Irene Adler?"

"Yes. She was blackmailing the King of Bohemia."

"I know it," he declared. "The German king, von Ormstein, was it?"

The lady nodded. "She wants to ruin him for ending their affair."

"Yes, yes," agreed the guvnor, crossing his arms. "Von Ormstein is about to be married to the King of Scandinavia's daughter, but Miss Adler has threatened to send a compromising photograph to the lady's family. He's afraid the scandal will cause his fiancée to call off the marriage, and so he offers Holmes seven hundred pounds to steal the photograph."

"A thousand, sir," she replied, sitting forward. The train rattled suddenly, causing her to grip the armrest. "Seven hundred in notes, three hundred in gold."

"Of course." The guvnor glanced at me in disgust. "A thousand pounds! Holmes runs off to watch Miss Adler's house and within a day or two has retrieved the picture."

"He plans it all out, sir. It's quite genius." Here the young lady looked at me and explained. "Sherlock Holmes sends a whole crowd of people outside Irene Adler's house to create a stir. Then he pretends he's been injured so that Miss Adler will take him inside her house. When he's got inside, Watson throws a smoke rocket through the window. "Fire, fire!" they all shout. Miss Adler runs to rescue the photograph, revealing its hiding place. But just before she pulls it out, Holmes calls out that it's a false alarm." She looked back at the guvnor. "But he doesn't retrieve the photograph, sir. Irene Adler realizes it's Sherlock Holmes and has a coachman watch him so he cannot get to it. Even so, it's enough to put her off her blackmail plot. She goes abroad with her new husband, leaving a letter promising not to publish the photograph."

"And the case is solved, do you think, miss?" asked the guvnor kindly.

"Yes. The king is safe. He believes Irene Adler will keep to her word."

"Indeed he does. Tell me, miss. Does something strike you as odd about it all?"

"What do you mean?"

"Well, as you say, the king believes she won't go back on her word. That is to say, he trusts her. But how is it that such an honourable woman, whose word can be trusted completely, how is it she would consider blackmail in the first place? Are these not two opposing characters?"

"Yes, I suppose," she replied slowly, searching his face. "I didn't think about that."

"What do you think is her motive for blackmail?"

"She wants to ruin him."

"But why?" he whispered, leaning forward in his seat.

"Because he ended their affair," she said with a shrug. "We know this from the story."

"But now she has a new husband. Indeed, they've been married only a day. In her letter she declares she's in love with this man, and that he's a much better man than the king."

The young woman nodded. Her eyes narrowed. "That was what I couldn't fathom. If she has all this, why does she care about the king so much to put it all in peril?"

"I wondered the same!" exclaimed the guvnor in triumph. He edged his heavy hocks even further forward, so his knees almost touched hers. The young woman pushed herself back in her seat, alarmed at his agitation. He spoke with urgency now. "Irene Adler has been a successful opera singer. She has an impressive house. She's adored by all who meet her, and she has found love. This is not what a woman in her position would do. Now, what does she say in the letter to Holmes? That the king has cruelly mistreated her. Cruelly mistreated her, miss. If I was the detective, I would wonder what that meant. I would not take a bow and declare the case solved. I would want to know!"

"What do you think it meant, sir?" she asked. The emotions on her face were mixed, not wanting to excite this fat stranger more, yet feeling compelled to ask.

"Well now, miss," he replied, his finger waggling above his greasy head. "Here's a story for you. The king had promised himself to Miss Adler two years before. She even wore his ring. Unknown to Miss Adler, this was going on at the same time as he began courting the lady from Scandinavia."

"Then she wanted revenge?"

"No," replied the guvnor. "Remember, she's now married to a better man. The truth of this case is that she wanted to expose the king for his deception. She wanted to warn his fiancée about what sort of man he was."

The young lady clenched her lips together. I could see she wasn't convinced. "But he made his choice. He changed his mind about who to wed. This isn't so bad. Anyone may change their mind before they are wed."

"That's a very modern opinion, if I might say," said the guvnor, his nose wrinkling in disapproval. "But there's more, miss. Before the king broke with Miss Adler, she began to suspect him. She had him followed by an enquiry agent of her own. This agent discovered he'd been consorting with two other women at the same time, and one of them an actress."

"An actress!"

"At the same time. While he prepares to wed the daughter

of the King of Scandinavia, he is making love to three other women. But listen. There's more. The other was a chambermaid at the Langham, where he had a suite. After some months the girl discovered she was with child. When that poor creature told him of her situation, he arranged with the manager to have her dismissed." Here the guvnor paused and lowered his voice. "That very night she threw herself off Waterloo Bridge."

The young woman gasped, looking at me in despair.

"The enquiry agent discovered this from the girl's friends at the hotel. This is why Irene Adler wanted to expose him. She wanted to warn his fiancée that this was the type of man he was. A cruel, deceitful man. It was the only way she knew without exposing herself to libel."

"So the villain was not Irene Adler?" asked the lady as the train began to slow.

"It was the king. Irene Adler was trying to protect her rival. And events have since proved her correct. It's widely known that the king keeps his wife's cousin in a villa in Prague. He does it right under her nose and he doesn't mind who knows it. His wife lives in misery."

Shaking her head, the young lady closed the magazine and placed it on the seat next to her. The train pulled into a station. An old man with a doctor's bag got in the carriage.

"But why didn't Sherlock Holmes see that the king was deceiving him?" she asked as the train pulled off again.

"Perhaps he didn't notice the clues. Perhaps his famous perception was affected by the status of the man who had come for his help. After all, it isn't only Sherlock Holmes who assumes the nobility are more trustworthy than the rest of us. Or perhaps, and I hesitate to suggest it, but perhaps the exceedingly large fee caused the great detective a temporary blindness. He sees women as emotional creatures, he says this often in his cases. He doesn't take them seriously."

"Oh dear," said the lady. "But why does Miss Adler promise not to expose the king in her final letter?"

The guvnor shrugged. "No doubt she's intimidated to be against the famous Sherlock Holmes. After all, he put on quite a show to get inside her house, and all the world knows how those in high positions respect him. Perhaps she hasn't the strength for the fight. I don't know."

The lady collected her hamper and placed it on the seat. Then she looked back at him with suspicion in her eyes.

"How do you know this?"

"I don't." The guvnor smiled and folded his hands on his belly. "I made it all up."

Her mouth fell open. Her face was such a picture of astonishment that I couldn't help myself laugh.

"But it could have been true, miss," he continued, becoming animated again. "That's the point. There's enough doubt in what we know to suggest more enquiries were needed. Holmes never questioned who the real villain was in this case. He trusted rank and ignored the signs that there was another story buried there. And the one part of my story which is true is that now they are married the king does keep his wife's cousin as his lover and the whole of society knows it. His poor wife has become a recluse."

The train pulled into the next station. The woman, shaking her head as if she had just had her day-trip spoiled, rose from her seat and collected her bag and hamper.

"My stop," she murmured.

"Good day, miss," said the guvnor, cheery as you like. As the door shut behind her, the pages of the abandoned magazine fluttered in the gust.

When we were nearing Croydon, he reached into his coat pocket and pulled out a small case of red velvet.

"I bought it this morning," he said to me. "Do you think Isabel will like it?"

Inside was a thin gold chain, in the centre of which hung a teardrop opal.

I looked at his lumpish, hopeful face.

"She'll like it," I replied.

He smiled and put it back in his pocket.

"What'll you do if she's not coming back?" I asked him.

"We were happy once. We might be so again."

"You didn't make life easy for her. She might have found another bloke by now. One with more money than you."

"I've learned my lessons, my friend." He put his elbow on the window ledge and watched the rows of cottages below, their grey roofs, their sooty chimneys slick with the summer rain. "I'll be different this time."

"How?" I said, more harshly than I intended. "You're the same. There's still no money."

"I feel we've reached a turning point, Norman, after all the work we've done, all we've learned about this profession. If we expose how Cream's been obtaining British Army rifles, we'll be heroes."

"But we don't know how he's getting the rifles."

"We're getting close. It must involve Venning and Longmire. We've only to piece it together. And when we do, the papers will talk about it for months. People will understand that Holmes isn't the only private investigative agent in London and then we'll get better cases. You could even produce stories like Watson." He laughed. "If only you could write, old chap."

"It wasn't just down to money that Isabel left," I said, ignoring his joke.

"But that's what made things difficult. If she can see that I'm a success and that we'll be comfortably off…" His eyes fell to his shoes. "If she can be proud of me."

"I hope so."

"What else can I do?"

Looking at the guvnor perched there on the edge of his seat, hoping so hard I could almost feel it in the air, I felt sad for him.

"But you must keep your eyes open, William. I don't want you to be hurt."

He looked at me through his eyeglasses and blinked like he might be holding back tears. I offered him a toffee.

"Thank you," he said, plugging it into his mouth.

After we'd chewed for a while, he said, "Tell me, Norman, what did you think of Miss Cousture's reaction yesterday?"

"I thought she recognized Longmire."

He nodded. "Her face betrayed her. Mr. Darwin says that expression is to the passions as language is to thought. She's a good liar—only a very strong emotion could give her away like that. But why did she hide it? And what emotion did you read in her face?"

"I don't know. She's out of her depth, maybe?"

"It was hatred. That's what I saw in her eyes."

"I'm not sure you can read a person's eyes, sir, with respect. I don't know if it's possible."

"Listen and I'll explain," he said, shaking his head. "The Fontaine is a dark place. In darkness the pupil opens, greedy for what little light there is. In the sun it shrinks so as not to receive too much brightness. This is simply physiology. Did you watch her eyes?"

I shook my head.

"As we began to speak they were wide as coal-holes. As were yours, as no doubt were mine. But the moment I described Longmire and that mole on his face, they clenched. Her pupils became smaller than peppercorns. It was as rapid as a hand recoiling from a hotplate."

"This is a new trick of yours?"

"It's no trick. I think it's a way of reading emotions. I provided her mind with a picture and her eye tried to prevent its entry. But then the hatred departed and something curious took its place. Did you see how she couldn't clear her throat? Tell me, what did you feel at this point?"

"I can't remember that clear."

"I felt queasy," he declared. "I had the damnedest feeling that her emotions had transported themselves to me. It was uncanny, Barnett. Tell me, do you think that's possible?"

"I don't know. Anything's possible, I reckon."

"Say it's true, then why would she react this way?"

"Fear maybe? You can be sick with fear."

"Sick with fear?" he said with a frown. "Interesting. Let's keep that idea. Perhaps now that we've found Thierry she'll tell us. Perhaps now she'll be honest." He shook his great head and sighed. "Half of this case seems to be solving the problem of Miss Cousture."

As we worked on our toffees, we watched the suburban houses run past our windows. He didn't speak again until we drew into Victoria.

"We might have found Thierry, but our case isn't solved, Barnett. You know that, don't you?"

"Yes, William."

"We must find Martha's killer and bring him to justice. I couldn't live with myself if we failed."

The train stopped and we dismounted, following the crowd along the platform to the exit.

"And if we can help Miss Cousture in her project of exposing Cream, so much the better for us," he said once we'd gone through the ticket gate. "Tomorrow I'll be with Isabel. I want you to go to Alexandra Park. There's a race meet at noon. Find Gullen and take him along, offer him a couple of shillings. See if he can identify the burglars. You remember the description of Paddler Bill? Big red-headed fellow with an American accent. He's the leader. Follow him. Find out where he lives. If he's not there, see if Gullen can recognize any of the others. Take Neddy as well. You'll look like a father and son on a jaunt."

"Will do, sir."

"And Norman. Please be careful. My sister and I are lucky to be alive. If there's a hint of danger, get Neddy away. Don't let them find you out."

Chapter Thirty-Two

❖———❖———————————————————————❖———❖

NEDDY AND GULLEN WERE BOTH HAPPY ENOUGH
to come with me to the Frying Pan, and the three of us
took the crowded train up to Alexandra Park the next morning. Outside the station was a protest by the National Anti-
Gambling League: two men and a dozen women holding
placards saying "Betting degrades manhood!" "Racing leads
to ruin!" and other well-intended half-truths. As we passed
them, a man with bushy whiskers accosted me.

"How dare you take a child in there, sir!" he barked. He
wore a new satin top-hat; his shoes had a high sheen.

Neddy stared in fear at this angry gent.

"You'll infect your son with the same degeneracy as has in-
fected all these thousands of fools come to throw away their
wages," the gent continued, holding my arm. "Be responsible,
sir. Do not introduce an impressionable mind to this vice."

Three of the women had now also gathered around us.

"Shame on you," declared one.

"Take the boy home," demanded another.

"He should be in school!" cried the first.

I took Neddy's hand and pulled away. We entered the
ground as the first race was starting. It was packed out. Neddy

jumped up and down in the crowd, trying to get a glimpse of the horses, but the press of bodies was too dense, and the boy was just too small. There was a roar as the horses came down the back straight, then it was over. Tickets were ripped and dropped on the floor; knots of men turned back to the beer counters.

"Where'd you see them last time?" I asked Gullen.

"I always stand over there, to the right of the grandstand," he said, pointing at the other side of the crowd. "Not so many people there, and the trees don't block the traps. That's where they usually are."

It took us ten minutes to get through the mess of men, most of them already half-drunk, talking loudly, checking their papers before the next race. Finally, we reached the other side of the grandstand where there was a long beer counter. Men were sat on benches between the counter and the bookies' stalls. Gullen pointed. Over there by the bins," he said, pulling his cap low over his face lest they recognize him.

They were exactly as George had described. The tall one had to be Paddler Bill. Beneath his black cap a great bush of red hair fell out, mixing in with his thick beard. His laughter pealed out over the babble of men's voices. Next to him, studying a paper, was a broad man with a neat black beard, a derby on his head, a new-looking three-piece suit. Talking to them was a nasty-looking fellow with long yellow hair, his trousers too long for him and dragging on the ground. A chill ran through me to lay eyes on them.

"What's up?" asked Gullen.

"Nothing."

Another joined them with four tankards in his hand. He wore a brown suit, a red neck-handkerchief tucked into his shirt. Bill took his pint and wandered over to the bookmakers to lay a bet.

"How about that pint then?" asked Gullen.

We got ourselves a drink, then found a place on the far side where we could keep an eye on the Fenians. Neddy ran off when the next race began so as to squeeze through to the front. We finished our pints.

"I couldn't have that two shillings, could I?" asked Gullen. I handed them over.

"Do you need me any more?" he asked.

"Thanks, mate. You can go home."

He screwed his face up and looked at the bar. "I might stay. You ready for another?"

The gang were there all afternoon. One or other of them would go to the beer counter or the bookmakers or the pisser and then come back. Watching them was easy; they didn't even know we were there. We were just a couple of men and a boy amongst thousands. Gullen stayed with me, out of sight behind a post. It turned out he wasn't as bad as he looked. Good company, in fact.

"You ever need some help, I'd be happy to oblige," he said later in the afternoon. We'd just picked up another pint.

"I'll tell the guvnor."

"Must be an interesting life you have. I've read all the Sherlock Holmes adventures. He's a wonder, all right. Pretty much a genius."

"I'd keep that to yourself if you want to work with us again," I told him. "The guvnor can't abide Sherlock Holmes."

After the last race, the Fenians made their way to the exit with the rest of the crowd. We followed them to the train, making sure to keep back, and pushed our way onto the same carriage. Gullen left us at Kings Cross to take a different line home, while Neddy and me followed them onto the Metropolitan Line. This time we were more careful, getting into the next carriage and watching them through the joining doors. They were in good spirits, talking madly, laughing, throwing their hands in the air. It looked like maybe some of them had come out ahead at the races. Anyways, they weren't looking for anyone following them. They all got down at Westbourne Park and crossed the canal to a pub. I parked Neddy outside, telling him to follow the big red-haired fellow should he come out. Once inside, I took a pint and sat on a bench on the other side of the room. It was early evening now, and there were about twenty or thirty others in there. A bookie made his rounds, the Fenians took out a few more bets with him, then in came the winkle seller and I had myself a pot of eel jelly. Nobody took no notice of me. Presently two ladies came in, both with flowery summer bonnets and bustled petticoat skirts. All heads turned their way. Paddler Bill stood.

"Polly! Mary! Come over here while I get you a drink."

The ladies laughed and pushed their way through to the Fenians' table where they were greeted with hugs and kisses from the men. The noise grew.

Soon the black-bearded man left. I took myself another drink, and, as I turned back from the bar, the door swung open. There in the doorway, in the same tattered winter coat, stood the other man we'd been looking for all these weeks. His face was pinched and wet with sweat, his oily grey hair stuck on his forehead. In his hand he clutched *The Times*. It was the man who'd killed Martha.

I didn't know for sure if he'd got a look at me that day I chased him, and for a moment I froze. My hand reached for the cosh in my pocket, then I edged behind a big coalman, trying to put another body between us. The killer's eyes swept the room. They fell on me and he seemed to wonder about something. I was ready to make a dash for it out the door to the saloon bar when he frowned and looked away, his eyes finally resting on the gang. I breathed again.

He pushed through the other drinkers to the Fenians and threw the paper onto their table. I couldn't hear what he said, but Bill took up the paper and examined it. He frowned and spoke, angry as hell. He hurled the paper down. They bolted their whiskies, collected their hats, and left the pub, Polly and Mary protesting the end of their party.

I took my empty pot up to the bar and on my way back glanced at the paper left on the table. On the front page was the headline: *Sir Herbert Venning Murdered!*

I found Neddy outside and we followed the gang, keeping a long way back this time. Although the streets were busy enough with omnibuses and wagons and folk trudging home from work, it was getting more likely we'd be spotted. It would only take one of them to recognize us from the races to make them suspicious.

Soon they stopped outside a small shop called Gaunt's Booksellers. We watched from a doorway further down the street as the man who'd killed Martha pulled out his keys and opened the door. They filed in and the door was shut. A lamp came on in the upper window. A few minutes later a potboy trundled along the street; I asked him who kept the bookshop.

"That's John Gaunt's shop, sir," he said.

"Is he Irish?"

"Most of us is Irish here, sir."

"Is there an alley behind there?"

"Not as I know," said the lad as he pushed his cart away.

It was getting dark. We moved to the other side of the

street, where we hid under the stairs of a lawyers' office for an hour before Paddler Bill came out again. When he turned at the end of the street, Neddy chased after him and waited for me at the corner.

"He went down the other street, there," he said pointing.

"Go on then."

He hurried to the next corner and waited for me again. We carried on this way for another five minutes before we saw Bill pull out his keys and let himself into a tall house right opposite a school.

It was dark now. We hid ourselves behind a brick gatepost in the schoolyard. Dim lights were on in three of the four front rooms, and soon the flicker of a gaslight came on in the basement too. We waited for another half hour but nothing changed: it looked like Paddler Bill was in for the night.

I stood up. All day I'd been thinking about the guvnor and his meeting with Isabel. I was afraid that by now he'd be miserable and in need of a helping hand.

"Let's get going, lad," I said. "I've got to get back to see Mr. Arrowood."

"But he might come out again, Mr. Barnett," replied Neddy, looking up at me. I could see a little twinkle of light in his eyes.

"So he might, but we've got to get home."

"I'll stay, sir."

"No, Neddy. You come with me. I don't want you left out here on your own."

"But I done it scores of times! And didn't you say I was all trained up?"

"I know, but—"

"You can trust me, sir." His face was serious. He shoved

his hands in his coat pockets. "I won't let anyone see me. It ain't dangerous."

"I don't think so."

"Please, Mr. Barnett. Honest, I'll be all right. Please."

I looked around, thinking about what the guvnor had said about Neddy wanting to please him. I could see how important it was to the lad to stay. The street was quiet. It didn't look like anything else would happen tonight.

"All right, lad," I told him. "He's probably gone to bed, but you might as well wait and see if anyone else comes to see him. If nothing happens in half an hour, come home. But be extra careful. Don't take no chances. Don't go following anyone this time. Stay hidden here in the shadows and don't let anybody see you." I squatted down so I was on his level and gripped his shoulder. He looked at me serious. "Can I count on you not to take no chances?"

"I'll be real careful, sir. He won't know as I'm here."

"Promise me you won't follow no one."

"I promise." A serious look came over his face. "Mr. Barnett?"

"What is it?"

"D'you think they killed Terry?"

"No, matey. We found Terry yesterday, down in Sussex. I forgot to tell you that, didn't I? He's safe and well. Working in a bakehouse."

"So we solved the case?"

"Almost. We've just a few ends to tie up."

He nodded, very serious. My knees were starting to pain me, so I stood up again, flicking his cap as I did so.

"Couldn't you get a smaller one?" I asked. "This is for a man."

"I like it."

"It's too big for you. And it's torn."

"It's better than yours, sir," he said. His little face was offended.

I laughed.

"Come see us at Lewis's house tomorrow," I told him.

I bought him a hot potato from round the corner, gave him his bus fare, then left him crouched in the schoolyard, chewing on the skin of the spud.

Chapter Thirty-Three

— ◆ — ——————————————— — ◆ —

I REACHED THE HOUSE AFTER TEN THAT NIGHT.
Lewis answered the door; Ettie stood behind him in the small
hallway.

"He didn't return from dinner," he said, standing aside
to let me in. The corridor was dim: only one of the gas taps
was working. While it was warm enough outside, here in his
house it was cold.

"When did you last see him?" asked Ettie.

"Yesterday," I said. "When we came back from Sussex."

"Do you think he's still with her?"

I shook my head. "Can't see where they'd go for so long,
Ettie. She's no place in London, and she never approved of
pubs."

She gripped her hands one over the other.

"Oh dear. You don't think Cream's found him, do you?"

"Let me check the Hog," I said. "If Isabel told him she isn't
coming back, he'll have gone there. He'll be half-drowned
in gin by now."

"Shall I come?" asked Lewis.

"There's no need."

Ettie took my hand. "You look tired. Do you want something to eat?"

"I'm all right. I'd best be off and find him."

"Thank you, Norman. We'll wait up for you."

The truth was I was tired. The Hog was a half-hour walk from Lewis's house, and I was wore out. Though the swelling in my arm had mostly gone down, it started up aching again in the evenings. I needed another dose of Black Drop but knew it would make me want my bed even more than I already did.

The Hog was busy, the air thick with beer fumes and smoke. Most of them were drunk, a funeral crowd, all in black, all ages from toddlers to grandparents. They must have been drinking for hours. Two of the young lads were being held down on the benches and were struggling, glaring at each other across the room, red-faced and cursing, their shirtfronts torn. One of them had a bloody nose. A tiny old woman with hair down to her waist was standing on a table singing a hymn, a quart of gin in her hand. A boy who couldn't have been more than twelve lay under the table, a puddle of vomit by his lips.

The landlady I'd seen last time stood serving.

"Mr. Arrowood?" I asked.

Without speaking, she lifted the hatch and pointed at a door behind the bar. It led to a dark corridor lined with crates and barrels. I made my way down until I heard voices in a room at the end. I pushed open the door.

A middle-aged woman sat in her undergarments on the edge of a filthy mattress. Her hair was grey and curled, her lips painted red.

"We're busy in here, my dear," she said, peering at me with a crooked smile.

A single tallow candle flickered on the washstand, where a bottle of gin stood half-drunk.

The guvnor lay on the mattress, the great mound of his belly flesh spurled with black hairs, his breasts drooping to either side of his ribs. His trousers lay on the floor in a pile; his undergarments, grey and patched, were still where they should be. I was spared that; I was not spared his stink.

His eyes were shut, his mouth open. On the floor beside the bed was the red velvet case he'd showed me on the train.

"If it's business you're after, you can wait out front," the woman explained, her voice croaked but friendly. "I've got my hands full as you might see with this gentleman here right now."

"Is he asleep?"

Hearing my voice, he grunted.

The woman stood.

"Go on, darling," she said, pushing me out. "I'll be there in half an hour."

"No, mum," I said. "I'm here for Mr. Arrowood. I'm here to take him home. I'm his assistant, Barnett. You're Betts, are you?"

"That's me, my dear. He told you about me, did he?"

"Sure he did."

"Well." She screwed up her face and thought. "He ain't paid me yet, that's the thing."

"How much?"

"A crown."

I bent for his trousers and found a coin.

"Guvnor!" I said, shaking his shoulder. "Home time!"

He made a noise that sounded like a curse, then rolled over to face the wall.

"Come on, get up!"

"He's been in here since two," said Betts. She nodded at the gin. "That's the second bottle."

She helped me get him dressed, then the both of us got him up on his feet. When she was looking the other way, I scooped up the jewellery box and dropped it in my pocket. It was an effort, but we managed to walk him through the pub to the street, one of us on each arm. She hailed a passing cab. We squeezed him in.

He vomited just as we turned into Lewis's road, all over his shirtfront and the floor of the cab. The driver was fuming when we stopped outside the house.

"That's the third time this week I've had to clean out the cab for folk throwing up in there!" he complained. "I can't get the blooming stink off of my hands neither."

"Sorry about that, mate," I said. "You couldn't give me a hand to get him out before he does it again, could you?"

"Have to pay a boy tuppence to clean it for me, so I will. Can't stomach it again, no way."

"Help me get him out, will you, mate?" I asked again.

He stood his ground on the pavement. He was old and scrawny, and he looked like there was no pleasure anywhere for him in life.

"Give me an extra tuppence first," he said.

It was only when I'd coughed up that he helped me lug the guvnor out the carriage and onto Lewis's front step.

When I got back the next morning, the guvnor was sat in the parlour. He held a sheet of brown paper soaked in vinegar to his head; on his knee was a mixing bowl. His face was white, his hand trembled. Lewis sat opposite him with the newspaper, his black waistcoat unbuttoned. His one good sleeve had an elastic armband above the elbow, as if he was a croupier.

"A cup of tea, Norman?" asked Ettie. She wore her Sunday

best: a blue silk dress tight at the waist. Her hair had a high cushion. She touched me on the shoulder and smiled.

"Yes, please, Ettie."

"And for you, Lewis?"

"That would be perfect, Ettie. There are some biscuits in the kitchen."

"Extra sugar for me, please, Sister," said the guvnor in a weak voice.

She glared at him.

"Has Neddy been yet?" I asked.

"We haven't seen him," replied Ettie. "Perhaps he's at church."

"If he is, it'll be the Unitarian. Minister there gives out thruppence each to those that need it. Second Sunday each month."

I said it quite hopeful, trying to persuade myself there was nothing to worry over. I'd started wondering as I walked home last night whether I should have left the boy there on his own. Maybe I wasn't in a proper state to make that decision, what with all the ale and the Black Drop I'd had to keep me going, but Neddy knew all the tricks. He'd kept watch for us many times and we'd taught him how to keep hidden, how to keep quiet. I looked at the carriage clock on the mantel: it was still early.

When Ettie left the room to make the tea, the guvnor turned to me.

"What happened yesterday, Barnett?"

When I'd told him everything, he said, "You should never have left him there." His voice was weak with sickness. "Not after last time."

"He always does it safely."

"Not last time. You should have stayed yourself."

"I would have if I didn't have to come and pull you out of the mire," I said sharply.

"I didn't need your help last night," he snapped.

We glared at each other.

"Anyways, I'm sure he'll be here soon," I said.

"I hope you're right, Barnett."

We didn't speak for a few minutes. Finally, Lewis broke the silence.

"So, the one who killed the girl is with the Fenians?"

"Looks like it," I replied. "But there's something else going on. You know I saw him with Coyle the other day? One of the SIB officers that took us in? They were very friendly, I'll tell you that."

"The one who gave you a hiding?" asked Lewis.

"The same."

"Oh dear. I wonder where his loyalties lie?"

Ettie came in with the tea tray.

"William told me of your trip to Hassocks," she said, handing me a cup. "You had no inkling that Miss Cousture was a whore?"

"None. Not I nor William."

She frowned.

"This house she lives in. This shelter for unmarried women. Where did you say it was?"

"Lorrimore Road. Behind Kennington Park."

"Is there a plaque of any kind by the door?"

"Just the letters CSJ."

"Christian Sanctuary and Justice," she declared, passing a cup to Lewis but not her brother. "We left a girl with them only last week. It's a sanctuary for fallen women. Run by a very earnest young man, Reverend Jebb."

"For God's sake!" exclaimed the guvnor, suddenly coming to life. "Why the blazes didn't you tell us this before?"

"I didn't know she was there."

"Oh, Ettie!" he spluttered. "We could have done with that information some time ago!"

She ignored him, turning to me. "Well, it does make sense now that we know her history. Tell me, what happened yesterday at the races?"

She listened carefully as I described what we'd seen at Alexandra Park and the pub.

"The news of Venning's death was a surprise to them, you say?" she asked.

"They were enjoying themselves proper till he came in and showed them the newspaper."

"And you say they were angry?"

"Paddler Bill had a barney when he saw it."

"Of course he did," said Lewis, helping himself to a handful of Peak Freans from the tray. "Sir Herbert's an important man. The police will put extra men on the case. The papers are going to be following it. The Fenians won't want all that attention, that's for sure. It endangers their operation."

"Nolan says they've been burgling embassies and the like before this," I said. "Didn't do them no harm then."

Lewis put a whole biscuit in his mouth and began to chew.

"True," he said. "But this is the murder of a high government official."

"You're right, Lewis," said the guvnor, serving himself a cup of tea from the tray. He was beginning to get a bit of colour back. "But there's another reason they're angry. Longmire lied to us about his affair with Martha and about the bullet. He didn't want us to think it was important. The rifles Thierry found must have come from the War Office. Nobody else has these new Enfields. When we confronted Longmire with the bullet he went first to Cream and then to Venning."

"He said he wanted advice from his friend about the blackmail," I said.

"But who better to supply the rifles than the Quartermaster General? Now, my friends, if this is true, why else would Paddler Bill be angry that Venning was dead?"

"The Fenians are buying the rifles from Cream?" suggested Ettie.

"Precisely," said the guvnor.

"But where does the burglary fit in?" I asked.

"I don't know, Barnett. I just don't know."

"Why are they buying rifles now?" asked Ettie. "The bombing campaign ended ten years ago."

"Not all of them wanted to go with the Parnellites," said Lewis, lighting a cigar. "Some of them don't believe a political solution will ever come. They've seen the Home Rule bills defeated in Parliament, that's why they split off from the organization. And it isn't the first time they've tried to seize weapons from the army. There was Chester Barracks."

"Yes," agreed the guvnor. "And Clerkenwell—destined for a fighting force in Ireland. We can assume they've been buying rifles from Cream, and they want more."

"They're planning an uprising," said Lewis.

"And Venning's death cuts the supply line," added the guvnor.

We sat and thought on that for a while. Ettie poured herself another cup of tea and sat chewing a biscuit.

"Is Cream a Fenian?" she asked at last.

"Cream isn't political," said the guvnor. "He's only interested in money. He's a hereditary criminal, Ettie. Four years ago I made it my business to find out about him. His father killed his mother for an insurance policy when he was a child. The man was hanged for it. Cream was raised by his mother's brother, a minister. But crime was his inheritance."

"I don't believe that theory," replied Ettie. "The bible tells us each person must choose their path."

"No, Ettie. Crime is born into Cream's instinct so strongly that he must follow it, and with it comes a wild animal talent. Crime's as natural to him as killing rabbits to a hawk."

"But that means he isn't responsible," protested Ettie.

"I'm not saying he mustn't be punished, Sister."

There was a knock at the door.

I jumped up, hoping it was Neddy. When I opened the door, the street was empty but for a boy running away towards the synagogue. An envelope addressed to the guvnor lay on the mat.

I knew it was bad as I handed it to him. He tore it open. As he read it, dread appeared in his eyes. He groaned, crushing the letter in his fist.

I took it from him and read.

Mr. Arrowood,
I trust you have recovered from the conflagration? If you want the boy back, bring the Frenchman tomorrow midnight to Issler's Warehouse. Park St. Next to Potts Vinegar. If you do not come, the boy will die. If you bring police, the boy will die.
With respect, your most faithful friend.

I sat heavily on the chair, my strength gone, my head swirling.

"What is it?" asked Ettie. "What's happened?"

"They have Neddy," I heard the guvnor say. His voice came from far away.

"Who has Neddy?"

"Cream."

Ettie gasped. "Again? But how did they get him?"

"The Fenians must have picked him up on the street and passed him to Cream."

I held my head in my hands. It was my fault. What was I thinking of, leaving him there like that? What sort of bloody fool would do such a thing? What with the Black Drop and the beer I hadn't looked out for the boy as I should. I was weak. It was my fault.

The room was silent. I couldn't look at them; I'd have been grateful if the Lord had struck me down right then and there.

"It was me," I said, my head clasped in my hands. I didn't want the guvnor to protect me from what I'd done. "It was my fault. I left him keeping watch."

"Oh, Norman," said Ettie. "You didn't! How could you leave that child in danger?"

I couldn't answer her. I stared at the fringe of the carpet, disgusted with myself. A fury was rising in me.

"But what do they want?" asked Lewis.

"They want Thierry," said the guvnor. He placed the bowl on the floor and stood, peeling the paper from his forehead.

"We must get Inspector Petleigh," said Ettie. "He can search the Barrel of Beef."

"They won't be holding Neddy there," said the guvnor. "Or at the cooperage, or Milky Sal's. Cream knows they might be searched."

"Will they hurt him?"

The guvnor said nothing. I rose from the chair, my mind flooded with the hideous memory of the copper's body.

As I spoke, I could hear the words tremble in my throat.

"I need a pistol, Lewis."

Lewis nodded and stepped over to the cabinet.

"No, Norman," said the guvnor. "What do you think you'll do with a pistol?"

"He'll tell me where Neddy is if his life depends on it."

"Who? Cream? You'll be killed before you even get up-stairs!"

"This is my fault. I'm going to fix it."

"Lewis, do not give him a pistol."

Lewis looked from me to the guvnor.

I stormed out of the room and down to the kitchen. There I found a bread knife. The three of them were in the hallway as I returned.

"Stop, Norman!" said the guvnor, trying to hold on to my coat. I pushed past him and gained the front door.

"Norman!" cried Ettie. "Please, wait!"

I ignored her. When I got outside I opened my legs to run, but just as I took the first leap my foot was wrenched from under me. I crashed down onto the pavement, right on my smashed-up arm. From the ground I looked back to see Ettie holding one end of an umbrella, the handle hooked around my ankle. Quick as I could I freed myself and was scrambling to get up when she threw herself on top of me.

"Stop resisting me," she said in my ear, her voice hard. "You'll be killed, and that wouldn't help the boy."

I lay there, sick at the pain in my arm and the shame at what I'd done.

"You've been a fool, Norman," she said, the whole length of her body on top of mine. "You cannot make amends by being an even bigger one."

When she saw the fight was gone out of me, she took the knife and raised herself. Lewis helped me to my feet.

"I'll go and see Neddy's mother," said Ettie. "She'll be worrying again."

"Thank you, Sister," said the guvnor. "Come, Norman. Let's walk. We must think of a plan."

He picked up his walking stick and stuck his hat on his head.

"We have to get him back, William," I murmured as we gained the street. My eyes were fixed on my feet: I couldn't look up for shame.

"I know, Norman."

It was Sunday morning. The shops and pubs were shut. The sound of bells from the neighbourhood churches filled the air, quarrelling with each other happily in the breeze. Families in their best marched down the street, returning from church, visiting. Except for his wheezing, the guvnor was silent, thinking as we walked.

The memory of the poor lad in the Betsy case came back to me, the innocent lad caught up in something that wasn't his business and losing his leg for it. I thought of Neddy's dirty little face and his eagerness to help and I never felt more sick of myself as I did right then. We walked up Blackfriars, then along the river by the cranes of Bankside, where the lighters and barges were moored. It was their day off too.

Finally, Arrowood spoke.

"Neddy must have told them we've found Thierry."

"And he wouldn't have told them unless…" I couldn't bring myself to finish it.

The guvnor sighed. "We must give them Thierry. There's no other way."

"He'll never agree to come back. It'd be suicide."

"He might, if we can convince him it's safe. We'll get Petleigh to be there with some officers. How can he refuse to help save the life of a child?"

We walked on in silence. As we approached Southwark Bridge, he spoke again.

"Miss Cousture must bring him back. Remember, her case is not finished. She wants to bring Cream to justice. Perhaps this is her chance."

"But we've got nothing on Cream. Terry's the only one who could give evidence, and all he knows is they had rifles in the cellar. We've got nothing."

"Cream's kidnapped Neddy. Petleigh can arrest him for that. And one of those girls from Milky Sal's might give evidence that she was imprisoned."

"They'll charge Long Lenny or Boots or Milky Sal. Not Cream. They never get Cream."

We walked on down Southwark Bridge Road. In the recreation ground on Newington Causeway, children were playing. Men were selling spice cakes and sherbets. Outside the Elephant and Castle station, a boy had a stack of *Daily News*. The guvnor was deep in thought.

"Latest on the Venning murder!" cried the boy in his high-pitched voice. "Get your latest here!"

The guvnor fished in his pocket for a coin.

"Perhaps there's some new information," he said, taking the paper.

As we walked away, the boy struck up his pitch again.

"Get your latest on the Venning murder! Sherlock Holmes to help the police! Latest on the Venning case!"

The guvnor reacted on instinct. He spun around, raising his walking stick, his eyeglasses falling to the pavement.

"Stop shouting, you little cur!" he cried. His face, quite pale until now, was purple. The veins stood out in his temples. "Stop! D'you think we're all interested in Sherlock Holmes?"

The boy crouched behind his pile of newspapers, his arms

covering his head. The guvnor took a swipe at the stack, sending the top copies flying into the road. He swiped again. An infant in a perambulator began to shriek in terror.

"Control yourself, sir!" ordered a gentleman stepping down from a cab. "Leave the boy alone!"

I pulled a tuppence from my pocket and dropped it in the boy's pocket. "Get up, lad. We're sorry for scaring you. The gent's got a bad head, is all. Shouting at everyone today."

No sooner had we crossed the road than the guvnor turned on me.

"How dare they bring in that charlatan! We've been on this case for weeks! When I see Petleigh I'll throttle him. I swear, Barnett, I'll throttle him. But we'll get there before Sherlock Holmes. I swear we will!"

We took a turn into the park and crossed to the other side. The guvnor now looked morose.

"What did Isabel say, William?" I asked.

He swung his stick, cracking it against the railings.

"She wants to marry a lawyer she's met in Cambridge," he replied, his voice clear and exact. "She wishes us to divorce and for me to sell my rooms and give her half of the proceeds."

"Christ. Is there no persuading her?"

"We will see," he replied, cracking his walking stick hard on the railings again. "We will see."

Chapter Thirty-Four

AS WE APPROACHED MISS COUSTURE'S LODGINGS, A
minister was walking ahead of us. He reached the house before us, turned up the path and inserted a key into the door.

When he saw us, he smiled.

"Good day, gentlemen. I presume you are Mr. Arrowood
and Mr. Barnett?"

He was a young man, thin and earnest, his black topper well
worn, his white collar high up his long neck. In one hand he
clasped a bible held shut with a brass clasp.

"Yes, sir," replied the guvnor. "And who are you?"

"Reverend Josiah Jebb. We've been expecting you." He
opened the door wide and stepped aside. "Come in, please."

"Miss Cousture has spoken to you?"

"Indeed she has."

He led us into the parlour and invited us to sit.

"I'll get Caroline. She's anxious to talk to you."

Outside the sky was low with thick grey cloud, and little
light made its way through the heavy red curtains. The same
piano stood in the corner, the same sofa along the wall, the
same silver Christ nailed to the wall. We sat in the same two
ragged chairs.

Presently Miss Cousture entered the room and greeted us. She wore a simple black dress over which was a white pinafore. Her hair was gathered up inside a white headscarf.

The minister followed, he standing up straight and holy by the fireplace, she sitting on the same orange wing chair as before.

"May I ask the name of your church, Reverend?" said the guvnor.

"We're not a church. We're a mission called Christian Sanctuary and Justice. We rescue women who've been ill-treated. We offer them a chance to make a new life for the glory of the Lord."

"I haven't heard of your mission."

"That's how we prefer it, sir. Some of our womenfolk have escaped from dangerous persons who would have them back."

He looked at me, then at the guvnor.

"Reverend, I hope you don't mind, but we need to speak to Miss Cousture urgently on some rather sensitive personal business," said the guvnor. "Would you allow us a few minutes of conversation?"

"Reverend Jebb knows everything," said Miss Cousture. Her French accent was now so soft I could barely make it out. "You can speak in front of him."

The guvnor nodded slowly. "Well then, Miss Cousture. We've found your brother."

Her eyes fell to her hands clasped on her white apron.

"I know," she replied softly. "He came yesterday."

"Miss Cousture, you've told us lie after lie. Why didn't you tell us what you wanted from this case from the beginning? It would have made everything more straightforward."

"Because you wouldn't have taken it," she declared. She looked at him calmly. "Everyone knows how dangerous Stanley Cream is. Who would tackle him? Even the police leave him alone. Mr. Arrowood, I confess I've used you, but what choice did I have?"

"We thought it best," said Reverend Jebb.

"Josiah wanted me to go to Sherlock Holmes, but I chose you instead."

This gratified the guvnor, and his stern face melted. He glanced at me, making sure I'd heard it, then sat back, crossing his stumpy legs one over the other.

"My dear lady, I'm flattered that you put your trust in me."

She continued as if he hadn't spoken: "I thought Holmes would find Thierry too quick, and then we wouldn't learn enough about Stanley Cream and his business."

At first the guvnor didn't see what she was saying, but soon enough his face pinched up again. He got to his feet.

"You mean to say you employed us because you didn't think we'd find him?" he exclaimed.

"No, no, Mr. Arrowood," said the minister. "She means that with fewer resources at your disposal you'd have to gather more information about Cream's network before you could locate Thierry. That is the information we wanted."

The guvnor looked suspiciously at Miss Cousture.

"Yes," she agreed. "That was it. Please sit, Mr. Arrowood."

He crossed his arms over his belly and considered it, his face like a babe about to weep.

"Why didn't you tell Thierry that Martha was dead?" he asked at last.

"I was afraid he'd come back here for vengeance," she replied. "He would have got killed. But now he's angry with me for not telling him."

"We have a problem, miss," I said. "Cream's taken our

lad, Neddy. He wants to swap him for Thierry and he's set a meeting for tomorrow night. He's threatened to kill the boy."

Her brow tensed. She glanced at the minister.

"Who's Neddy?" she asked. "Your son?"

"He's a boy we use for keeping a watch on people," I said. "We got to get him back, miss. He's only ten years old."

"You've been using a child to watch criminals?" asked Reverend Jebb.

"I assure you it's quite normal," said the governor. "Sherlock Holmes has a whole band of them working for him."

"But how could you let him get caught?" demanded Miss Cousture.

"It just happened," I said. "This hasn't been an easy case."

"I didn't pay you to send a child after criminals!" she exclaimed, her eyes wide with anger. "*Mon Dieu!* How could you do this?"

"Listen," I said, irritated with her for getting on her high horse after all the lies she'd told us. "We're worried half to death about him. It'll do no good your telling us we made a mistake. We did. We made a bad mistake, but we need your help to save him."

"Miss Cousture," continued the guvnor firmly. "We need you to go down to Sussex and persuade Thierry to come back immediately. The meeting is tomorrow at midnight. Tell him there's no danger: we'll only pretend to give him up. Inspector Petleigh will be waiting nearby with his constables and they'll intervene once Neddy has been produced. But you must persuade him to come. Tell him we're going to bring Martha's killer to justice. We only need to get Cream to admit he ordered the murder while Petleigh's listening. That'll be enough evidence to charge him."

"What if he doesn't admit it?" asked Jebb.

"Then we encourage him to talk about the rifles, or Sir Herbert, or the girls he sells. It's all we can do. If he speaks in front of police witnesses we can use it as evidence in court. Even if he doesn't talk, he can be arrested for imprisoning Neddy."

"I can't do it," declared Miss Couture suddenly.

"What?" cried the guvnor. "But you must try!"

She shook her head.

"Thierry left on the midday boat. He's on his way back to France. He'd stay for Martha, but not for me. Not after what I did."

The guvnor groaned and slapped his forehead. He began to pace the room, his brow knitted in thought.

"We must send a telegram immediately," he said at last.

"He hasn't gone to Rouen," she replied. "He's gone to Paris. I don't know where."

"Then you must follow him."

"I'd never find him. Where would I start?"

"Damnation!" cried the guvnor, stamping his foot.

"Mr. Arrowood," said the minister. "I would ask you not to curse in our house."

"But we need him! How else can we save Neddy?"

"What I don't understand is why he wants Thierry so bad," I said, looking at Miss Couture's sad face for a clue. "He only saw the guns. He's gone off and disappeared and hasn't caused them any trouble since. I just can't see it. He doesn't know enough to be a danger. There's something else you haven't told us, miss, that's what I think."

Her mouth fell open, revealing her one chipped tooth. She shook her head.

"I don't know why he wants Thierry," she said.

"Cream's trying to tie up the ends, Barnett," said the guvnor. "My guess is that he wishes to do away with anybody who knows about the rifles. It would explain Martha, the SIB man, Sir Herbert." His nose twitched; he looked uneasy. "Thierry's next."

"And us?" I asked.

The guvnor nodded. "All three of us, Barnett. And we'll all be there tomorrow."

"You mean he'll try to kill you all tomorrow?" demanded the minister.

The guvnor took a deep breath. "I think so," he whispered.

"You cannot take that risk."

"We must try and save Neddy."

"But what are we going to do without Thierry?" I asked.

The guvnor continued to pace, his back bent, muttering something under his breath. He glared at me, at the minister, and Miss Cousture in turn. The three of us kept quiet. He would stop, open his mouth, then shake his head and begin to pace again.

Finally, he straightened his back.

"You must come tomorrow, Miss Cousture. You must pretend you have Thierry hidden nearby. Tell them you'll bring him when we see that Neddy's safe."

"That will put her in danger," said the minister.

"It's all right, Josiah," she said. "I've put everybody else in danger. It's my turn."

"I'll get Longmire and Paddler Bill there as well," said the guvnor. "The more confusion there is, the more chance we have to avoid being killed, and the more chance they'll say something that can be used for evidence."

"Or the more dangerous it is for us," I said.

"It's all or nothing now, Barnett."

"Yes," said Miss Cousture. "It's our only chance."

The guvnor turned to her. "How do you know Colonel Longmire?" he asked suddenly.

"I don't."

"What's the point in denying it?"

He paused. She looked at him calmly.

"We're at the end of the game, Miss Cousture. Don't you owe us honesty now?"

Still she didn't reply.

"We might be killed," he whispered.

She said nothing.

"I see," said the guvnor. "So you won't tell us."

"No, sir."

The guvnor picked up his walking stick and hat.

"We'll pick you up at nine fifteen tomorrow. Be ready."

Back at Lewis's house the guvnor explained what we were going to do. He sent two messages. To Longmire he wrote:

Bring £25 to Issler's Warehouse, Park St., at ten minutes past midnight tomorrow. Tell nobody. Come alone. If you are not there, if you are not alone, or if we hear you have told Cream about this meeting, our information will be on the desk of the Pall Mall Gazette by midday.

He signed it: *Locksher.*

To Paddler Bill, he wrote:

You have an SIB informant in your organization. Be at Issler's Warehouse, Park St., at ten minutes past midnight tomorrow. Bring all your men but do not tell them the purpose. Bring £25 and the traitor will be revealed.

I got myself over to Park Street to have a look at the warehouse. It being Sunday, all the businesses were shut and the street was quiet. The warehouse was between a vinegar works and the Crosse and Blackwell pickle factory. It was derelict, its doors and windows charred from a recent fire. The wide entrance was locked, the windows boarded up. Round the back an alley ran from the chimney of Barclay Perkins brewery along the yards of all the warehouses. I hoicked myself over the fence into Issler's yard. There were a few outbuildings— storage sheds and workshops—and a couple of big doorways into the warehouse as a horse and wagon could fit through.

I stood in the yard feeling numb, like there was an extra distance between me and everything around. I knew I had a job to do but my mind kept turning to Neddy, wondering what they'd done to him, wondering how he was. Thinking about it made me sick, made me weak. Staring up at the grey sky, I fought against it.

I got out my betty and had the lock open quick. The air smelled of smoke. I lit up my lantern: it was a wide open space, with hundreds of barrels of all different sizes stored there, from small pins and firkins to beer barrels, hogsheads and butts, and tuns the size of haystacks. Above was a balcony that went around the four walls. More barrels were stacked there. In one corner, built under the balcony, were a couple of office rooms with open windows onto the warehouse floor. Pigeons were nesting high above in the rafters, where watery moonlight found its way through holes in the roof. The walls were stained with smoke; the floor was strewn with ash. The barrels must have been put in since the fire, since there were no signs of charring or soot on them.

I called out Neddy's name a few times, but the only noise I could hear was the pigeons shuffling in the roof. I walked about, my steps echoing around the high walls, looking for somewhere Petleigh and his officers could hide. Maybe the outbuildings or the dark spaces between the barrel stacks. Over on one side, separated from the main part of the warehouse by a concrete dyke filled with stagnant water, there were rows of tuns that could each hold a few men standing up.

By the offices I found a hatch in the floor. Underneath was a ladder leading down to a cellar. If there was one thing I never liked it was cellars, but I knew I had to go down for Neddy's sake. I took a big lug of fresh air and climbed down the ladder. At the bottom was a long, low room, cold, dark as the devil's backside and damp-smelling, with piles of rotting rags and spills of oil on the floor. I didn't like it one bit. Before going on I waited, listening. There was only the scratch of rodents and a slow drip somewhere in the blackness. When I was sure I couldn't hear anything else, I hurried the length of it, checking with my lantern in the corners and crevices in case Neddy was down there. It looked like nobody had been there for years.

"We'll get Petleigh in there before they arrive," said the guvnor when I was back at Lewis's. "Cream will be there early, so we must be earlier still. Ask Sidney to come and pick us up at nine. He'll have to wait nearby. We might have to make a run for it."

"It's too dangerous," said Lewis. "There's too many of them, William. You can't rely on the police to protect you."

"We've no choice, Lewis. The police could question Cream but he'll swear he knows nothing about it, and you can be sure they won't have hidden Neddy in the cooperage again. Don't worry, friend. Petleigh's agreed to bring plenty of men."

Lewis sighed. He struggled out of his chair and crossed the parlour to a cabinet. From a drawer he took a cherrywood box. With a small key attached to his watch-chain, he unlocked the box.

"Have you used a pistol before?" he asked me.

I shook my head.

He took out a silver gun and offered it to me. It was heavy and cold, and I felt sick to hold it. He gave another to the guvnor, then explained how to load it, how to hold and take aim, how to fire it.

He asked us to pretend to fire at a bust of Alexander the Great that stood by the door.

"I don't like this, William," he said, wiping the sweat from his head. "You've been a friend for too long. I don't want to lose you."

I didn't like it either, but I said nothing. I didn't know what else we could do.

"We have to get Neddy back," said the guvnor.

Lewis nodded. He turned to me.

"Protect him, Norman."

I hoped he couldn't see the fear in my face.

Chapter Thirty-Five

WHEN WE ARRIVED AT ISSLER'S WAREHOUSE THE doors were still locked. Apart from the brewery at the end of the road, which had lights on inside and smoke rising from its chimney, all the other factories and warehouses were shut up for the night. If there was going to be shooting, nobody was around to hear it.

We left Sidney by the chimney and walked round to the back alley where the guvnor had arranged to meet Petleigh. Reverend Jebb had insisted on coming with us, thinking that Cream might moderate himself in the presence of a holy man. I doubted it, but was happy to have him there. The more of us the better.

Miss Cousture was dressed as a man, in a tattered black suit the minister had found for her. He'd thought it safer somehow. As the guvnor couldn't climb over the fence to the yard, I had to jemmy out a few boards to let him squeeze through. Inside the warehouse I lit a couple of candles to show them the layout. As we walked around, our boots echoing in the great black space, I kept my hand on the cold revolver in my pocket.

"We'll use these barrels over here in the corner for the police," said the guvnor, approaching the rows of tuns stacked on their sides. "Two men can go in each. Even if Cream's men search the place, they won't open all these barrels. Two more can hide in the cellar."

The darkness of the warehouse had silenced Miss Cousture and the Reverend, and they did not speak until we were outside again.

"What do we do now?" asked Miss Cousture. Her voice trembled.

"You two go back and wait with Sidney," replied the guvnor. "We'll join you when Petleigh arrives."

We stood in the alley as they walked away.

"Have you loaded your revolver?" asked the guvnor when they were out of hearing.

"I have."

"Lewis did mine. Here, take these extra bullets just in case."

"I never thought we'd be using guns in our work, William."

"I only wish we'd had them for the Betsy case," he said.

"We still would've got there too late for John Spindle."

He turned to me. His little derby hat sat on his head like a chocolate cake on a pig, and in the moonlight his whiskers seemed to drift around his face in a fog. I could smell wine on his breath. He farted.

"Norman, I wanted to tell you how much I rely on you, how much I've always relied on you. I wanted to tell you I appreciate it before…" He hesitated. "We're a proper team, you and I."

I put my hand on his fat shoulder.

"I know, William. You don't have to say anything."

He offered me a cigar and we had a smoke while we waited. A ragged dog came sniffing around, hoping for a bit of food. Ten o'clock came and went.

"Where the devil is he?" asked the guvnor.

"Are you sure he said ten?"

"Of course I am."

Ten fifteen came. Then ten thirty. There was no sign of Petleigh. The guvnor had been pacing for half an hour.

"What the blazes is he playing at?" he exclaimed, then checked himself and whispered, "If he doesn't come soon they won't be able to take their positions."

Reverend Jebb came running down the alley towards us clutching his hat.

"Is there a problem?" he asked, breathless.

"They aren't here yet," I replied.

"Oh dear, oh dear. What do we do if they don't arrive in time?"

"They'll come," the guvnor assured him. "Petleigh promised me. Now go and wait in the cart with Miss Cousture."

At a quarter to eleven, the alley was still quiet.

"Something must have happened, Norman. I cannot understand why he's not here."

"Maybe they had an accident."

We both gazed down the deserted alley.

"He promised me he'd be here."

"What are we going to do if they don't come?" I whispered. "We'll get no evidence."

"We'll get no protection, more to the point."

"I don't fancy our chances with these revolvers. There'll be too many of them."

He nodded, his face grim. "Damn it, Barnett. We've no choice but to go in without them."

"What'll they do when they find out we don't have Thierry?"

The guvnor took in a long breath of the night air and lit another cigar.

"In the worst case…" he said slowly, "… they'll try to beat his location out of us. Then they'll kill us."

I was scared before, but him saying it like that made it even worse. The guvnor reached into his pocket and offered me his hip flask. I took a couple of good swigs. My hand trembled as I passed it back; his trembled as he took it.

"Damn it!" he said suddenly, the words echoing in the dark alley.

The dog came back and sat looking at me with sorrowful eyes.

"We'll think of something," I said.

"And if we don't," said the guvnor, "we'll have to start shooting."

Just after eleven we heard the big doors at the front of the warehouse slide open and bootsteps echo in the great building. It was Cream and his men. The guvnor took my arm and we moved further down the alley, hiding ourselves behind a great stack of crates. Half eleven arrived and still no Petleigh. I knew then the police weren't coming. The guvnor and me were both keeping quiet now. I was thinking about dying and I suppose he was too. I was ready for it, if it came tonight. You don't know you're dead when you're dead, that's what I was telling myself. What did I have to live for, anyway? A body that was finding it hard to take the beatings these days and a cold and empty room that I didn't want to go back to no more. That was all I had. But even so, I knew I didn't want to die that night. Not there, and not by Cream's men.

As the notes of the midnight bells began to rain down in the streets all around us, we gave up waiting for Petleigh. We collected a couple of lanterns from the cab and walked down to Park Street with Miss Cousture and Reverend Jebb. The guvnor gave them the chance to stay back with Sidney, telling them it was too dangerous without Petleigh and his men, but Miss Cousture wouldn't have it. She wanted to help save Neddy. The minister agreed, but he was rattled. He insisted we stop to pray on the corner. He wanted to know what we were going to do. We couldn't answer him.

"We'll trust in the Lord, then," he said. The authority in his voice that was so clear the day before was gone. The young minister was out of his depth.

Miss Cousture walked next to us as if she was already dead. She didn't speak. Her face was calm under her cloth cap. She didn't even seem to breathe.

All the windows in the factories and warehouses of Park Street were dark, but the bright moon cast a soft glimmer over the cobbles. A carriage was outside Issler's. The guvnor nudged me and pointed: a man stood further down the road. Another lingered in a doorway on the other side.

I knocked on the great warehouse doors. Piser opened them, his cap pulled down low over his eyes. He held a lantern in one hand and a revolver in the other. After peering up and down the street, he stepped aside. Inside, in the middle of the great space, stood Cream, the lantern in his hand lighting up his white topcoat and brown topper. In his hand was an ebony cane. Next to him stood Boots and Long Lenny. Boots also held a revolver; Lenny had a long poker which he tapped on his hand.

"Who are these people, Arrowood?" demanded Cream.

"This is Thierry's sister," declared the guvnor. His voice was altered, like he had a sore throat. "This is our colleague, Reverend Jebb."

"You may leave, Reverend," said Cream.

"No, ah, n-no," spluttered the minister. "I would…p-prefer to stay."

"Lenny," said Cream.

Long Lenny advanced, his boots crunching on the cinders.

"Let's get going, Father," he said, holding his poker out before him.

Reverend Jebb, though tall himself, was not as tall as Long Lenny. He backed away slowly, protesting, until Lenny grabbed hold of his coat and hauled him out the door. Piser banged it shut after him.

"Now to business," said Cream. "Where's Terry?"

"We have him nearby," said the guvnor. "Where's the boy?"

Cream nodded at Boots, who took the lantern and walked across the warehouse. He stopped just before the oily dyke and let the lantern down to the floor. There, curled in a ball, was Neddy, his head covered in his hands. His clothes were wet and filthy. We couldn't see his face, but even from fifty yards we could see he was trembling.

I ran over and picked him up. He groaned as I touched his leg; as soon as I'd got him in my arms he buried his face in my chest.

"It's OK, matey," I whispered, stroking his hair. "I got you now."

I felt a shudder run through his little body. He pushed his face harder into my shirt, but didn't speak. His leg hung at a queer angle over my arm.

"What the hell have you done to him?" said the guvnor.

"Where's Terry?" demanded Cream.

"Once we have the boy out of here we'll bring him," said the guvnor. "Barnett, take Neddy to the cab."

"Don't move," snapped Cream. "I have charge of this situation, not you, Arrowood. The young lady will take Boots to retrieve her brother. We'll wait here."

"Best if I go," said the guvnor. "Thierry might need some encouragement."

"Boots will encourage him," replied Cream with a nasty laugh. "Encouragement is his speciality."

Boots came over, his gun held before him. Miss Cousture looked at the guvnor, unsure what to do.

"I cannot understand why you're so eager to get hold of Thierry, sir," said the guvnor, stepping between Boots and Miss Cousture. "He's no trouble to you: all he's done is see a box of rifles. He's too scared to talk. If you harm him it's only more risk to yourself."

Cream laughed again. He stretched his arms in front of him and walked towards the guvnor.

"Is that what he told you?"

"He did."

"He didn't tell you that he stole a portmanteau from me before he left?"

The guvnor turned to Miss Cousture. She shook her head.

Cream swung his walking stick and continued. "He didn't mention a portmanteau containing over a thousand pounds in Canadian railway bonds?"

"*Putain!*" exclaimed Miss Cousture. "Idiot!"

"Did you know this?" the guvnor asked her.

"No. I swear, sir. He didn't tell me."

The guvnor threw me a glance. We were thinking the same thing, neither of us knowing whether to believe her any more.

"Take her, Boots," said Cream.

Boots took her arm roughly and began to lead her to the door. I put Neddy down as careful as I could and stepped forward, knowing I had to stop them. Boots turned and pointed his gun at me.

There was a knock at the door.

Everybody froze.

Cream nodded at Piser, who opened it a crack and spoke. I tried to listen, hoping it was Petleigh's voice on the other side, but it was too far away to hear.

Piser swung open the door and in stepped Paddler Bill, a lantern in his hand. He was followed by the bald American, then the little fellow with the yellow hair. Last came Gaunt the bookseller, the man who had killed Martha, his tattered winter coat hanging open, his head uncovered. He stood out of the lantern light, behind the rest of them. While the attention was on the Fenians, I bent down quick and whispered to Neddy.

"Get behind those barrels, lad. Keep out of the way."

I saw his face proper now. His lip was split open and swollen worse than last time. Dried blood covered his chin, and I could see sores like burns on the back of his hand. He looked at me but didn't move.

Piser bolted the door behind them.

"Bill?" exclaimed Cream. "What are you doing here?" For the first time he didn't seem so sure of himself.

"I got a message," said Bill. He spoke real quick, so quick you had to listen hard to follow him. He was bigger all round than his mates, dressed in a fancy three-piece suit and an American hat out of which his storm of red hair exploded. "Don't know from who. Thought it might be you, partner."

"Ah," said the guvnor. "That was me, I confess."

"And who the hell are you?" demanded Bill.

"He's a private detective, Bill," said Cream quickly. "He's looking for that lad who stole our railway bonds. I don't know why he's brought you here. This has nothing to do with you. We've got the situation under control."

"I'll hear what he has to say," said the big American.

There was another knock at the door.

"Who the blazes is this now?" cried Cream.

Again Piser opened it a crack, then he looked back at Cream, puzzled.

"It's Colonel Longmire, Mr. Cream."

"Let him in!"

Piser opened the door and Longmire stepped inside. He must have come from the theatre, with his evening dress, his cape, his velvet hat. He stopped just out of the light of Piser's lamp, startled to see so many people there.

"What's this?" he exclaimed. "Stanley, what's happening here?"

"So you've invited Longmire as well," said Cream. "Bravo, Arrowood. You've succeeded in surprising me, and that doesn't happen often. However, it isn't going to help you."

As he was talking, Miss Cousture stepped away from Boots and pulled what looked like a shoemaker's knife from her sleeve. She seemed confused for a moment, turning to Cream as if ready to go for him. Then she turned again, and, with a low groan, flew at Longmire. It happened in a flash. He cried out, clutching his neck, falling back onto Piser and then onto the floor. Blood shot from between his fingers, shrieks from his mouth.

"Get her!" cried Cream.

Piser seemed stunned. He stood with his mouth open, as if he couldn't credit what his eyes were telling him.

"Piser!" screamed Cream.

Miss Cousture fell to her knees, raised her arm, and plunged the knife twice into Longmire's chest. With each blow he writhed up, his shrieks drenched in the gargle of blood. Piser came to his senses now and grabbed her hand, wrenching the knife off her. Boots took her other arm and they pulled her to her feet.

She stood looking on Longmire's body as they held her, her breast heaving. The colonel groaned like an animal, then held his hand up, as if reaching for something in the air. Blood filled his mouth and spilled down his chin; he fought for each breath.

"Go to hell," she said, and spat on his face. She was awash with blood—it covered her cheeks, her neck, the white shirt beneath her black suit.

Longmire uttered one last, long gasp, then stopped moving.

Piser and Boots pulled her away from the body. She wouldn't take her eyes from Longmire's corpse.

"What the bloody hell's going on here?" boomed Paddler Bill. "Who is she?"

"Terry's sister," said Cream.

"Terry?"

"The one who stole our bonds." Cream turned to the guvnor. His voice was filled with venom. "You've ten seconds to tell us what's happening, Arrowood, or we'll start breaking your fingers."

The guvnor stood with his mouth open, looking from Longmire to Miss Cousture and back.

"Five seconds."

"I don't know," said the guvnor, shaking his head. I caught his eye, trying to signal to him that we had to do something now otherwise we were done for. I saw his hand reach into his pocket to clasp his revolver. Inside my coat I cocked my trigger. The vein in my temple throbbed: my heart was thumping in my ribs. It was sure the shooting was about to start, and

I couldn't see any way we would get out alive. Christ, Pet-leigh. Where are you?

"Don't you know me, Mr. Cream?" said Miss Cousture, her arms held behind her back by Piser.

Cream picked up the lantern and shone it on her.

"You think I should?"

"You should, but of course you don't," she replied calmly.

"Tell me why you killed Longmire."

"Because he deserved it."

Cream stepped over to her and lashed her across the face with his hand. "Get on with it, woman," he barked. "How do you know Longmire?"

She took a long draw of breath and shut her eyes before she spoke.

"He violated me," she said at last.

For a moment nobody spoke.

"For God's sake," said Cream. "Is that all? You killed a man for that? Look at you. You're healthy. You've survived."

"Let the girl speak," hissed Paddler Bill. He looked at her. "Explain this to us, missy."

She turned to the big American.

"Thank you, sir." She stopped to take a long, slow breath. "When I was thirteen years old my mother heard there were positions in service for girls in France. There was a notice in the paper. I had four brothers, all younger. Mother couldn't keep us all. Couldn't earn enough to feed us all on her own."

"We're not interested in your history," said Cream. "She knows where our railway bonds are, Bill. That's why we're here."

"Let her speak, Cream," barked the Fenian again, his voice booming in the great warehouse.

"So we went along to see the agent," she continued, turning back to Cream. "You know her, Mr. Cream. Sal's her name. She works for you. She said there was a good family in France waiting for a girl like me, only when I got there it wasn't a family, was it?"

"I'm already weeping for you, girl," said Cream, an ugly grin on his face. In the dark of the warehouse his perfect teeth still shone. "Good God, how old are you? This must have been years ago!"

"Let her talk," commanded Paddler Bill.

"I get taken to an accoucheuse that very first day to check I'm unspoiled." She spoke like she was in a trance. "Then I get taken to the house I'll be kept in for more than ten years, to be ill-treated every night. To be ill-treated by man after man. Night after night. I was made into a whore. You sold me to a brothel, Mr. Cream."

"Seems to me it's him you should have stabbed, miss," said Paddler Bill. His three men laughed.

Cream pointed his gun at her, nodding at Boots, who twisted her arm further up her back. She gasped, ghostly in the dim light from Cream's lantern, bruised with the patterns of Longmire's death.

"On the second day they wash me and dress my hair and put powder and rouge on me. Then they hold me down and give me chloroform, just enough so I can't think straight. A man comes in the room. A rich man from London. I still didn't understand what was going to happen."

"Longmire," said the guvnor.

She nodded.

"And then it did happen," she continued. "And after he finishes he starts up beating me with his fist like it's me that violated him. He starts on my face." She pointed at her chipped front tooth. "My arms, my chest. He beats me again and again on my belly and…" Her voice dropped to a whisper. "He stamps on my legs. I was abed a month before I could get up again."

She stared at the guvnor hard, her eyes on fire.

"I never seen so much anger in a man in my life, and all because of what he did to me."

"That is what this case was about?" asked the guvnor quietly.

"I've been looking for him since I stepped off the boat." Her voice was flat, the anger gone.

"So let me get this straight," said Paddler Bill. His great, red head shook in disbelief. "Cream sells girls to men for the maiden tribute? That's one of his businesses, is it?"

"There were other girls after me," whispered Miss Cousture. "Just as young as me. From London."

"That's enough," protested Cream, his hands in the air. "I'm not the devil here. Remember, the age of consent was only raised ten years ago."

"I did not consent."

"Now, now, dear." A sickly smile held on his face; his voice was like curd. "I'm simply a businessman. The sin is with the men who have these desires." He looked at Paddler Bill. "The lady killed Longmire, Bill. She's had her vengeance. I've only ever tried to do business."

"That's a poor argument, Cream," I said.

He wheeled round to me and spoke quickly, anger in his voice.

"Listen while I explain this, you fool. Powerful men are like thoroughbred horses. They lead the country because they are superior. If they aren't kept happy they couldn't fulfil their positions in society. I don't expect a man such as you to understand. These men are of good stock, but inside them are a labyrinth of needs and urges, animal as well as civilized. They need whisky and wine to help them think—someone supplies it. They need laudanum—someone supplies it. They need a wife and a home. They need sport."

Cream began to walk slowly around us, moving towards Boots and Piser, who still held Miss Cousture. We kept our eyes on him, ready to draw our revolvers. I could feel he was working up to something.

"They need fine food, clothes, good furniture. Someone supplies them, keeps them comfortable. Maids, butlers, valets—all take care of them so that they can take care of the country. I understand them. I was at school with Colonel Longmire, we shared a room at Marlborough. He entered the army while I was more suited to business. He disapproved of me, and yet I came in useful when he needed certain things. I helped him serve his country, that's all. And I didn't create any of his desires—nature did that."

He looked around the faces of his men, who nodded. He looked for support from the Fenians, but they only stared at him, their lips shut.

"How do you think I found out about Sir Herbert's photographs, Bill?" he asked. "It was through Longmire. They shared the same interests. They exchanged photographs."

"You didn't tell me that," said Paddler Bill.

"You're in this just as much as I, Bill. You passed the photographs to me."

"I thought I was buying the rifles from you. I wouldn't have done business with Longmire if I'd known what he was."

"Longmire didn't get a penny of your money, Bill. Not a penny. I went to him because I knew he could obtain the rifles for us, and he knew I could cause him a scandal. Longmire only cooperated because he was afraid of exposure. That's why he killed Venning. But he never had a penny of your money, Bill."

Paddler Bill shook his head.

"Did you tell him to kill Venning?"

"No!" cried Cream. "When these two fools started asking questions about the rifles, Venning flew into a panic. He was ready to turn king's evidence. Longmire couldn't allow that as it would bring him down as well. I told Longmire it was his problem to solve. He did the rest himself."

"Mr. Cream, sir," interrupted the guvnor. "You say you're blameless because you're only a businessman?"

Cream wheeled round. He looked pleased to end his conversation with Paddler Bill, yet at the same time impatient with the guvnor.

"Yes," he said sharply.

"And do you apply the same argument to the supply of these rifles?" asked the guvnor, moving closer to the Fenians and away from me.

"Of course it's the same! The one who shoots the rifle bears the responsibility, not I. I don't murder anyone. I have no dog in the fight."

The Fenian with the yellow hair stepped forward, his eyes narrowing. Paddler Bill glanced over his shoulder at him and gave a slight shake of his head.

Cream's face contorted. "And now, Arrowood, I've had enough of—"

"You're a worthless scurf, Cream!" barked the guvnor in a sudden temper, his voice rising above Cream's and echoing in the great warehouse. "You're involved quite as much as those who fire the rifles, but you're worse because you deny it! They're trying to do something outside themselves at least. What are you doing?"

"I don't kill women and children!" Cream snapped. "Don't put those crimes on me! I'm no more than a tool of the market. I buy. I sell. That's all. The sin is in the passion. There's no passion in what I do." He cracked his stick against his boot. "Listen, Arrowood. I'm not driven by hatred. I can see that look of condescension on your face, but you've no right to judge me. I employ twenty-one. How many do you employ? Twenty-one mouths I feed, and their families and their children. See Lenny here. I employ him. I feed his wife and three children. He spends his money at the pudding shop, the cookhouse, the chandlery, the market. He spends it at the pub. So the money I give him circulates further. The good multiplies. It's businessmen like I that feed this country. I'm not pure, I know that, but you must weigh the bad against the good I do."

"D'you really see yourself like that, pal?" asked Paddler Bill, crossing his arms.

"What do you mean?" Cream had been so involved in his speech he seemed surprised to hear the big American speak.

"That you're better than us?"

Cream twitched. He shook his head quickly. An ingratiating smile appeared on his face. "No, no. I didn't mean to say that. Arrowood was provoking me. You know I have great respect for you and your campaign. I was only saying I'm a middle-man, Bill. That's all. People like me have to stay out of it, otherwise what service can we be?"

"But you think we're only driven by hatred?" asked Paddler Bill.

"Bill, no. Arrowood was provoking me. I didn't mean to say that."

Paddler Bill turned to the man with the stringy yellow hair.

"Now that Sir Herbert and Longmire are dead, would that mean our business with Mr. Cream is complete, Declan?"

"I'd say so, Bill," said the man.

"And would you say that the lady's been avenged?"

Declan looked over at Cream. "Not completely, Bill, no. I wouldn't say that."

Paddler Bill turned back to face us, only now he held a pistol.

"Bill!" cried Cream.

The shot rang out. Cream staggered back, then fell to the floor. Boots and Piser raised their guns but Declan and the black-bearded American now had rifles pointing at the two men. Long Lenny just stood there, his poker swinging at his side.

"We've no quarrel with you men," said Bill. "Throw your guns down."

They did as he asked.

"Now get out of here. And don't think about getting yourselves some revenge on us. We've eyes everywhere. Your employer's dead. You owe him nothing."

Long Lenny, Boots and Piser turned and hurried out of the warehouse.

Paddler Bill walked over to us.

"Now what about you?" he said. "I reckon it was you who sent me the message. What have you got to tell me?"

I pointed at Gaunt, who stood behind Declan, a knife in his hand. He was the only one of the four without a gun.

"That man there's working for the SIB," I said.

"It ain't true, Bill!" cried the bookseller in a hoarse voice. Then to me: 'I'll kill you for that, you lying fuck!"

He flew at me with his knife, but the bald American got him first and held him back. I pulled my revolver out of my pocket.

"No, Bill!" cried Gaunt. "It's a bloody lie!"

Paddler Bill ignored him. "How d'you know about this?" he asked me, his eyes on my gun.

"I was held by the SIB last week. When I came out of Scotland Yard I saw your man having a meeting with Detective Coyle in a coffeehouse. Works with Detective Lafferty, both of SIB. Coyle and him were very friendly with each other."

"No, no, Bill," said Gaunt. "I never heard of no Coyle, honest I ain't. He's only trying to save himself by fitting me up."

Bill ran his fingers through his wild beard and looked for a long time at Declan.

"Bill! He's lying to you!" cried Gaunt. "I swear it!"

"You were right, Declan," said Bill at last.

"Declan?" cried Gaunt. "What have you said?"

Bill walked over to him and struck him hard in the belly. As Gaunt was bent double, Bill searched his pockets. He pulled out a key and put it in his own waistcoat pocket.

"No, Bill," pleaded the bookseller, gasping for air. "It ain't true what he's saying. I swear it, Bill."

"Put him in the wagon," said Bill, turning his back on them.

Declan and the bald Fenian dragged him away, kicking and struggling, swearing he hadn't done nothing. It was the desperate voice of a man who knows he's on a journey to the gallows, and it made me sick. Bill didn't look at him. He waited until they were outside before speaking again.

"We had word from the organization a few months back. A few of his stories didn't add up. We've been watching him. Declan had his doubts about him from the start."

"Price was twenty-five quid," I said.

"So it was," he replied. His gun was trained on me. Mine was on him. Now was the time for the guvnor to bring out his pistol, but he did nothing.

The warehouse door opened and the bald American stepped back inside. He levelled his rifle at the guvnor.

"Put your hands on your head, fat man," he said.

The guvnor turned and raised his hands.

"Drop the gun," said Paddler Bill to me.

I thought for a moment about firing it, but saw I had no choice. I dropped it, cursing the guvnor for not pulling his pistol when he could.

"Tell us something," said the guvnor, turning back to Paddler Bill. "Why did Gaunt kill the serving girl?"

"I wouldn't know anything about a serving girl."

"Did you order him to do it?"

"I just told you I don't know about it."

"What about the plainclothes detective? Did you kill him?"

Paddler Bill shrugged.

A strange silence fell over us, like no one wanted to make the next move. I looked down at my gun on the floor, thinking that if the guvnor pulled his at the same time I dropped to the floor we still might have a chance.

"You going to kill us?" I asked at last.

Paddler Bill sighed.

"Let me explain something, pal. Our goal's to free Ireland from slavery. Independence is coming, that's for sure, but blood seems to be the only language your government understands. Parnell could never persuade them through peace."

"I'm for a free Ireland," said the guvnor. "Many of us in England are."

"Well those that rule you aren't. But listen. We didn't invent violence. The English taught us that. We only kill people to help the cause."

"Innocent people," said the guvnor.

"As in every war," replied Paddler Bill. "As in every war."

The big American picked up Miss Cousture's knife, which Piser had dropped as he left. He pulled Cream's body over to where Longmire lay and dragged him around the bloody floor until his white topcoat was soaked wet. Then he lay him by Longmire's corpse and dropped the knife next to his hand. He put his own revolver into Longmire's hand. Finally, he picked up my gun, put it in his pocket, and walked towards the door where the bald fellow stood, his rifle still raised at us.

"Killing you wouldn't help the cause," said Paddler Bill. "Your deaths would be linked to Cream's operation, not the movement. Anyway, we're not in the business of terrorizing London any more. There'll be an uprising and it'll be in Ireland. Everybody knows it'll come."

He opened the door and turned back to us again. I realized at last he wasn't going to shoot us; it was only then my body began to tremble.

"You won't tell the police what happened here because we'd have to explain to them that it was the lady who killed Longmire. She'd be for the gallows, and I guess not one of us believes she deserves that. So you'll keep quiet. But I'm warning you: keep out of our business. If I ever see any of you again, I won't be so generous."

Chapter Thirty-Six

I PICKED UP NEDDY WHILE THE GUVNOR SEARCHED Longmire's pockets for the twenty-five quid he owed us. Outside the street was quiet: the Fenians were gone. I looked up at the dark sky, at the moon and the stars. They were still there. Reverend Jebb came out of a doorway to meet us, and we walked back to Sidney's cab.

I held Neddy in my lap as we set off to the mission. He was quiet and still, his face turned in to my chest.

"You're safe now, Neddy," said the guvnor. "You're a very brave lad, you know. Did they hurt you?"

In a very small voice, Neddy whispered, "Sorry."

"Sorry?" said I. "You've nothing to be sorry about, son."

With his face still buried under my arm, he said, "I told them where Mr. Arrowood was. I told them you found Terry."

"We don't blame you for that, lad," said the guvnor. "They're evil men."

He reached out to stroke Neddy's leg, but as soon as he touched it the boy pulled away with a sudden groan. It was a deep sound, like a grown man was inside him, and I felt it gnaw right into me.

"What's wrong with your leg?" I asked him.

He sniffed and pressed his face into my jacket. We could hardly make out his muffled words.

"They smashed my foot." He did his best to hide it, but as he spoke he began to cry. "They had a hammer."

"I think they burned his hands too," I said.

"You're a hero, boy," said the guvnor, his voice almost cracking. "We'll get you a doctor the moment we get back. He'll give you something for the pain."

The minister, who sat squeezed in the corner, watched the boy in silence. Miss Cousture, sitting next to me, began to stroke Neddy's hair. I wondered if what she'd done would heal her. It didn't seem so. As she gazed out at the dark streets her eyes still shone with anger, but it seemed to me the strength that propelled her since the first day we met was gone. The guvnor looked out the window too: his blood-raddled eyes bulged with tears that sparkled as we passed under the gas-lights. We rode on in a dazed and solemn silence.

As we approached the mission, the guvnor said, "Miss Cousture, there's something I don't understand. How did you really come to be working in Fontaine's photo studio?"

"Eric had nothing to do with this," she said, her hand resting gently on Neddy's back. "Thierry got a job in the Beef first. He had to take packages around the city for Cream. He opened everything; he knew how to seal them again so nobody knew. Some of the packages were from Eric's studios. You wouldn't imagine the pictures he was delivering. I mean…" She paused, glancing down at Neddy, then whispered, "Intimate pictures. Men with men, groups of people, young girls as well, anything you could think of. Cream was selling them or using them for blackmail. We thought maybe the man we were looking for could be buying photos like this. His appetites wouldn't change. We weren't sure, though, so Josiah helped me get the job in the studio. He offered me so cheap that Eric dismissed his assistant and hired me. But Longmire and Venning never came to Eric. Other men like them, but not them."

"So you were in this from the start, Reverend?" asked the guvnor.

"It's part of the mission's work," replied Jebb. "We offer salvation, but we aim to bring those who abuse our women to justice. An eye for an eye, Mr. Arrowood."

"Pardon me, Reverend, but I don't think you're cut out for this work."

"I'm learning, sir."

We pulled up outside the mission house.

"What'll you do now, Miss Cousture?" I asked.

She thought for a moment, her face sad and serious. She seemed unconcerned with the blood that stained her.

"I think I'll go to Paris to try and find Thierry. I think he owes me half those railway bonds."

"Well, best go first thing in the morning," said the guvnor. "The police will be investigating the deaths. Be assured we won't tell them it was you."

"Thank you, Mr. Arrowood."

"You really didn't know he'd stolen them?"

She shook her head.

"Well, good luck, miss," I said.

"If you need any help finding him… " said the guvnor.

She looked at him, surprised.

"…Please do not come to us."

It was the first time I'd seen her laugh.

Ettie and Lewis were waiting for us when we returned. We sent for the doctor, then put Neddy to bed. The guvnor brought out a bottle of brandy; Lewis laid out a spread of bread and ham. We sat in the parlour, talking over what had happened.

"Then Longmire didn't get a share of the money?" asked Lewis, having a struggle to cut the bread with his one arm.

"It appears not," replied the guvnor. "I'd thought he was partners with Cream in selling the rifles, but Longmire was coerced, just as Venning was. Cream had threatened to expose him if he didn't obtain the weapons. No doubt Cream and Milky Sal had been providing for his perversions for years."

I got up to help Lewis.

"Longmire was reckless to trust them," said Ettie.

"Longmire and Cream were at Marlborough together," explained the guvnor. "I suppose he trusted the old school tie."

"And Sir Herbert?" asked Ettie.

"Longmire couldn't get the weapons on his own. He needed his friend Sir Herbert to provide a way, and since they shared the same interests—" The guvnor stopped and turned to Ettie. "I mean sexual interests, Sister."

"I know what you damn well mean, William!"

"Well, anyway," he continued, taken aback. "He knew how best to blackmail him."

"You mean the maiden tribute," she said.

He nodded. "Pictures of girls under the age of consent. No doubt the same type of poor girls you've been ministering, Ettie. Twenty years ago this might not have been such a scandal, but they no longer look kindly on men such as Sir Herbert. When we began to ask questions, Venning took fright and was ready to turn king's evidence. Longmire couldn't allow that to happen. He tried to make it look like suicide, forgetting Sir Herbert's disfigured hand."

"You were lucky to get out alive," said Lewis, his mouth full of ham. "I still can't believe it."

"No thanks to that imbecile Petleigh," said the guvnor. "I knew our only chance was to cause as much confusion as possible. That was why I wanted the Fenians there. That was why I wanted Miss Cousture and Longmire there. But it was only partly luck, old friend. This has been a long case, and cases like this don't get solved, only concluded. We've done many things along the way to bring us here."

"And are you satisfied with the conclusion?" asked Lewis.

"For Miss Cousture the case is complete. She has what she wanted. And we tracked down Martha's killer. That was our case. Her death would otherwise have been forgotten. I hope in some way we've atoned."

"But couldn't you have turned him over to the police?" said Ettie.

"How, Sister?"

"Norman was a witness. Gaunt would have been convicted."

"Gaunt had friends in the SIB. He would have been protected."

Ettie shook her head. "You cannot be sure. By identifying him to Paddler Bill you sentenced him to death. Doesn't that make you uncertain?"

"I didn't make the laws of their world, Sister. These men lived in it. They understood."

We sat for some time, each deep in our own thoughts. When the clock chimed, Ettie turned to me.

"Were you afraid, Norman?" she asked, her head tilting to the side. Her collar reached up to her chin, and I could see now how tired she was.

"Never been more scared in my life," I replied. "There was

so many of them. And when William started up shouting at Cream I thought it was goodnight for sure. If Bill hadn't shot Cream, we'd be in the river now."

"Oh, William," she sighed. "Why can't you keep your temper?"

"It was a blind, Ettie," said the guvnor. He put down his plate and sat forward. "Cream was going to kill us. I was searching for anything I could use to give us a chance. Bill was unhappy that Cream had taken advantage of the maiden tribute to procure the rifles. Bill was also angry about Venning's death and losing the supply of weapons. It wasn't enough on its own, but it was something to build on. As Cream spoke I watched the Fenians, and there came my chance. When he argued that no blame attached to him, when he said the Fenians were murderers, Declan stepped forward. Anger passed over his face and I saw a chance. In a group like the Fenians there are many types. Perhaps some enjoy violence and want revenge. Perhaps others desire the status. But others, and Bill and Declan are no doubt amongst those, take up arms because they believe it's the only way. Cream didn't understand that. That's why I provoked him to say more. For Cream to claim he was better was abhorrent to them. Bill's friends were executed for the cause at the Invincibles trial. He was the only one who wasn't sentenced. To accuse him of acting without morals is like setting a bomb in his heart, especially from one so low as Cream. I saw the trigger. I pulled it."

He took his pipe from the table and uncapped it.

"But why didn't Cream see what he was doing?" asked Ettie.

"If you've ever made a speech you'll know how easy it is to lose your sensibility. The attention of a crowd is like a strong brandy: you feel full of yourself." He stopped a moment to light his pipe. "And of course evil men are sometimes convinced they are good."

"But, that means you were trying to make them kill Cream," said Ettie softly.

The guvnor did not reply.

"Oh, William. You've made too many decisions."

"Ettie, it was justice. For all the young girls. For Miss Cousture. For the policeman. But even if you don't agree, you must see it was our only chance. We'd be dead. Neddy would be dead."

It was shortly after this there came a hammering at the door. I checked the window before opening it, fearing it might be Boots and Piser, but it was only Petleigh.

"I've just come from Issler's," said he as he stepped into the hallway. Although it was late he smelled of scent, and his jet-black moustache had recently been waxed. "What the blazes happened there?"

"Where in Christ's name were you?" called the guvnor from his chair. "We were almost killed!"

Petleigh entered the parlour before replying.

"It wasn't my fault, William," he said. "At the very last minute, as we were preparing to leave, the assistant commissioner ordered us to go with Sherlock Holmes on a raid. I told you they'd asked him to help on the Venning case?"

"The whole of London knows it," replied the guvnor, furiously puffing his pipe, a great cloud of smoke rising around him.

"The minister himself demanded we provide every assistance to Holmes. It seems the War Office knew about the theft of the rifles and Venning was suspected of being involved. He'd been interviewed on the matter the very same day he

died. All efforts were to be made to find those weapons before they fell into the wrong hands."

"You knew we were in danger!" cried Arrowood. "The
boy! What about him?"

"Where is the boy? Did you get him?"

"He's safe, but had he been killed I would have held you
responsible."

Petleigh now became angry. He jammed his hands in his
pockets.

"I tried to get away, William, but I had no choice. The assistant commissioner put myself and twenty constables on the
raid. It was too late to alert you, and I don't have the authority
to disagree. It's as simple as that. If I'm told to do something
by my superiors I must do it. But look, you're safe."

The guvnor snorted, then tipped a whole glass of brandy
down his gullet.

Ettie came into the room. Petleigh bowed and kissed her
hand.

"Delightful to see you again, Ettie," he said. "You're up
late. Waiting for William, I suppose?"

"Why didn't you arrive to help them, Inspector?" she demanded. "You said you'd be there."

"I was ordered by the assistant commissioner to help Holmes
tonight. I tried to get away but it was quite impossible."

She frowned and sat next to me on the sofa.

"I suppose Holmes solved the case?" asked the guvnor.

"He's been quite brilliant," replied Petleigh, leaning his
elbow on the mantel and gazing at Lewis's decanter of brandy.
"Luckily for us, he's been keeping information on the Fenians and their allies since the bombing campaign. He has the
most comprehensive information system, you know. I think
he said he has records on every important crime in London

over the last twenty years. I don't understand how he did it, the man is quite simply a genius, but he tracked the guns in their passage right across London."

"I suppose they were stacked amongst his own books?" muttered the guvnor.

"What do you mean?"

"In the bookshop."

Petleigh stiffened. "But how did you know the rifles were in a bookshop?"

"Gaunt's Bookshop, unless I'm mistaken, Petleigh?"

"You knew where the guns were?"

"We've been working on this case for weeks," said the guvnor dismissively.

"Then why the blazes didn't you tell me?"

"Unless you've forgotten, we've been rather busy, Inspector."

"Those guns would have killed British soldiers!"

"We've just saved a boy's life," retorted the guvnor. "And anyway, do we not ourselves use ri—"

"Shut your mouth, William," warned Ettie. "You'll end up in the gaol yourself."

Petleigh, not understanding what had passed between brother and sister, waited for some clarification. When it didn't come, he said, "Well, you'll be glad to hear we retrieved all sixty of them, and a dozen crates of bullets as well as a good amount of nitroglycerine. The minister's delighted. Unfortunately, the owner of the shop wasn't there, but we'll pick him up tomorrow no doubt."

The guvnor snorted.

"Why did you snort?" asked Petleigh.

"You'd be better to look for him in the river."

"Tell me what happened at Issler's," demanded Petleigh. "There are two corpses."

"Ask Holmes to solve the mystery."

"Tell me, William. Two have been killed."

"I'll come to your office tomorrow and explain," said the guvnor wearily. "Barnett and I have been through a lot tonight. We're too tired to think straight."

Despite his anger, Petleigh saw it was true.

He paused in the door as he was leaving.

"Shall we arrange a day for the luncheon you mentioned, William?"

"It'll have to wait until we're back in our home, Petleigh."

"Ah, yes," said the inspector, and there was a little sadness in his eyes. At this late hour of the night, he looked old.

He wished Ettie and Lewis goodnight, bowed, and was gone.

"How did you know the guns were in Gaunt's?" I asked when we were sitting again.

"Bill removed a key from Gaunt's pocket before they took him away," replied the guvnor. "Do you remember? It had to be the key for the bookshop."

"It could've been for a lock-up."

"But if they'd hired a lock-up they wouldn't have entrusted the only key to a man about whom they had suspicions. The key must have been to Gaunt's own shop, and the storeroom of a shop is an ideal place for stolen goods. I suspected it might be the location when you told me of the place."

With a groan he pushed himself out of his chair and crossed the parlour.

"I'll visit the privy and then it's bed for me."

"William," said Ettie. "Sherlock Holmes is a great detective. Nobody else could have found those rifles in two days. When will you finally admit it?"

The guvnor stood in the doorway, and it seemed that all the tension of the night had drained away. His shoulders fell, his face relaxed into a smile, and I thought at last he would give Holmes his due.

He opened his mouth to speak, then seemed to think better of it. Instead he shook his head, picked up the lamp, and took himself off to the outhouse.

I left soon after. The guvnor walked me to the door and there he held out a fiver, still wet and stained with Longmire's blood.

"Here's your share, Norman."

I stared at it some time, chewing my lip, looking as dubious as I could.

"Oh, for goodness' sake," he said finally, in a defeated tone. He pulled another fiver out of his pocket and pressed them both in my hand. "It's too late to argue."

Chapter Thirty-Seven

I SLEPT ALL DAY. WHEN I AWOKE IT WAS ALREADY late afternoon. There was one more job to do. I took the bus across town to Scotland Yard and waited outside the pub, watching the entrance as the coppers came and went. Night fell and the cold crept in; my arm started to throb again. It was dark when Coyle finally came out. I tracked him down the length of Victoria Embankment, where he turned north. I followed him for another ten minutes until he crossed an empty park and there I saw my chance. He was the type of man who is very sure of himself, and he didn't look behind him when he heard me approaching. It made it real easy. I took a good big swing at him and it felt fine. Very fine indeed. His legs gave way the moment the poker hit him, and he cried out with a sound like a horse having a burp. I fell on him at once, digging my knee into his chest, my hands tight around his throat, choking him. His arms scrabbled at my coat, his legs writhed, but I was too heavy for him. The spit oozed out of his mouth as I squeezed tighter. His eyes were popping, tears running down the sides of his head.

As soon as I stopped he started coughing and choking, trying to breathe again. I got to my feet and put one boot on his wrist, the other on his shoulder. Then I raised my poker high and brought it down on his arm, in just the place he had beat me with his truncheon.

He howled.

I dropped with my knee onto his belly.

"Hurts, doesn't it, Coyle?"

He was coughing again now, his arms pawing at me, gasping for breath.

"I owed you that. Now, I want to know one thing, otherwise I give you another. Why did your agent kill the serving girl?"

"Fuck you," he wheezed.

"Right." I stood again and raised the poker.

"No!" he cried. "No. I'll tell you."

He started choking again. I waited until he was ready to talk. He raised himself till he was sitting, holding his throat with his good arm. "He thought the Fenians were onto him," he said, his voice hoarse and rasping. "He had to prove he was loyal. They was worried about what your Frenchman found out and what he'd told his girl. They'd heard you two'd been to see her, asking questions, so he took it on himself to kill her. He thought it'd convince them he wasn't no double agent."

"You told him to do it," I said.

He shook his head.

"We didn't know about it till after. I swear it. That's the way our agents work. They make decisions. Sometimes they make good decisions, sometimes they don't."

"But you didn't arrest him. You knew he'd done it and you didn't arrest him."

He looked up at me, his ugly face weak and beaten.

"He's too valuable. He's given us a lot of information over the years. If there's another bomb plot, it'll be him that tells us."

"I don't think so," I said.

"You don't know what you're talking about."

I got a sovereign out of my pocket and dropped it in his lap. "Goodnight, Coyle."

I tramped back across town, over Waterloo Bridge, where the barges and wherries were tied up for the night. There was a pub down there that was open late and nobody knew me. I didn't want to go back to my room. It would be like it was every night since Mrs. Barnett died: cold and dark and empty. The two silhouettes we had done when we got married hung by the window like ghosts, all the features and life erased from them. I couldn't bear to look at them no more. Her memory suffocated me in that empty room.

I'd tell the guvnor when I was ready. Now I needed to keep busy, to keep out of that room for as long as I could. What I needed was another case to come along, and soon. The guvnor and me, we both needed a case to come along soon.

★ ★ ★ ★ ★

Author Note

THANK YOU TO VINCE FOR HIS KINDNESS IN READ-ing more than was reasonable over the years, to Jo, Sally and Lizzie for helping breathe life into this book, and to my friends for all the talks we have had. I relied on many books and on-line sources for the historical background. These included (among others) *The Invention of Murder* and *The Victorian City* (Judith Flanders), *War in the Shadows* (Shane Kenna), *The Suspicions of Mr. Whicher* (Kate Summerscale), *London's Shadows* (Drew D. Gray), *How to be a Victorian* (Ruth Goodman), the National Library of Scotland's georeferenced maps (maps.nls.uk/geo), Lee Jackson's The Dictionary of Victorian London (victorianlondon.org) and Booth's Poverty Maps (booth.lse.ac.uk/map).